SURVIVAL OF THE FITTEST

Daniel shuffled over to Jack who seemed to be coming round, his face bone-white under a mudpack.

"Love what they've done with the gate room." Jack blinked up at the canopy. "Where the hell are we? Mato Grosso?"

"Doesn't look like Brazil to me." Daniel sniffed, squinting at the blur of a monumental structure behind them. High in the wall, the gate formed the third eye in a stone-carved mask that placidly gazed down at him. "My money's on Angkor Wat."

"What encore?"

"You know. The Khmer temples in Cambodia."

"Didn't know they kept a Stargate there."

"Uh, they don't, I guess. If they did, somebody'd have found it by now." Glancing at fuzzy walls and reliefs again, Daniel said, "This is amazing. We definitely need to check out this place. It could—"

"Daniel!"

"Hmm?"

"We don't know where we are, we're hogtied, we've got no weapons or supplies, and we— Holy buckets!" Jack had finally turned his head to get a spectacular view of Daniel's face. "You know, you're... Nah, I won't say it."

"Won't say what?"

"Uh-uh."

"Jack?"

"I'm not gonna say you're a sight for sore eyes."

"Very funny."

"That's why I didn't say it."

STARGÅTE
SG·1™

SURVIVAL OF THE FITTEST

SABINE C. BAUER

FANDEMONIUM BOOKS

An original publication of Fandemonium Ltd, produced under license from MGM Consumer Products.

Fandemonium Books
PO Box 795A
Surbiton
Surrey KT5 8YB
United Kingdom
Visit our website: www.stargatenovels.com

STARGÅTE
SG·1

METRO-GOLDWYN-MAYER Presents
RICHARD DEAN ANDERSON
in
STARGATE SG-1™
AMANDA TAPPING   CHRISTOPHER JUDGE   and MICHAEL SHANKS as Daniel Jackson
Executive Producers ROBERT C. COOPER   BRAD WRIGHT   MICHAEL GREENBURG
RICHARD DEAN ANDERSON
Developed for Television by BRAD WRIGHT & JONATHAN GLASSNER

WWW.MGM.COM

ISBN: 0-9547343-9-4
Printed in the United Kingdom by Bookmarque Ltd, Croydon, Surrey

To Tanya—beta extraordinaire and the one
who's responsible for Everything!

PROLOGUE

The childlike face—she'd been a child, first and foremost, a smart, needy, tantrum-throwing teenager who'd made an awful mistake—never moved. Jack reached for her neck as if to feel a pulse they both knew had never been there. It wasn't the pulse he was after, Daniel realized. Below her right ear a hidden catch activated and released the energy cell that had powered her. The crystal fizzed briefly and winked out, looking dull and dead; its removal a clear case of overkill. Nothing would revive her now. After all, Jack O'Neill, ex-Special Ops, was a crack shot.

"You stupid son of a bitch!"

"Hey, you're welcome."

Daniel wanted to hit him, for the glib reply alone.

Someone up in the control room gave the *all clear*. The klaxons stopped their wailing, and the gate room fell quiet enough to hear the soft clickety-click and clatter as all throughout the base Reese's 'toys', bereft of the life-force that had fuelled them, disintegrated to a harmless rain of metal wafers.

Rain or tiny needles of snow. Daniel felt cold. Another difference not made, for Reese and for an entire race of beings who were getting their little gray asses whupped by the offspring of her 'toys'. Too many differences not made. Maybe it was time to leave. No point in staying and pretending things were just fine when everything had changed. Or perhaps nothing had changed.

He heard himself start up an argument, because he was Daniel and Daniel always argued, pitting the ever-same reasoning against the ever-same justifications and with the ever-same results.

"Look, I'm sorry," Jack said finally. "But this is the way it had to go down, and you know it."

Now brush your teeth and go to bed!

He stopped short of that. Instead he turned away, muttering into his radio, and began walking off toward the blast door. He'd still be holding the gun, always would. No difference.

Daniel didn't look up, afraid of what he'd see, of the decisions it'd force on him.

CHAPTER ONE

Convergence: *The development of similar features in distantly related lineages due to the effects of similar evolutionary factors.*

The subject, strapped to a gleaming metal table inside a gleaming surgical lab, opened his mouth for a scream. Thankfully that particular audio channel had been set to mute. The scream was enduring and heartfelt, which didn't come as any great surprise. Suddenly the subject's eyes rolled up, and he stilled. The solemn face of a white-clad doctor interposed itself between camera and surgical table. The doctor shook his head. Another failure.

How many had there been? Eight? Nine?

It was high time to consider the alternative. Frank Simmons switched off the aftermath of the experiment and turned to the central monitor bank. Each screen showed the same image, just from a different angle. The backgrounds varied. French doors and a glimpse of a garden or pristinely starched curtains or a blank white wall. However, all of them showed bars in the foreground and, behind the bars, a man. Or what looked like a man.

He was dark-haired, tall, and heavily built, and he moved with a curious absence of grace, as though mind and body hadn't really connected. Which might be the case after all. Some of the guards called him Herman. The likeness was indisputable, but Simmons discouraged the joke. Herman Munster was a cretin. This… thing… on the screen was highly intelligent and commanded the entire knowledge and viciousness of his species. Prettifying him would be lethal.

Until quite recently the man-thing had been a person called Adrian Conrad. Obscenely rich and incurably ill and unwilling to appreciate, let alone accept, the irony of it. And so he'd paid a large amount of money for a larval Goa'uld and let it infest his body. The alien parasite had cured the disease but usurped the host's mind in exchange when the removal process had run into a hitch. Tough luck.

Good luck for the NID. Thanks to Simmons, the secret government agency owned the Goa'uld exclusively. Right now, the thing that had been Conrad sat inside his cage leafing through a textbook. Genetics. Suddenly, and with all signs of disdain, he leaped from his chair and flung the book against the bars.

"Where are you?" The harmonics of the distorted voice made the speakers hum. "I know you are there! I demand to speak to you!"

Simmons took another bite from his sandwich—pastrami and pickle, though they made them better in New York—and watched as Conrad paced the cell. Let him stew. Sooner or later he'd grasp that he was a prisoner. Maybe he'd learn some manners then.

Ten minutes later the sandwich was gone and Conrad had stopped pacing and slumped back onto the chair. It was time. Simmons scrunched the wrapping paper into a tight ball and pitched it at a trashcan. He missed, shrugged, and left the control center.

When he entered the prisoner's room, trailed by two guards armed with *zat'nikatels*, Conrad straightened up, his eyes glowing. "You are late!"

Ignoring him, Simmons nodded at the guards. "Unlock the cage."

Given the Goa'uld's immense strength, it posed a risk, but it also was a psychological necessity. Remaining outside the cage would have betrayed fear. More importantly, a face-to-face meeting suggested a degree of equality that would facilitate cooperation. The ploy had worked before, it would work now.

The door of the cage fell shut behind him, and Simmons picked up the book, leisurely flicked through its pages. "Not to your taste, I take it?"

"It is puerile! Your so-called scientists do not know half of what they ought to know. Even the men my host employed were amateurs." A sly glint stole into the alien's human eyes. "You killed another one, did you not? That is why you are here. But I can only tell you what I have told you before. Your plan will fail."

"Not if you help me."

"Why should I help you? So that you can assemble an army of warriors to destroy my kind?"

"Your *kind*?" Simmons leaned back against the bars of the cage and started laughing. "Since when did you develop feelings for the family? Your *kind* would kill you just as soon as look at you, and you know it."

He did, of course. For a second, the eyes flared in annoyance. Then he rose and approached until he was mere inches away, towering over Simmons. From somewhere outside the cage came the dissonant chime of *zat'nikatels* being readied.

"Stand down!" Simmons snapped and, more quietly, added, "We're having a friendly discussion."

The parasite molded his host's face into a smile. "Indeed. Suppose I could help you, human, would you accept my price?"

"Freedom? Not just yet. You're a little too useful for that, I'm afraid."

"No. Not just yet." The grimace deepened, bared teeth. "But if I give you those warriors, you are to send them against whom I tell you when I tell you."

When hell freezes over! Simmons stared past Conrad and at a strip of sunlight that dissected the white floor of the cage. The reflection was painfully bright, and he closed his eyes, hiding a flicker of triumph. It was true. The Goa'uld's arrogance was their greatest weakness.

"Why not?" he said. "With the one obvious exception, of course."

"Of course. Unfortunately, I cannot help you."

"What?" Simmons's eyes flew open in time for him to watch Conrad back off in a show of boredom. "What do you mean, you can't help me?"

"I mean what I said. I do not have the skill. However…"

"However?" It took some doing, but Simmons managed to bite back a more suitable reply. *However*, once he'd squeezed that punk dry, he'd kill him personally. Slowly.

"My mistress possesses the skills you require."

"Your *mistress*? Forgive my skepticism, but *mistress* implies that you do what she says, not the other way round."

"The price I have named will be ample to buy her assistance."

"I see." Simmons allowed a trace of interest to creep into his voice. "And how would I invite your mistress to join us for negotiations?"

"I assume there were communication globes among the loot you took from our worlds?"

"Of course, but… What about range?"

The NID's tame Goa'uld smiled.

CHAPTER TWO

The place was vast, gutted, and its acoustics stank. Which was to say you twitched an eyelid and got an echo. Consequently, Colonel Jonathan 'Jack' O'Neill, USAF, wasn't considering any twitching. What he had been considering for the past ten minutes or so was getting up and stretching his legs. His knees were very unhappy with the current state of affairs, a reminder that, maybe, he was getting a little long in the tooth for this.

This spelled waddling along a metal catwalk in stealth mode and a crouch. And anyone who thought it was a piece o' cake could be his guest and try it in combat boots. *This* also was the only way of getting anywhere near the enemy position. The enemy, quite unfairly, had displayed unforeseen tactical originality. Okay, not unforeseen, but Jack still felt a little insulted. Tactical originality was *his* department.

Then again, he wasn't doing too badly himself. The gallery lining the room fifteen meters above the ground seemed inaccessible. The staircases leading up had either collapsed or corroded to brittle red trash, and if, for some perverse reason, you had your heart set on getting up here, you were in for a stint of shinning up the side of the building, forcing a window, and carefully dislodging a bunch of loose bricks. Which they'd done—having the aforementioned perverse reason—and it had paid off. This was the last place the enemy expected them to be. You could tell.

The hostiles had a three-strong sentry unit holed up amid a few dozen bales of molting white stuff. Cotton, by the looks of it, though what it was doing here beat him. Part of the enemy force was prowling the grounds outside, led on a wild goose chase by Teal'c and his team. The rest were in the building, securing a stairwell Jack wasn't interested in. Yet. Below, Larry, Curly, and Moe felt safe as babes in arms—never a real smart proposition, in life or in warfare. It got you dead. So far none of them had bothered to check above.

They'd better not. If they did, things would get ugly in a hurry. Fallback options were at a premium up here. On the bright side, even if they did check, they'd have to look closely. The windows in the two outer walls were blind, encrusted with decades of industrial dirt. The only light trickling in filtered through a handful of broken casements, and the room, nearly a hundred meters long, half as wide, and about thirty high, was mired in almost solid gloom.

The enemy position sat smack in the northeastern quadrant, beautifully chosen, because it covered both ground floor entrances. Jack O'Neill wanted it. In fact, he coveted it. Once he took it, it'd be like shooting fish in a barrel. His teams would be able to pick off the hostiles as they came home to roost.

A faint whiff of herbal shampoo announced that his 2IC had caught up with him. He turned, saw her grin, teeth flashing in a face blackened by camouflage paint. Then she shucked a stray coil of the zip line back onto her shoulder and gave a thumbs-up. Evidently Major Samantha Carter was enjoying herself.

He signaled her to keep going. With a brisk nod she crept on, followed by Pancaldi and four others. They did good, moving quickly and quietly, until they reached the corner where the catwalk turned along the short wall, some ten meters on from his own position. Perfect. Now all he needed was the third prong of his attack force. And there it was, right on time. Diagonally across, six ghostly shapes settled in behind the railing.

Daniel and his braves had taken the other way round, with the braves gamely submitting to the command of a geek. Well, if truth be told, Dr. Daniel Jackson had lost his official geek status quite some time ago. Whether he liked it or not, he was getting good at this. Very good. Now he peered over, waiting for the signal. The Stooges down below still were blissfully oblivious. They'd have a rough awakening.

Showtime.

Jack raised his hand, thumb, forefinger, and middle finger extended, and slowly began to count down, folding in his thumb, three, then the forefinger, two, then—

A whirr and a whoosh, five, eight, ten times over, zooming down from the ceiling.

No! Goddammit, no! He felt himself go ice-cold, knowing what he'd done in one terrible instant, knowing that he'd pulled the screw-up to end them all—the same dumbass stunt as the Three Stooges. He hadn't bothered to check above, because he'd felt too damn sure of himself and his brilliance. It'd make a great epitaph: *Here lies Jack O'Neill, Smug Bastard.* And not just he. Not just he…

"Take cover!" he roared.

Too little, too late. Besides, there wasn't any cover to be had.

Black-clad and masked, they hovered on their zip lines like so many giant spiders, and they moved with the same eerie speed, instantly opening fire. Like a mad lightshow, the thin red streaks of laser sights crisscrossed through dust-laden air, hit walls and struts and bodies. One drilled toward him, and Jack rolled away, brought up his own weapon, fired, missed. Somewhere behind him rose a cry. Chen. Chen was down, his group of five a man short now, and it was only the start. Chances were he'd lose them all. The red streak swiveled back, still searching for him, then it went wild. Daniel had taken out the shooter. Go, Daniel!

Giving up on the non-existent cover, Jack got to his feet, found another target, and had the satisfaction of seeing the man sag into his harness. Next! By now there was a fairly constant barrage from Carter's corner. She and her group took out three attackers in quick succession. Daniel's gang clocked up two more. If they could keep it up then maybe, just maybe—

"Stevens!" he shouted back over his shoulder. "Get the lines ready! We're going down a floor."

"Yessir! On your—"

Stevens toppled as the wall burst outward. It did the same thing in two other places, behind Carter's and Daniel's teams. A piece of mortar ricocheted off Jack's head, picking up some skin and hair along the way. He reeled back, and the groans volleying from various locations on the gallery told him that the flying masonry casualties were mounting. It was the least of their problems. Through the holes in the walls piled more guys in ninja outfits. Twelve in all, four to each breach, they exploded onto the catwalk like the wrath of God.

Jack never even had time to aim. He fired anyway, from reflex and an instinctive urge to stop the nemesis thundering toward him. The shot went high, and all he could do was brace for the onslaught. His dance partner was a woman, surprisingly enough, at least an inch taller than he and built like a Russian shot-putter. Etiquette would have to suffer, he concluded, and rammed the butt of his rifle into her midriff. It didn't slow her down. Miss Universe bellowed like an ox, one beefy hand slapping away the rifle, the other delivering a roundhouse blow that tore Jack off his feet and flung him against the railing.

It sounded like someone clearing his throat, and he felt it before he heard it—the dry crunch of ancient metal deciding that enough was enough. The railing gave. There was an endless, weightless moment of teetering on the edge and Carter screaming his name. As if it'd been waiting for that chance, a red streak leaped through dusty air and at the middle of her forehead, shearing off the scream. Gravity kicked in the same instant, and Jack fell, ass over tit and almost grateful, still hanging on to his gun, knowing this was it. *Here flies Jack O'Neill, Smug Bastard.* He'd be lucky if he *didn't* survive.

He landed on something soft and squishy that compacted under his weight. Teeth still rattling from the impact, he lay inside a crater of white fluff. Over its rim gawked the baffled faces of Larry, Curly, and Moe.

"Hi," Jack said grimly and brought up his rifle. "Just thought I'd drop in."

A curiously Dopplered yell from above cut off whatever else he'd meant to say or do. By the time he'd located its origin, it was too late. Miss Universe came hurtling through space like a monster fruit bat, on a trajectory that ended smack atop one Jack O'Neill. Who, knowing what would happen, closed his eyes in silent resignation.

The First Aid tent had adopted all the atmosphere and civility of the catering marquee at a biker shindig. People were guzzling or spilling coffee of every description—cream and two sugars left the best stains on lab coats—and dropped empty paper cups where they stood. Sergeant Pancaldi had eviscerated an MRE pack to get at the candy bar—which, frankly, he could do without—and sat on a spare gurney, a happily munching nucleus at the heart of the mayhem. Calories or no, you couldn't discount the curative properties of chocolate. Pancaldi was the only satisfied customer in the entire tent. Everybody else, including the female contingent, was squirting testosterone.

"... could have killed her!"

"It was an accident! Besides, she—"

"*Accident*, my ass!"

"I can spell it out for you, jarhead!"

"*Jarhead*? Wanna take that up with an officer?"

The participants in this lively conversation had surrounded a portable defib unit and were threatening to come to blows over it. A shy-looking orderly took his life into his hands and tried to rescue the equipment. "Excuse me?"

"What officer? Somebody's actually in charge of you hood-lums?"

"Excuse me!"

"Yo, flyboy! Butt out!"

"Muscles are required, intellect not essential. Can you string the initials into a word, *jarhead*?"

"Excuse me!" The orderly made a grab for the defibrillator and got in the way of a shove.

That did it. Dr. Janet Fraiser was all for healthy social exchange between the service branches, but this was getting a little too tactile. She'd either have to start administering chocolate or clear the tent. The latter was better for her nerves, and never mind the patients' welfare.

"Shut it! That's an order!"

The bellow stalled arguments, made Marines and Airmen flinch, provoked ducked heads among nursing staff, caused Pancaldi to choke on his candy bar, and trailed blessed silence in its wake. Inevitably, really. Most mouths hung open. Yep. Meet the mouse that roared. Janet Fraiser was five foot three in heels and not of a build anyone would associate with Pavarotti volume. A good diaphragm had its perks. What made it especially rewarding was the fact that at least half of this mob didn't even know her.

She smiled winningly. "Ladies and gentlemen! Now that I have your full and undivided attention, listen up. Anyone who can walk and doesn't have a job to do, get the hell out of my tent and *don't* step back in unless you're dying!"

From the gurney to her right came a rustle, followed by a strangled moan. Without even looking, she snapped, "That doesn't include you, so stay put! Sir!"

The rest of the delinquents were still gawking at her, though some of the mouths had started to close.

"Well? What are you waiting for?"

"Shorry, Doc," mumbled Pancaldi around a chunk of chocolate. Then he slid off his perch and led the exodus.

Two minutes later the tent had cleared, except for three patients—well, two patients and an immovable object—and two nursing staff. The daredevil orderly still clucked over the defib unit like a hen over her chicks. He had a slightly nervous disposition, but he was a cracking triage nurse.

"Stand down, Corporal. I think it's safe," she said, trying hard not to sound patronizing. "Can you see to Private Lamont? The morphine should have kicked in by now, and her jaw needs bandaging. It'll have to be wired shut, but I don't want to do that here. The ambulance is standing by, so whenever you're done, she can go."

"Yes, ma'am!" The corporal relinquished the defibrillator and headed for the opposite corner of the tent, where PFC Lamont lay sprawled on a gurney, humming tunelessly. The morphine had kicked in alright.

Now for the fun part. Fraiser squared her shoulders and turned to the would-be absconder who, unlike the now departed multitudes, knew her exceedingly well—too well to even have tried to vamoose. The back of his gurney had been raised, bringing him to eyelevel with the immovable object, which was delivering a hushed lecture. The patient, not in the mood for sermons, dispensed one of his patented glares.

"Dammit, Daniel!" His outburst stopped the lecture in its tracks and rattled the tent poles. Then he lowered his voice. "Can the pep talk already. I screwed up."

Sitting in a chair next to him, Daniel Jackson sported a first-class shiner that was only partly concealed by an eye patch. Shiner and patch were down to a close encounter with an airborne brick. His glasses were trashed, though they hadn't done any further damage, and he squinted myopically at his friend. "Guess what, Jack? We all do. Live with it."

Whereupon Colonel O'Neill looked ready to throttle an archeologist.

The temper was only a first reaction, and Janet Fraiser knew it. She sure as hell didn't want to be there when it all sank in. He wasn't exactly adept at forgiving himself. If this had been for real, eighty percent of his men, Sam Carter included, would be dead and it would have been his fault. *If* it had been for real... Well, it hadn't been!

She sighed and moved in to join the fray. Nothing like a good distraction. Which really was the reason why she'd allowed Dr. Jackson to stay. That and the fact that, for the first time since Reese's death, there seemed to be a spring thaw in the cold war between him and Jack O'Neill. Maybe the accident hadn't been such a bad thing after all. "Let's check you out, Colonel," she said.

"I'm—"

"Peachy. Yeah. I heard you the first six times. Newsflash, sir: you're peachy when I say you are and not a moment sooner."

"Na—"

"—poleonic power monger. So you keep telling me."

"I was going to say 'naturally'." For a split-second his gaze met hers, and he shot her a grin that was as brittle as glass.

"The Marines who pulled him out said he had trouble breathing," Dr. Jackson offered, which earned him a sour snarl.

"I'd like to see them breathe with a mature killer whale landing on their asses."

"It wasn't your ass, and she didn't mean to. One of our guys knocked her off the gallery."

"Didn't *mean* to? She took *aim*! Just keep her the hell away from me!"

"She—"

"You won't have to worry about her for a while," Janet cut in. "Private Lamont's worse off than you, Colonel."

His scowl crumbled into concern. "She gonna be okay?"

"Eventually. She struck the stock of your rifle face-on. Her jaw's fractured pretty badly. She'll need some new teeth, too."

"Ouch." Dr. Jackson winced.

"Yeah. *Ouch.* Speaking of which." She nodded at O'Neill. "Can you take your shirt off for me, sir?"

He tried. The result were clenched teeth and a grimace and something that sounded like *cannelloni herbs and summer fish*.

Janet blinked. "Come again, Colonel?"

"Can't sit up." He made an elocution lesson of spitting out the words. At a guess, the respiratory problem had resolved itself. "It hurts like a son of a bitch!"

"Ah. Good job I didn't let you sneak out then."

"It wasn't that bad a while ago."

If he actually admitted to it, it had to be *really* bad. She peeled the shirt apart. His skin had barely left the flushed stage for indigo, but tomorrow it'd be a dozen shades of purple. About five inches wide at its broadest, the contusion looped from the lower right front of his ribcage up the side and disappeared under his arm. Superficially nothing seemed to be broken, which was great news — if not entirely pleasant. Deep bruising could be more painful than a fracture and for longer.

"Sorry," she announced. "This'll hurt."

"Ya think?"

As gently as she could she probed for injuries, bits that moved when they shouldn't or were stuck where they didn't belong. He didn't say a peep, but by the time she finished his face had turned pale under the tan and glistened with sweat.

"Sorry," Janet said again, meaning it. "I had to make sure."

"Sure of *what*?" he panted. "My pain threshold?"

"Didn't know you had one, sir." Eyebrows arched in mock surprise, she grinned. "Button up. The shirt, I mean. You're lucky. When Lamont fell on top of you, those cotton bales absorbed most of the impact. No broken ribs this time."

"Then how come —"

"*But* you've got severe contusions, and I don't have to tell you that those always are fun. They've triggered something that's called intercostal neuralgia."

"Panama Canal?"

"*Costal*, not coastal!" Across the gurney, Dr. Jackson rolled one eye. "That was crap, Jack, even by your standards."

In Janet Fraiser's experience, the safest course of action lay in ignoring the pair of them. "I'll give you some Demerol, Colonel, but other than that it'll just have to heal on its own."

"I don't need painkillers."

The phrasing was disputable, though she knew better than to quibble. He didn't *want* painkillers. He thought he deserved everything he got and then some. Janet pasted on an innocent smile. "Oh, you'll need them. Sooner or later you'll find it necessary to take off your pants or tie your shoelaces."

Assertions of the contrary were cut off by a commotion at the entrance. The ambulance crew was about to stretcher off PFC Lamont, and two visitors were trying to get past it into the tent. Her orderly made the most unlikely bouncer you could ever hope to meet.

"Sorry, ma'am. Uh…" With an uncertain look from the blond Major to the enormous black guy whose rank, if any, was a mystery, he added, "Sir. You can't come in unless you're dying. Dr. Fraiser's—"

"It's okay!" Janet called before the corporal, in the line of duty, committed a folly he might regret. "Let them in."

Dusty, disheveled, streaks of camouflage paint still decorating her nose, Major Carter pushed past the orderly. She came to an abrupt halt in the middle of the tent, the relief on her face boundless and, for once, unguarded.

Teal'c filled in what she didn't say. "O'Neill. Daniel Jackson. I am pleased to see you alive."

Trust him to come straight to the point. His dark voice rang with genuine warmth, and it had the added effect of shaking up Sam Carter. She snapped back into her usual efficiency, just about jumped to attention, and said, "Sir. Daniel. Debrief's over at the factory in fifteen, if you're good to go."

Major General George S. Hammond's chair—an exquisitely uncomfortable creation in orange plastic—crowned one end of two stained tables, which had been pushed together lengthways to create a debriefing venue for this debacle. At the other end, too far to kick the man's ankles but not far enough to miss the smirk, sat Lieutenant General Philip 'Alistair' Crowley, USMC. Whoever had dreamed up that call sign displayed commendable insight into the human psyche. The key members of his coven sat along one side of the makeshift conference table, looking as superior as their intrepid leader. The Air Force participants opposite looked anything but.

The room itself was high in ambience, a former cafeteria on the top level of an abandoned factory building on the outskirts of Colorado Springs. The floor was padded with newspaper where the linoleum had cracked, the windows were dirty and streaked by drizzle, and yellowing acoustic tiles drooped from a damp ceiling. Atop two crates in a corner sat a TV/VCR, screen snowy with static. Up until two minutes ago it had been playing video footage of the Armageddon that had taken place two levels below.

All in all, Hammond wished he were in a galaxy far, far away, where they had comfy chairs. Where the people voted least likely didn't suddenly commit catastrophic deployment errors. Where one's superiors didn't insist on scheduling exercises that did more harm than good and only served to stroke inflated egos. Maybe he wasn't entirely objective. Losers rarely were. He closed his eyes. The galaxy far, far away didn't materialize.

The underlying mistake had been his, of course. He should never have agreed to it: a handpicked crew of Recon Marines against the finest the US Air Force had to offer. Okay, he *hadn't* agreed to it. Staging an exercise like this at a time when the Navy was at the Air Force's throat, and the Air Force at the Navy's, and the Army at everybody's because they'd all been led to believe it was a matter of survival? Madness. Waste. To the best of his knowledge, rivalry among the forces had never won a war yet, and fact of the matter was that they *were* fighting a war—the most crucial war ever. Even if only five people in this room were aware of it.

So he'd said *no*. Once, twice, a half dozen times. But Crowley had been more insistent than an insurance salesman. He also was well-connected. After all, the Marines guarded you-know-whom. The final invitation had arrived via that red phone on General Hammond's desk, and its phrasing had been along the lines of *Do it! RSVP*. If he weren't up to his eyeballs in politics, struggling to keep Senator Kinsey and the NID at arm's length, he still might have talked his way out of it—he'd done it before—but giving in had just seemed quicker. Easier. Safer. The hallmarks of a poor decision.

In consequence, a bunch of good people who should be out there doing it for real had got the crap kicked out of them for kudos, and one of them had damn near got himself killed.

Christ almighty, Jack! What the hell went wrong?

Rejoining the proceedings might be one way of finding out, Hammond figured. To his dismay, the room hadn't magically transformed into a desert island when he opened his eyes. At least the timing was perfect. Crowley was through pontificating on the merits of inter-service competition. *Gives the men an edge, and that's what we want, right?*

Rah-rah!

"So, let's assess this, ladies and gentlemen, shall we?" brayed Crowley. "George?"

Hammond dumbly nodded his assent—what else could he do?—thinking all the while that, if anything, Colonel O'Neill might have *lost* his edge. Under the circumstances, eighty percent casualties were indefensible. It had been a simple raid scenario. The rules allowed each team to carry laser-sighted *intars*—the Marines had been told they were a new type of long-range stun gun—and basic equipment and two cutting charges. Specialized gadgets, even radios, had been off-limits. Straightforward stuff, in other words. Which, in the way of any decent circular argument, led right back to *What the hell went wrong?* If Hammond were to play it by the book, today's performance should be Jack's ticket to a desk from where to organize supplies. Under strict supervision. But when it came to this particular officer, Hammond rarely played things by the book, and he wanted to know a lot more before he even contemplated going down the supplies route. Question was whether he'd learn it in this room.

Chest feathers puffed, Colonel Pete Norris, the CO of the Marine teams, had begun outlining his strategy, which boiled down to *Take It And Keep It*. Pragmatic, if hardly novel. Either side of him, his team leaders dutifully scratched the highlights onto notepads. Crowley interrupted here and there, asking through a benign smile for reiteration of choice moments.

"That's correct, sir," replied Norris. "There were those steel girders under the ceiling. I ordered ten of my men up there when I realized that the gallery could be critical."

"That's a considerable proportion of your manpower, Colonel,"

Crowley observed. "Wasn't that a bit reckless?"

"With respect, sir, no. We had the ground floor entrances covered. Same goes for the only staircase to the upper levels. I had twelve people on standby there. Those are the ones who were then deployed to break through the walls onto the catwalk."

"Hang on a minute." Dr. Jackson, who until now had been listening with sullen forbearance, started scribbling numbers onto the notepad in front of him. Once he was finished, he frowned at them. The eye patch made him look like a kid who'd come to the Halloween party in a pirate outfit two inches shy of menacing.

"You've got a question, Doctor?" Crowley was craning his neck, trying to see what Jackson had written.

"As a matter of fact, yes. These figures don't add up. We were allowed no more than twenty-five men each. Now, even if the unit that Murray"—he cast a quick glance at Teal'c whose tattoo was safely hidden under a watch cap—"and his team chased around the grounds was only half the strength we assumed it was… still seems like Colonel Norris had about five men too many."

"That's exactly why civilian contractors shouldn't be allowed in the field!" Norris snarled. "How can you folks even start to comprehend tactical issues?"

Slick as a buttered bun, Crowley cut in. "Dr. Jackson, have you considered that Murray was chasing his own tail because Colonel O'Neill's reconnaissance wasn't quite what it should have been?"

"No, because that's absolutely—"

"Colonel Norris, please continue," said Crowley.

And on it went. With the one difference that Major Carter had furtively swapped her notepad for Dr. Jackson's and was adding some scribbling of her own.

At last Norris ran out of brilliant ideas to present for applause, and Crowley thanked him and turned his gaze on Jack O'Neill. "Colonel O'Neill? Your take on it, please."

Face rigid, Jack abandoned an ongoing attempt to skewer his notepad with a pen and stared at the window. "Yessir."

He kept staring at that window throughout a clinical analysis of his actions that lasted a fraction of the time Norris's homily had taken and was twice as brutal. Largely on himself. Halfway through, Hammond heard the door open and close. Somebody had stepped into the room, silently hovering in the background. Whoever it was could wait while Jack relentlessly approached the crux of the matter. He had failed to correctly assess the tactical situation inside the factory. The problem was, George Hammond still refused to believe it.

"I screwed up. Sorry, sir." Jack finally gave up on the window and glanced at Hammond. For once, he looked his age. "I'm just glad it was an exercise. God help me if it hadn't been."

"That's one reason why we stage these things," intoned Crowley. "We all can do with a wake-up call now and again. Now, ladies and gentlemen, I think that wraps it up. Thank you all for your efforts, and hopefully we can arrange a rematch at some point. Dismissed."

There were perfunctory handshakes across the table, then the Marines rose and Norris went to collect his pat on the back from Crowley. In a cloud of chatter they filtered out the door. The Air Force contingent all but ignored their exit. Colonel O'Neill had resumed his scrutiny of the glassware. Dr. Jackson and Major Carter were huddled over a notepad. Maintaining his quiet air of aloofness, Teal'c didn't huddle but peered over sideways and evidently didn't much care for what he—

The slow, deliberate claps echoed through the empty room like gunshots, startling them all.

"Astonishing. I didn't think I'd ever have the privilege of seeing you eat humble pie, Colonel. Actually, for a moment there I thought you'd choke on it." The man slid off a chair by the door and ambled toward them, perfectly groomed in a suit by Armani or Boss or some other designer that didn't tailor for people of Hammond's stature. The urbane façade was as deceptive as quicksand, of course.

Sam Carter's face suggested that somebody was trying to feed her live slugs. "What are you doing here?"

In a way, Hammond was grateful she'd beaten him to it. He couldn't have risked infusing the question with quite the same amount of venom. Then again, he didn't have quite as much reason to hate the man. "Simmons," he ground out.

"Oh yes." Colonel Frank Simmons smiled. "Surely you were made aware that the NID had assigned an observer to this... masterpiece?"

CHAPTER THREE

"**C**ome on, Gus! Don't go official on me," Sam Carter purred, grimacing—partly at herself for the purr, partly at Gus and his habit of making people woo him. She wasn't a wooer.

Eighty-seven degrees through a monumental eye roll she caught sight of Daniel who came strolling into her lab, Teal'c in tow. Pinning the handset between ear and shoulder, she gestured for them to grab chairs. At the other end of the line, in an office in Chantilly, Virginia, Augustus 'Gus' Przsemolensky was graduating from *No way!* to *I'm not supposed to*.

"For old times' sake. Gus! This is *me!*"

Teal'c's left eyebrow did a pull-up, and Dr. Jackson mouthed *Gus?* with such an exaggerated look of surprise that Sam exploded into a snort.

"No! I had to sneeze. Dust." She glowered at Daniel. "Look, *if* somebody asks… Yeah, blame it on CORONA… You will? Great! Got something to write? Here goes…" Sam reeled off a set of coordinates, date, and time and repeated it all for good measure. "You got my email address. Ten minutes would be good… Okay, okay… Half an hour. Thanks, Gus."

She put the handset back into the cradle and sagged onto her lab bench, forehead resting on folded hands. "Talk about giving birth to China," she muttered at a technical drawing.

"Gu-u-us," sang Daniel, drawing it out over three syllables. "Anything you want to tell us, Sam?"

Raising her head just enough to glare at him between bits of disassembled particle accelerator and mummified donuts, she growled, "Not really. How about you?"

Daniel's glee evaporated. "Looks like they're here to stay."

"Damn! Have they talked to either of you yet?"

"They have not, Major Carter." Teal'c sounded like a funeral director.

"What about the Colonel?"

"No idea. I doubt it, though," said Daniel and shrugged. "I tried to phone him a few times. Don't know how he did it, but his service is redirecting all calls to the talking clock in Tokyo."

"It's *what*?" Sam straightened up, knocking a donut mummy off the bench. It bounced. "That's... impressive. How do you know it's the talking clock?"

"I speak—"

"Japanese. Of course."

"Anyway, I guess even those NID jerks would have got the *Do not disturb* part."

Yesterday, three days after that misbegotten exercise, two faceless, flavorless NID agents of unspecified rank and sublime dress sense had descended upon Stargate Command. Over the protests of General Hammond. The protests had been silenced by a call from Washington. It wasn't the first time it had happened, it sure as hell wouldn't be the last—unless somebody finally grew the balls to shut down that nest of vipers—but usually you found out in a hurry *why* the NID came at you. If only because they came at you with all the diplomatic finesse of an Abrams M1A battle tank.

Sam winced at the memory of her own interview with Frank Simmons a few months back. He'd made a damn good bid at dismantling her professionally, mentally, emotionally. Halfway through she'd grasped that Simmons had to be the illegal user who'd hacked into the SGC mainframe. Thinking she could rattle him, she'd accused him point blank. Water off a duck's back. He hadn't even tried to deny it, and the threat implicit in his indifference had scared the hell out of her. Eventually, Simmons had left. The threat hadn't. It lingered like a bad smell. His impromptu appearance at the debriefing four days ago had reinforced it nicely. And now his henchmen were here, sniffing after—

"Major Carter."

"What?"

Teal'c silently pointed at her computer. In the lower right-hand corner of the screen the mail icon was flashing.

"That was quick. I think Gus is a little overeager." Daniel's eye patch rode up his forehead, and he grinned. "Want me to check?"

"You wouldn't be able to read it. Besides, it can't be him yet. He's never in his life been ahead of a deadline."

Then again, stranger things had happened. She darted out from behind the lab bench, pushed aside her computer chair, currently inhabited by Daniel, and opened the email.

From: augustus.przemolensky@nro.mil
To: cartersmaj@norad.mil
Subject: Long time no see
Sam, great to hear from you and thanks for thinking of an old flame. Do as you promised and drop in on me next time you're in this neck of the woods. Gus xoxox

No attachment. More significantly, no encryption. Gus encrypted his shopping lists. She should know because, once upon a time, she'd played Crack The Algorithm with him. Either Gus wasn't the author, or he'd wanted to demonstrate to somebody standing over him that this was perfectly harmless—and at the same time warn Sam Carter. She felt a lump of ice congealing in the pit of her stomach. "Oh crap," she whispered. "Crap!"

"Hey! He did sign off with hugs and kisses. There's hope yet." Daniel was scanning the mail, then his gaze arrested on the sender's address. "National Reconnaissance Office? Friends in high places, huh? All the way in orbit. *Now* care to tell us what this is all about?"

Sam dug a crumpled piece of paper from her back pocket and tossed it at Daniel. "Your little math problem."

"My what?" Smoothing out wrinkles between thumb and forefinger, he stared at his own writing. "Oh. Well, that got slapped down alright. *Dr. Jackson, have you considered that Colonel O'Neill's reconnaissance wasn't quite what it should have been?*" His rendition of Crowley's adenoid twang was flawless. "So what about it?"

"Daniel, we both know that the Colonel's reconnaissance was just dandy. Teal'c did most of it."

"Indeed." The Jaffa had risen from a chair that seemed two sizes too small for his frame and wandered over to them, all elegance and contained power. "O'Neill had no reason to assume that there were sufficient numbers for the kind of ambush we experienced."

"But telling that to Crowley would have gone over like a pregnant pole-vaulter," Daniel glumly completed the thought. "Jack must have realized when I got my butt kicked by Norris. Maybe I should have just kept my mouth shut."

"O'Neill would not have told General Crowley under any circumstances."

"Teal'c's right," said Sam. "The Colonel *believes* he's to blame. No points for guessing what that means."

"Yeah," grumbled Daniel. "Anybody who wants to tell him otherwise can go have a heart to heart with the talking clock in Tokyo."

"Which is why Major Carter attempted to obtain independent evidence from Augustus Przsemolensky."

"Yup." Sam nodded at Teal'c. "Your momma didn't raise no dummies."

"She did not." The smile was there if you knew him, quirking just beneath the dignified surface. "I am an only child."

"Sooo…" Pensively shredding the notepaper, Daniel gazed at the computer screen and then back at Sam. "You asked your friend Gus at the NRO to get you a satellite picture of the factory grounds at the time of the exercise. The idea being to run a headcount of everybody outside. How am I doing for a civilian contractor with no grasp of tactical issues?"

"Not bad." She grinned. "Colonel Norris would be shocked."

"I don't see a picture."

"No."

Her grin died, and Sam crossed her arms in front of her chest as if to protect herself. The iceberg in her stomach wanted to stage a comeback. For a minute or two she'd allowed herself to push aside the implications of Gus's email. They meshed perfectly with the diffuse sense of dread the presence of the NID agents had triggered. But none of this would go away just because she ignored it. Simmons wouldn't go away. She drifted back behind her lab bench, feeling safer among the familiar clutter of research and experimentation. At least that was predictable, obeyed rules. By and large.

"Somebody intercepted my phone call," she said at last. "My money's on the NID. Unless Gus told them, they won't know what I asked him to do, because the call was scrambled. But they *do* know where it came from and where it went, and they got to Gus by return post. There's no chance of him sending me any pictures now. No chance of proving anything, either way."

"*Oh crap*, huh? But you're wrong." The corners of Daniel's mouth twitched, and he looked nine shades of smug. It went well with the eye patch. "They've shown their hand. They've just told us loud and clear that there *is* something to prove. All you've got to do is find another way of proving it."

"There is no other——" Her eyes arrested on the dismantled generator and a clutch of tools. Research and experimentation. Predictable. Obeying rules. By and large. Sam gazed up and smiled. "Okay, scratch that. Gentlemen, we're going on a fieldtrip back to the factory."

As they left the lab, klaxons started wailing, signaling an incoming wormhole five levels below. Habit tugged at her and demanded she head down to the control room. Sam made for the armory instead. There were some props they needed to collect, ideally without answering questions. The well-timed excitement in the gate room would keep the NID creeps occupied.

The stowaway stepped from the chill, liquid embrace of the *Chappa'ai*. Behind her the wormhole destabilized and died, and the barrier, which the Tauri thought could protect them, slid into place. Before her two of them slowly marched down the ramp, supporting a third. He was injured. So fragile, humans. So ignorant.

Little did they suspect that she had caused the injury, caused the man to trip and fall down a ravine and break his leg. She had heard the bones snap. It had amused her. Fragile indeed. And because they feared their own fragility, they had invented a goddess of deceit and destruction to appease. Destruction and deceit were apt enough, but there was much more.

"So much more, my children." Her lips moved, but she did not utter a sound. Not yet.

For the ones who appeased her enough, there were rewards—screaming, blood-sweet turmoil of body and mind. If, ultimately, the rewards pleased her more than their recipients, it was only due tribute to a deity.

The humans had eased their injured comrade onto a step at the bottom of the ramp. Others, clad in black, swarmed around them. Toward the edges of her vision they appeared increasingly distorted,

grotesque gnomes brandishing grotesque weapons. The phase shifting device smudged her view of their reality into a gray-in-gray perspective through shattered glass. A noise to the left made her turn her
head—too fast—and her eyes snapped shut against a jagged blur of
images. She blinked and saw the healer rush into the room. No black
for this one. This one wore white. For purity, she presumed, snarling at the thought. Not so pure, this one. Not above destruction and
deceit, just like her.

She remembered this diminutive woman pointing a weapon, large
and out of place in too-small hands. This healer, so-called, had forced
her to reverse the maturing of the first viable *hak'taur*. Centuries of
labor destroyed at the cusp of fruition... She felt a swell of rage, let it
fill her, relishing its heat. No weapon now. It would be easy to crush
the healer's body. It could be achieved in a heartbeat, and the humans,
fragile and ignorant, would be helpless to prevent it. But this was not
the time, and it was enough to know that she *could* do it. That knowledge held a satisfaction all of its own, an assurance of godlike power
over life and death. She smiled.

Their fat, bald leader had joined the group around the injured man.
"What happened?" he barked.

Did it matter? And did anyone believe this show of concern?
Apparently they did. Excited voices chattered out a garbled account
of an accident that had been no accident. Humans. How they bored
her! Most, but not all of them. She scanned the room for more adequate entertainment and was disappointed. Then again, she would
have wanted to meet him alone, like the last time...

*"In your place I doubt I would have done the same." The fact that
she concedes even that much is remarkable, and she does not quite
know why she has admitted the truth or what it means. A grudging
tribute or a warning against future folly. At any rate, a challenge.*

*Dark eyes unreadable, he turns it back on her. "I'll keep that
thought alive."*

*About to step onto the ramp, she throws a last look at him—tall,
lean, gray-haired, fearless. A worthy adversary. Better yet, a complex
one. Life has scored that handsome, narrow face, and hidden behind
his eyes lies a much older man's experience of bliss, agony, death.
A lot of the latter, she suspects and idly wonders what it will take to*

*break him. Deceit and destruction? Perhaps. Perhaps she will find
out. Perhaps not. But whatever the answer, they are not finished yet.*

She smiles a promise, and he understands her perfectly.

The memory was shattered by two more men entering the room
below, their clothing markedly different from the others'. These were
the ones the human Simmons had advised her to contact. She briefly
recalled the image of his face in the communication globe. No secrets
here. The mouth alone, sensuous and cruel, betrayed his thirst for
power, and the long, fleshy features held a haughtiness that rivaled
her own. He could be trusted, because his most fundamental trait
could be trusted: greed.

Noiselessly she glided down the ramp and toward the new arrivals. Slipping in behind the younger one, blue-eyed and innocent, she
caressed his neck. He would not be able to feel her touch in his phase,
not completely. It would seem like a breath of cool wind to him, she
assumed. She had assumed correctly. Fine blond hairs stood on end.
A second gentle stroke across soft skin, and he shivered impercepti-
bly, which pleased her. Perhaps she would reward him. A poor substitute, but a substitute nonetheless.

At the third touch he nudged his companion, who turned around,
frowned, shrugged. They had been told what to expect but still hesitated to accept what they could not see. So very human. It did not
matter, however, as long as they obeyed their instructions.

A mere two paces away, the injured man was carried from the
room. Behind him followed the healer and the human leader. The
elder of the escorts stepped forward and addressed him. "General
Hammond?"

"I don't have time for you now, Kyser!"

"This won't take a moment, and I guarantee you'll like what you
hear." The man Kyser gave a tight smile.

The General stopped in his tracks and whirled around, nimble for
a man of his girth. "Make it quick!"

"Simply a courtesy, General. We're finished here. You can expect
Colonel Simmons's report within a day or two."

"Fine. Don't let the door hit you on your way out." The human
leader strode off.

"Don't let that head of yours get too big," Kyser hissed into thin air. "One of these days, it's gonna roll, General. Real soon." Then he nodded at the younger man. "Let's go."

She followed them through a maze of drab corridors, into two elevators for an endless journey toward daylight, and finally out into a manmade cavern. This area accommodated surface conveyances, and it smelled acrid with fumes. Her escorts stopped at a vehicle, large and sand-colored. The young one unlocked its doors.

"Now what?" he asked.

"We wait a few minutes, then we make tracks," replied Kyser. "If she's in the car, great. If not, I won't complain. I'm not exactly keen on spending hours on a plane with an invisible snake at my back."

"Would it make you feel more confident if I were visible?" She enjoyed the effect immensely. The man stifled a scream and staggered against the rear of the vehicle, staring at her in pure terror. She approached until she stood pressed against him, fingers playing across his cheek. Without warning they clenched in his hair. "Be grateful that I choose not to punish you for your insolence!"

"Yes, ma'am."

"Now take me to your master."

"Yes, ma'am."

Daniel watched the anchor-like metal contraption reach its zenith and stall. It hovered for a moment, then it flipped downward and nosed into yet another plunge, trailing rope. He clamped his hands over his ears, winced. The noise of a grappling hook striking concrete, amplified by God knew how many thousand cubic feet of empty space, was cataclysmic. It seemed to drill through his hands and into his ears, after which it converged somewhere behind his shiner to pound around a bit. Wonderful. By the end of this he'd probably be deaf *and* blind.

Eventually the echo died down and Sam shouted, "That was great, Teal'c! Nearly there. Try again!"

Oh for cryin' out loud... to coin a phrase. "Sam, I really—"

"Major Carter." Teal'c actually looked frazzled. "A Tauri scientist named Albert Einstein devised a most apposite definition of insanity. Are you familiar with it?"

"Yes. Doing the same thing over and over again and expecting different results."

"I assure you, the result will be no different however many times I attempt this." Which was the sound of a Jaffa digging in his heels.

Cross-legged on the floor, Sam hunched over her laptop, keying stuff that presumably made sense to her. Now she gazed up. Just how she did it was a mystery to Daniel, but her smile lit up the gloomy factory hall and raised ambient temperatures by several degrees. A select few had been known to say *No* to the killer beam. Jack, for instance, though he probably practiced in front of the mirror. On this occasion, the full force of it was directed at Teal'c, who wasn't in training. His resistance wilted, and he wordlessly began coiling the zip line attached to the grappling hook. Take umpteen.

"Your last two tries were really close," she said, faintly apologetic. "I've computed the kilopond necessary to get that hook up there. That's easy, just a function of weight and distance, with the aerodynamic drag of the rope factored in. I've also downloaded your physiological profile from Janet's databank, which allows me to calculate the force you put into a throw like this. Now, given that the differential between—"

"Major Carter. I am ready, and it is getting late. We shall not be able to continue after sunset."

Teal'c's methods were somewhat more gracious than Jack's but equally effective. Sam abandoned a lecture, which, in the simplest of terms, came down to *If a Jaffa can't get the damn hook up there, nobody can.* She nodded. "Go ahead."

After a glance at the girder thirty meters above, Teal'c stepped back and measured out some slack on the zip line. Then he began swinging rope and hook in a diagonal circle over his head. Once, twice. The third time he let go, his body extending as if he meant to take flight himself. The grappling hook soared upward and did what it'd been doing for the past hour. Five meters or so short of the girder it ran out of steam and stalled. Crash-bang-boom.

"Well, I think that settles it." The words mixed with the echo still caroming through Daniel's sinuses, and he yawned to ease the pressure. Then his mouth snapped shut with an audible clack. "Uh-oh."

The man stood motionless just inside the open gate, outlined by a wedge of copper evening light. Terrific! If not entirely unexpected.

The ongoing racket was bound to have brought security guards on the plan sooner or later. Of course they'd hoped to be out of here sooner. Strictly speaking, what they were doing could be considered trespassing at best, breaking and entering at worst.

"We've just come to collect some leftover equipment." Sam had risen, arms slightly spread to indicate that she was unarmed. "There was a military exercise here a few days ago. If you want to—"

"I *know* there was an exercise, Carter. I got you killed, remember?"

"Sir!" Chiseled by a sharp breath, it sounded like a sob.

"O'Neill," said Teal'c.

"The one and only."

Fists sunk into the pockets of a leather jacket, he started walking toward them, affecting the nonchalance of a tourist at some historical site. *Gee, that's a real neat battlefield!* Except, it didn't quite come off as planned. He moved as though somebody had strapped him into a corset, and when he finally stepped out of that glaring backlight, Daniel was startled to see how drained he looked. Drained and wound more tightly than a wristwatch.

"What the hell are you doing here, Jack?"

"The perp always returns to the scene of the crime. Never heard of it? We also tend to turn up at funerals."

By Jack O'Neill's standards this was a whole encyclopedia of information, although Daniel was willing to bet a month's paycheck that Jack had had no real intention of carrying the conversation even this far. If they hadn't noticed him, he'd have beat a quiet retreat until after they were gone. And then? He'd have come in here and made himself relive every second of the exercise, compulsively listing and re-listing everything he thought he'd done wrong.

"Where's the crime?" Daniel asked, aware that it was the next best thing to poking a tiger's abscessed tooth.

"We've had this discussion. We're not having it again," snarled the tiger. Then his curiosity asserted itself, and he took in the zip line, the hook, the laptop, and the piece of equipment sitting next to it. "What the hell are *you* doing here?"

"Sir, we—"

"Observe, O'Neill."

Obviously Teal'c had concluded that a demonstration would be
more beneficial than Sam's treatise on kilopond and differentials. The
grappling hook flew, stalled, plunged, and made that infernal noise.

Jack never even twitched. "You missed."

"That's precisely our point, sir." Sam allowed herself a small,
hopeful grin. "If Teal'c's throwing short, Norris's team—Marines or no—wouldn't have had a prayer of catching the girders.
Unless"—she picked up a bulky gun that had the business end of a
hook sticking out its nose—"they had launchers."

Settling the device against her shoulder, she took aim, fired. The
hook soared, rope rippling after it, and neatly wrapped itself around a
girder. Just like that, and with considerably less noise, too.

"That's the only way they could have got up there, Colonel," she
added. "And we both know that launchers weren't permitted. Norris
didn't play by the rules, sir. Nobody can blame you for not anticipating that they'd cheat."

"Oh no?" Jack's voice could have cut glass. "Tell me something,
Major. When the Goa'uld pull the next new and improved doomsday
machine out of their collective hat you gonna come running to me
and bawl, 'They're cheating! They're not permitted those, so I don't
wanna play!'?"

"No, sir." Her jaw worked, but she refused to be drawn into a
fight.

Sensing it, Jack wouldn't let up. "That's what the enemy do. They
cheat. If you haven't grasped that by now, you're in the wrong job,
Major! They cheat because it gives them an advantage. We do the
same damn thing, and anybody who doesn't anticipate that is a liability."

"Your comparison is flawed, O'Neill."

"Is it?" Jack whirled around, grimacing when the abrupt move
jarred his ribs.

"Indeed." Slowly and methodically, Teal'c was coiling his zip
line. Each coil punctuated a sentence. "It was a game. Games have
rules. You abided by these rules and expected your opponent to do the
same, because you *knew* it was a game. But the rules were broken.
Who is to blame? You or the one who broke them?"

As so often, Teal'c's unshakeable calm deflated Jack. Sighing softly, he hunched his shoulders. "I *know* it was a game. What I *don't* know is that I'd have done anything different if it'd hadn't been. If it'd been for real... Sergeant Chen's wife had a little girl two weeks ago. If it'd been for real, that kid would grow up without a father because of me. You'd be dead, too, Carter, and I'd rather not think about the ways in which Jacob would rearrange my anatomy. As for you"—he tossed a wry grin at Daniel—"you'd probably have got your head in the way of some obstacle no matter what, so I won't plead to that."

"Jack—"

"Ah!" One hand held up, he wandered away, aimless until he was caught in the gravitational pull of the cotton bales and veered toward those. His left hand slipped from the pocket and started picking fluff. At last he turned back. "I appreciate what you're trying to do, kids. I... Look, I'm sure Carter could get Norris sent down for grand larceny, but it's not gonna change anything. So do me a favor and forget about it. I'd like get out of this with a few shreds of dignity intact."

The *get out of this* part was unequivocal and triggered something of a flashback. As far as thoroughly miserable conversations went, that one had been a doozy. "That's... uh... that's funny, because I didn't figure you for the early retirement type anymore," Daniel said quietly.

Jack shot him a sharp glance. He remembered it too. Those words and what had come next.

"So, this friendship thing we've been working on the last few years..."

And he stares at Daniel point blank and finishes that half-formed question, "Apparently not much of a foundation, huh?"

He had the same steady, determined, goddamn implacable look now, though the veneer of arrogance was missing completely. "This is different, Daniel, and you know it."

It was. This time it wasn't a lie. This time it was for real. The question was if it'd be worth fighting. For a split-second, Daniel saw Reese's dead face and asked himself if things weren't just dandy the way they seemed to pan out now. Then he banished the thought to where it'd come from, ashamed of himself. Twisted and battered and bent out of shape, yes, but that friendship was still there, still for real, and as long as—

"Sir, you can't!" Sam had gone white as a sheet. "Not over this. Not when—"

"*When* what, Carter?" Jack asked almost gently. "Always boils down to the same thing, see? Liability. In every sense of the word. Besides, I already have. The letter should be on Hammond's desk tomorrow. The only alternative would be me pushing paper till the end of my days. You can see that working? No, wouldn't have thought so. I can't either."

Bits of cotton floated in the air, and he caught one, picked at it, blew it away again. Abruptly he turned and headed for the door. He looked surprisingly small in the vastness of the room, a black silhouette outlined by a wedge of light that had deepened from copper to burgundy.

"That's pathetic!" yelled Daniel, furious at him, Norris, the world at large. "The hero walking off into the sunset! It's such a cliché, Jack!"

For once there was no comeback. He just kept going. Daniel started after him, and was stopped by Teal'c's large, strong hand clasping his arm.

"Not now. You will not dissuade him now, Daniel Jackson."

Colonel Frank Simmons had monitored the car's approach from the control center. The vehicle had passed the gatepost at the outer perimeter of the safe house and gone on a winding journey through a mile of lush countryside. When it emerged from a pine copse and entered the last stretch toward the house, he'd gone outside to wait. Now he regretted it. The night air was freezing.

Next to him Conrad shuffled, one finger stretching the collar of his turtleneck sweater. In all likelihood his discomfort was caused not by the collar but by the safety device it concealed; a remote-controlled choker studded with parcels of naquadah-enhanced explosive. One wrong move and it would literally blow Conrad's head off—and kill the Goa'uld. It was the price he had to pay for attending the meeting.

"Tell me one thing," Simmons asked. "How can she be your mistress? You were stuck inside a Jaffa's pouch when you got here, then you spent some time in a fish tank, and then you ended up inside our friend Adrian."

Conrad gave up fidgeting and condescended to answer. "You know nothing, human. The Jaffa who nursed me once belonged to her. The Goa'uld queen who bore me belonged to her. Therefore she is my mistress."

Headlights doused, the government-issue sedan pulled into the circular driveway in front of the house. The slamming of the doors and crackle of feet on gravel sounded overly loud in the stillness of the night, and Simmons finally admitted to a mild case of nerves. It had set in about six hours ago, when his operatives had informed him that they'd made contact and were en route to Peterson AFB where their jet was waiting. Even then Conrad had refused to reveal the identity of his 'mistress'—another one of the pointless power games the Goa'uld seemed to enjoy so much—but it didn't matter now. Simmons was about to find out.

A blond agent held the door open for her, and she got out of the car with the grace of a debutante. The first thing that struck Simmons was how delicate she looked. Then she turned, and the light of a lamp below the portico illuminated a chin-length bob of raven hair, black almond eyes, a deceptively generous mouth, and a narrow nose. A diamond-shaped Bindi on the Chakra point between the eyebrows underlined the exotic flair of her features.

Simmons resisted an urge to laugh. Not that he'd ever met her, of course, but he'd seen archive pictures and read the SGC reports, and by God, her credentials were perfect. More than that, she would be amenable to the offer. She needed all the help she could get. Slipping into his role of host—a rather worrying term, come to think of it—he glided down the steps to greet her.

"Lady Nirrti. I'm delighted that you chose to accept my invitation."

The sardonic tilt of her eyebrows suggested that either the address had been too baroque or she'd seen through the formulaic courtesy. She swept past him and toward Conrad, eyes flaring. "What made you think you could allow this human to summon me here?" The distorted voice sounded almost masculine.

It also sounded utterly cold, and Conrad, whose mask of superiority had slipped out of sight the moment she approached him, seemed tempted to prostrate himself. "Forgive me, mistress. I meant no offense. I acted merely from a wish to aid you."

The veiled reminder of her precarious standing—if any—among the System Lords caused another baleful flicker in her eyes, but she was smart enough to concede the truth. "Very well. I am willing to discuss this proposal."

"In that case, please follow me." Grateful to get out of the night chill, Simmons led her and Conrad into the library on the first floor. The ambiance would be sufficiently pompous, even for Goa'uld tastes. The room smelled of old leather bindings and faded parchment, and in the open grate roared a fire, the shine of its flames dancing across walls and a parquet floor. Atop a priceless Persian rug sat a cherry wood table, surrounded by high-backed chairs.

Nirrti stopped dead in front of the grandfather clock by the door, listened to its ticking, suspicion contorting her face. "What is this device?"

Not so omniscient after all. The urge to laugh threatened to return, and Simmons stifled it ruthlessly. "It measures time. It's quite harmless, I assure you. Please, take a seat."

"How... quaint." As she eased herself onto a chair, a sneer told him exactly what she thought of antique timepieces. Then her gaze fell on a crystal decanter and three glasses that sat on the table. "I am thirsty. Pour me some water."

Almost obeying, from reflex and the dicta of a conservative upbringing, he caught himself at the last moment. It was part of the power game, and if he gave in to her in the first round, she would have the upper hand throughout. Simmons ignored her and sat down in the chair opposite.

Face stony, eyes simmering, she engaged in a staring contest. "Pour me some water."

Conrad broke. The command had never been directed at him, but he was hovering behind Nirrti's chair like one of those... what did they call their loyal and trusted servants? Lotus? Luther? *Lotar*... like one of those *lotars*. Now he reached out, poured the water, handed the glass to her. "If it pleases you, mistress."

She took the glass without thanks and set it down on the table.

When she looked up, she was smiling. "You have my attention, Simmons."

Simmons smiled back at her. "Any progress on the *hak'taur* yet?"

"What do you know of the *hak'taur*? You could not possibly comprehend what it means!" It had rattled her, as it was meant to, and the hostility was back.

Good. He preferred to confront the real nature of the beast. Smiling sharks were unpredictable. "I think I comprehend enough: *hak* means 'improved' and *taur* is a slang term for 'Tauri'." Dr. Jackson, tedious and rude as he was, had his uses. That report had been eminently informative. Without waiting for an answer, Simmons carried on. "Put together, you get a human with superhuman abilities. An über-host, in other words, which is what you're after. You had to start from scratch, because Stargate Command, and specifically Dr. Fraiser, prevented you from using the Hankan girl, Cassandra. So I repeat: any progress yet?"

"It took me more than two hundred of your human years to achieve what I had achieved with the Hankan girl. How much progress do you think I have made in the two months since?"

"Not much I would assume." Simmons schooled his features into a kindly frown. "And in the meantime you are virtually unprotected—one mothership and barely enough Jaffa to man it isn't exactly a defense force, is it? Is Lord Yu still hunting you?"

"What if he were?" Her fingers caressed the stem of the water glass, twisting and turning it. "What is it to you?"

That was a yes. So much the better. "I'm asking because I would be prepared to provide you with protection."

"What kind of protection?"

"The kind only you would be able to create."

"You are talking in riddles!" Nirrti's eyes brightened to neon-white displeasure.

Conrad leaned forward and began whispering to her in rapid Goa'uld.

"Speak English!" Simmons snapped. Neither of them gave any indication that they'd heard him. That little problem had to be solved and solved decisively. He rose. "This discussion is terminated." Without another word he headed for the door.

"Wait!" And then, as if it were causing her throat to ache, "Please."

"Yes?" He slowed to a halt and carefully wiped the smirk off his face before turning back to her.

"I have no wish to offend you. Certain things are easier to understand in my own language. Sit." It was as close to an apology as she would ever get. Nirrti watched him with the stare of a snake charmer while he resumed his seat. Suddenly she burst out laughing. "You amuse me, human. Be glad you do. So you thought it was a question of a simple surgical procedure?"

"Of course not! We—"

"Tried to implant the pouch. Then you tried to prevent the inevitable immune response by applying the crudest chemistry imaginable. Without success, of course. Each one of your subjects rotted slowly, from the inside out. Did it ever occur to you that the very thing that causes rejection would be integral to the process? A protein. Such a tiny thing. So small that you cannot see it with the naked eye. Tauri scientists call it a 'building block of life', yes? For once they are correct. And yet, this tiny thing will cause death if introduced into a body that responds improperly. Why do you think it is called *symbiosis*?"

"Spare me the biology lesson!" Simmons placed his hands on the polished wood of the table and studied his fingernails. "I don't care *how* it's done, as long as it *is* done."

"What makes you think it *can* be done?"

"The fact that it wouldn't be the first time." His gaze drifted up from his fingers, and he met her eyes. "Hathor did it."

Nirrti's face twisted in a grimace. Apparently she and Hathor hadn't been in the habit of sharing girlie secrets. "Hathor was a queen. I am not."

"*Don't* take me for a fool!" In a deliberate show of anger, his right hand had slammed down on the tabletop. The glasses sang. "It had nothing to do with her being a queen and everything to do with a tasteless piece of costume jewelry. If I had to guess, I'd say it's a close cousin to a Goa'uld healing device."

The shark's smile returned, and she slowly inclined her head. "You say you would protect me? How?"

"Some of the warriors you create would be at your disposal."

"*Some*? Are you aware that Lord Yu can command thousands?"

"It's a question of quantity versus quality, isn't it? The more advanced your product, the safer you will be. Pick the best and see what you can do. I trust this will aid in your own research?"

"Conceivably." Barely contained excitement supplanted her feral posturing. She looked almost childlike—the kind of child who would gut a live cat to hear it squeal. "How would I obtain the raw material?"

"You won't have to worry about that. I've made arrangements to ensure a steady supply of elite troops." Elite troops, Simmons didn't bother to explain, whose motto was *Ever Faithful* and who would always choose to protect the interests of the United States of America rather than those of a Goa'uld.

"You forget that they cannot survive without a symbiote. I told you, I am not a queen. I shall not be able to provide the larvae."

"I haven't forgotten." He nodded at Conrad. "The scientists his host employed took live tissue samples. We cloned him. Right now, there's about three hundred of him."

For the first time something like respect stole into her eyes. "Very well. I have a small additional request. Grant me that, and I shall give you what you ask."

CHAPTER FOUR

Selection: Inducing, through natural or artificial processes, the survival of one type of organism over others that die.

"Chevron seven... locked," Sergeant Harriman concluded the ritual chant. Then he watched, like everyone else in the control room and for the thousandth time, as the event horizon whirled out in a cascade of glacial blue and retracted to a pool across the Stargate.

"Seems to be engaging fine," muttered Major Carter and bent over the dialing computer, backpack already on her shoulders. She'd been recalled from the embarkation room when the wormhole to M3D 335 had failed to establish. "It's all nominal, and the diagnostics came up okay, too.

"Alright, ma'am. It's just..." Harriman frowned a little. "Well, it's not the first time."

"I know. Could be an orbital thing. I'll look into it while I'm there. For now, and as long as it locks eventually, just roll with the punches. I don't want to risk messing with the failsafe..."

She left it hanging, but George Hammond knew what she was thinking: *again*. The last override on the failsafe had damn near annihilated a planet whose primary had taken none too kindly to being skewered by a wormhole.

Recently two out of seven attempts to establish a connection to M3D 335 had failed, but if and when the wormhole chose to engage, everything worked. Hammond hoped it stayed that way. The last thing he needed was Simmons or Crowley accusing him of trying to sabotage their bright idea.

The moon—ten days into the program '335 was uniformly referred to as Parris Island, though Hammond still refused to adopt the habit—had been declared a training and selection camp for a whole new USMC unit. The jury was still out on how to name the child. Crowley had mooted 'Force Galaxy'. The various proposals circulating among SGC personnel weren't quite as swanky. George Hammond favored 'Space Cadets'.

Whatever it was going to be called, it would be an elite attack force operating independently from Stargate Command. As promised, Hammond had received Colonel Simmons's report within a day of the NID agents' sudden departure. It had been delivered in person and informed him of the *fait accompli*. Use of the red phone was discouraged. Given the outcome of that exercise two weeks ago, the President had already approved the report's central suggestion and ordered the SGC to assist in any way necessary. To underline the point, Simmons had brought along ten Marine instructors and technical specialists who, accompanied by SG-3, had gated out to set up camp on '335. During the past week, fifty men had deployed with equipment and supplies.

At this moment, another ten troops were gathered in the gate room, waiting to embark. Some distance apart stood Teal'c and Dr. Fraiser, the only people not to jump sky-high when the wormhole engaged. Colonel Norris, who apparently was joining this trip, approached them. There was a brief exchange of words, then he glared up at the control room window, spun around, and stormed out through the blast door. Seconds later Hammond heard him clattering up the stairs.

"General! I'd requested an—" Norris caught sight of Sam Carter in full gear and bellowed, "You gotta be kidding me! Not her, too?"

"We're good to go, sir," Major Carter interjected sweetly.

"Wait a minute! I'm not prepared to drag along God knows how many babysitters, including one who isn't even... American!"

"Would you prefer a Russian babysitter?" Hammond smiled when Norris broke into the expected grimace. "It can be arranged, Colonel."

"I don't—"

"You requested an expert on off-world medicine and alien diseases to brief your men. I gave you my CMO who, incidentally, is this world's leading authority in the field. However, Dr. Fraiser is *not* a combatant, and I've therefore decided to have Major Carter and Teal'c escort her." Which wasn't entirely accurate, though Hammond felt no stirrings of guilt. Major Janet Fraiser was an experienced soldier and more than capable of looking after herself. The simple truth was that SG-1 still remained on stand-down, and Teal'c and Sam Carter were getting a little stir-crazy. A friendly snoop around the Marine camp would take the edge off it — and give General Hammond a better idea of what he was up against.

Norris blustered some more. "My men are perfectly—"

"I'm sure they are. *My* men are going to accompany Dr. Fraiser, and that's my last word, *Colonel*!"

"General Crowley will hear of this."

"I'm counting on it." Knowing he'd won this round, Hammond briefly berated himself for deriving quite so much satisfaction from it. Then he shot a pointed look at Sam Carter. "You have a Go, Major. Godspeed."

"Thank you, sir!"

The clipped nod was a military caricature, as was the brisk parade ground turn she executed. Norris seemed to suspect that somehow he was being sent up, but he had no time to dwell on it. Major Carter headed down the stairs, and he all but ran after her, determined to beat the SGC team through the gate.

Minutes later the embarkation room was empty, the wormhole winked into oblivion, and the iris slid shut across the Stargate, obstructing the view of gray concrete behind. Hammond gazed at it for a moment, as though it might present him with an excuse to post-pone the return to his office a little longer. Nothing was forthcoming. Stifling a sigh, he made for the staircase and the inevitable.

The inevitable had been sitting in the in-tray on his desk for ten days. So far he hadn't even opened it. Neither had anybody else, given that the words *Private and Confidential* leered from the enve-lope in a sprawling hand that was only too familiar. He could guess the contents, which was reason enough to take a leaf out of their author's book and pretend he wasn't getting all his memos. Unfortunately, ten days was pushing the limits, and the only miracle was that Jack O'Neill hadn't called him yet.

Hammond slid behind his desk and into the sumptuous orthope-dic chair, which, as so often, offered no real comfort. *Private and Confidential* stared at him accusingly, and he finally fished the letter from the tray, poked a finger under the envelope flap, and started ripping as despondently as he knew how. Halfway through, a knock rattled against his office door.

"Come in!" he called, grateful for a reprieve, however temporary.

The door opened on an uncommonly bashful Dr. Jackson. He'd abandoned the eye patch for an eggplant raccoon effect that suggested he'd led the mother of all bar brawls. "Am I interrupting, General?"

"Sit down, son." Hammond waved at a chair and waited. Somehow he had the feeling that anything as overtly aggressive as a question would make Daniel run for the hills.

Whatever had prompted this visit, it wasn't a request for a pay raise. As Dr. Jackson settled in the chair, his gaze fell on the semi-opened letter Hammond was still holding, and he obviously recognized the handwriting too. "Not getting all your memos, sir?"

George Hammond smiled momentarily, then turned serious again. "I take it you know what's in here?"

"Kind of. Jack, uh, dropped a hint." He paused, cleared his throat for the third time since entering the room. "General, supposing it is what you and I think it is… What are you going to do?"

Good point. Then again, Dr. Jackson's points usually were. If truth be told, Hammond's gut instinct and fondest desire was to feed the damn thing to the shredder unread and plead ignorance, but he couldn't say that, much less do it. Instead he opted for rational if unpleasant ground. "You got a few minutes, Dr. Jackson?"

Daniel nodded, eyebrows arching in surprise.

"Let me tell you a story."

The only thing to set the tale apart from hundreds like it was the fact that Lieutenant George Hammond had been there and come out the other end. It had happened during his first—no, second—tour in 'Nam. They'd got reports, fabricated by the Viet Cong as it would later turn out, that a whole platoon was nailed down in the jungle, some fifty miles northeast of a village whose name he didn't care to remember. His CO, an experienced officer, had decided to go in. And in they'd gone, twenty men in all, including Colonel Freeman, and parachuted straight into a killing ground. Only three had made it out alive: a private who subsequently lost his arm, Lieutenant Hammond with a bullet in his leg, and Freeman who, by some cynical twist of fate, had suffered only minor injuries.

"You might say it was a clear error of judgment on Freeman's part." Hammond leaned back in his chair. "He relied on the intel, because confirming it would have cost too much time while good men might be dying out there. There never was a choice, really, but he'd committed a horrific mistake all the same."

"What became of him?" Dr. Jackson asked softly.

"Freeman was, without a doubt, the best commanding officer I ever served under. Bright, gutsy, unconventional, a tactical genius, and he cared about his people to the point of running himself into the ground—and if you think that sounds like somebody we both know, you'd be right. But he made a serious mistake in a situation where he couldn't afford to make any." Suddenly Hammond had no wish to go any further. Funny how the grief was still fresh, so many years later. Funny how things didn't seem rational at all anymore.

"What became of him, sir?"

"He retired. He felt that he'd failed us, which was a mortal sin in Freeman's book. According to him, he didn't *deserve* to lead anyone. He never said it in so many words, but we knew. The irony was, we'd never stopped trusting him. A few months later he drove his car into a ravine. They only found bits of him among the wreckage."

"So you're going to run this"—Daniel nodded at the letter clutched in Hammond's fingers—"through the shredder?"

Occasionally, the young man's mind-reading abilities were a little on the disconcerting side. Nevertheless… "I'm afraid I can't do that, son. I can't—"

Dr. Jackson got up, stared through the window out into the briefing room, fists jammed into pockets, shoulders rolling with tension. "Jack didn't—" Suddenly he whipped around. The words tumbled out like water through a breaking dam. "General, this is strictly between you and me. Jack didn't want us to take it further, and Sam and Teal'c agreed. But I'm not military, and sometimes I find that military notions of honor, ethics, idealism, whatever, get in the way of facts." His good eye narrowed, and he grinned. "Go ahead, sir. Don't choke on it."

Sound advice. Hammond let out the chortle that had been creeping up his throat. "That's a fascinating observation, Dr. Jackson, especially coming from you. And yes, we'll keep it in this office, if that's what you want. Go on. What *are* the facts?"

"You can't let Jack go, sir. Because he *didn't* make a mistake."

"That's not the way it—"

"The exercise was rigged. Jack never stood a chance. It was a no-win scenario, designed to get that Marine base up and running... I think."

"Care to elaborate, Dr. Jackson?"

Five minutes into the explanation, General Hammond had lost any desire to chortle and silently congratulated himself on sending Major Carter and Teal'c to Parris Island.

A saffron expanse with cinnamon clouds filled what little was visible of the sky, and Teal'c instantly succumbed to a sense of oppression. The Stargate was located at the end of a deep, narrow gorge. Either side rose vertical rock walls, a hundred meters high or more. Looking up it was impossible not to conceive the notion that the planet above was about to crush its moon, settle on the surface, and suffocate anyone trapped inside the valley.

"Should have brought a helmet," muttered Major Carter.

Dr. Fraiser seemed unaffected. "Oh, I don't mind. At least you know you're off-world."

This probably was true, though Teal'c found it difficult to share the sentiment. Most of his life had been spent off-world on one journey or another; indeed, twice in his one hundred and four years he had been forced to make a home of planets not his own. His birth-world was long lost to him, but at least among the Tauri he had found acceptance and kinship.

Behind them the wormhole disengaged with a finality that appeared to disturb even Colonel Norris. "Welcome to M3D 335, Marines!" he shouted, a little too forceful, a little too loud.

"Sir! Thank you, sir!" came the reply, molded into uniformity by years of training and rigid discipline.

The same training and discipline had compelled these ten young men—mere children by a Jaffa's reckoning—to arrange themselves in a perfectly straight line and to adopt a stance that evoked pride and a readiness to fight. In truth, they were afraid. Teal'c saw it in their eyes. They were apprehensive of this alien landscape that looked nothing like the Moon they had learned about in their schools, and, more than that, they were apprehensive of admitting their fear. Because they were afraid of Colonel Norris. The discovery was unsurprising. Unlike O'Neill, Colonel Norris did not inspire trust or confidence. Unlike O'Neill, Colonel Norris would never consider punishing himself for failing those who relied on his guidance.

"What are you waiting for?" he barked. "Move out! On the double!"

A ripple of hesitation traveled down the line, barely perceptible and instantly overridden by the mechanisms of unquestioning obedience. They took up formation, five rows of two, and broke into a brisk trot. Colonel Norris followed them, an avenger alert to any faltering in their step, any sign of uncertainty.

O'Neill would have been attuned to their apprehension and, knowing that, of all the ways to combat fear, laughter was the most formidable, would have found some joke, absurd and out of place. And they would have loved him for it.

"Don't look like that, Teal'c." Major Carter had concluded her routine test of the DHD and gave a crooked smile. "Colonel O'Neill's the exception, not the rule."

"I am aware of it." He was, after all, Jaffa. And while Master Bra'tac's leadership closely resembled that of O'Neill, there were many, too many, who acted like Colonel Norris. "It is one more reason to discourage him from his present course."

"Good luck," Dr. Fraiser replied dryly. "You know what he's like. Anyway, I suppose we'd better catch up with Colonel Congenial and his cohort."

"Did you say *catch up*?" enquired Major Carter, evidently not relishing the idea of an unwarranted run. The moon's atmosphere was thinner than Earth's.

"Well, I would have said *overtake*, but what's the point in embarrassing them?"

"If you put it that way. I mean, two women and a guy who's not even… American?" Grinning, Major Carter adjusted her backpack and set out.

Twenty minutes later Teal'c passed the Marine camp's outer

perimeter at a steady jog, barely having broken a sweat. Perhaps it was petty, but he felt he owed O'Neill this victory, inconsequential though it might be. At any rate, it would not have occurred had Colonel Norris not spurred his men to a faster and faster pace once he noticed the SGC team's approach.

Ignoring the bemused faces of the guards, Teal'c came to a halt and turned to review the situation behind. Dr. Fraiser had fallen back a little, but Major Carter kept abreast of the two Marines in the lead, not forcing a race but making plain that she could match any further increase in speed. Not so Colonel Norris.

Teal'c conceded another stab of furtive pleasure, propped himself on his staff weapon, and awaited the column's arrival. While Major Carter and Dr. Fraiser broke left to join him, the Marines slowed and reformed their line. Some doubled over, gasping for air. Most faces had reddened dangerously. It had been foolish to subject them to such exertion without permitting them to acclimatize first.

"Well, that was bracing." Major Carter dragged her forearm across her face to soak up sweat. "I need a shower."

"That was idiotic," panted Dr. Fraiser, echoing Teal'c's own thoughts. She bent over, hands pressed onto her knees, and tried to catch her breath. "The kid over on the right looks like he's gonna crash! This kind of thing's alright for you two; you guys swap atmospheres twice a week, but for the rest of us..."

"So why didn't you slow down?"

"What? And let *him* win?"

"Attention!" Colonel Norris tone had lost some of its vigor, breath failing him mid-word. Nevertheless, the ten men pulled themselves up straight, some with obvious difficulty. Their unease was overt now. With reason. "You are pathetic! So I'm telling you right now, shape up or ship out! If you want to lose, join the Air Force. They love losing. I don't."

"Yeah, we noticed," murmured Major Carter. "*You*'d rather cheat."

Colonel Norris's rant continued, the men before him shrinking under every word. Suddenly a hand clasped Teal'c's shoulder, and an amused voice noted, "Wow! You people sure put a burr up his ass!"

"Hi, Warren." Turning to the speaker, Dr. Fraiser gave a soft laugh.

"I don't think we were supposed to keep up with them."

"Oughta know better, Doc. After all, they're Marines. Teal'c. Carter. Nobody told me you guys were gonna join the fun." Major Warren, himself a Marine and SG-3's commanding officer, peered in the direction from where they had come. "Where're Colonel O'Neill and Dr. Jackson?"

"Neither of them's fit for active duty yet," Dr. Fraiser answered, a fraction too quickly perhaps, wishing to avoid the subject.

However, the major failed to notice. "My men and me still can't believe that General Custer got the upper hand on O'Neill of all—"

"*Who*?" asked Major Carter.

"General Custer." Major Warren grinned. "Norris's nickname. Not that anyone's ever risked calling him that to his face."

"Didn't realize that Custer was a Marine."

"Neither's that chicken shit," he replied. Then his gaze roamed over their packs and weaponry. "Anyway, welcome to Parris Island, folks. Let's find you a place to bunk down, whaddya say?"

As with most linguistic peculiarities of the Tauri, it had taken Teal'c some time to establish the workings of this last phrase. It did not, in fact, require the addressee to say anything. Agreement was a foregone conclusion, as indeed it was in this case. They abandoned Colonel Norris who was still punishing warriors better than himself for his own weakness and followed their guide along a broad, dusty trail toward the camp.

Teal'c was unsure at which point during the moon's diurnal cycle they had arrived, but it seemed to be getting close to nightfall now. The hues of the giant planet above had gradually changed to greens and blues and bathed the landscape in a sallow light.

"One good thing about this place, it never rains, though temperatures actually are pretty moderate," said Major Warren. "No open bodies of water, of course, just a few shallow wells. Most moisture precipitates as morning dew."

This much was evident. The moon's surface showed no sign of climatic erosion. Its only remarkable geographic feature was the rock formation where the Stargate was hidden. Once past it, they had emerged onto gently rolling plains, dotted with tussocks of short, wiry grass and low brush and extending as far as the eye could see. The encampment was visible for miles around, which posed a danger to say the least. There was a further ramification, and Teal'c found it odd in the extreme. Was it not the purpose of a facility such as this to accustom warriors to a *variety* of terrains?

A little later they reached the central square of the camp. One side was taken up by a large metal hut, along the others stood several smaller structures. East of the square stretched rows of tents. Nothing differed from the arrangements Teal'c had come to expect in a Tauri camp, except—

"That's the commissary *cum* class room," said Major Warren, pointing at the large building. "You'll be doing your lecture in there, Doc." Dr. Fraiser nodded, and his finger moved on, indicating the smaller huts. "Ammo, communications, sickbay, storage, and lavatory... Uh, I guess we gotta think of something for you ladies. At the moment it's Boys Only." He broke into a sudden grin. "Something's telling me you're gonna be hugely popular."

"Not if Colonel Norris has anything to do with it," Major Carter groused. "Is there someplace where I can set up a temporary lab? We've been having trouble establishing a wormhole to '335, and I'd like to check it out." When she noticed the major's frown, she hastily added, "Nothing to worry about. Probably to do with the moon's orbit causing some intermittent gravitational distortion. You won't get stuck here, Warren."

"I damn well hope not! But yeah, we can rig something for you. I'll see to it in the morning." He jerked his chin at the tents behind the square. "Right now quarters are more important. Nights can get chilly. Carter, I hope it's okay if you and the doc share a tent, and Teal'c, you can move in with me, unless you mind."

"I do not, Major Warren."

"Alright then, let's go."

Teal'c was about to follow when he realized that Major Carter had remained in the same spot, looking around in puzzlement.

It was then that he recognized the cause of the subliminal worry that had bothered him since arriving here. The camp was uncommonly quiet. Too quiet.

"Warren?" asked Major Carter. "Where *is* everybody?"

"Where *is* he?" Dr. Jackson muttered under his breath, hopping from foot to foot and wishing he'd brought a jacket. Even at the end of April, Colorado nights could get fresh. He stabbed the doorbell again, listened as the chime ding-donged through the house and faded. Nothing.

Okay, so maybe he should have tried calling first, but Daniel seriously doubted that the soft-spoken Japanese lady with the clock fetish would pass on messages. At least the truck was parked in the driveway. Chances of Jack having shot off to Minnesota were slim, which came as a relief.

A few months later he drove his car into a ravine.

He couldn't have gone for a run either. Janet Fraiser had said the bruising would get worse for a couple of weeks before it got better, and even Jack's masochism had limits. Probably. Knowing him, he was standing on the other side of that door, pulling faces and whispering *Shoo!*

Daniel was in no mood to be shooed. General Hammond's little story had left him rattled, which explained why he was here—Jack's admirable efforts to avoid communication notwithstanding. He shivered, blamed it on the night temperatures, and gave up his attack on the doorbell in favor of a reconnoiter around the house. The living room curtains were open, and as he peered in from the deck he saw a light in the kitchen. Just a light, no movement. No movement anywhere else either. Unless Jack was hiding in the basement, he—

"D'oh!" Daniel leaped back onto the walkway, tore around the corner and past some bushes, and ducked under the low-hanging branches of a tree to get to the ladder.

Halfway up, the beam of a flashlight exploded in his eyes, and a disembodied voice asked, "Drew the short straw, Daniel?"

Had he mentioned that, in addition to a finely honed sense of personal accountability, Jack O'Neill possessed the stupendous talent of making Dr. Jackson spit tacks in two seconds flat?

"Dammit, Jack! I can't see a thing!" The beam slid away to illuminate the rungs and allowed Daniel to discern Jack's silhouette above. The rooftop should have been the first place he looked. "You must have heard me down there. I don't suppose you could have shouted or something?"

"I knew you'd figure it out eventually, and if not…" The silhouette gave a shrug.

"You want me to leave?"

"Would it make a difference?" The beam danced back into Daniel's face and was followed by an appreciative whistle. "Shame you haven't got green eyes."

"What's wrong with blue?"

"Well, one's red. If you had green eyes, you'd pass for Milton's devil. One red, one green."

Squinting, Daniel heaved himself onto the roof deck and swatted the flashlight away. "You've read *Paradise Lost*?"

"The abridged version. Though it doesn't explain why the guy's running around looking like a traffic light."

"There's an abridged version?"

"One word: *Oops*."

Daniel hadn't really meant to groan—the less encouragement Jack got, the better—but it slipped out anyway, if only because *Paradise Lost* seemed strangely apposite. "Remind me not to discuss literature with you. Ever."

Without warning the flashlight winked out and left Daniel blinking. He heard footsteps, the scrape of metal on wood, and knew that Jack had retreated into the chair by the telescope. Gradually the neon spots in front of Daniel's eyes receded and solid darkness crumbled to shades of gray as his night vision returned. Jack sat in his chair, hunched over the eyepiece, fingers playing with screws to adjust angle and magnification. The tension in his shoulders and neck gave him away. Half of this was show. All of it was screaming *Leave me alone!* If Jack had looked any less lonely, Daniel might have taken the hint. As it was, he leaned against the railing, folded his arms across his chest in hopes of warding off the cold, and waited.

"So, if not literature, what *do* you want to discuss?" Jack said at last.

"Should we discuss anything?"

"You tell me."

Great. They could engage in the question and counter-question game until the cows came home. Better to hop off that particular merry-go-round. And maybe just being here was enough. "Looking at anything nice?"

"Check it out." Jack shifted over and surrendered the eyepiece.

It was a pale beige speck on black velvet. Stifling a yawn, Daniel straightened up and returned to his perch. "Exciting."

"Yeah. It's Io."

Their solar system's own version of Netu. Not unlike the stuff you saw when you opened a medical textbook under 'A' for 'Acne'. Only worse. Usually even the wildest zits didn't spontaneously erupt. This did. Close up, Io's surface would be a heaving, angry mêlée of reds and oranges and black.

"A moon of Jupiter, right?" Daniel asked, curious to discover where this was going.

"Innermost moon. Jupiter's gravitational pull exacts huge pressure on Io. Its crust shows a tide of up to one hundred meters. The moon gets squeezed out of shape, hence the eruptions. I know how it feels," Jack added and resumed his study of Zit Central.

Daniel bit his tongue. Hard. You didn't have to be a genius to guess that Jack's empathy with a volcanic moon wasn't open for discussion. "What are you going to do?" he finally asked.

"About what? Io?"

"Yourself. What are you going to do with yourself?"

"Don't know. Move to Minnesota, start up a fishing business."

"There are no pesky fish in your pond, Jack."

"Yeah, well, that's par for the course, isn't it?" It was trailed by another silence, vast enough to swallow the Rockies whole. After an eternity and a half, he enquired, "So, *did* you draw the short straw?"

"No straws. Why do there have to be straws?"

"I don't see Teal'c or Carter."

"I'm sure they would have loved to join this lively little get-together, but they're off-world."

For once the reaction was completely unguarded. Jack's head snapped up, and his voice held an odd mix of disappointment, regret, and more than just a trace of jealousy. "Where?"

"You miss it already. It's only been two weeks, Jack. How long do you plan for this retirement thing to last?"

The dark shape by the telescope stiffened, fingers clenching in an effort to contain either a sharp reply or the longing to be out there and do what he'd always been meant to do. "Technically I'm still off-duty. Where?"

"M3D…" A premature mosquito zeroed in on Daniel. He slapped at it, slapped again, missed again. "335."

"Of course! M3D 335, the marvel of the galaxy—Goa'uld fashion malls, Tollan karaoke clubs, and Nox hairdressers. Care to be a little more specific? What's there?" And that sounded completely like Jack. Whether he liked it or not, leadership was second nature. If he couldn't physically command a team, he did his clucking vicariously. "Daniel? What's there?"

"A Marine base."

"A *what*?"

The temptation to spill everything he'd told General Hammond was so strong Daniel had to grit his teeth against it. It would be counterproductive. Any mention of the exercise having been rigged would be a red flag to Jack, who'd already made abundantly clear that, for him, ignorance was no excuse. The trick lay in feeding him just enough information to keep him interested. As long as he was interested, he'd stay away from cars and ravines.

Daniel pushed himself off the railing. "Look, I'm freezing my butt off up here. Let's go downstairs, have a beer, and I'll fill you in."

"I thought you didn't like beer."

"I've been known to make exceptions for friends."

CHAPTER FIVE

"I think this'll do, ma'am." The corporal, detailed by Major Warren, twisted and squirmed and yanked until he and the table he was carrying popped free of the frame and catapulted through the door.

They'd cleared out half a storage hut—well, mostly they'd just pushed and piled crates together—to make space for a desk and Sam Carter's laptop, a few other bits of electronic equipment and a small naquadah generator to supply the power. It still looked like a derelict woodshed, but this was as good as it got and besides she'd only be stuck here for a day.

"This'll do nicely, Corporal," said Sam.

"Anything else I can get you, ma'am?"

She squinted at an indecisive patch of brightness in the side wall. "A bucket of hot water and a rag to clean the window, maybe."

"I'll do that." His indignant tone implied that the mere idea of an officer fiddling with buckets and rags was a court-martialable offense. He made to leave, hesitated, turned back. "And ma'am?"

"Yes, Corporal?"

"Yesterday… that was pretty damn impressive, ma'am."

If truth be told, the compliment came as a surprise. It could as easily have been resentment, given that he was one of the new arrivals who'd got their heads ripped off after that impromptu little race. She decided to return the favor.

"Look, Corporal, under normal circumstances you guys would have outrun anyone but Teal'c. Once you're acclimated to the thin air, you'll leave the rest of us standing."

"That's good of you to say, ma'am." He shot her a crooked grin, blushed. "'Cos Colonel Norris—"

"Corporal, between you, me, and the crates, Colonel Norris had no right to treat you like that. If you were any less fit, you'd have keeled over."

"Thanks, ma'am. I mean it. I…" The blush deepened, and he stared at her with open adoration until he caught himself. Whereupon, and despite the fact that the major wasn't covered, he saluted crisply and fled the hut.

Sam clamped down on a laugh and set about installing her equipment, soon accompanied by the squeak of leather on glass. Her corporal was spit-shining the window. Just over an hour later—the squeaking had ceased by then—she sat on a crate, elbows propped on the desk, chin on her fists.

"Okay, *that* is weird," muttered Major Dr. Carter, ogling the graph on her computer screen.

"What is?" asked a voice from the door. "Morning, Sam."

She gazed up and at Dr. Fraiser, swathed in the freshly-scrubbed glow of a recent shower. "Hi, Janet. Anybody ever tell you that you snore?"

"Hey! Being field personnel doesn't give you the right to get mouthy."

"It does, according to Colonel O'Neill." As soon as it was out, Sam wished she hadn't said it and forced a smile.

Very few things got past Janet. "You miss him."

Of course she did. Who wouldn't? But, to quote the Colonel, she and Janet had had this discussion, and they were not having it again.

"Parris Island to Sam. Come in, Sam." Head cocked, Janet gazed at her. "This anything to do with why you got up in the middle of the night?"

"Uh, no. It's just… Pull up a box and look at this."

"How about you scoot over?" Janet squeezed next to her onto the crate and stared at the innocent graph. "So, what's so remarkable about this?"

"Nothing. That's what's remarkable." Despite the claustrophobic skyscape it created, '335's primary fundamentally consisted of a lot of hot air. It had nowhere near enough mass and was too far away to mess with the moon's orbit. "Obviously gravitational fluctuation isn't what's interfering with the gate."

"Is that good news or bad?"

"Don't know yet." Sam shrugged. "I'll just have to go back to the drawing board."

"Yeah, but not now. I'm about to go sing for my supper, and I need moral support."

"What about Teal'c?"

"I haven't seen him since last night. Warren says he took off at first light, probably reconnoitering."

"Oh." Sam was surprised that Teal'c hadn't let her know. Then again, this wasn't a mission, and she hadn't been put in official command. "Well, the problem's not gonna go away." Closing the lid of her laptop, she rose. "Shall we?"

Though the planet overhead had gone back to its killer satsuma look, the day was pleasant enough. A gentle breeze sent streamers of dust swirling around the square, and halfway across Sam decided that joining Janet had been a very good idea. From the commissary drifted the unmistakable aroma of fresh coffee.

Inside, somebody had arranged tables and chairs classroom-style, facing the short wall and a blackboard. Janet took one glance, sighed, and dragged her feet to the lectern. Leaving her to her fate, Sam veered off to the bar to get that coffee. As she sipped the hot, bitter brew she watched the Marines trickle in, ignoring a mix of come-on grins and hostile glares—the latter from Colonel Norris and his cronies.

Yesterday they'd been told that two thirds of the men were assigned to night maneuvers, which explained why the camp had been so quiet. This morning it did seem a little more populated, but there were sixty men supposed to be permanently stationed here. Right now, the commissary held just over thirty and all chairs were occupied. So where was the rest? Not interested in alien diseases?

Major Warren marched to the front and introduced Janet. The response was a polite smattering of applause and a nucleus of hoots and whistles that pinpointed SG-3's position. A scowl at his team clashed with the emcee routine, and Warren said, "Over to Dr. Fraiser."

Janet was a natural. Within five minutes she had the Marines eating out of her hand. Of course, the subject wasn't exactly boring. Glowy, aerobic, intelligent bacteria that proposed to take over Earth and eat a conveniently skewered officer alive while they were at it… That one had been a joyride and a half, thank you very much. Sam, who'd witnessed the effects of most and fallen victim to a representative selection of alien organisms, wasn't really keen on a trip down memory lane.

"The trick actually is lateral thinking," said Janet. "Sometimes what you'd consider to be a common garden variety remedy can be life-saving. How many of you suffer from allergies?"

Twelve hands went up.

"Got antihistamines on you?"

"Yes, ma'am," chorused a few voices.

"Congratulations. You guys won't get the Neanderthal bug. About four years ago…"

Sam had sudden visions of sweet little tank top numbers, locker rooms, and alpha males, felt a hot tingle across her chest and up her neck, and knew she'd just gone bright scarlet. If Janet so much as breathed a word of who and what had been involved in that incident, she'd kill her.

Mercifully, at that moment the door opened and a few stragglers trudged in, temporarily interrupting the lecture and bringing the attendance total up to thirty-six. Right behind the stragglers entered Teal'c, and Sam didn't like the expression on his face. At all. She'd seen it only a few times over the years, but on each occasion the crap had started raining from on high shortly thereafter. Putting down her coffee mug, she began sidling over to him. A barely perceptible shake of his head stopped her, and Teal'c casually leaned against the wall by the door, pretending to be enthralled by the lecture.

Sam followed his lead, picked up the mug again, and tried to look fascinated between halfhearted sips. From the corner of her eye she watched the newcomers move up along the counter. The guy in front was about four meters away from her when she sensed it and instantly knew what had rattled Teal'c so much.

It wasn't really a feeling, at least none she could describe. Some kind of amorphous tug, a forgotten scent, a caress of cobwebs, everywhere and nowhere and completely unique. Like other people could taste the coppery tang of blood, Sam could taste naquadah. She tasted it now. The three Marines who ordered coffee at the bar carried Goa'uld.

Conrad's upper lip curled a little as though he'd smelled a stealthy fart. His version of a sneer, quite understated for a Goa'uld. It was directed at the jerry-rigged communication globe, which admittedly wouldn't win any beauty contests. The design was courtesy of Harry Maybourne who'd been in the habit of tossing alien gadgetry at his renegade geeks and saying *Make it work!* The geeks had been incapable of reproducing Goa'uld anti-grav technology, and so, instead of hovering gracefully, the globe was hardwired into some sort of metal briefcase.

Frowning, Simmons decided to ignore the design flaws. "What are you waiting for? Turn it on!"

"Yes, my lord." Conrad's sneer lost any trace of understatement.

"Considering that I can make your head blow off at the push of a button, I suppose that, yes, I *am* your lord. And you heard me. Turn it on!"

As Conrad activated the globe, a flare of his eyes incinerated the smirk. Obedience didn't sit well with him.

Opaque gray began to swirl, like ink in water, and cleared to show a vast, ancient hall half eaten by the jungle; a ruin, long abandoned, throttled by creepers snaking up pillars and across stone tiles and pierced by dazzling shafts of sunlight that broke through a rotting roof. For a moment Simmons could almost feel the heat and humidity. At the far end of the hall, past a wide archway, cascaded a waterfall, cool counterpoint to the steaming rainforest. Then a man came into view, dragging himself from pillar to pillar, nails torn and fingers bleeding. The tan desert uniform that made him stand out like a sore thumb among the greenery was ripped and streaked with dirt and blood. Down his back and under his arms spread dark patches of sweat, gluing fabric to skin. His face wasn't visible, only an island of hair left after a crew cut, stiff with filth and perspiration and bristling from a square skull. He twisted a little to check his six, and Simmons could make out the insignia on his sleeve.

One of the very first group. If he'd survived out there for ten days, he was more than capable. The indigenous life forms were a force to be reckoned with, but of course there was an added bonus, just to turn this into a real challenge. And weed out the candidates who weren't suited. This one had salvation in his sights now. Ten more meters, and he'd be home free.

"He shall not succeed," Conrad declared with supreme certainty.

Around his mouth played a cold smile, advertising that he looked forward to failure and, beyond that, to failure's consequences. "How many more, Simmons?"

"As many as it takes, not that it's any of your business!"

The man, so close now that Simmons saw sweat beading between stubbly hair and rolling down the sunburned neck, raised his head. The face was coated in mud—a hopeless attempt at camouflage—and scored with white lines where perspiration had dissolved the dirt. White patches, too, around eyes slitted with fatigue. Suddenly the eyes went wide. He finally had seen the stealthy predator lying in wait for him. Conrad had been right—or maybe not. It all depended on what the man would do next.

There was a hint of motion. Was he reaching for the submachine gun he carried? Perhaps. Perhaps he even aimed it. But then his mouth opened, showing blood-smeared gums and teeth; likely the result of trying to live off the land. Most types of local vegetation disagreed with the human physiology.

Please, he mouthed. *Please*.

"Wrong answer. Thank you for playing," Colonel Frank Simmons said dryly and through a sliver of dissatisfaction. Passing it on would help. He turned to Conrad. "Switch it over. I want to talk to your 'mistress'."

"I wish to—"

"Switch it over!"

An occasional demonstration of power could only be salutary. The Goa'uld had to be kept in his place. Besides, Simmons enjoyed his frustration. Gray swirls obscured the image in the globe and, moments later, parted on Nirrti, whose expression was as sour as Conrad's or his own and for pretty much the same reasons. She must have deliberately underdressed for her visit to Earth. Back then she'd worn a nine-year-old's idea of a ninja costume—just as well, considering the alternatives. Today it was a pink sari with heavy gold trim, whose gaiety contradicted the lady's mood.

"Is this what the Tauri call elite soldiers, Simmons? They would not survive a Jaffa child's training."

"Forgive me if I doubt that." Simmons shrugged, unwilling to submit to the exquisite tedium of her bullying. "How many so far?"

"Eleven." She stared at him blankly.

For a second he wondered if she was lying, then discarded the thought. The men were loyal to him, to Earth, and the only way for her to reap the benefits was through full cooperation. He'd made that clear enough. But eleven were deplorably few. "What about the others?"

The image switched to a view of the outer wall of the ruins and the native predators fighting over a mangled body. When Nirrti reappeared she was smiling. "Alas."

"All of them?" he asked.

Her turn to shrug. "Some of them are still alive in the forest. I do not know how many. They will either reach their destination or they will die. Unless, of course…" She stepped aside. "I have taken the liberty of retaining one of the rejects. He pleases me."

Standing behind her was a man in his mid to late twenties, clad in a pair of voluminous oriental pants of blue fabric and little else, apart from leather bands around his biceps and neck. The well-muscled chest was bare and scored with angry red welts—marks from claws or fingernails—and the hairstyle gave him away. One of the Marines.

"Come here," crooned Nirrti, and he took a few steps toward her, knelt, eyes downcast. She languidly slipped a hand under his chin, yanked up his head. "Who am I? Tell me who I am!"

"The one I love. The one I die for. The one whose will is my command."

On his face stood an incongruous blend of abject terror and mindless devotion. Simmons recognized the look. He'd seen it in the eyes of one of the escort agents, the morning after that same agent, a strapping blond farm boy, had spent the night supposedly guarding Nirrti's quarters. Favoring prevention over cure, Simmons had ordered the man shot. Now he ground his teeth. What if she did the same thing to others? Then again, would it matter? She'd already given him eleven Jaffa, and as she'd said, this one was a reject.

"Dispose of him," he ordered, careful to keep his voice even.

"He pleases me."

"He doesn't please me. Dispose of him!"

"Why?" Nirrti's features contorted to a moue that clashed with the cold, dangerous gleam in her eyes.

"Because this isn't part of our agreement. And because," he added to sweeten the demand, "you'll be otherwise engaged. Your… additional request?"

"Yes?"

"It's about to be fulfilled."

"I am pleased."

The smile flashed up with positively alarming speed. At the same time, the palm-piece of the ribbon device on her left hand and wrist began to glow. Slowly, sinuously, the hand came up until it hovered above the Marine's head. The light intensified, the beam melting into his forehead, soaking his upturned face in golden radiance. Simmons was beginning to think that it actually looked quite beautiful. Then the man's mouth opened in a silent scream. Seconds later he collapsed, blood trickling from his nose and ears.

"You drive a hard bargain, Simmons," said Nirrti, her voice holding a note almost akin to regret.

Without warning, gray ink obscured the globe. End of conversation. When Frank Simmons glanced up, Conrad was sneering again.

It was late—very late—afternoon by the time the last members of the audience stopped flirting with her and filtered out the door. Dr. Janet Fraiser wished she hadn't touched the camp cook's idea of a gourmet lunch. To make matters worse, in the course of two lectures and two Q&A sessions she must have drunk at least five gallons of water. While it hadn't stopped her throat from going sore with talk, it'd made her bloat like a dead fish. Slipping behind the lectern, she unbuttoned the top of her pants. Better. It would get better still once she grabbed a chance to declare the lavatories *Girls Only*. Which had to happen within the next ten minutes, else—

"Dr. Fraiser!"

Janet swallowed a groan and wondered how she could square it with the Hippocratic Oath to give Colonel Norris a lingering disease. *First, do no harm.* Mono sprang to mind. She'd do the universe a favor by putting the guy out of commission for a couple of months. Then again, he'd probably turn out to be a carrier and not go symptomatic. It'd have to be something more reliable. Rabies, maybe…

For the time being, she pasted on a grimace that might or might not pass for a smile and watched Norris slalom around orphaned chairs; a cadaverous six-footer in desert fatigues and thinning hair who looked like he had yet another axe to grind.

"Colonel. What can I do for you?"

"Dr. Fraiser. That was"—bony nose twitching, he gagged on the praise long enough for Janet to contemplate botching a Heimlich Maneuver—"useful."

"Thank you," she said noncommittally. Past his left shoulder she saw Sam Carter closing in on them. Weird, actually. She hadn't expected Sam to stay all the way through. "Was there anything else, sir?"

"Yes. When are you and your escort planning to leave?"

"Well, I was going to—"

"We're leaving tonight." Sam had arrived, and her voice held an edge that preempted any contradiction. "As I understand, General Hammond had agreed to Dr. Fraiser delivering two lectures, nothing more."

"Already tired of our hospitality, Major?" Norris grinned an ugly little grin.

Sam returned it in kind. "That would be virtually impossible, Colonel. Fact of the matter is, I ran some polarization spectroscopy measurements early this morning. The moon's gravitational acceleration shows a distinct abnormality, which may or may not affect the functioning of the Stargate. Unfortunately, I can't complete the tests with the equipment I've got here. I'm guessing that you and your men intend to get back home at some point, so it's in your own best interest if I return to the SGC and continue my work."

By the end of this speech the colonel's complexion had assumed an attractive shade of green. Dr. Fraiser, on the other hand, was hard pushed to sustain her expression of polite interest. For one thing, she rather enjoyed the sight of Norris just about wetting himself. For another, Dr. Samantha Carter had just completely contradicted her previous findings.

"I've been assured that this was safe!" yelped Norris. "Hammond himself told me—"

"General Hammond had no reason to suspect a problem. The

MALP readings came back normal. The odds of this happening are one in a—"

"You're suggesting we evacuate?" Norris's splutter notwithstanding, he seemed to be hoping for an affirmative answer.

"I'm not suggesting anything, sir," Sam replied, her studied indifference unnerving Norris even more. "There's a chance that it's nothing at all. However, you might want to order everyone back to camp, just in case."

"Yes. Yes, I'll see to it. I'll also detail an escort for you."

"That won't be—"

Norris was already scrambling for the exit, practically at a run.

"—necessary." Staring after him, Sam Carter expelled a slow breath. "Get your things, Janet. We're leaving."

"What's polarization spectroscopy?"

"Something some guys at JPL are working on," she murmured absently, still watching the door. "Sounds great, but they haven't cracked it yet."

"You are aware that you just lied to a superior officer?"

"He'll get over it. Besides, I'd dispute the *superior* part." Suddenly she whipped around, face tense, a small muscle in her jaw twitching with impatience. "What the hell are you waiting for?"

Up until this moment Janet Fraiser had nursed the admittedly improbable idea that, somehow, this was an elaborate hoax at Colonel Norris's expense. Of course, Major Carter wasn't in the habit of playing practical jokes. Nor did she snap at her friends—unless she was hip-deep in command mode. Like now.

"For God's sake, Sam, what's—"

"Later, Janet. Let's go." She started moving toward the door.

Dr. Fraiser scooped up the lecture notes and hurried after her. "Where's Teal'c?" Like some of the audience, the Jaffa had left after lunch.

"Keeping an eye on some… relatives. He'll be meeting us at the tent."

Relatives? And what exactly was that supposed to mean? On the other hand, it might be wise not to examine the question too closely. It opened up some nasty possibilities. Without noticing, Janet picked up her pace.

Out in the square, Marines flocked in small gaggles to chat and enjoy the spectacle of 'planetset'—not that the ugly menace ever really *did* set. It just slipped two thirds of the way under the horizon and turned brown. Norris was nowhere to be seen, but at least he hadn't galloped through camp, hollering *To arms! To arms!* The place still seemed drowsily quiet, and Janet suddenly realized that, if there was a command barrack somewhere, Warren had omitted to point it out during their guided tour yesterday. So who was running this show and from where? *Later*, she reminded herself with a last wistful glance at the lavatory and stumbled after Sam.

When they got to their tent, Teal'c was there already, posted outside and looking grim. Okay, grimmer than usual. For the first time, Sam's poise faltered. "Where are they?" she hissed softly.

"Together with five others they set out in the direction of the Stargate approximately thirty minutes ago," Teal'c replied just as quietly. "I considered it imprudent to follow."

"Crap," muttered Sam, a worried crease between her eyebrows deepening.

"As O'Neill would say, we shall traverse that viaduct when we reach it."

Jack O'Neill wouldn't say anything of the sort, at least not in these terms, and Teal'c damn well knew it. It had to be a Jaffa joke. His attempt at lightening the mood was partially successful. Dr. Fraiser grinned. Major Carter probably grinned internally.

"Can you stay with Janet, Teal'c? I need to fetch my equipment. After the yarn I've spun for Norris, somebody might get suspicious if I leave it."

He solemnly indicated the aluminum case strapped to his already sizeable backpack. "I understand the naquadah reactor is part of the onsite facilities."

"Should have known." Sam gave a hint of a smile. "Thanks, Teal'c."

His only reply was a wordless incline of the head. During the five minutes it took to gather their belongings from the tent and fling them into backpacks, Sam waxed equally chatty and her movements were stiff and over-controlled. Finally she asked, "Ready?"

Strictly speaking, it wasn't a question. Janet hadn't heard a question mark, and that was the straw that broke the camel's back. "No! I gotta go pee, if it's the last thing I do."

The doctor's flippant remark kept playing in Teal'c's mind, mostly because he dreaded her being proven correct. In the cold actinic light of the planet the rock formation looked like one of those forbidding glass-fronted edifices the Tauri liked to erect. Directly ahead yawned the black chasm at whose end waited the Stargate. Not for the first time, he marveled at the purpose of its location. What had been the intent of the Ancients or Goa'uld who had put the *Chappa'ai* there? To hide it? Or to control access?

Without a doubt, the answer to the riddle would be given sooner than Teal'c preferred, and so he turned once more to survey the plain behind them. Far off twinkled the lights of the Marine camp, drowning in a sea of blue gloom. This moon knew no true night, which might be of advantage before long; even sparse light was better than none. Out on the plain, nothing stirred. Or at least nothing stirred that should not have, and he still puzzled over the whereabouts of the men absent from the camp. In the course of his search this morning, he had been unable to find any tracks, save those that led to the Stargate valley. Even now, after Colonel Norris presumably had undertaken to recall the troops, the only discernible movement and sound came from dry grass brushed by the night breeze. And from the four Marines who constituted their escort and followed at a short distance behind Teal'c. Their presence, though unwelcome, provided some vague reassurance. None of them was anything more than he seemed.

The gamble of waiting until the end of Dr. Fraiser's lectures and leaving in a normal manner appeared to have borne fruit. Their departure had drawn stares from a handful of men gathered in the camp square, but otherwise it had attracted little notice. However, this could have been a ruse as ingenious as the one that Major Carter had devised to hoodwink Colonel Norris. They would not know for certain until they entered the gorge. Teal'c turned back and broke into an easy lope until he caught up with his companions.

"Anything?" asked Major Carter.

"Nothing as yet. Although I fear that we may be intercepted at the

Stargate."

"You and me both, Teal'c." Her fingers closed more tightly around the P90 strapped across her midriff. "You and me both."

"I know you sensed *them*." Dr. Fraiser had been apprised of the situation as soon as they had left the camp and its potential eavesdroppers behind. Though seasoned with a pinch of disbelief, her mood had improved since. "But are you sure they sensed *you*—or Teal'c, rather?"

"You can't help sensing it, Janet," replied Major Carter. "It's just *there*. It's the naquadah in the Goa'uld's blood. They get close enough, the alarms go off, no matter how preoccupied you are, and it works both ways."

"Perhaps Dr. Fraiser's question is valid." Teal'c had not considered this before, but it was entirely possible. "The men did not act like Goa'uld. There is another way of carrying a symbiote, Major Carter."

She looked at him sharply. "Jaffa? You're saying those guys are *Jaffa*?"

"Not true Jaffa." They did not wear tattoos to visibly brand them a system lord's slaves. But, again, there were other ways. "Jaffa can be created, as you are well aware."

"Don't remind me," she glumly said over Dr. Fraiser's soft groan. After a second, Major Carter added, "Even if they're Jaffa, it doesn't make any difference. They would have sensed you."

"Indeed. However, when I first encountered them on my return to the camp this morning, they did not react to me. I thought it was subterfuge." Teal'c pondered this briefly and continued, "But if these men were not brought up Jaffa, they would lack the training and skills to fully benefit from the advantages a symbiote bestows. They may not have known what it was they were sensing."

"Teal'c, I wasn't brought up Jaffa—or Tok'ra for that matter—but I still know what's what."

"Because, in addition to the symbiote and that protein marker, you got Jolinar's memories. Unabridged edition," the doctor interjected.

"Dr. Fraiser is correct. You did not have to learn, because you were blended. These men are not."

"Well, let's hope you're both right. Because, if they're Goa'uld after all and realized we're on to them, I'd really hate to meet them in there."

They had reached the entrance to the gorge, and Major Carter brought up her weapon. The beam of its small, strong flashlight bored ahead into a passage barely four meters wide and seamed by rock too sheer and smooth to be scaled. From here it would be approximately five minutes' march to the Stargate. Teal'c's every instinct balked at the notion of proceeding into this trap, but there was no choice. He accelerated his pace to take point.

A minute smile audible in her voice, Major Carter stopped him. "Teal'c, if you don't mind, I'd rather have you watching our six. It's that whirling the staff weapon and shooting backward trick."

"I see." And he did. Their escort was an unknown quantity.

For a while they walked in silence, all senses keyed to their surroundings. Teal'c heard the whispered footfalls of a small night creature scampering to safety at their passing; the far-off cry of a bird of prey and its mate's answer; the muted voices of the men behind him, discussing a variety of subjects, from commanding officers to sexual exploits. The Marines, at least, felt at ease in this place.

Suddenly Dr. Fraiser murmured, "Sam? Did you warn Warren?"

The flashlight's beam jerked up a fraction and settled back onto their path, telling Teal'c that Major Carter had flinched. He knew why. It had been the only possible course to take, but it went against the one rule O'Neill held immutable, for himself and for his team. *Nobody gets left behind.*

"No," she said softly and then, more to herself than to Dr. Fraiser, "I couldn't risk it. We'll brief General Hammond and be back with reinforcements by tomorrow evening at the latest. If Warren's involved in whatever this is, he'd have stopped us. If he isn't, he'll be safer not knowing."

The gorge took a sharp bend to the left, the rock barriers narrowing. Teal'c remembered this feature. Past the bend, the ravine would open abruptly into the crater that held the Stargate. If there was to be an ambush, it would be his task to prevent the Marines behind from closing the narrows. Ahead, Major Carter and then Dr. Fraiser disappeared from view and his immediate protection. An impulse to race after them screamed to be obeyed. Teal'c curbed it, fell back even further so as not to lose the Marines, and followed the shimmer of the light that hovered along rock walls like a ghost. His world shrank to this dancing glow, the white plumes of his breath rising in the air, and the echoes of footsteps before and behind. No sight or sound out of the ordinary.

When he emerged from the narrows, a familiar sensation leaped at him with painful acuity.

Major Carter and Dr. Fraiser stood motionless, staring at the Stargate and the three men posted in front of it. Only three. The five who had accompanied them were nowhere to be seen. Deep within his pouch, Teal'c felt a ripple; the symbiote stirring, affected by its carrier's tension—or the proximity of its kind.

This time the men did react. Their weapons came up. One of them, tall and heavily muscled, slowly walked down the steps of the dais.

"Where the hell do you think you're going?" he demanded, his submachine gun aimed at Major Carter.

"Drop the Rambo act, Poletti! They're going home!" The voice at his back very nearly startled Teal'c into a jump. Their escort's leader stepped out in front of them. "You hear me, you dumb guinea? It's Johnson. Stand down and breathe, will ya?"

Approaching, Mr. Poletti swore, lowered his weapon, and signaled his comrades to do the same. "Jesus Christ, Johnson! Nobody told us you guys were coming!"

"Yeah, well. Nice to know you weren't asleep."

"Who'd wanna sleep in this creepy shit-hole?" Mr. Poletti seemed to reflect on his choice of words and, with a nod at Major Carter and Dr. Fraiser added, "Sorry, ma'am, Doc. Uh, I really enjoyed that talk of yours by the way. Shame we had to leave."

"Thanks," Dr. Fraiser said weakly, her tone betraying an uncertainty Teal'c shared.

Of one thing, however, he was certain now. These men were not Goa'uld. A Goa'uld never would have countenanced an insult, no matter how jocular. They had to be Jaffa therefore—although it still did not explain by whom and for what reason they had been created.

"Look, gentlemen, it's getting a little chilly, and I'd hate to catch a cold. So, if it's okay with you?" Major Carter motioned at the DHD, her weapon lowered but still unsafed.

"Of course, ma'am." Mr. Poletti moved aside, smiling. "All

yours."

While Major Carter stepped to the DHD and dialed, the other two men moved down from the dais and joined Mr. Poletti in a tight group. Their backs were turned on Teal'c, who could hear them whispering. It disturbed him, but there was no palpable reason to interfere.

One by one the chevrons locked with reassuring clanks and the wormhole established in a splendid flare of power. Teal'c released a breath he had been unaware of holding and, as soon as Major Carter had entered the ID code, nudged Dr. Fraiser forward. The doctor hurried past the men, up the dais, and disappeared in the event horizon. Over by the DHD, Major Carter had turned to face him, her eyes issuing a silent command. This time he refused. He would not leave M3D 335 until he knew her safe. A slight nod conceded his choice, and she went to follow Dr. Fraiser.

"Well, it's been a pleasure," said the escort's leader.

Teal'c inclined his head in acknowledgment and walked toward the Stargate, acutely aware of the Marines' stares. Their eyes seemed to be burning his back, but the men never moved. Then he was at the dais, and four large strides carried him up the steps and into the wormhole.

The fractional part of his higher consciousness that always remained alert to the journey registered the wrongness now, and it was screaming. Untold forces tore at him, intent to shred his every fiber until he was nothing but dust drifting in the vastness of space. Wrapped in icy agony, he howled his defiance, was still howling when the Stargate spat him out onto spongy ground, wet and redolent with the stench of decay.

Impossibly far above him the wormhole disengaged, leaving the Stargate a gaping hole in the forehead of a face carved into ancient masonry. Above that mask soared the impenetrable canopy of a rainforest.

Groaning, every joint aflame, Teal'c pushed himself to his knees. A few meters to his right lay Dr. Fraiser, unconscious, bleeding from a head wound. She had struck the root of a giant tree. Not far from her, Major Carter was drowsily struggling to her feet. He saw her eyes widen when the realization hit home.

"Where the hell are we, and where's the DHD?"

"I do not—"

As silent as it was ferocious, the attack came without warning.

CHAPTER SIX

Reward Pathway: *Areas of the brain stimulated while a subject is engaged in pleasurable activity.*

General Hammond contemplated a heap of unattended paper-work—taller by three inches than the sheaf of documents in his out-tray—and wondered why vital matters such as parking permits for visiting officers couldn't be authorized by someone of less exalted rank. Then again, the whole point of doing paperwork was to avoid witnessing the deployment of another twenty Marines to '335. If Crowley kept going at this clip, he'd run out of Earthside personnel by the end of next week.

Holding on to that thought, Hammond peeled a two-page document from the heap, this one a request from SG-11 for permission to wear sneakers instead of combat boots on archeological digs. Apparently artifacts, when trodden on, responded better to sneakers. Well, that was painless. Next. Next was an advisory to the engineering unit, which shouldn't have landed on his desk in the first place. From underneath peered Colonel O'Neill's letter, still half-opened, the way he'd left it after Dr. Jackson's remarkable disclosure.

In the four days since that conversation, Hammond had called in a handful of chits and launched some very hushed enquiries into General Crowley and his connections to the NID. So far it'd got him zip. He'd even formalized Major Carter's rather inspired call to her friend, Augustus the Unpronounceable, only to receive a terse email from Mr. Przsemolensky's superior at the NRO, informing General Hammond that there were no satellite pictures of the Colorado Springs area taken at that time. He didn't know what annoyed him more: the man's low opinion of his mental faculties—Cheyenne Mountain rated twenty-four hour satellite surveillance—or the sheer frustration of it all.

Still, something needed to be done. Hammond tugged at the letter. Its tattered flap caught on a paper clip, with the result that the whole stack of correspondence keeled over and spilled onto the floor. The ensuing blue streak was interrupted by a rap on his office door.

"Come in!" grunted Major General George Hammond, doubled over in the chair and gathering the equivalent of a medium-size forest from the carpet.

"Ah. I'll come back later, sir."

Hearing the voice, Hammond shot up abruptly. The impact of his skull on the underside of the desk loosened a tooth or two. Biting back another curse, he bellowed, "You'll do nothing of the kind, Colonel! Sit down!"

By the time Hammond had extricated his head from under the desk and straightened up, Jack had eased himself into a chair. He wore civvies, looked like he'd been subsisting on a diet of coffee and next to no sleep, and did a great job of avoiding Hammond's gaze. Which admittedly wasn't all that difficult, given the mess.

Jack studied it intently and finally looked up. "Bad day, General?"

"I've had fourteen of them so far, and counting."

"The Marine base?" Seeing his CO's frown, he added, "Don't blame Daniel, sir. He couldn't help it. I plied him with beer until he talked." The grin he was aiming for didn't quite materialize. "It's my fault, isn't? If I hadn't blown the exercise, they—"

"The exercise was rigged."

The anger coiled behind Jack's eyes erupted. "I told them I didn't want it to go any further! Who was it? Carter? Daniel?"

"I may be an old fool, son, but there's still a thing or two I can figure out for myself." Technically, it wasn't a lie. Hammond felt rather pleased with himself.

Not least because it took the wind out of Jack's sails. To an extent. "Like what, sir? The infamous grappling hook theory? I suppose it didn't occur to you or my team that it'd be a piece of cake if you did it in two stages: get up to the gallery first, and from there to the girders."

"And on the gallery you hook onto what? An antique railing that broke when you fell against it?"

"It could have been a weak spot. Look, sir, one thing that's not gonna happen is me trying to avoid the consequences by accusing another officer."

At that moment the klaxons went off. Jack's hands closed on the armrests of the chair, as though he were about to push himself up and run downstairs to the control room. And then it passed. He sank back, a look of defeat in his eyes.

George Hammond had seen that same look thirty-odd years ago, and it scared the hell out of him. It always was the best who were hit hardest, because you didn't get to be best if you didn't care. And yes, you knew that death was on the cards every time you led a team out there. Jack knew it as well as Freeman had known. But seeing people you care about die—even in an exercise—because of a mistake you've made... now, *that* was a whole different ballgame. After that, you ended up doubting your choice of toothpaste and breakfast cereal, and never mind your ability to lead a team.

Aware of the scrutiny, Jack tried to dodge Hammond's gaze again. He zeroed in on the wad of papers rescued from the floor and, as luck would have it, the letter lay topmost. "I'd been wondering why I hadn't heard from you. It's why I'm here, really."

"I tried to call you a couple of times, Jack. Kept getting a lady who speaks Japanese."

"Oh." For a second he looked genuinely puzzled, then he nodded at the letter. "You should read it, sir. I'm saying some pretty nice things about you."

"It's the rest I'm worried about. I—"

The knock was vigorous enough to make the door hinges rattle.

"That's gotta be a Marine," muttered Jack.

"Behave, Colonel." Hammond stepped on a grin. "Come in!"

It turned out to be an admirable piece of divination on Jack's part. The door opened on the somewhat crumpled shape of Major Warren, fresh through the gate and obviously in one big hurry.

"General Hammond. Colonel. Sorry to butt in, sirs."

Grimacing, Jack hauled himself from the chair. "I'd better—"

"Stay put, son! We're not finished yet," snapped Hammond and, just to be on the safe side, waited until the delinquent had sat back down before addressing Major Warren. "Good to see you back, Major. What can I do for you?"

The expression on Warren's face plainly said that, whatever he'd expected, it wasn't this. "Major Carter's lab results, sir. Has she come up with anything yet? Colonel Norris is getting a little antsy and... Well, he wasn't real happy about you letting those troops gate out to '335."

Whatever General Hammond had expected, it wasn't this either. "Care to run this by me again slowly? I've got no idea what you're talking about. Major Carter, Teal'c, and Dr. Fraiser have been *on* '335 for the past four days and, frankly, I'd been hoping to have at least my chief medical officer back by now."

The expression intensified, graduated from *What the heck?* to *Oh crap! The old man's cracked*, and Hammond felt a chill crawl up his neck and raise his hackles. Finally, carefully almost, Warren offered, "Sir, they gated back here three days ago."

"What?" It had come from Jack.

"You heard me, sirs. They stayed for one night; next day the doc gave her lectures, and then Carter told Colonel Norris that she'd found some kinda gremlin messin' with the gate... Well, she didn't say it like that."

"Wouldn't have thought so," Jack grumbled.

Momentarily thrown, Warren cast a sidelong glance at him, sniffed, and continued, "Anyway, she told the colonel she needed to get back here PDQ to figure it out, and that's when they left."

Hammond's mind was racing through a whole kaleidoscope of possibilities, from busy signals and secondary gates in cold places to people's matrices being stored inside the gate in ways even Sam Carter could barely explain, let alone remedy. None of these possibilities seemed desirable, and so he latched on to the obvious. "Major, they're not here. Take my word for it. So I'm suggesting they never left. There *was* a minor anomaly, but that only affected outgoing—"

"General, they had an escort, and those guys *saw* them go through the gate. As a matter of fact, the..."

Warren trailed off, mystified by the antics of Colonel O'Neill who'd leaned forward, reached out, and gingerly removed an unopened letter from the base commander's desk.

"Something on your mind, son?" Hammond asked quietly.

"I'd like to return to active duty, sir." The letter disappeared into the inside pocket of Jack's leather jacket.

"You sure about this? What about your ribs?"

"My ribs are fine."

"Uhuh. I can tell by the way you move like you've swallowed a poker, Colonel."

"It's the deportment classes I've been taking. Sir, please. I want to go to '335.'"

"With respect, Colonel!" spluttered Warren. "If you're imply-ing—"

"I'm not *implying*. I'm *noting* that two thirds of my team and Dr. Fraiser have gone missing. Now, I don't know about you, Major, but I'd like to find out what the hell happened."

"Yes, sir. Sorry."

Going by the way Jack heaved himself from the chair, the deport-ment classes hadn't yet advanced to Lesson Two, *Rising Gracefully*. He hid a wince, turned to Hammond. "Request permission to gate out to M3D 335, sir."

Past experience showed that Jack wasn't going to take *No* for an answer. Besides, Hammond had got what he wanted, and if cir-cumstances had been less worrying, he'd have called the situation a Godsend. "Permission granted, Colonel. Take SG-3 and—"

"No. Sir. I'm going on my own. It's a whole moon full of Marines, General, and I don't... I don't want to put anybody else at risk."

The toy huddled in a corner, and he pretended to be asleep. He was not. His eyelids fluttered in an involuntary spasm. Fear made it impossible for him to relax. This attempt to deceive her was the first vaguely amusing act he had conceived in three days. Perhaps she should not have revived him. But it had been worth it, if only for the knowledge of having flouted the will of that arrogant human, Simmons. Besides, it could be remedied. Quite easily, in fact.

Nirrti nudged the toy with her toes and found a fleeting spark of enjoyment in the way a shudder racked his body and his eyes snapped open on a look of pure terror. Maybe not?

No. It was time for something new. She turned away, heard the toy sob with relief, and smiled. The room was splendid, and this was an opulence that would never pall. Intricately carved pillars of wood, hard and small-grained and with a reddish sheen, supported a low ceiling. From the beams hung curtains of sheer silk that partitioned the space into a gently swaying maze in all shades of red and orange. One entire wall was taken up by a mirror of polished silver. Savoring the whisper of cool fabric on her skin, she parted the curtains to step through and study her own image.

How long had it been? Seven hundred years? Eight hundred? She barely remembered. The host's body had worn well, still retained a fair measure of its former owner's youthful allure. But it would not last, could not last. She thought of the Hankan girl, the boundless possibilities and power open to a *hak'taur*, and felt the rage rise again. A new host was another debt the Tauri owed her.

A touch on the bluish gem set in her ribbon device released an invisible burst of energy that altered the molecular structure of the mirror. Like oil welling from a vent, viscous grayness pooled and obscured Nirrti's reflection, then cleared to a jungle vista. Deep within a closed-off part of her cortex, her host dreamed of home, while she watched, once more and as if through a window, the events of three days ago.

The Chappa'ai, *inset in the outer wall of the temple, fills with liquid azure gleam, and Simmons's gift is flung from the wormhole in a graceful arc. Once, twice, the healer spins in the air and comes down heavily on the root of a thousand-year-old tree. In coarse tan clothes, not in white today, she lies motionless. Stunned? Dead? The latter would be inconvenient. But no. She lives. Near her slack mouth a leaf shivers under shallow puffs of breath. Nirrti, too, breathes again, entranced by the stirrings of the leaf.*

And so she starts when a second traveler seems to fly straight at her. For a second their eyes meet, black on blue, although the woman, tall and blond, is unaware of it. Nirrti sees shock, pain, and a gleam of avid curiosity. This intrigues her—more than the leaf—because curiosity would have been her own first instinct. Curiosity and the need to examine just how the Chappa'ai *could have deceived them to such a degree. Maybe she will reveal the secret. After all, this Tauri woman probably has saved Nirrti's life by staying the healer's hand and she will bear closer scrutiny. In good time. Is it possible that Simmons has given more than he intended? For the moment, though—*

Incredibly, a third figure hurtles from the Chappa'ai. *Now Nirrti is sure that Simmons has not intended this. Greed and caution would not have permitted it. For the third is male, but not human. He is Jaffa, the* shol'va *who denied his god. A memory of Apophis's fury makes her smile. She herself relishes the illusion of divinity and the terrified veneration it brings, but she is a scientist and has never been deluded enough to believe her own lie. The key to immortality is, after all, knowledge not godhead.*

Mouth gaping, teeth bared in a scream of rage and pain, the shol'va *hits the ground hard. When, at last, the* Chappa'ai *winks out, the blond female is the first to discover that they cannot leave this place. One terror compounded by another. And it is only the beginning. What the Tauri and even the Jaffa cannot hear are the vibrations that whip the beasts into a frenzy and lure them to their prey. Hungry and swift-footed, they fly from their lair, dark, bristling shapes unlike anything the subjects have ever seen. And, as planned, the subjects are driven apart in the struggle for their lives.*

"A gift. My, what a gift," Nirrti murmured as the image dissolved into the silver surface of the mirror.

Slowly, her fingers curled and clenched in a fight to resist temptation. She wanted to bring them in now, break them now, use them now. But it would not be the same. The true triumph lay in their willing surrender when the horrors out there had piled despair upon despair and even servitude seemed preferable to further endurance or lingering death.

Exhaling, she relaxed, clapped her hands once. One of her beautiful new Jaffa entered instantly and quietly, anticipating every whim of his mistress, as a good servant should. He had brought a flowing red robe, held it out for her approval, and she raised her arms and permitted him to clothe her. When he was done tugging folds into place, he took a step back, eyes averted, as though he had anticipated this need, too. For a few moments she studied him, appreciated the nervous play of muscles under milky skin dotted with freckles, the almost imperceptible flaring of nostrils when he sensed her gaze on his face and the new tattoo on his forehead—the golden shape of a dove in flight. At last she reached out, fingertips caressing the sensitive flaps of his pouch.

"You please me, child," she said.

His smile was beatific. "You honor me, Lady Nirrti."

"Yes, I do. The question is whether you deserve it." She increased the pressure of her touch just enough to suggest the potential for exquisite pain, but not enough to hurt him. Yet.

Only the slightest squirm betrayed his desire to back away. Excellent. He had been one of the first, and he had come far. "How can I make myself more deserving, Lady Nirrti?"

Yes, he had come far indeed. But was it far enough? "What is your name?" she asked.

"Master Sergeant Charles Macdonald."

She almost laughed. Such a waste of time, Tauri names. "Master Sergeant Charles Macdonald, I have a task for you."

"Please, Lady Nirrti, name it."

"Dispose of the thing in corner."

"As you wish, Lady Nirrti."

He disappeared through the curtains, and she curbed an impulse to follow and watch. Let him believe he was trusted. Shadows danced and from behind sheer fabric rose the toy's cracking voice.

"Sarge, what are you doing? Hey, come on, Sarge. It's me, Gonzales. Gonzo… Come on, you remember me. You gotta remember me! Please, Sar—"

When her Jaffa returned to drag his prisoner before her, the toy's eyes, unearthly pale in an olive-skinned face, appeared to scream.

"How do you wish me to dispose of him, Lady Nirrti?"

"Take him to the temple. And"—she smiled at the thought—"make my pets jump."

BDUs and combat boots felt uncomfortable and alien after a couple of weeks of jeans and sweatshirts and walking barefoot round the house.

Bull, Jack decided, suddenly angry at himself.

It was neither the BDUs nor the boots. *He* felt uncomfortable and alien. Though not usually prone to fits of nostalgia—God knew he had little enough reason to be—right now he wished he were in his twenties again, a stupid kid off on his first mission, young and eager and full of himself. Not exactly ideal either, but preferable to middle-aged and jaded and full of something else.

"Chevron five engaged," chanted Sergeant Harriman.

Five? Thirty-nine, more like. What the hell was taking so long? The gate's inner ring seemed to be spinning at half its usual speed and doing it on purpose.

"Chevron six engaged."

Harriman's contributions to this interior monolog were a tad predictable. Why couldn't he say something interesting like, *The balalaika-type thing's just got a triangle clamped over it*?

"Chevron seven locked."

Locked. Now there was a plot twist!

Jack O'Neill watched the event horizon roar out at him; a blaze of glory that momentarily froze all thought. It always did. Given a chance, he'd look at it all day. Of course it didn't stand still long enough. It sloshed back into a luminous membrane across the gate and sent blue reflections rippling around the room.

At which point Hammond was supposed to say *Colonel O'Neill, you have a Go* or *Godspeed, Colonel* or both. He didn't.

Now what?

Clutching his P90 until he thought either the gun or his fingers would snap, Jack refused to turn around. The last thing Hammond needed to see was him getting jumpy. *Getting* jumpy?

Just stand here and breathe, O'Neill. He's gonna say it. Any second now…

He didn't.

Instead the blast door rumbled open. The noise was followed by the clatter of boots on concrete. *Hurried* boots on concrete. There was only one person who regularly entered the gate room at this pace. Something to do with time-keeping issues brought on by a propensity to lose himself in dictionaries or similarly riveting literature.

"Come to kiss me goodbye, Daniel?"

The boots clattered to a halt beside him. "Uh, nothing personal, Jack, but no."

Jack whirled around, stared up at the control room window, just in time to see Harriman take cover behind his computer screen. Hammond next to him didn't move; a burly, implacable rock who stared right back.

"General, we had a deal!"

"That's right, Colonel. The deal was for me to pretend I've never received a certain piece of correspondence and let you go through that gate. But you either go *with* Dr. Jackson or not at all."

The SFs dotted around the room began to look interested, and Jack began to feel no longer uncomfortable and alien but slightly nauseous. "Daniel's half blind! He's not fit for duty!"

"Neither are you," Daniel muttered helpfully. "Want me to poke your ribs?"

"Daniel—"

"They're my friends, too. I know the score, Jack. I've always known it. I was the one who took us to Abydos without having the coordinates to get back, remember?"

Oh yes! How could he possibly forget? The first of three supremely joyous occasions on which Daniel Jackson had died. Jack's nausea ratcheted up a notch. If he ever went through that wormhole, he'd sail out the other end barfing. "Is this supposed to convince me?"

The response didn't come in quite the way Jack had anticipated. Instead of waiting for General Hammond's blessing, Daniel took the steps up to the ramp two at a time and steamed for the Stargate at flank speed.

"Dammit, Daniel!"

It was pointless, and Jack knew full well that he'd lost this argument. He only had two options. One—staying put—was absolutely out of the question. And thus Colonel O'Neill, for the umpteenth time, found himself running after an enterprising archeologist. Halfway into the event horizon, he heard Hammond's voice rattle over the PA.

"Godspeed, Colonel."

Very funny, sir.

The thought melted into rushing, star-streaked black.

Stumbling out onto orange air and looming rock, Jack decided that the trip through the wormhole had left him more than usually chilled. His first impression of M3D 335 didn't help. The gate sat at the bottom of some humungous hole, which in turn was capped by a planet that looked set to belch in his face. Apart from the Stargate, the only access to this tomb was by parachute or through a narrow gorge opposite. And if the locals didn't want you to come calling, they either whacked you upside the head as soon as you poked your nose into said gorge, or they lined up around the crater to shoot fish in a barrel. Or both.

Jack sensed a cold prickle of paranoia seep up his back and tried to ignore it. At least he had an answer to Question Number One. Part of him had been hoping for a forest with thick underbrush to hide in. But, given the terrain, there was no way in hell that Carter, Teal'c, and the doc could have gone anywhere, except where Warren said they'd gone. Unless the escort had been lying. But why would the Marines lie? Why indeed? The query brought to mind his team's interesting theory about the—

"DHD seems okay to me," said Daniel who'd crouched in front of the Dial-Home-Device, tinkering with some diagnostic tools. Now he stowed them and rose. "Of course, Sam's the expert, but I can't see anything wrong with it."

Daniel's words sounded flat and sank like lead under the weight of the planet above, but at least they'd fractured the eerie quiet of this place. Too much quiet. No wind, no trees, not even a pebble clattering down the cliffs. Why were there no guards at the gate? Warren had mentioned guards, three of them. Maybe only after dark. Maybe. But still…

"Jack? Are you listening?"

"Yeah. The DHD's fine."

Which led straight to Question Number Two. Harriman had corroborated that the gate malfunction was intermittent and affected outgoing wormholes only. That aside, whatever had caused the problem, it seemed to have resolved itself. During the past few days there'd been no further glitches. So why would Carter concoct some cockamamie tale to scare Norris?

"… unless she had a damn convincing reason to get off this rock," Jack mused aloud. "A reason she didn't want to air to the gentlemen of the Marine Corps."

"What are you—" Daniel stiffened suddenly and turned toward the gorge. "Shh!"

"I wasn't saying anything."

"Shh! Somebody's coming."

Almost of its own accord, Jack's hand flew into a sequence of signals. A swift memory flashed up, of the last time he'd done it and what had happened next. When the image receded, he already was running for a boulder to the left of the gorge, keeping an eye on Daniel who'd headed right as ordered. On the dusty ground their footfalls made virtually no noise, but the tracks would be visible. Couldn't be helped. They'd just have to be fast.

Pretending that the activity his ribs currently engaged in was normal, Jack skidded into cover behind the boulder. Nice view. Across the mouth of the gorge he saw Daniel peer around the edge of his rock, giving a thumbs-up. Like Carter, just before— Throttling that thought, Jack brought up his gun. The metallic click of the safety coming off sounded perversely loud. He flinched and forced himself to go still. Never easy for him, more difficult than ever now.

The gorge funneled noises into the crater like the an old gramophone tube. Out there the ground had to be covered in shale. He could hear the crunch of boots on stone. Four sets of boots… probably. Voices. No. One voice. Barking commands. In English. He relaxed a fraction. It ruled out Goa'uld or Jaffa—unless they were practicing. Well, they had to sometimes, right?

Daniel had heard them, too, raised an enquiring eyebrow, and Jack shook his head. Before he indulged in prospects of a happy reunion with his pals, the Marines, he needed to have these guys where he could see them—or draw a bead on them if necessary.

The footfalls grew louder. The visitors were moving fast, carelessly, which was good news one way or the other: they either had no idea that somebody was expecting them, or their intentions were as pure as driven snow. Okay, there was a third way, and it wasn't such good news: they knew they owned the goddamn place. Eyes fixed on the cleft in the rock wall, Jack spot-welded the P90 against his cheek and waited.

A minute later Larry, Curly, and Moe trotted into view, as unwholesome as he remembered them from the exercise. Behind them followed their CO. All things considered, a bunch of Goa'uld would have been preferable.

CHAPTER SEVEN

He stands right at the lip of the Stargate, arms flung wide, body curved in a fluid arc, like a gymnast on a beam, trying the impossible, trying to regain balance broken. She knows what will happen, knows that gravity will win, because that's what gravity does, it always wins, immutable and uncaring. A tiny shiver ripples around the edges of weightlessness, grace collapses, and he falls. Watching helplessly, she knows what awaits him on the ground, knows because—

"No!"

Sam Carter shot from a sweat-soaked, troubled sleep, listening to the echo of her own scream. It shook loose a cacophony of chatters and screeches in the canopy above. Curled up into a tight ball, she nestled further into the crook between bole and branch where she'd spent the night and wished she were invisible. Gradually the noise died down, and no one found it necessary to check on the intruder or come shopping for breakfast. Thank God for small favors.

After a few minutes of listening for stealthy approaches, she decided it was safe and awkwardly uncoiled. In the process she discovered several muscle groups she hadn't known she owned—amazing what an extra-hard orthopedic tree could do for one's anatomy. Not that it made that much of a difference, and these kinks at least would work themselves out once she was on the move again. As for the rest…

She rolled up the tattered leg of her pants—damp. Everything was damp and never dried. Had the fabric started rotting yet? Maybe. A flap of material came away under her fingers. Unless she managed to get off this adventure playground sometime soon, she'd be running around in her bra and panties. Of course, in order to get off she'd have to find the DHD, and in order to have any hope of finding that—if it even existed—she'd have to find the gate, and before she did any of the above, she'd have to find Teal'c and Janet. If Janet was still alive. It'd been three days now, three days of plodding through the jungle looking for them. She was less worried for Teal'c; Teal'c had that air of indestructibility—deceptive, yes, but he *did* have a symbiote—and he knew how to take care of himself, better than any of them. Janet on the other hand…

The image popped into Sam's mind unbidden; her friend sprawled between the roots of one of those giant trees, unconscious, blood trickling from a head wound. It might have been something as relatively harmless as a concussion, but she'd never got a chance to make sure. Those… things… had poured from the open maw of the stone face beneath the Stargate, dozens of them, huge and black and brutal. The nearest way to describe them was a cross between boar and hyena, five feet tall and armor-plated under the bristles. She'd emptied a whole magazine into one of them before it finally broke to its knees, juddering. Even then it'd managed to gouge her leg. Howling in pain and fury and without time to reload, she'd switched to her handgun, then to her knife.

Teal'c had fared a little better. His staff weapon gave them pause if not much else, and he'd been able to reach Janet and cover her. Sam had figured that he might stand a chance if she could draw off at least some of that vicious mob. Ignoring Teal'c's roar of disapproval, she'd backed away from the pack that was trying to have her for lunch and allowed the hell hogs to chase her into the jungle. Only when they'd suddenly stopped hounding her and disappeared, she'd realized that, of all the mistakes she possibly could have made, this had been eminently the most stupid. Limping for her life, tripping over roots and dodging branches, she'd stumbled into an unnerving green maze without landmarks or any other means of orientation. The attempt to retrace her steps had led her in circles for seventy-two hours.

"And now it's time to greet another fun-filled day," Sam muttered and tugged at her pants some more.

Under the rolled-up end appeared a makeshift bandage; sterile gauze strapped to her skin with tape. She ripped it off, wincing. At least it took care of the fact that she hadn't shaved her legs. A deep gash gaped from the side of her calf to the back of her knee, and at its center gleamed white bone. It hadn't even begun to close, and the torn flesh suppurated. So much for antibiotics. Whatever else they killed, giant hog germs obviously weren't on the list. One more reason for finding Dr. Fraiser.

Reaching behind her, Sam fished the medikit from her backpack, opened it, and frowned at the dwindling supplies. With sudden determination she grabbed the disinfectant, unscrewed the cap, and liberally squirted the liquid into the wound. The trick was not to scream your head off. She bit her hand instead, drew blood. It hurt like a son of a bitch. Not for the first time she longingly eyed the two ampoules of morphine. She'd left them untouched so far, knowing she'd need them if she was faced with the choice of either dying of gangrene or losing a leg.

When the throbbing ebbed, she packed the wound in sterile bandages again and taped it shut, which started a whole new round of throbs. As she wiped her face, sweating with pain, the back of her hand struck something lumpy high on her cheekbone.

"Yuck!"

Her stomach flipped, and she got within an inch of crying. Hell, the beasts had made Bogey cry! Just watch *African Queen*. Of all the disgusting… Leeches! God, she hated them. It wasn't the first leech she'd picked up, wouldn't be the last. She'd have to twist it off—and head out of here before this tree threw any more surprises at her. That aside, she needed food and water.

Two minutes later, she'd shouldered the pack and was rappelling down a vine, which, coincidentally, was a darn sight more difficult than Tarzan made it look. Largely because it was a good way of flaying your palms if you didn't do it slowly. Except, *slowly* required a strength she no longer had. The branch where she'd set up camp was some sixty feet above ground. Gazing down now, Sam figured she'd gone maybe a third of the way, and her arms were already rattling with fatigue.

Below her the thin thread of a path snaked through relentless vegetation. She'd found it late yesterday afternoon, followed it until dark, and she'd follow it some more today. Probably not the safest thing to do—although she'd seen no spoor, it had to be a game trail, and if the hell hogs were anything to go by she didn't care to meet the rest of the wildlife. Then again, her options were limited.

"Right. Onward and downward," she murmured. What was it they said about people who talked to themselves?

Another fifteen feet down she froze, not sure if she'd really heard what she thought she'd heard or if the fever was getting to her. No. There it was again. Soft, rhythmic squelching. She knew that noise. She'd been listening to herself making it for the past three days; footsteps on soggy ground. Then a sharp crack. Somebody had trodden on a branch, and he/she/it was coming her way.

Now what?

Play possum.

Easier said than done. Below, the hiker was closing in, and she hung barely twenty feet above his head. If he looked up, he was bound to see her. Like the exercise. The Colonel had drummed it into them with a sledgehammer: *Don't give them reason to look up. Don't even breathe.* And then it'd all gone wrong. Why?

She held her breath, ignoring the tremors that racked her arms and shoulders and promised to explode into a full-blown cramp. When the hiker came into view, Sam stifled a gasp. The snazzy hairstyle pegged him as a Marine, but the outfit and weaponry made him something else entirely—unless the USMC had radically changed their dress code and equipment during the past three days.

Then, almost directly under her, his step faltered, he stopped, looked around and finally, inevitably, up. She knew why. She'd sensed it practically the same moment as he. It explained the costume.

"Well, lookee here." The upturned face was smirking.

Its owner had participated in the exercise. Except, back then he hadn't worn a tattoo on his forehead. A bird in flight. Whose sign was that? Daniel would know. Sam decided against asking and just stared back at the man. What was his name? Burger? Somebody had called him Burger. King? Surely not Dairy Queen? Macdonald. That's what it was. Master Sergeant Macdonald.

Macdonald kept smirking, and it gave her the creeps. A shaft of sunlight stabbing through foliage picked out the tattoo, lost it again when he raised and primed the staff weapon he carried. "Okay, sugar. Let's have a little competition, huh? Let's see if you can climb faster than I can shoot."

The practical part of the competition would be wholly redundant. The state she was in, Sam couldn't climb, period, and never mind fast. There was no point in even trying.

... gravity will win, because that's what gravity does...

And sometimes this was an advantage. Returning the ex-sergeant's smile, Major Samantha Carter did the one thing he hadn't expected her to do; she let go of the vine.

The impact was crushing, strained ligaments, bruised bone, sent agony boiling up her leg. Her trajectory had been just so, bringing her down smack on top of him. The crumpled heap beneath her lay motionless—dead or out cold, right now she didn't give a damn. Groaning, she crawled off, rolled him on his back, undid his chest armor. Lifting the coarse shirt, she found it; an x-shaped incision on his abdomen, edges of the flaps curling up slightly. A Jaffa's pouch.

"Damn," she whispered, shaken although she'd known it'd be there.

At that moment he gave a low moan. Not dead, then. Time to haul ass. She struggled to her feet and, using his staff weapon as a crutch, slipped off the path and into green, dripping undergrowth.

Far off, in the direction from where he'd come, rose a scream, human and desperate.

"Seeing that you insist on pleasing your whims, Colonel... Then again, I suppose that's the one thing you actually excel at." Norris sneered and pointed across a dusty square kept in the moon's color scheme of titillating beige. "Over there's the mess. I reckon that'll do."

Daniel, normally all in favor of a non-violent approach, was beginning to hope that Jack would deck the creep. The needling had been going on non-stop for the entire three klicks from the gate into the camp. Obviously Norris had an ego to massage. Might have to do with the fact that he'd been caught with his pants down and jumped sky-high when Colonel O'Neill and Dr. Jackson had ambled from cover back in the crater.

Eyes hidden behind shades, Jack was taking it with a forbearance so out of character as to be positively unsettling. Okay, like it or not, they needed Norris's cooperation, but usually Jack didn't let minor issues such as that stand in his way when he was pissed. And he ought to be well and truly pissed by now.

"That'll do fine," he said, face stony, except for a tense white line around his mouth that betrayed the effort to keep a lid on whatever he felt. "Thanks."

Thanks? Talk about gilding the lily. Daniel had heard just about enough of this crap, and if Jack didn't put a stop to it soon, he would.

"Make yourselves at home in there," Norris offered; the sudden generosity probably due to his having placed yet another successful kick in Jack's teeth. "I'll round up the men who were on escort and guard duty that night. You can ask them if you don't believe me or Major Warren."

With that he strode off toward a cluster of huts. Jack gazed after him for a moment and then headed for the mess. For once, Daniel resisted the impulse to rush in where angels feared to tread. Given their history over the past months, it might get him punched in the nose. And in truth, he didn't really want to find out. If this was what he thought it was, he had no idea what to do about it. Besides, now wasn't the time.

The camp was oddly quiet. He'd been to the Alpha Site once, and at the base there folks had been falling over themselves in a constant bustle. Here he'd counted maybe ten people so far, excluding the perimeter guards. By a stack of crates across the square loitered a couple of men, casting furtive glances his way. A third one stepped out of a squat building nearby—latrines, going by the way he adjusted his pants—and he was staring openly, a look of surprise and suspicion on his face. At his nod, the pair by the crates joined him, kicking up dust, and they set off in Daniel's direction like a bunch of hoodlums spoiling for a fight. They passed him at shoulder-brushing distance.

"Hi, Dr. Jackson," Latrine Boy said. "Hope you'll enjoy your stay."

Then they were past and disappeared around a shack, which probably was where the good citizens of Stepford kept their wives. And just how had that guy known his name? Conference with Norris in the Fonz's office? Daniel felt his skin crawl. The place had him spooked in broad daylight. Coffee would help. Definitely.

The mess offered all the coziness you would expect from a corrugated steel hut, but at least it was more or less empty. And the smell rising from the coffee machine suggested something freshly ground. Not necessarily coffee, but still. At a table by one of the windows sat two men—one of them actually smiled. Jack had grabbed a perch as far away from them as possible and was staring holes into the wall. Daniel sighed, got two mugs of coffee and wandered over.

"Here," he said, putting a mug in front of Jack. "Not sure about the taste, but it's the right color."

"Thanks," muttered Jack, tried a sip, and grimaced. "Love the color."

"Yeah." Daniel gave a brief grin. Maybe now was the time. After all, the shades had come off for the time being. "Look, Jack, are you gonna tell Norris where to shove it or—"

"It's the only thing that *is* right about this place."

"—shall I?"

"What?"

"What do you…?" It gradually dawned on Daniel that every single one of Norris's snide comments might have missed its target. He started laughing.

"What's so funny?"

"Me."

"Yeah, well, that's a given, but now isn't the time."

"I know. Welcome back." The wry look it got him made plain that Jack understood exactly what was on Daniel's mind and that there was some truth to it, too. But he was back. Daniel grinned again, harder. "Okay. You first."

"For starters, the training. This is a Marine camp, for cryin' out loud. There ought to be lots of muscular guys running around, singing cadence. So where the hell are they?"

It really was only for starters. Ticking off points on his fingers, Jack reeled off a list that proved he hadn't missed a trick since stepping through the gate. Some of the items—like the conspicuous absence of people—Daniel had noticed himself. Others—the unsuitable terrain, for instance—hadn't registered.

"Ten," said Jack, left pinky raised. "What's with the location of this place? I mean, three klicks from the gate and wide open? Does it get any more unsafe? Makes no sense."

"So, you're— Yuck!" Daniel realized that his coffee had gone cold, which did nothing to improve the taste. "You're saying that—"

"Carter or Teal'c would have picked up on most or all of these things and smelled a rat. Somebody may have taken exception to their keen sense of smell."

"Norris?"

Jack snorted. "My good friend Colonel Norris couldn't find his own ass if you lit it for him. Partly because he's so far up it. I'm starting to think you could be right, by the way. Anyhow, he's a straw man. He hasn't gone to get the escort or the guard. He's gone to ask what to do with us. Somebody else is running this show."

"How do you know—" Suddenly it hit Daniel. His eyes narrowed. "You're starting to think I could be right about what?"

"*You*, plural."

By Jack's standards the answer was straightforward. Daniel considered a celebratory sip of gross cold coffee but refrained when he saw the door open. Not Norris. His three pals from the square, steering for the table next to his and Jack's.

"What?" Jack had clocked the frown.

"The bouncers who just came in?" Daniel murmured into his mug. "I, uh, met them earlier. One of them knows my name, and I swear I've never seen him in my life before."

"Should have told me," Jack murmured back. Aloud he said, "Wonder what's taking Norris so long."

As if on cue, the colonel strode in, self-importance wafting behind him like cheap aftershave. "I'm sorry, O'Neill, but the men aren't available. Their units are conducting night maneuvers. So you might as well head back."

"I don't think so, Pete." A thin smile edged onto Jack's face. "I think I want to wait till they're back, and then I want to talk to them."

"This whole thing is outrageous," spluttered Norris. "I told you a half dozen times that they won't be able to tell you anything new. Chances are that the Stargate malfunctioned, just like Carter said. Too bad, but there it is."

The smile got thinner, verging on predatory. "I want to talk to these men. I don't give a damn how long it takes."

This wasn't quite the tune Norris had got accustomed to on their trek from the gate. He hesitated for a second, then snapped, "What is this, huh? Trying to come over concerned or something? You weren't that worried about your team when you screwed up the exercise, were you?"

The look Jack gave him was on a par with liquid nitrogen. Just as quickly as it had flashed up it was gone again. He waved Norris closer as if for some confidential revelation and gently, if rather loudly, asked, "Tell me something, Pete. Do you actually have to work on being such a pr... preternaturally offensive jerk or is it a gift?"

Somebody at the table across the room seemed to have swallowed the wrong way. A frantic wheeze resolved into a protracted coughing fit. Norris straightened up, bright red in the face, and sent the cougher a glare that made Daniel want to extend his condolences to the victim. Jack had pasted on a mask of pure innocence and contemplated the coffee dregs in his mug.

Finally, Norris turned back to him. "Fine, O'Neill. Have it your way." And, with a nod to one of the Marines at the neighboring table, "Poletti, find these... gentlemen... quarters when they're ready."

"Yessir." It was the man who'd addressed Daniel by name.

On the way out Norris slammed the door hard enough to set the window panes rattling.

Coming out of a wince, Daniel smirked. "Personally, I'd have gone with the first 'pr'."

"Oh, I dunno." Jack cocked an eyebrow. "Now he's gonna go find a dictionary to see what 'preternaturally' means. Broadens his horizons."

Her prison was dark and dank and stank of rotting wood and fungi and mold. There was enough of the stuff in here to keep a pharmaceutical plant busy for decades. Not that it did her any good. Through a knothole a million miles above her head a trickle of light seeped into the hollow bole; just enough to extinguish the faint, pulsing glow of whatever organism it was that ate this tree from the inside out. Like everything in this place — or the place itself; it ate you from the inside out. She shuddered, pushed away the thought, and dug in the dirt until she found her weapon again. Not a real one, of course. He'd disarmed her when she'd tried to resist capture, and God only knew where he'd stashed her handgun and knife. Out of her reach, anyway.

The only weapon she had was a tent stake, slim and light and blunt. Well, not so blunt anymore. She'd slipped it from the back-pack during their first night here, while her captor had believed her asleep and kept watch outside. Even from out there he'd heard the soft clinking of metal on metal and crawled back inside the tree, to check what she was doing and drag her back onto a makeshift pallet of leaves and twigs.

Her pulse leaped into a frantic race at the mere memory of it. She couldn't recall ever having been so scared in her life. If he'd caught her... If he'd caught her, she wouldn't have had to worry about her heart rate ever again—it was as simple as that. But he hadn't caught her. All he'd done was take the pack outside with him. By then she'd already removed and hidden the stake.

Digging some more, sickened by the slick, moist earth squeezing between her fingers like a living thing—just as well her nails were short—she found the whetstone. It was a small piece of rock, rough and hard as flint, pushed up a few hundred years ago by the sapling tree. She rubbed it over her pants to clean off the dirt and settled back to do what she'd been doing whenever her captor was absent during these past three days. He was absent often and for long periods of time, and she knew he was searching for another victim.

It wouldn't be long now. The tip was already sharp, and she'd managed to hone an inch or so to an edge. She'd come to love the rhythmic swishing of stone over metal. The sound promised escape and a return home, and it calmed her. It also was a kind of medita-tion. While she whetted the stake, her mind rehearsed the plan for the hundredth time; the small, vital details of where to position herself, when to strike, where to place the dagger. There would be no second chance. If she hesitated for even a fraction of a second, gave him the slightest opening, he would crush her. The images were perfectly clear now, and she could almost feel the gentle pop of the point pierc-ing skin. Like bursting a zit.

The notion made her laugh, quietly, briefly, snapping her out of her reverie. Good. She needed to stay focused, and never mind that her head was pounding. Her attention fixed on the boulder that blocked the entrance. Had it moved? No. He wasn't back yet, though he would be soon. He always came back several times during the day, to make sure she hadn't found a way to free herself. When he'd first left her here, she'd tried to shift the boulder. Tried for hours, straining and swearing and angrily refusing to admit that it was hopeless. Physically he was so much beyond her it defied description. But she still could outthink him. He'd shift the boulder for her, unblock the narrow gap in the tree, and then—

She drew a hissing breath, froze. There! There it was again. A soft squelch of boots on wet ground; the kind of noise you'd associate with a maiden aunt dispensing sloppy kisses. Kissy-kissy, louder now. Bigger. Because it wasn't an aunt, it was an uncle. She giggled, instantly recognized the hysteria and wrestled it down. No time for that. The steady, insistent voice that had kept her sane until now demanded action. This was it. If she spent another day in this hole, she'd lose it.

Suddenly her palms were slick with sweat. Railing under her breath at the vagaries of physiology, she ripped a strip of fabric from her shirt and wrapped it around the stake to give her a secure grip. Then, inch by inch, so as not to make the slightest sound, she edged off the pallet and over to the entrance. Back pressed into the digestive slime that coated the tree's interior, she stood and waited, half convinced that he would hear the hammering of her heart. She barely heard anything beside it. But then she *did* hear something else. The scrape of stone on wood.

He was back.

She'd been watching carefully whenever he'd opened the entrance. He always rolled the boulder from left to right. Perhaps it was easier that way, perhaps he'd done it once and, finding that it worked, did it the same way each time after that without giving it any thought. It didn't matter. The only thing that mattered was the fact that he rolled it left to right now. Once the gap was clear, he'd pause, not entirely immune to the exertion, then he'd push himself off the boulder and duck and turn to enter. At that moment, and at that moment only, his jugular would be exposed.

The scraping was loud now; scraping and harsh, labored breath. A thin slice of light cut into the gloom inside the tree, broadening slowly, winking in and out as he moved. Another push, another, and another. Then stillness, no more winking and scraping, only the unbroken strip of light and his gasps.

It brought the familiar urge to fling herself past him and flee. She'd tried that, too. He'd moved faster than she ever could have imagined, caught her, and carried her back inside. After that he'd always made sure that his legs partly blocked the gap, as they did now. But he'd have to turn.

Wait. Not yet. Wait!

It was a second. Only a second, two perhaps, but it seemed to grow out of all proportion, stretch into infinity. Her fingers cramped around the grip of the stake.

Relax. Relax your arm. Relax your fingers.

If the muscles got too tense she would have neither the speed nor the accuracy she needed. The bacterial goop that clung to the bark was beginning to seep through her shirt, sticky and moist on her skin. She concentrated on the discomfort, allowed it to distract her just enough to breathe again. Very, very softly.

And then he turned and ducked into the opening.

Her arm flew up, fist tight around the stake, just as she'd rehearsed it time and time again in her mind. He saw the movement from the corner of his eye. His head snapped around, but he was helpless at that moment, broad shoulders wedged inside the gap, arms still caught outside.

"Dr. Fraiser! No!"

Perhaps it was the sound of her name, perhaps the look in his eyes. It dredged up words of a promise she'd made; more than a promise, a command: *First, do no harm.* Fierce and compelling and almost enough to stop her. Almost. Her arm kept moving, needing to find its target, but its thrust changed, thrown off course by four words. Instead of slicing the vein in his neck, the stake plunged into the hollow above his clavicle, destroying a nexus of nerves and disabling the right side of his upper body. He bellowed in pain, reeled back, and crumpled against the boulder.

Now, as she watched his large hand clutching the wound, she knew she'd done the right thing. Hadn't she? He was looking for the weapon. Wasn't he? Looking to pull it out and turn it against her. She had to hold on to it. And she did. There was blood dripping from it, rich and dark, like the blood that trickled from between his fingers.

First, do no harm. Take a sterile bandage and apply pressure to staunch the bleeding. Probe for tissue and nerve damage and for any contamination introduced into the wound canal. Administer— No. Not for this patient.

He wouldn't need antibiotics. Infection wasn't an issue. But how did she know that?

Her gaze slid from those twitching, bloodied fingers up to his face, his eyes again. Deep brown—black almost—and patient and concerned. And still not angry. At that instant the veil tore, and she moaned, dropped the stake. It landed with a muted thud.

"Teal'c," Janet Fraiser whispered, choking on the horror of what she'd done. What she'd almost done. "Teal'c…"

His eyes slid shut, severing the tenuous link she'd found, and the voice floated back, steady and calm and convincing. So convincing.

His symbiote will heal him, and he will come after you. Kill him. Kill him now.

Stare fixed on him she crouched, moving as through treacle, groped through the mud until her fingers struck metal, curled around the stake, raised it. Then she stepped through the gap and out into freedom, half expecting his legs to shoot up and trip her. But he never stirred, either having resigned himself or unconscious. An insect landed on his face, flexing iridescent wings, buzzed and traipsed around and flew off again. To spread the news and bring others to the feast?

Kill him, the voice murmured.

"He's already dead," she replied through a shiver of anxiety. What if the voice noticed she was lying?

It didn't. It simply fell silent, quietly content.

This puzzled her. She'd assumed the voice had all the answers. But she wasn't going to quibble with it. Not now. Not while she still… Not while *it* still was fooled. She took a step back, and another, and stopped, hands shaking, body shaking. Then, before the need to obey became overwhelming, she spun around and headed into the jungle at a dead run.

"Your lunch, sir." As usual, Delores objected to having been dispatched to the deli—or maybe she was vegetarian and had ethical reservations against Pastrami sandwiches. Two French manicured fingernails clamped the top of the paper bag, swung it over the desk, let go. Like a logging crane. "Anything else I can get you, sir?"

"Write out an expense claim form for this and bring it in for me to sign. I assume you'll want your money back." Frank Simmons didn't have to look up to know that her pretty, inane face was twitching with annoyance right now. "You *did* get a receipt, didn't you?"

By ways of an answer, she flounced out, letting the door slam behind her. Simmons supposed he should sack her on the strength of the attitude alone. Truth was, though, she had a fairly high entertainment value. That aside, Delores was blessed with the intellectual brilliance of a Scheffleria, which wasn't actually a bad thing. Intelligence bred curiosity—not a trait to be encouraged in the person who handled his diary. Somebody with two brain cells to rub together might have asked questions about his recent extended absences or about the fact that he'd shown up for a whirlwind tour his office and would vanish again tonight without leaving a forwarding address. She'd figure he had a lover, if she figured anything at all. Like most stupid people, she was wholly unimaginative. Again, a bonus. Unimaginative people were impervious to bullying. As she'd proved conclusively on at least one occasion. Nobody else would have possessed the nerve to keep Jack O'Neill from entering the office for a full two hours.

Frank Simmons pried apart the folded top of the bag and chuckled. It'd been priceless. Little Jack, all dolled up in a neatly pressed dress uniform, cap balanced on his knees—hell, he'd even bothered to do something about that hair of his—and trying to be on his best behavior. Which admittedly didn't amount to much, but by the time he'd lost it and stormed Simmons's office, you could tell it was virtually causing him physical pain. And then he'd crashed head first into a brick wall and slunk away again, tail between his legs. Priceless.

Of course, afterwards his behavior had deteriorated dramatically. He'd gone ahead and solved the riddle of where Major Carter was held and why. As a matter of fact, he'd damn near caught Conrad before Simmons could get to him. The amusement factor of that hadn't been anywhere near as high, so, all things, considered, it probably was best if O'Neill dropped out of the picture permanently.

Simmons took a bite from his sandwich, chewed contentedly—the pickle was homemade—and wished the good colonel hadn't been

wearing a vest that day. Then again, odds were that the joint Marine/
Air Force exercise, beneficial in oh so many ways, had taken care of
this problem, too. In other words, the kinks had worked themselves
out on their own, thank you very much. Too bad that O'Neill refused
to be more flexible. For the price of a little moral malleability somebody like him could have had a stellar career in the NID.

Halfway through the second bite, the door flew open, and Delores
leveled a smug smile at him. "You've got a visitor."

"I'm busy," Simmons managed around a mouthful of Pastrami
and rye.

"It's Lieutenant General Crowley."

Crap! Crowley knew better than to just pop in for a chat. Whatever
reason he had for coming to the office, it wasn't to enquire after
Colonel Simmons's health. More likely the reason would render the
Pastrami indigestible. So much for kinks working themselves out.

Simmons finally swallowed, sank the sandwich bag in a desk
drawer, and said, "Show him in."

Her face registered disappointment, as though she'd hoped for
open signs of irritation, and she stepped back to clear the way for
Crowley—who gusted in like a tropical storm, only drier. Delores
closed the door behind him.

"General. What can I do for you?" asked Simmons, certain that he
didn't want to know.

Complexion florid under a nearly white crew cut, Crowley flung
himself into a chair. It groaned. At five foot eleven, the general
weighed about a hundred and ninety pounds, all of it muscle. "Where
the hell have you been?" he hissed.

Okay. Moderate misconception right there. Simmons straightened
up, shot his cuffs. "With respect, sir, that's none of your business. So.
What can I do for you?"

Needless to say, the reply wasn't designed to calm Crowley down,
but at least he accepted it. Most of the stuff the NID did was classified
up the wazoo. In fact, Simmons had been at the safe house, trying to
cajole a digest of Jaffa training methods out of Conrad, but he had no
intention—or obligation—to reveal that. Not even the President was
cleared to know about the Goa'uld.

"You assured me that he wouldn't be a problem!" Crowley

snapped.

"That *who* wouldn't be a problem?" From the desk drawer wafted the scent of Pastrami, and Simmons was still feeling hungry.

"O'Neill! You said Hammond was bound to bench him and that he'd retire rather than fly a desk." The general gave a dyspeptic snort. "Well, guess what? Your guy's surprisingly active for a retiree. He's snooping around on '335."

"He's *what*?" All of a sudden, Simmons lost his appetite.

"You heard me. He's got that nerdy civilian lapdog of his with him."

"Dr. Jackson? How do you know?"

"Major Warren came back. He told me. I practically had to beat the report out of him. You'd think he's Air Force, the way he—"

"How did they get there?"

"It's a safe bet that they didn't hike," snarled Crowley, peeved at being cut off. "So I'm assuming Hammond sent them."

It was an equally safe bet that someone, somewhere along the line, had perpetrated a cataclysmic foul-up. Otherwise Hammond would never have deployed a man whose fitness was questionable. For all his good ole country boy demeanor, the general was one hell of a smooth operator and way too shrewd to lay himself open like that.

"Any particular reason why he'd do that?" Simmons asked, keeping his voice as calm as he could.

Predictably, it let some of the air out of Crowley's bluster. Squirming, he muttered, "There was an unforeseen complication. The doctor wasn't on her own. Carter and the Jaffa were with her. Our men didn't know what else to do, so they delivered all three of them."

"They did *what*?" Simmons all but screamed. Never mind loss of appetite; he felt distinctly bilious.

"What's the big deal? You authorized the doctor as part of your agreement with that alien. So they lost two people more than expected. Tough."

"General, did you actually *read* O'Neill's file?"

"No. Why should—"

"Because ten years or so ago he did a four-month stint as POW in Iraq and came back a few cards short of a full deck. Eventually he recovered, though some people would argue with that. What a herd of shrinks didn't manage to shake loose, despite their best efforts, was an obsession with never leaving any of his team behind. When you kidnapped Carter and the Jaffa, O'Neill was bound to go after them. And Hammond, with his sentimental fetish for honor and self-sacrifice, probably shoved him through the gate. I guarantee you, between them they're not gonna leave a stone unturned."

"Oh, now it's my fault, is it?" Crowley asked testily. "May I remind you that it would have been your guys who gave the order?"

"I didn't say it was your fault," murmured Simmons, hating to be on the defensive and wishing, for the hundredth time, that he could be out there and run the show himself. The enforced lack of communication was a serious weakness. Unfortunately, his face was too well known around the SGC, and even in a Marine uniform he'd never have made it through the Stargate unnoticed.

"So what do you suggest we do? Any ideas?" snapped Crowley.

"You got somebody who can deliver a message?"

"I've got another unit on standby. They're to gate out whenever I give the word."

"Good." Simmons experienced a wary tug of relief and tapped a pen on his desk blotter. "O'Neill and Jackson can't stay on '335. We can't afford witnesses. Nor can we afford my dear friend, Lady Nirrti, vacuuming Major Carter's head, which she's perfectly capable of doing." Dropping the pen, he leaned back in his chair. "I'm afraid SG-1 will have to go missing in action."

"That's your solution? Make them go away?" Crowley's already livid face reddened alarmingly. "And you think Hammond's gonna sit still for that? He's investigating me, for God's sake!"

"Don't worry about Hammond. I'll take care of him."

"He's gonna go MIA, too? Subtle, Colonel. Real subtle."

"Oh no. I'll just keep him busy." Simmons smiled. "Now, by the beginning of next week you should have ten new Jaffa, bringing the total up to twenty-one. Once they arrive, we ought to give them a road test, see how efficient they are."

Somehow he didn't think he was going to apprise Nirrti of this idea.

CHAPTER EIGHT

*Reversal: Process whereby a derived character state changes back to
the ancestral state through mutation or selection.*

M3D 335's primary was doing a pretty convincing impression
of his ribcage, though Jack O'Neill felt certain that the phe-
nomena were unrelated. Turning green and purple, the bloated per-
il—the planet, that was—had sagged to half-mast and leered over
the horizon. Whoever was responsible for the design sure knew how
to enhance the warm fuzzy feeling the rest of this place evoked.

The blighted eggplant backlit a handful of huts and the ten-strong
unit of Marines who had arrived half an hour ago, yipping in the rari-
fied atmosphere. They were still being briefed by a pair of sergeants,
and something about these two guys irked Jack. They fit in like trans-
vestites at a Revivalist meeting.

The crate that currently served as his bench was getting uncomfortable. Shoulders resting against the wall behind him, he slid forward a little, stretched his legs, and yawned to reinforce the large,
lazy cat look.

Daniel, who'd been ogling one of Mr. Poletti's braves across the
square, turned around to observe Jack's shufflings and asked, "Am I
boring you?"

"Not yet."

"Oh good. If it gets to the point, let me know and I'll start tap-
dancing."

"In a feather boa?"

Jack didn't hear the reply. Out on the square new and exciting
things were happening. The men had been dismissed, but one of them
now addressed the two sergeants. As Newbie's hand dipped into a
pocket, Sergeant A's fingers locked around his wrist, stopping him
from taking out whatever it was he meant to deliver. The sergeant's
hand let go and slipped to the man's shoulder for a pat. Meanwhile,
Sergeant B kept smiling and chatting. All very low-key and expertly

done, and if Jack hadn't been watching out for this type of thing he'd have missed it.

What happened next was just as slick. The sergeants casually herded Newbie in the direction of the communications shack—it'd been introduced as such to Colonel O'Neill. While Sergeant A swiped a keycard through the door lock, B sent a furtive jerk of the head at Mr. Poletti's brave, whose lips began to move. In other words, the brave was either nuts and talking to himself, or wired and inviting other guests to the party. Whom? Newbie and the sergeants entered the com shack. A minute later the guests arrived: Norris and Poletti showed up, collected the brave, and also felt the urge to communicate. If nothing else, it answered one question. The two sergeants who looked like they ought to be wearing suits instead of BDUs were the ones calling the shots around here. NID sprang to mind. Sweet.

By now the eggplant had darkened to a color combination exclusive to Gothic novels, and the men milling around the square were beginning to disperse. The only one dragging his feet was the guy who'd suffered that nasty pulmonary incident in the mess earlier.

"Jack?" Daniel said softly. He looked worried.

It probably wasn't a good idea to admit that his commanding officer shared the sentiment. "I've seen him. I'm just not sure which club he belongs to."

"What?"

"The ape who went into the hut last was the *real* tail. This one's a freelancer." Easing himself from the crate, Jack swore under his breath. How come it hurt that much if he didn't even have a fracture to show for it?

"You okay?" This from the man with the world's worst shiner.

"Fine. Let's go."

Jack ducked into a short alley between two huts and broke into a run, Daniel right behind him. At the other end, they whipped around the corner and stopped dead. Their shadow was following doggedly, his footfalls getting louder. Timing the noise, Jack stuck his leg out and was treated to a rather nice forward flip. The pursuer hit the ground oomphing, rolled onto his back, and found himself staring up the business end of Daniel's Beretta.

"Hi," said Jack, patting his P90 to indicate politely that, on request, they also did fifteen rounds a second instead of two. "Anything we can do for you?"

The man didn't look as though he was going to make any requests. Front paws raised, like a puppy waiting for a belly-rub, he yelped, "Colonel O'Neill?"

"Who wants to know?"

"Corporal Lon Wilkins, sir." Corporal Wilkins seemed to want to salute but didn't dare to move his hands. "Permission to speak freely, sir?"

Well, that held a certain comic piquancy. As far as Jack could recall, he'd never got that type of enquiry from a Marine flat on his back. He grinned. "You heard the corporal, Daniel. He said *freely*. Put the gun away and help him up."

"Thanks, sir." Duly restored to an upright position, Wilkins dusted himself off, came to attention, and said, "You're looking for Major Carter, right, sir?"

The blush triggered by Carter's name revealed that Wilkins carried a torch the size of a young lamppost for the Major. For some reason it irritated Jack. "*And* Dr. Fraiser. *And* a big black guy who variously goes by Murray or Teal'c. You know where they are?"

"No, sir. They did leave for the Stargate, though. I saw them. But that's all I can tell you. That and…" The corporal swallowed, looking sick all of a sudden. "I don't usually— Look, I heard what Colonel Norris told you in the mess. It was a lie. The guys who guarded the gate that night? They sat right next to you, sir."

Poletti and the Braves. That put an interesting spin on things. Jack filed it away. "Thanks, Corporal. Now beat it. You don't want to be seen with us."

"Uh, no offense, but no. Sir!" He got that salute in at last, then hesitated for a moment. "Watch your back, Colonel. I don't know what's going on, but it's weird." With that profound observation Corporal Wilkins sprinted into the alley and out of sight.

"*Weird*, huh?" muttered Daniel. "One way of putting it. Now what?"

"Now?" Jack poked his head around the corner, saw that the passage was empty, and started heading back toward the square at a leisurely pace. "Now we're gonna sit tight till lights-out, and then we'll pay a visit to the radio shack, pardon the pun."

"Why?"

"Because that's what passes for headquarters around here. The two guys who masquerade as sergeants went in there for a confab with the messenger boy, Norris, and the Poletti gang. To discuss new orders, I assume."

Daniel cast him a sidelong glance. "How can you possibly know all that?"

"Afraid I'm committing a tactical error?" snapped Jack, instantly regretting it. Daniel wasn't afraid. He was. And maybe Daniel *should* be afraid. Because it was conjecture, and it was the best Jack had right now.

He stormed out into the deserted square, staring at the planet, at the quiet barracks that seemed to be flattened by oily light. What the hell was he doing here? If he was all the SGC had to offer, then God help Carter and Teal'c and Doc Fraiser.

"Jack!" Daniel's hand on his arm, insistent and not letting go.

Stuttering to a halt, Jack turned around. "Sorry," he ground out. "Must be the light. Feels like I'm floating through a fish tank covered in green goop. Green makes me cranky."

The look gave it away. Clearly, Daniel found the image intriguing but didn't buy the excuse for a second. "What I was trying to convey back there—and I can see where it gets confusing—is my apprecia-tion for those deductive reasoning skills of yours."

"Ah," mumbled Jack and shrugged. "No big deal. You know what I've been doing in the bad old days. It involved a lot of that."

"Glad we cleared that up." Daniel broke into a cautious grin. "Now can we get some dinner?"

"You got a death wish? If the rest of the place is anything to go by, they serve boiled newt as— Oh crap!" Watching his nemesis approach, Jack wondered if it was too late to change the entree back to boiled newt.

Poletti in tow, Norris had emerged from the com shack and strut-ted across the square. "O'Neill! Sergeant van Leyden wants to see you."

"In which case *Sergeant* van Leyden can drag his ass out here. If he asks why, tell him to read up on privileges of rank." Norris's face said that this was exactly the reply he'd hoped for. Jack didn't like it. Time to stir things up a little. "By the way, Norris, what were you doing at the gate this morning?"

Haughtiness gave way to consternation, and Norris's jaw worked hard. Eventually he snarled, "I was waiting for Major Warren. We were expecting him back. Not that it's any of your business."

"*We*? Who's *we*? That happy little family you've got here?"

This time the shock tactics didn't work. Norris smirked. "Look, O'Neill, you two can either come with us or—"

The motion, a blur in his peripheral vision, told Jack that the unspoken threat had just become the only option and that it was gonna be ugly. He spun around, managed to block a blow that nearly broke his arm. His fist, aimed at Poletti's solid gut, missed by a mile. God, this guy was fast, way too fast! Jack was going for his gun when a punch to the kidney made him arch back helplessly. As he sank to his knees, pain tinted the planet's crescent brilliantly red, until the Stooges appeared out of nowhere to join the fun.

Curly's face smiled down on him, and Norris bleated a lame, unexpected protest. Then they were all over Jack, pinning him down, flex-cuffing his wrists, leaving his ribs screaming. Six feet away lay Daniel, tied up and motionless, nose busted, lip split, blood glaring from an ashen face.

"Take them to the gate," a whole new voice ordered, sounding like its owner was enjoying the spectacle. "Send them... home."

Sergeant van Leyden, Jack presumed.

It was near sunrise by the time Teal'c awoke, remembering little, except that the injury must have been grievous, else he would not have slipped into a healing trance. Then the forest, alive with the howls of its creatures, brought the events back to him.

He cautiously pushed himself upright, neck craned to look at his shoulder. A large bloodstain had soaked from where the fabric was torn and down the front of his shirt. Drenched by the pervasive damp, it was already beginning to blend with dirt and sweat. The wound itself had closed. Only a rosy scar, standing out starkly from dark skin, marked its location. That and perhaps some minor twinges and residual stiffness in his shoulder. In time, scar, twinges, and stiffness would fade, and they were a small price to pay for his folly.

"*Shek kree a kek, hasshak!*" he hissed, furious with himself.

Had he let himself be fooled like this as a raw recruit, Master Bra'tac would not have wasted any time or effort on whipping him. Master Bra'tac would have sent him home to his mother, to learn how to spin wool and tend small children, because Teal'c was not fit to become a warrior.

"*Hasshak!*" He spat again and pushed himself to his feet.

The shelter in the tree was empty, as he had feared. Dug into the ground he found a deep hole, filling with moisture. This was where Dr. Fraiser had hidden her dagger. Near the hole lay a small piece of rock; a whetstone, no doubt. There was nothing else the tree could tell him, and Teal'c stepped back out into the open, noting with some astonishment that she had not taken the backpack or any of the weapons, despite the fact that he had hardly been in a position to stop her.

Why had she left without supplies or arms? And where had she gone?

He could not visually recall her leaving, because he had been slipping from consciousness, but perhaps… Teal'c returned to the boulder that had secured the entrance, sat down once more, and closed his eyes. In his mind he saw the doctor's drawn face, her gaze lucid for the first time in days, agonized with the realization of what she had done. Then the image went black. This was when he had begun to drift. But he had still been able to hear; the sounds as clear and precise as they became in the split-second before sleep.

He's already dead.

Said aloud as if in response to something or someone—what or whom?—and with a distinct undertone of apprehension. The doctor had told an untruth, and she had been afraid of being found out. Not just about the lie. She had had the opportunity to kill him and refused to take it. Twice. First when she had only wounded him; the second time when he had lain helpless. Instead of striking, she had backed away, slowly and with great difficulty—a child, aware of the cost of disobedience but disobeying nonetheless—and then she suddenly had turned and run.

With perfect accuracy, his memory mapped out the volume and direction of the sound her footsteps had made. When his eyes snapped open, he stared at a tight gap in the undergrowth. Teal'c rose and retraced her path, unsurprised when he could not find boot prints. The ground, bog-like and resilient, returned to its original state within minutes. However, on the bushes themselves several thin twigs were broken and leaves crushed; unmistakable tokens of passage.

Dr. Fraiser's choice of escape route bewildered him. To the east, the terrain became easier, sloping gradually into a broad river valley. Logically, if a person were fleeing from something, they would tend to take the easiest path for best possible speed. Indeed, Teal'c himself had done so three days ago, fleeing from the beasts that had attacked them. Dr. Fraiser had done the opposite. She had turned west, choosing the most difficult and dangerous route, uphill into the mountains and back toward the Stargate—and the beasts. Why?

"To go home," he murmured in answer to his own question.

In her ramblings, she had repeatedly expressed a wish to return home. At the time, it had struck him as the most rational thought she was conceiving. Now he wondered.

Even when she had shown no sign of improvement, he had clung to the hope that the condition would be temporary. But he was no longer sure that it was madness at all. The assault on him, in its preparation and execution, spoke of a cunning that was fundamentally unlike Dr. Fraiser. Not because she lacked the intelligence and determination, but because she lacked the callousness. The fact that he was still alive proved it. If not madness, what then?

Teal'c knew of one thing that would explain it, and the thought sickened him to such an extent that he refused to entertain it. But whatever the case, he needed to find her, even if it meant temporarily abandoning his search for Major Carter. At this moment Dr. Fraiser was the more vulnerable of the two, although Major Carter, too, had been injured, and it was impossible to predict her current state of health.

In the name of a false god Teal'c had led men into battle, more than once, and thus the weight of responsibility he felt was as familiar as it was unwelcome. Unwelcome not because he sought to shirk it, but because he knew the consequences error could entail. His own father had fallen victim to them, murdered for failing to please the whim of a would-be god and win an unwinnable skirmish. Holding himself accountable, he had calmly accepted his punishment—as indeed had O'Neill, who had become his own judge and jury. Neither man had conceded that responsibility without error could not exist.

If there were no risk of error, what weight could there be to responsibility? They went hand in hand, one the dark side of the other, and the conclusions O'Neill had drawn were wrong. The penance he inflicted on himself was unjust and would be warranted only if he were a god possessed of omniscience.

Teal'c decided that, should he escape with his life, his friend and brother would need to be reminded of his patent lack of divinity.

Fuelled by sudden resolve, he turned back, collected the pack and his staff weapon, set off on the doctor's tenuous trail of broken twigs, crushed tendrils of creeper plants, bark scraped from tree trunks. Irrespective of the difficulty of the terrain, all traces were on a line that led uphill and west as straight as a bird flew. It was as though Dr. Fraiser followed a beckoning voice, imperious and seductive.

Further up in the mountains, the ground became marginally drier, and here he found footprints—mostly indentations made by the tips of her boots. She had been moving fast, running at times, and continued for longer than she should have been able to sustain such a frenzied pace. If Teal'c was right, the will that governed her would drive her on relentlessly and past the point of exhaustion. And if he was right, it meant that a Goa'uld was on this planet.

More than four hours into his pursuit Teal'c reached a small stream and followed it upriver, until it widened into a pool. Halfway along its northern shore, he discovered the impression in the mud. During his first winter on Earth, O'Neill had explained to him a game Tauri children liked to play. It was called Snow Angels, and O'Neill had obliged by throwing himself to the ground and demonstrating its mechanics. This looked similar—the shape of a body etched into the soil, legs splayed, arms stretched wide.

Dr. Fraiser's physical strength seemed to have flagged at last. She had tripped over a root and fallen face down into the mud. From there she had gathered herself and crawled to the water's edge, presumably to drink.

"*Shek kree*," Teal'c muttered, dismayed.

He knelt, scooped up a handful of water and, careful not to swallow any, sloshed the sweat from his face. Tepid and smelling sickly sweet, the water was less than refreshing. It also was tainted, Teal'c knew not by what substance. When he had first come upon the creek two days ago and several miles further downstream, he too had drunk from it, but his symbiote had neutralized most of the contaminant. Other than a passing dizziness there had been no ill effects. However, he could not tell what harm it would do to Tauri physiology.

Some, he surmised. Dr. Fraiser had risen again, but the footprints, plainly outlined now, were uneven and staggering like a drunkard's. He trailed the unsteady path and two hundred meters further up found a rock where she had rested. Though not in the position he would have expected. Instead of slumping onto the smooth stone directly, she had walked around it and sat facing uphill.

Why? Whom or what had she been watching?

Teal'c eased himself onto the rock, absently noting that his shoulder ached; a reminder that, while the symbiote was able to accelerate his body's healing process, it required the rest of *kelno'reem* to do so properly. It would have to wait. Rotating his arm to loosen cramped muscles, he suddenly realized that the maddening cackle and chatter of the jungle had ceased. The only sounds were the tap of condensation dripping from branches and the splash of a reedy waterfall at the western end of the lake. Other than that, the forest was quiet.

His fingers inadvertently tightened around the staff weapon, and he fought off a sense of foreboding. Then his gaze traveled upward, against the motion of the water, over black rock and plants shining with moisture, until at last he saw what Dr. Fraiser must have seen.

Atop the cliff and its cascade rose, gray as ghosts, the ruins that housed the Stargate.

Dr. Daniel Jackson felt distinctly claustrophobic. The rock walls reared toward a starless corridor of olive drab sky, and the uneven ground wasn't designed to enhance physical or spiritual balance.

Send them… home.

As he walked—alright, tottered—Daniel mulled the three words over, the linguist in him fascinated by that beat before *home*. Somehow the pause suggested that there was no place like… home. It could be interpreted in all sorts of ways, none likely to coincide with his preferred definition. For instance, the—

He stumbled, felt a hot bolt of pain rattle through his head, heard the snigger of the goon behind him, and swore under his breath. You'd think that, if people insisted on converting your face to raw hamburger, they'd at least have the decency to order a sedan chair for you afterwards.

"You okay?" whispered Jack.

"Shut up!" barked Mr. Poletti, the echo of his voice bouncing through the canyon.

"Fine," Daniel said quickly, careful to keep Jack on his right, in order to hide the left side of his face. The goons—dead ringers for a mob of Jaffa—hadn't been kind enough to give him a moment to take off his specs. That pair, too, was trashed now, though it didn't make that much of a difference. He couldn't see out of his left eye anyway, and so far he'd been unable to ascertain if this was because the eye had swollen shut or because, this time round, he'd actually lost sight in it.

Either way, it livened up the hike. One of the rarely considered benefits of stereoscopic vision was the fact that it allowed for depth perception. He'd found out the hard way while running around in that stupid eye patch—one of the reasons why he'd discarded it three days earlier than prescribed by Doc Fraiser. His shins had been unable to stand the strain.

Right now, his shins didn't worry him. What *did* worry him was being funneled through the canyon that led to the gate. That meaning-ful pause seemed to preclude the literal meaning of *home*, which left a euphemism popular among romantic novelists—along with *eternal rest*. Odds were that he and Jack would be lined up against the cliff for a quaint old execution by firing squad—blindfold unnecessary in Dr. Jackson's case—with subsequent disposal of their remains through the Stargate.

What do you mean, General Hammond? They gated back three days ago.

The thought that this might be precisely what had happened to Sam and Teal'c and Janet made him sick. Only sheer, undiluted fury at the prospect of never finding out why kept the churning in his gut at bay. It wasn't just scientific curiosity. Daniel wanted to know whom to haunt.

The goons prodded them around a narrow bend, and suddenly the rock walls parted and opened out into the crater.

"Keep going," advised Mr. Poletti.

More prodding, but strangely enough not toward the cliff but toward the gate. One of the Marines broke into a trot, overtook, and headed for the DHD. He made no attempt to conceal the address he was dialing. He didn't need to. Daniel himself had dialed it countless times over the years.

Earth.

He heard Jack's sigh of disbelief, seconded the motion, and wondered how General Hammond would respond to having them returned in this not quite factory-sealed condition. With a decidedly undiplomatic note of protest, Daniel assumed. The thought was cut off by the whoosh of the event horizon, and then the wormhole established, drilling a clear blue circle into murky air.

"In your own time, gentlemen," said Poletti.

"You'll have to uncuff me," Jack muttered. "I need to enter the IDC."

"I'll do the honors." Poletti smirked and started punching numbers into the transmitter on his wrist.

So this was how it'd go. No blindfolds and last cigarettes. Just bugs on the windshield, and next time Sergeant Siler cleaned the iris, he'd wipe off some familiar-looking subatomic particles. Daniel never for a moment believed that Poletti had entered a valid code.

Glancing over his shoulder, he saw that five of the goons had formed a semi-circle behind him and Jack, discouraging any fool-hardy notions such as running. Out front, Poletti had climbed the dais.

"Bon voyage, gentlemen," he brayed.

Jack started walking. Evidently he wasn't immune to niceties of phrasing either. If he thought they were going home, he'd leave last, after seeing his one-man-team safely through the wormhole. Daniel caught up with him in front of the event horizon.

"Stop jostling for pole position," he hissed.

"They say it hardly hurts at all," Jack hissed back.

"Who says?"

"The particles." And then Jack was gone.

Two seconds later Daniel concluded that the particles were lying through their teeth. But conscious thought and sensation folded into merciful black, until he shot from the far end of the wormhole, screaming and in free fall. Images took on a snapshot quality; an oppressive flood of green, age-old masonry, the still figure sprawled between ferns below. He hit the ground hard, though moss and mud cushioned most of the impact.

The Hereafter didn't exactly live up to the advertising. Then again, there always was the possibility that he wasn't quite dead yet.

Groaning, he rolled over and struggled to his knees. The gymnastics shook loose an avalanche of throbs that felt like it wanted to exit his head through his left eye. He ignored it and shuffled over to Jack who seemed to be coming round, his face bone-white under a mudpack.

"Love what they've done with the gate room." Jack blinked up at the canopy. "Where the hell are we? Mato Grosso?"

"Doesn't look like Brazil to me." Daniel sniffed, squinting at the blur of a monumental structure behind them. High in the wall, the gate formed the third eye in a stone-carved mask that placidly gazed down at him. "My money's on Angkor Wat."

"What encore?"

"You know. The Khmer temples in Cambodia."

"Didn't know they kept a Stargate there."

"Uh, they don't, I guess. If they did, somebody'd have found it by now." Glancing at fuzzy walls and reliefs again, Daniel said, "This is amazing. We definitely need to check out this place. It could—"

"Daniel!"

"Hmm?"

"We don't know where we are, we're hogtied, we've got no weapons or supplies, and we— Holy buckets!" Jack had finally turned his head to get a spectacular view of Daniel's face. "You know, you're... Nah, I won't say it."

"Won't say what?"

"Uh-uh."

"Jack?"

"I'm not gonna say you're a sight for sore eyes."

"Very funny."

"That's why I didn't say it." He winced. "Can you see anything at all?"

"Not out of the left eye."

"Crap."

Accompanied by a lurid selection of curses, Jack maneuvered himself onto his side, facing away from Daniel. Who was watching the performance, knowing that it had to hurt like merry hell and wishing he could make himself useful.

"You need a doctor," he offered lamely.

"I'll consult the first medicine man who's got his shingle out." Jack wiggled his fingers. "Chew through the flex."

"You're joking!"

"No."

Sighing, Daniel dropped into a patch of mud and scooted down until his teeth were at a level with Jack's wrists. "Fart and I'll kill you!"

There was no reply, and Daniel resigned himself. Bits of his face that desperately wanted to be left alone were chafing against Jack's arms, and the plastic was no real winner for taste and stuck between his teeth. Jack kept quiet. He'd either passed out again or he was brooding.

Daniel stopped and sat up, trying to relax his shoulders. The sun had crept over the treetops and onto their little patch of forest floor. It occurred to him that they'd been cheated out of a night and some much-needed sleep.

"I didn't fart!" So Jack *had* been brooding. "Keep going!"

"How about you entertain me by telling me why you retired?"

"You know why. You were there."

If there'd ever been a moment when Daniel wanted to cross his arms this was it. "Don't bullshit me. You quit—which isn't exactly a specialty of yours. So what's going on?"

"Daniel, I—"

"Spill it, Jack. I mean it."

Jack shifted over a little further, staring at a lump of moss. "This last year—"

"You mean the one when you were too busy being the alpha male to see daylight?" And Daniel had risen to the bait every damn time, until their usual banter deteriorated into personal insults. "Sorry. Just gag me."

"Can't. I need you."

"Oh right. The flex."

"What else?" O'Neillese for *the friendship's still there*. Twisted and battered and bent out of shape, but still a friendship. Solid foundations.

"What about this last year?" Daniel prodded.

"You mean apart from the fact that I was prepared to blow up a spaceship with you in it? Or that I shot to kill when I shot Carter? Or that I left Teal'c to get his matrix stored in the gate? Notice a pattern? Too many bad calls, Daniel. The only reason why any of you's still around is that I got lucky each time. I can't afford to rely on that. *You* can't. The exercise sent up a red flag. That's what happens when luck runs out, Daniel." His fingers balled into tight fists. "The other day, when I shot that robot—"

"She was sentient, Jack."

"When I shot Reese? I shot her because I couldn't gamble. I was scared stiff of luck running out. I've lost too many people already, and so help me, I'm not going to lose any more."

You stupid son of a bitch!

Daniel grimaced. "Look," he said at last, "for what it's worth, I've always been convinced—still am—that, if I buy it out here, it won't be because you're there but because you're *not*. You've pulled our asses out of the fire more times than I care to remember and long may you continue to do so. Because I have every intention of living to a ripe old age, and I'm counting on you to keep that little fancy of mine viable."

"Gee! Thanks, Daniel." Jack sounded raw, but the attitude was encouraging. "Anything else I can do for you?"

"As a matter of fact, yes." Daniel grinned. "Try stretching the flex. It might pop."

"You sneaky, underhand, devious little… You mean there was no reason for me to—"

"I didn't say that. I said it *might* pop. So it *might* still need some nibbling."

"And you *might* just stay cuffed!" growled Jack and did as he was told.

The flex popped. Ten minutes later, Daniel's hands were free, too. Rubbing his wrists, he looked for a doorway that would lead to the interior of the ruins, but all he could see was the gaping mouth of the stone face that held the Stargate. Not likely, despite the stone tongue that lolled out into the clearing like an entrance ramp. Besides, the maw stank of feces and God knew what else, and even Daniel's investigative fervor had limits. He began trailing the wall into the forest, noticing for the first time that the noises you'd expect in a jungle were absent. Except for an unnerving, insistent buzz. Following the sound, he rounded a huge tree and froze, bile rising in his throat. So much for peace and quiet.

From somewhere behind him drifted shouts. "Daniel! Wait up! I can't find the"—Jack came trotting around the bole and ground to a dead halt—"DHD..."

Clouds of flies dancing around it, the body hung suspended from a protrusion in the temple wall.

CHAPTER NINE

"**O**kay, sirs. That's it for today. As you can tell from your sched-ule, the role play exercise is slotted first thing tomorrow morning, so you might wanna go over your notes tonight. Thank you all, and I'll see you tomorrow." The hollow-chested lecturer, a war-rant officer in academic uniform—baggy chinos, checked shirt, and beige corduroy jacket—shuffled down from the dais in front of the projection screen and immediately was mobbed by a gang of teach-er's pets.

Like high school, George Hammond thought in disgust. Except, he himself had never hung around after class. He'd been too busy trying to set new records for the run between classroom and bleach-ers. Nothing to do with baseball. More to do with Betty Mae Turner. He smiled briefly—Betty Mae had ended up marrying one of the teacher's pets and produced a houseful of organ-pipe offspring.

However, this wasn't high school and more's the pity. If it were, or if he had more of Jack O'Neill's blithe disregard for institutional authority, he'd have carved *This sucks!* into the desk with a penknife. As it was, he simply gathered his—unused—notepad and sidled out of the row of seats and toward the exit. Below, the eager beavers were still wooing the lecturer, who was lapping it up. Presumably it was more attention than the guy otherwise got in a year.

Good for him. And good for Psych Ops. If they were striving to imbue their existence with some meaning, that was a laudable under-taking and all very well with Major General Hammond. However, he signally failed to understand why he should have to be involved in the ego salving. He had better things to do. More urgent things. That aside, a little advance warning might have been nice. The order for Hammond to participate in this extravaganza for general staff had landed on his desk yesterday morning.

The three-day seminar at Bolling AFB (*Enhanced Understanding of Leadership and Dealing with Subordinates*) seemed to be part of some obscure drive toward fluffier armed forces, and it was as redundant as a pair of left shoes. A lot of wishy-washy psycho-babble that had nothing whatsoever to do with real life. Real life was fifty percent of SG-1 and Dr. Fraiser missing.

Hammond stormed down the corridor, dodging clumps of chatting people. His interest in discussing this afternoon's lecture (*Voluntary Separation and How to Handle It*) was strictly limited. Besides, his personal method (*Wait Till Half a Team Disappears and See How Fast Their CO Bounces Back*) wouldn't meet with the attendees' approval. As he rattled down the stairs he thought he heard somebody hollering his name, opted for temporary deafness, and ducked out the door. He needed to contact the SGC and check if there were any news, but he didn't want to make the call from Bolling. He had friends elsewhere whose phones would be secure.

Outside, the wind was driving sheets of rain across the lawn. The weather suited his mood. Head bowed and shoulders hunched, he hurried along the access road and through the main gate, guessing that it would take him at least half an hour to find a taxi at this time of day. He'd guessed wrong. Stepping out onto McDill Boulevard, he saw a yellow cab tearing toward him, and the driver actually responded to his wave. The cab pulled over, and Hammond, eager to get out of the rain, hopped in before it'd even screeched to a complete standstill.

"Andrews Air Force Base," he said, in a tone proven to discourage any outbursts of verbal diarrhea on the part of cabbies.

Apparently it worked. "Okay," said the driver and left it at that.

It took Hammond exactly five minutes to realize that the cabby's reticence wasn't based on sensitivity. Instead of driving east into central Washington, the cab sped into the maze of roads along the river, weaving in and out of traffic and steadily heading north toward Interstate 66.

"Hey!" He rapped against the glass partition. "Where the hell do you think you're going?"

The cabby, bearded and in a brown, wooly Afghan hat, cast a quick glance in the rearview mirror but didn't turn around. "Check your six, General. The beige sedan, three cars behind us? They're after you. I'm trying to lose them."

Terrific! A conspiracy nut! Next he'd confess that he got this intel from the Cigarette-Smoking Man in an underground parking lot.

Could this day possibly get any worse?

Then again... As instructed, Hammond checked his six. Sure enough, there was a beige, government-issue sedan three cars behind, and while this wasn't an uncommon occurrence in DC, its driver did look a little more intense than the rush-hour traffic warranted. The guy next to him was talking into a cell phone.

Hammond settled back into the seat. "Who the devil are you?"

This time the cabby did turn, grinning broadly and revealing a sturdy set of teeth with a pronounced gap between the upper incisors. "We'll chat soon, but right now you don't wanna distract the driver."

With that he goosed the engine to 70 mph, nearly clipped the rear bumper of a black Lexus in front, cut right across an eighteen-wheeler that tooted Beethoven's Fifth on its horn, and shot over three lanes onto the ramp for Custis Memorial Boulevard. The beige sedan missed the exit and drove on straight, its co-pilot gesticulating furiously.

At least Hammond's question had been answered. The day had got worse. By a considerable margin. He was trapped in a speeding cab, steered by a convicted traitor, rogue agent, and con artist. On the upside, this promised to be more diverting than tomorrow morning's role play exercise. The cab was out on the I-66 now and doing 80 mph.

Thirty-five minutes later they were passing Dulles International, and his chauffeur finally slowed down a little to retrieve a sports bag from under the passenger seat. He slid open the partition and shoved the bag into the rear.

"I suggest you change, General. It'll attract less attention than a dress uniform. I won't peek, I swear."

The bag contained a pair of jeans, trodden-down sneakers, a wind-breaker, and, to Hammond's dismay, the man's favorite fashion state-ment, an unbearably lurid Aloha shirt.

It'll attract less *attention?*

By the time he'd zipped the windbreaker up to his neck to tamp down the effect of the shirt, they were pulling into the parking lot behind a seedy truck stop.

"*Now* are we safe to talk?" Hammond snapped.

His chauffeur backed the cab into a slot beside a forty-foot

Winnebago. "Inside," he said. "They do a great chocolate meringue pie. I've been looking forward to it all day."

Then he killed the engine, exchanged the ethnic headwear for a dozer cap, and got out of the cab. He was wearing grease-stained mechanic's overalls to go with the hat. Climbing out, Hammond figured that dressing up as Bobo the Clown still beat running around like the Trucker King of Hicksville.

A state cruiser parked directly outside the café, and as they ambled closer a trooper back-pushed and rotated through the door, balancing two cups of coffee on a box of donuts. It probably explained why they hadn't been caught speeding.

"I should just hand you over to them," Hammond muttered angrily. "For reckless driving, if nothing else. You're a menace, Maybourne."

"Please, General. I just saved your butt, and I'd prefer it if you called me Hutch. For, uh, personal reasons." He shot a sideways glance at Hammond. "Maybe I should—"

"Absolutely not! Whatever else happens, you will *not* call me Huggy Bear. Do I make myself clear?"

"Just a thought."

"Do the world a favor and stop thinking!"

The interior of the café lived down to expectation; dark and dingy, with the smell of old fries thick in the air and Formica tables stuck between tattered red seats. They also were out of chocolate meringue pie, as George Hammond noted in a bout of petty satisfaction. Maybourne had picked a booth at the back of the room, directly under an antique speaker that hissed and drooled country music between the static. A waitress brought two mugs of coffee and a plate of apple pie—runner-up, going by Maybourne's face.

The coffee wasn't too bad, and Hammond took another sip and waited until the girl was out of earshot. "Right. What the hell is going on? And don't even think of bullshitting me. Kidnapping's a federal offence, in case you'd forgotten."

Tearing into his apple pie, Maybourne observed, "Our boy Jack's got himself in trouble again, hasn't he?"

"What do you care? You shot him!"

"I'm hurt!" He put down a heaped fork and sent Hammond a

baby-blue look of wounded innocence. "You mean Jack hasn't told you? I *didn't* shoot him. I can guess who did, but it wasn't me. I mean, why would I?"

"I don't know. Why do you do anything, Maybourne?"

"Hutch. I'm serious, George." The baby-blues turned cold as he finally dropped the Endearing Goofball routine. "If you're in my… predicament… you've got to keep an ear to the ground. I do. So I hear things. Lately I hear that Jack screws up an exercise past recognition, decimates his own team, and resigns. Then I hear that somebody out Cheyenne Mountain way is sniffing at a high-ranking Marine who happens to have organized said exercise. Then I hear that the NID doesn't want said high-ranking Marine sniffed at and is proposing to remove the sniffer. And *then* you get sent to DC, which is the last place you ought to be, on some lame excuse and with a couple of NID heavies on your tail. How's my hearing so far, George?"

Wondering who'd redefined the meaning of *Top Secret* and when, Hammond snarled, "Accurate. Except for one detail. Colonel O'Neill didn't resign."

"Where is he? He isn't at home. I tried to get in touch with him."

"Off-world, and I shouldn't even tell you that much."

"General, what do you think those guys in the sedan were going do to? Ask for directions? They had orders to solve the NID's problem. You're hip-deep in it, and I'm the only ally you've got right now. You'll have to trust me."

Trust Harry Maybourne. As far as George Hammond was concerned, the ex-colonel had all the credibility of a psychotic rattler. On the other hand there was no getting away from the fact that Jack O'Neill trusted him, and Hammond knew better than to ignore Jack's instincts. Repeated threats to shoot Maybourne notwithstanding, Jack actually liked the guy. Not that he'd ever admit it. And Jack *had* publicly revised his opinion as to who'd parked that bullet in his arm.

"What's in it for you?"

Maybourne smirked. "Jack's got that quaint loyalty thing going. If anything happens to you and he finds out that I could have stopped it, he's gonna come after me and bust my ass. I'd like to avoid that scenario."

"Christ! I could get court-martialed just for being seen with you," drawled Hammond. Then he leaned forward, nearly knocking over his mug. "If I ever hear so much as a whisper of this from any source other than you or me, *I*'m gonna come after you and bust your ass. Are we clear on this, Colonel?"

"Crystal."

Doubting his judgment all the way through, Hammond laid out the entire story for Harry Maybourne. Who rapidly lost interest in the apple pie. By the end of it he was attacking the tabletop with his fork.

"This is uglier than I thought." He quit stabbing, rummaged through his back pocket, produced an envelope, and slid it across the table. "I'm hoping the Air Force'll pick up my expenses."

"For what?" asked Hammond.

"Two tickets to Seattle. I gotta show you something."

The faces, serene and beautiful, seemed to be smiling at her in approval. They were everywhere, on walls, pillars, doorjambs, and they wore elaborate hairstyles and headdresses shaped like pagodas. There were full-length statues, too; countless round-busted, wide-hipped women, their arms raised gracefully, and men almost too pretty to be male, though you could hardly miss that they were boys. Some talked to her, or so Janet thought. Or perhaps it was the voice speaking through them. It had got louder and more distinct since she'd entered the city. Another sign that she was close now. Close to home.

But mostly she knew because she felt at peace. There was no noise at all. The cackle of the rainforest had stopped as soon as she'd stepped through the great gate. No noise, and none of that merciless itch to run, run, run that had driven her to collapse yesterday. She could take her time now. And she would. So much to see, and it would be a shame to rush. Suddenly she realized that this had to be the same kind of excitement that drove Daniel.

Whom?

Janet gave a small mental shrug, unwilling to get into an argument, and went back to studying her surroundings. The voice acquiesced. In front of her stretched a broad corridor—well, not exactly a corridor, seeing as it had no roof—that led to a sun-flooded hall of pillars. The ground was covered with grass, short and thick and velvety.

"So who's mowing the lawn around here?" She giggled.

Obeying an impulse, she took off her boots and socks. The grass felt as luxurious as it looked, warm and springy under her feet. It practically begged her to skip, and so she skipped all the way into the hall, finally forcing herself to stand still and look around. The ceiling soared sixty feet above her head, crumbling with age in places. Plants had nudged their way through brittle masonry, and some of the vines, studded with delicate, fragrant blossoms, brushed the ground. No telling what this hall had been once. Perhaps a throne room, something out of *The King and I.* Janet started whistling a tune from the show, then cut herself off, surprised at a giddiness that wasn't normally hers.

There is nobody here to see or hear you. Why be embarrassed?

Because.

That is no answer.

"It isn't me!" she shouted, the sound whirling around pillars and vines and toward the lofty ceiling like a living thing.

Oh, but it is.

A second later it was her whirling and skipping around pillars and vines, whistling 'Shall We Dance?' and curtsying to an invisible king. The laughter of the voice bled into the hall and drifted through the ceiling on shafts of sunlight.

She wanted to scream, yell at it to stop, and found she couldn't, because she had to skip and whirl and whistle, whistle like a madwoman, whistle a tune she didn't recognize anymore, eerie and frantic and alien. Somewhere in her mind, compacted by utter panic, formed the thought that she was going insane.

No. No. No. No. No. "No!"

The wail, released at last, broke the compulsion, made her feet arrest mid-skip, and she stumbled and fell hard. No grass here. Red stone tiles, rough and unforgiving. She skinned her elbow and curled into a ball, whimpering like a child.

It was a joke. Only a joke.

"Leave me alone!"

No reply this time, but miraculously that indefinable pressure lifted. The voice was gone. For now. For the most part. She slowly pushed herself up, no longer trusting the peace, needing to get out of this hall never to return. Shadows of laughter still hung in the air like a foul smell, and she couldn't bear it.

Across the room, at the end of an alley of pillars, opened a tall arch, curtained by a cascade of water that glittered like diamonds in the sunshine. This was the only exit, unless she were to turn back, and she knew she couldn't do that. Not if she wanted to go home. Carefully groping her way from pillar to pillar, half expecting her body to go berserk again and trying to avoid the stares of the faces, she edged closer to the arch. It reminded her of the Stargate, and this familiarity calmed her.

She feared the water, though. Yesterday, parched with thirst, she'd drunk from the stream and got violently ill. As far as she'd been able to tell from the symptoms, it had been a mild form of botulism. *Mild* because you didn't usually survive once you experienced double vision and respiratory impairment. She'd dragged herself to a small, dank cave at the bottom of the falls where she'd spent the night, shivering and heaving. Some time after midnight she'd fallen asleep from sheer exhaustion, only to be woken at sunrise by the jungle's dawn chorus. She hadn't wanted to leave, but the voice had reasoned with her for a long time, warning her to climb the cliff, lest her captor would find her.

Not her captor.

"Teal'c," she whispered defiantly. "His name is Teal'c, and I'm glad he's alive."

There was no answer. She hadn't expected it, because she and the voice had had this one out, too. The voice had known all along that she was lying, seeming amused—pleased, actually—rather than angry about it. But she should move on. She had to. And the only way to go was through the arch. If she tried to turn back, the skipping and whirling and whistling would start again.

The cascade beyond the arch sparkled, painting rainbow patterns of light on the floor. It looked nothing like the water in the stream. This looked pure, utterly perfect. As she inched toward the brilliant curtain, one hand gingerly relinquished its contact with a pillar. The stone, unchanging and immobile on her skin had reassured her. Anchored her. She was scared of letting go, but unless she let go, she wouldn't be able to find the way home. Slowly she extended her arm, fingertips scoring transparent furrows into the veil of water.

It was cool. Cool and delicious and inviting, and it smelled of sun-yellowed summers and racing home after school to head out to the swimming hole. It smelled safe. She watched a sheet of water slide up her palm and to her wrist like a shimmering glove. It lifted bits of dust and dirt, rinsed them away, and left her feeling clean for the first time in days.

Smiling, Janet abandoned her last hold on the pillar, stepped onto the broad stone threshold under the arch and stood misted by spray for a moment. Something wonderful lay beyond that curtain of water. Home.

The thought drove her forward, through the cascade, her bare feet losing the ground almost instantly, and she fell, fell, fell, shattered the black mirror of a pool, and sank, aching from the impact, into airless silence. It was so cold, her first instinct had been to gasp. Icy water searing her throat and lungs, she slid deeper into blackness, unable to tell if her eyes were open or if her body even tried to swim.

Then her toes touched the bottom—soft and bumpy, though it wasn't silt. It felt like fabric and skin, but she couldn't allow herself to care, couldn't help whomever had drowned here before her. Pushing herself off with more strength than she'd believed she could muster, she shot back toward the surface, black fading to charcoal fading to insipid green.

Her lungs were screaming for air, and a madly sucked-in breath made her convulse with coughs and sent her under again. Flailing and kicking, knowing that, if she went back to the bottom, she'd stay there, she paddled for the rim of the pool, only to find shining stone walls; black obsidian, too high to reach the edge and too perfectly crafted to leave any cracks for purchase. And even if she could have reached, her arms and hands were cramping with cold.

Wasp, she thought. Wasp in the lemonade pitcher, flitting and buzzing until its tracheae were clogged with sugary yellow liquid, and then it suffocated. Very slowly. But first it'd go all still.

She turned onto her back, let herself drift to save what strength she had left. Shining black walls on three sides around her. Twenty meters away, in the shadows at the far end of the pool, tumbled the dark veil of the cascade, endlessly, brilliantly lit only at the very top, where the arch was.

Do you beg my forgiveness?

"I'm sorry," she croaked through a hurting throat. "I shouldn't have sent you away. It was disrespectful."

The surge of laughter, boisterous and mocking, was as awful as it had been in the throne room.

What makes you think you could send me anywhere?

"I—"

You are nothing. I am everything.

"I realize that."

Do you beg my forgiveness?

"For what?" She genuinely didn't know.

You did not ask my permission to bathe.

It was true. She hadn't. She hadn't even considered it. The voice was right to be offended.

"Please forgive me," she whispered, fighting back tears. "Please."

As the voice remained silent, the shadows deepened, and she began to sob, terrified of dying without having been granted absolution.

Very well. I shall forgive you this once. Have you finished bathing?

"Yes! Yes. Thank you. Thank you so much." Water lapped into her mouth and down her throat, tasting stale and putrid.

Then you must get out now.

"But I—"

Words turned into indistinct burbles as she sagged beneath the surface. Punishment. It was her punishment for refusing the voice. She had to get out. Had to try at least. The voice wanted her to. Choking and jerking desperately, she raised her head above the water.

A ray of sunlight pierced the foliage far above, burned the shadows of the pool, and picked out the relief in the pool wall. A hand, set in a circle, and the sunbeam seemed to have ignited a warm welcoming glow, a warmth that promised rescue and safety.

Janet knew she'd seen it before, couldn't recall when, but it didn't matter. All that mattered was that she touched it.

Breaths like hiccups, coming in short, ragged heaves and too loud. Way too loud. Sam Carter pressed her face into the crook of her arm to muffle the sounds. She shouldn't be cold. Not when she could taste the viscous heat of the jungle, steaming from black soil and trickling from leaves. Viscous, icy heat that hauled her body into a spasm of shivers. She fought it down, trying to remember why it was important not to be heard. Nobody here to hear her, was there?

Besides, it was raining. The monsoon cloudburst tattooed a machinegun rattle on the foliage and fizzed into vapor the second it penetrated the canopy. Humidity had to be at a hundred percent, and if you breathed it was instant emphysema. White mist everywhere, reducing her surroundings to coiling phantasms. Nothing seemed solid anymore, everything had become spongy and gluey, like the mire under her feet. Her fingers tightened around the air root of a mangrove she was clutching for fear of cutting loose and drifting away.

Ten yards to her left, invisible through the steam, though she would have found it blindfolded—she'd been staring at it most of the night—was the spot where the hell hog had died, flailing and snorting and screeching, fangs bared and slick with mud and blood. The others had trotted up and down along the edge of the swamp, agitated by the sight of one of theirs being killed over something as soft and weak as her; red marble eyes shining with scary intelligence, as if to say that, if she ever ventured out of the bog again, they'd be waiting and she'd be toast. Or maybe to tell her that the hog that had hurtled after her into the swamp would burrow up through the mud and—

"For cryin' out loud, Carter! Get a grip!"

It didn't work. The words were what the Colonel would have said—close enough, anyway—but her voice, reedy and cracking with thirst, sounded nothing like his. Didn't sound like her own either. Maybe the hell hogs had eaten that, too.

"Get a grip," she whispered. "Get a grip."

The one thing guaranteed *not* to get her out of this, were fever-addled speculations about porcines that IQ-tested in the top two percentile. And it wasn't just her who'd have to get out of this. It was Teal'c and Janet as well, and they were her responsibility.

Responsibility.

Good word. Six syllables that excused a multitude of sins.

Duty was good too. And shorter. Snappier. Best used for murder.

But it hadn't been murder, had it?

What then?

Mercy killing?

Where was the mercy in shooting a fellow human being like some lame horse or rabid dog?

But she'd done it. She'd done it, and there was no getting away from it. No escape. No choice. Just a duty.

After yesterday's—yesterday's?—encounter with Macdonald the Jaffa, she'd doubled back onto the path, retraced his steps, followed those ungodly, inhuman screams. Tactically stupid, yes, but what else was she supposed to have done? Could have been Janet screaming that way. Or Teal'c. Less likely, but still, he was her res-pon-si-bi-li-ty.

Whose responsibility had the kid been? Crowley's? Norris's? Who'd write that letter to his parents, his siblings, his partner?

We regret to inform you... of what? Training accident?

He'd been a Marine.

But he isn't a Jaffa, that much is glaringly obvious. Before suspending him from a lintel, somebody has seen fit to dress him in something flimsy with leather straps. All around him the hell hogs dance their frenzy, snapping and gouging. She seems to have forgotten how to move or feel and wishes he'd stop screaming, just for a moment, to let her sanity reassert itself. And then the screams do stop, just for a moment, just long enough for his lips to form one word.

Please.

He isn't asking for her to come and cut him loose. They both know there's no way to get to him, and even if she could, it would be too late.

Please.

Sam flees into the comfort of memory, back to an afternoon on the shooting range with her father, a lifetime ago. She unsafes the Beretta, adjusts her grip just like Jacob had shown her—

"There. Watch your right thumb, Sam. If your knuckle sticks up, the slide'll skin it on the recoil."

—and sights on a smile of pure gratitude that explodes the memory. Her hands start shaking, and she forces herself to relax and aim again, praying he'll forgive her relief at his being a stranger, not a friend.

She squeezes the trigger gently, oh so gently, a kiss of a kill, until the report of the gun smothers the roar of the hell hogs. In the leaden silence that follows the kid's scent must have changed. No more fear, no more pain, no more life, no more appeal. The beasts back off, squealing their displeasure, and wheel around to come for her. Against all instincts and training, Sam empties her last clip into the mass of bodies, howling out her grief and—

Mud-gloved fingers scrabbling for hold on the mangrove roots, she resurfaced coughing up a throatful of gunk. It was the third time since the hogs had chased her in here that she'd lost her grasp and gone under. There couldn't be a fourth. If they were still stalking her—well, too bad. She had to get out, get warm again, go back. She owed it to the kid. His screams had led her back the to ruins and the Stargate, and where the gate was, there had to be a DHD. Mostly. She pushed away insistent images of a prison world with no DHD and a charming old lady who could have taught Slobodan Milosevic a thing or two about mass murder. Hadante had been nearly as cozy as this, whatever it was called.

Hand over hand, arms and shoulders cramping with exhaustion, Sam hauled herself toward the edge of the bog. The mire sucked at her waist, her hips, her legs, unwilling to let go and give up its prize. Finally she crawled onto dry land—*dry* being relative. Not a trace of the hell hogs now, only the prints of countless trotters that had churned the ground. The devils had been dancing… She raised her head, letting the torrential rain rinse her face and clear her mind.

Getting to her feet took five fun-packed minutes, but eventually she was hobbling through the fog, propped on Macdonald's staff weapon, every step pumping liquid pain from her leg into the rest of her body. Halfway to the ruins the rain stopped and the sun came out again, stabbing through the canopy and infusing the mist with blinding radiance. It lit up a weather-blackened statue, overgrown with vines and purple orchids, that slouched between the trees. The face was long and patrician, almond-eyed, and the full mouth smiled. Sam didn't know or care at what. Daniel, were he here, might spin his own theories, doubtlessly bang on target, but as far as she was concerned the statue was a signpost. The outer perimeter of the ruins and the place where the kid had died lay less than two hundred meters east of here.

Still no hogs. The only sounds were the slow patter of drips on leaves, the tentative hoots of animals emerging from shelter after the rain, and her own breaths. She'd cut the kid down, she decided suddenly. Cut him down, bury him, get his dog tags, so that—

The twig snapped with the noise of a gun going off. It had come from behind and to her left, and if she'd had an ounce of agility left, she'd have dropped flat. Under the circumstances, her best option was to freeze in the shadows by the statue and inch around as quietly as she could until she had a fix on whoever or whatever was out there.

A few minutes later she knew that she was dealing with *who*ever. Two whoevers, to be precise. She'd smelled them. The Marine Jaffa obviously had a locker room somewhere around here; the bastards had the nerve to reek more or less clean. Soap, deodorant, mouthwash. Not too much, just enough to stand out from the pervasive backdrop of jungle rot and make her ache for a shower. On the upside, they didn't have a snowflake's chance in hell of sniffing her; she'd long lost the last whiff of civilization, thanks to a potent mix of fermenting swamp, stale sweat, and the fetid stench from her leg wound.

They were good. The breaking twig had been a glitch, perpetrated by Whoever Number One who'd now changed course and would pass her position somewhere to the right. Whoever Number Two was beyond good. He was spooky. You didn't hear him and you didn't see him—almost. He slipped through the forest as smoothly and silently as a wisp of fog, and if it hadn't been for Crest or Colgate, he'd have been on top of her before she knew what was happening. Sam could have admired his technique for hours. Unfortunately, after turning a wide circle to check his tail, the Phantom Menace came wafting straight at her and running was out of the question.

The staff weapon felt reassuringly heavy in her hand. She could take him out now, without his even noticing that she was there. Tactically it'd be wrong, though; Number One would hear the blast and ride to the rescue, and he'd be primed and ready to fight. She might end up killing them both. A waste, because she needed somebody to explain what the hell was going on in this place—and Number Two had just been volunteered for the job. She'd disable him and, if necessary, kill Number One.

Ahead, a dark shape glided in and out between patches of mist; the first time she'd actually had a visual on him for longer than a split-second. Oh yeah, Number Two was real alright, not the product of a fever dream. Fingers closing around the staff weapon in a combat grip, she eased further behind the statue. A human shadow filtered from the mist and flitted across sprawling ferns, and she heard his footfalls now, light and irregular, mimicking the random sounds a jungle creature might make.

Her body tensed in preparation for the attack. It was simple, all about angles and leverage; Teal'c had shown her the basics. The movement patterns were stored in her mind, an indelible blueprint. Ignoring the bolt of pain that shot up her leg as she stepped out for the turn, Sam whipped the weapon into a smooth loop to gather speed and momentum. Driven by the solid bud of metal at its tip, the staff swung out, sheared into an arc, sliced through a shout, hit its target. The force of the impact rattled through her arms, but she did as Teal'c had taught her, spun with the motion to face her prey, ready for attack, and… bit back a cry.

The blow, too fast—too goddamn fast!—for him even to bring up his arms and protect himself, had struck the side of his head. He looked at her, impossible and uncomprehending, then his eyes rolled back and he collapsed.

"No." Weak and pleading, the word rose on a tremor that racked her entire body, chilling her inside out. Her second homicide in as many days. And this one, this one—

A ferocious tackle ripped her legs out from under her. Tumbling into a white-hot sea of agony, she passed out before she even struck the ground.

CHAPTER TEN

Maternal Effect: Condition where the subject's visible characteristics are not determined by its own genotype but by that of the mother.

Nirrti regretted bringing the woman in so soon. Watching her bumble through the forest, hurting and muttering defiance, had been droll. But there were other considerations now; more important considerations. The human, Simmons, was playing his own game; one Nirrti was not privy to. Whatever his plans were, it seemed only wise to thwart them—without overtly appearing to do so. Who better to achieve this than the goddess of deceit and destruction? If she went about it intelligently, drollery could be derived from this, too. A great deal of drollery, she contemplated with a smile. Shame only that the latest installment of Simmons's gifts had arrived too unexpectedly for her to unleash the beasts. The fulfillment of that unspoken promise would have to wait a while, but anticipation was a thrill in itself.

Then her gaze fell on Master Sergeant Charles Macdonald, and her smile died. He cowered in a corner, drooling at her like a whipped dog. The raw flesh on his forehead where she had personally removed the skin and with it the tattoo—he was unworthy of wearing her sign—undoubtedly smarted less than her displeasure. On the table beside her couch stood a plate of chilled fruit; sliced mango, lychees, papaya, glistening with juice. A sweep of her arm sent the plate flying. It shattered on the floor, and her dog flinched at the noise. The stone tiles were spattered with soft, sticky wedges of fruit.

"Clean it up!" she snapped. "I do not want any more."

"Yes, mistress," whined the dog and came scuttling from his corner on all fours, not daring to raise his eyes now. At her feet he froze. "Mistress, please! I beg your forgiveness."

"No. And do not ask me again. Else I shall do what I ought to have done." Once more she felt like smiling. "Do you know what I ought to have done, slave?"

"No, mistress."

He did not dare to move when she reached out, briefly caressed the flaps of his pouch, inserted her hand. The symbiote squirmed, warm between her fingers. She tightened her grip, clutched it. Macdonald gasped, as much a reaction to his own discomfort as to that of the symbiote's.

Leaning forward, she murmured into his ear. "Shall I tell you what would happen if I crushed it?"

"Mistress, please," the man whimpered.

And why not? It did not matter. She squeezed harder, felt the symbiote's flapping panic, heard the man's groan. Harder still until she heard a soft crunch. "Its blood is bright blue and beautiful," she whispered. "It also is deadly to you, slave. The blood will mingle with yours, killing you slowly and very, very painfully."

Twitching and bawling as the poison took effect, he sagged into a heap, and she let go. A flimsy sheet of silk from the couch served as a towel to clean her hand. Finished with it—and him—she dropped it to the floor and rose. Her new First Prime abandoned his position by the door, gliding forward and sneering at the dying slave. Not as handsome as his predecessor, but perhaps smart enough to learn from poor example.

He lowered his head. "What is your desire, Lady Nirrti?"

"Take two others and accompany me." She brushed past him and through the door, his reply sliding from her back. It was predictable, anyhow.

"As you wish, Lady Nirrti."

Hurrying into the staircase, she could hear them fall in behind her, swift and silent, as they should be. Wide loops of stairs spiraled down into shadow and to the lower levels. Cool marble under her feet, she slipped past derelict floors, past the level that now housed over sixty new Jaffa, past the laboratory, and finally to the bottom, where the stairwell opened out toward the vault. The flickering distortion across the doorway indicated an exit secured by a force shield. From the inside it would seem opaque, allowing her to observe the new arrival without being seen herself.

Already small of stature, the Tauri healer was dwarfed by the dimensions of the room. The wet trail of footprints she had left reminded Nirrti of the puny, busy perambulations of an insect—an ant perhaps, separated from the hive and frantically searching for the other ants. Or at least a way out.

Now that the vibrations no longer warped the healer's mind, the woman was reacting normally again. The ant trail ran—pat-pat-pat—straight from the large puddle at the center of the room to the force shield where, no doubt, she had received a shock. For some reason they all tried at least once, believing themselves immune to physics. Then—pat-pat-pat—the trail doubled back on itself to where she had arrived. The rings were gone of course. At this moment—pat-pat-pat—she was traipsing along a wall, fingertips examining coarse stone, sooty from the torches that lit the room. Obviously she was hoping to find the controls for the ring transporter. Enterprising, if overly optimistic. The transporters inside the fortress could only be operated from a ribbon device.

Much like the force shield.

Nirrti touched a gem on her device, and a silent command neutralized photons and realigned the charges of the air molecules inside the doorway, until the air became just that—air—and lost its tense shimmer. The prisoner looked up, alerted by that indefinable sense of interrupted solitude all trapped animals seemed to possess. Her hair hung in limp red strands—amazingly it had changed color, chameleon-like, since Nirrti had last seen her on Earth—and she was soaked and pale and filthy, but there was no fear in her dark eyes. In fact, there was something almost akin to mockery. Mockery and contempt and collected stillness.

"I had a hunch it'd be you," she said. "The transporter control in the pool was a tad obvious."

Ah yes. The palm print. Originally designed for fever-ridden Hankan adolescents who, like the good little apes they were, could never resist placing their paws inside the relief to see if it fit. "Why modify a thing that serves its purpose?" Nirrti replied pleasantly. "It did for you, did it not? Without it you might have drowned."

The healer's fist scrubbed across her forehead, betraying her thoughts. "What did you do to me? Drugs? *Nish'ta*?"

"Nothing so crude. Think!" Her peal of laughter made the woman flinch, and Nirrti relished it. "When would I have administered a drug?" As she walked into the room, closing the distance between them, laughter was supplanted by just the correct amount of threat in her tone. "Do not underestimate me. I am not your prisoner now, and you do not have a weapon."

A flicker of defiance and raw hatred danced through the healer's eyes. "So that's what this is about? Revenge? Are you going to kill me or just implant me with a Goa'uld?"

"I told you not to underestimate me! Revenge? Do you really believe you can judge me by the paltry standards of the Tauri? Of course, should the chance for revenge present itself…" Nirrti smiled. "For now you shall make yourself useful. You are amply qualified, and you owe me a service."

The healer stiffened, brow furrowing in mulish refusal. A minute wave of their mistress' hand made the three Jaffa guards step from the shadows by the doorway. For a moment, the woman's eyes widened, and in that tiny frame of time puzzlement darkened to recognition and abhorrence.

Excellent.

Turning to share the healer's view, Nirrti herself found nothing abhorrent in her creations. "She will come with us," she said to her new First Prime and strode past him toward the doorway.

Lingering to watch was unnecessary. They would surround the prisoner, two either side, one at her back and, if called for, they would beat her into obedience. One way or the other, the woman would follow.

Nirrti scaled the stairs to the level above and headed down the hallway to the laboratory. The door that sealed the entrance opened noiselessly. Cold air hissed into the corridor, coating gilded walls and floors with moisture. Used to the brutal drop in temperature, she ignored it. Besides, she was able to adjust the host's body heat and barely noticed any discomfort. The healer, drenched from her bath in the pool and accustomed to the warmth of the jungle would suffer, of course. So much the better.

Overhead lights, activated by motion sensors, shed a pure white gleam on a facility that clashed with the opulence of the hallway and the rest of the palace. This was the domain of science, utilitarian and sterile by necessity, though to Nirrti it had a beauty of its own. Less sensual perhaps, but ultimately more enduring. The doors slid shut behind her Jaffa and their charge, and over their footfalls she could hear the woman's gasp. She knew what had provoked it.

The layout of the laboratory was that of a giant wheel. Its hub was occupied by a large surgical table, banks of equipment, and the climate-controlled vats that harbored swirling masses of larvae. The spokes radiating from the hub were dedicated to Macdonald, her new First Prime, and nine other warriors and held parallel rows of clear cylinders, each about seven feet high, three feet in diameter and filled with liquid. From some of the gestation tubes her creatures were staring at her, dawning recognition in their gaze. These would be mature soon, and they sensed the approach of their birth and *prim'ta*. The Macdonalds looked sullen, as though they realized that their prototype had been tried and found wanting.

She addressed the Jaffa escort. "You may go."

"Yes, Lady Nirrti," her First Prime responded.

All three of them bowed, identical movements; identical smiles on identical faces. Three sets of steps of the same length, three bodies swaying with the same little swagger, they left the laboratory.

"Clones," the healer whispered, her face deathly pale. She was hugging herself, seeking protection from the cold or the shock or both. "Why?"

Partly because she knew it would heighten her prisoner's discomfort, Nirrti laughed again. "How else would I obtain a sufficient number of subjects? Diversity is essential for maintaining a healthy stock."

"Sufficient subjects for what?"

"That is none of your concern. Your only concern is to assist me in creating more."

"No!"

"As you wish."

Nirrti's fingers found the contact on the ribbon device, activated it. The vibrations resonated through the room at a frequency far below human hearing. They once more rendered the healer's mind suggestible, open to Nirrti's invasion, the effect almost as pleasurable as taking a host. Pain and terror suffused the woman's eyes as she fought vainly to retain control of her will.

These are deficient. You may begin by destroying them, Nirrti thought at her, pointing at the endless rows of Macdonalds. *It is a task suited to you. As I recall you delight in destroying the work of others.*

"It's an acquired taste. Have another." Frank Simmons poured a second round of oak-aged Macallan at seventy bucks a bottle and returned to the fireplace to put the glasses on a low table. Playing butler. Why the hell not? "I'd suggest you drink it slowly this time."

Conrad, ensconced in one of the leather armchairs, picked up the tumbler and tossed back its contents. Then he studied the reflection of the fire in his glass. "My host is partial to wine—a type you refer to as Californian Shiraz—but he detests spirits. An instance of overindulgence in his youth, I believe. As for myself, ethanol has no effect on me. I can metabolize it into carbohydrates faster than you can pour. So you may as well abandon your attempt to intoxicate me."

"That wasn't the idea." Of course it had been precisely the idea of this companionable little get-together in the library of the safe house, but Simmons wasn't fool enough to admit it. He eased himself into his chair and took a sip of whiskey, savoring it. "I was trying to invoke a spirit of cooperation rather than opposition. We can both profit from working together. Partners, if you will."

"Is it customary among the Tauri to control their partners by leashing explosive devices around their necks?"

"Touché. On the other hand, it also isn't customary among us to control our partners by taking them as hosts, if you catch my drift."

"I have a host, Simmons. Admittedly, I would not have chosen him. As you would say, he is not my type. But neither are you." A sardonic eyebrow flicked up. Conrad actually had a sense of humor. "There is no sufficient enticement to switch hosts, so you are perfectly safe."

"Good to know." Simmons snorted. "What *is* your type?"

"Given the choice, I would have taken Conrad's assistant."

"A woman? I never considered—"

"Surely you are aware that the Goa'uld essentially are hermaphrodites. The gender of the host is irrelevant and purely a matter of personal preference."

In fact, Simmons's interest in the bedroom habits of a race of spiky reptiles was strictly limited. He'd read about it in the SGC reports and filed it away. And Conrad, under that personable mask he wore right now, was trying to play him. In a minute the bastard would claim he'd surrendered vital information and demand a cookie. Well, he could have a carrot. It was healthier all round.

"Prove to me that I can trust you, and the necklace goes away," Simmons offered over another sip of whiskey.

Conrad's hands rose in a mix of frustration and defensiveness. Sometimes the way he adopted human mannerisms was eerie. "I have already helped you by gaining Lady Nirrti's assistance. Is that not enough?"

"Nowhere near enough, my friend! You put me in touch with Nirrti because there was something in it for her, and you hoped the deal would get you on her good side. I'm looking for a slightly more disinterested show of faith."

"And how do I know that *I* can trust *you*?"

"I saved your life."

"Because I could be of profit to you."

Simmons laughed. "Do you have any idea how much more profitable you would be dissected and sold to the highest bidder? All the scientific benefit without the risks."

For once it gave Conrad pause. The silence was filled with the tap of rain against tall windows and the crackle of fire in the hearth. The Victorian idyll seemed custom-made to lend credibility to this charade of two old pals having an after-dinner chat. The only thing missing were the cigars. Simmons didn't smoke. Somewhere in the house a phone rang, muted and out of place. It jarred Conrad from his thoughts, remarkably without flashing eyes or vocal hi-jinks or any other theatrics.

"Very well," he said. "What do you wish to know?"

"What I've been wanting to know all last week. Jaffa training."

Conrad sighed, like a preschool teacher faced with a particularly imbecilic batch of toddlers. "And what I have been telling you all last week is true. I do not know. I am Goa'uld, not Jaffa. How the Jaffa train their warriors is of no concern to us as long as these warriors are skilled enough to do our bidding. One thing I *can* tell you, however.

Your men must be trained."

"Oh really?" snapped Simmons. "Wake me when you're through dispensing platitudes!"

"Listen to me, Tauri!" And now Conrad rolled out the whole sound and light show. "I assume Nirrti did not tell you this, because she seeks her own advantage—taking what you offer without surrendering anything in return. You never wasted a thought on the skills necessary for your men to wield the powers they are given. And you call the Goa'uld arrogant? We possess the entire knowledge of our race from birth. Learning is not a requirement for us. For you it is a matter of survival, as it is for the Jaffa. But, unlike you, the Jaffa are humble enough to know that they have to learn.

"Why do you think a Jaffa warrior begins his education even before he receives his *prim'ta*? It takes years to master *kelno'reem* and to school the senses for the presence of the symbiote. Unless your men receive proper training, they will weaken. Eventually they will die. Not straightaway, but they will die."

Simmons found that his fingers had clenched around the tumbler during this speech. If this was true... His hand shook, and he knocked back the whiskey in one gulp and deposited the glass on the table lest he broke it. "The tame Jaffa they keep at the SGC never mentioned any of this," he snarled at last.

"Why would he? Jaffa consider the relationship with their symbiote a private matter. Besides, he is a *shol'va*. Perhaps he had an ulterior motive for not mentioning it."

"So what do you suggest I do?"

"Is it not obvious?" Conrad's left eyebrow leaped up again, this time in disbelief. "Use the *shol'va*. Order him to train them."

Good thinking. Except, this obvious solution had an equally obvious hitch the Goa'uld wasn't aware of. Annoyingly, the hitch was of Simmons's own making. Which meant that Simmons would have to find a way around it.

His ruminations were interrupted by a knock on the door.

"Come."

An agent entered, brandishing a phone handset. He cast a quick, uneasy glance at Conrad before redirecting his attention to Simmons. "Call for you, sir."

"Dammit! I—"

"Sorry, sir. They said it was urgent."

Simmons snatched the phone. "What?"

The voice at the other end sounded sheepish. "It's General Hammond, sir. We, uh… we lost him."

The news was enough to make him jump to his feet and start pacing. "You did *what?*"

"He got picked up by a cab outside Bolling AFB. We're thinking it may have been arranged. We're also pretty sure the guy driving was Maybourne."

Maybourne. They should have executed him while they'd had the chance. Some days Simmons could swear the son of a bitch was going out of his way to make his successor's life hell. This was one of those days. "When did this happen?" he barked, staring through a rain-streaked window.

"Just after five this afternoon."

"And you've waited until now to tell me?"

"They were heading out I-66 last time we saw them from the car, sir. So we decided to check with the airlines at Dulles. Turns out two passengers who fit the description were booked on a United flight to Seattle."

"Did you say *Seattle?*" A silver lining. Maybe. If this was true, he had a fair idea of where to look for them.

"Yes, sir. We missed them by ten minutes."

"My congratulations on the spectacularly narrow margin. You still missed them, idiot!" Simmons disconnected the call and tossed the handset to the waiting agent. "I'm flying to Seattle tonight. Make the necessary arrangements. I'll be taking three men."

"Yes, sir." The agent left the library a lot faster than he'd entered it, undoubtedly grateful to get away from Conrad.

Who slowly rose from his chair and faced Simmons across the room. "May I accompany you?"

"Why? Homesick?"

"I suppose my host is." Conrad smiled a nasty little smile. "You appear to have been apprised of a problem. Perhaps I could make myself useful."

"*Useful?*"

"How can I gain your trust if you do not give me a chance to prove myself?"

True enough. And why not? Perhaps he really could make himself useful. At last, Simmons nodded. "Fine. But the necklace stays on. For now."

Jack carefully cranked one eye open. The world started to rotate around a hole in the ceiling. Through the hole snaked an arm-thick bunch of vines, and from their tendrils plopped a steady supply of water drops. Into his face. Which was what had woken him. He guessed.

Ceiling.

There'd been no ceiling before... before the cause of the headache. No ceilings in the jungle. And he was pretty sure he'd been in the middle of a jungle in the none-too-distant past. The ceiling belonged to a small room, stone walls blackened by age and slick with moisture. A single casement opened onto a dripping mass of green; foliage, trees, the whole nine yards of rainforest.

Ah.

The wall opposite was covered in intricate friezes, people and animals and ornaments, and Daniel probably would— Daniel!

Jack tried to sit up and promptly wished he'd opted for Plan B. Whatever that was, it had to be less nauseating. The room revved up to a brisk 90 rpm, and suddenly the face of Dr. Jackson spiraled into view, concerned, sweaty, with a paisley bandanna tied over the busted eye.

"Jack? Stay put, Jack."

By Jack O'Neill's estimate, he'd already done too much of that. "I'll be fine. Just give me a minute." An hour would be more realistic, but if things played out the way they usually did, he probably didn't have that long. "How did I get here? And where *is* here?"

"I carried you. The ruins weren't far. This must have been some kind of wardroom." Sitting on his haunches, Daniel slowly seesawed to a rest in front of Jack. Rumor had it he bought those bandannas on purpose. "You were out cold. I'm guessing it's a concussion."

"Ya think? What the hell happened? Did I get hit by a tank?"

"You got hit by a girl."

"I *what*?" The pieces fell into place. He remembered that indefinable sense of being watched and, seconds later, a slim, filthy, stinking figure whirling from the shadows. The business end of a staff weapon flying at his face, the shrill shock in her eyes when she'd recognized him, too late. "Carter. Did I mention I like her attitude? Where is she?"

Wincing, Daniel nodded toward a corner of the room, a makeshift pallet, and its occupant. "I, uh… You were down, and somebody was standing over you with a staff weapon. I kinda overreacted. Knocked her flat."

"Thanks."

"Nothing as inherently funny as misguided acts of heroism, huh?"

True. Except it could have been a real Jaffa with real Jaffa brethren lurking in the bushes. As far as Jack was concerned, heroism lay in the intention rather than the outcome. "Thanks anyway."

"You're welcome."

"Fraiser and Teal'c?"

Daniel gave a despondent little shrug. "No idea. All I know is that the staff weapon Sam used isn't Teal'c's."

"You can tell?"

"Sure. The markings are all different, depending on—"

"Make, model, and year."

"Something like that."

"Crap." *A real Jaffa with real Jaffa brethren lurking in the bushes…* and where there were Jaffa, there usually was a Goa'uld. "Crap," Jack muttered again. "So, where did Carter leave Teal'c and the doc? Did she say?"

Another wince. "No. I haven't talked to her yet."

"Come again?"

"She's in real bad shape, Jack."

Thankfully, the room was so small Jack could get away with just scooting over to Carter's pallet on all fours. Standing up might have been tricky. Daniel had cleaned her up as best he could, whittling down a solid layer of grime to smudges of dirt on a waxy face. Wrapped around one leg was a pristine bandage, looking absurdly out of place.

Jack stared at it. "What?" he said.

"It's nasty. Deep gash, and it's infected. I put antibiotics on it, but…"

The rest became a blur of sounds, throbbing in tune with Jack's headache. Not just infected, if the jaundice and the odor were anything to go by. He'd seen this once before, in a rebel camp in Honduras, and he'd hoped to hell he'd never have to see it again. Sweet Jesus, not Carter! He shouldered the thought aside. There was no place for it now. If and when the time came, he'd do what he had to do, but on the whole the preferable option was finding Fraiser. After all, they did have a tame doctor running around somewhere in this hellhole.

As gently as he could he patted her cheek. "Carter? Rise and shine. Time for a debrief." No reaction. Another pat. "Come on, Major. Sit-rep. Now! That's an order."

She moaned a little, and suddenly her eyes flew open on a flash of panic that melted into toe-curling relief. "Sir," she whispered, voice brittle. "I thought… dead… I didn't… I—"

"You whacked me upside the head, Carter. How's that gonna kill me?" He forced a grin, hoped she'd buy it. "If you'd whupped my ass, maybe, but my head? Hardest material known to man."

Bingo. It was wan and diffident, but it was a smile alright. Duration needed work, though. The panic crept back, in its wake something dangerously close to despair, and she pushed herself up on her elbows. "You shouldn't be here. You can't—" For the first time she seemed to clock Daniel. "You neither. What happened to your face?"

"Amazing, isn't it?" Jack said agreeably and didn't quite manage to evade a kick to his ankle.

Feigning innocence, Daniel crouched and handed Carter his canteen. "Nothing serious. Little difference of opinion with some Marines on '335."

The canteen jerked and spouted a splash of water. "Jaffa," she hissed.

Jack wheeled around; a move he immediately regretted, especially once the window had juddered into focus and he failed to spot any hostiles outside or elsewhere. "No Jaffa, Carter. We're—"

"The Marines, sir. The Marines are Jaffa."

Oh great. He exchanged a glance with Daniel, who barely perceptibly shook his head. Maybe he was right. Maybe they should just let—

"I'm not delirious, Colonel!" And maybe she was right, too. Her eyes were fever-bright, but she seemed lucid enough. Pissed enough.

"Okay, Carter. How about you start with *In the beginning* and work your way forward from there?"

Haltingly and with something less than her usual precision, she did just that. By the end of it she'd answered questions Jack hadn't even known he had. However, the two most important answers were missing. Where was the DHD? And where in the blazes were Teal'c and the doc? She couldn't say, and pushing her into speculations would get them nowhere.

"Good job, Major," he murmured. "Now grab some sleep."

"But, sir—"

"Sleep, Carter!"

"Yessir."

Five minutes later she'd dozed off.

Jack scrubbed a hand over his face, mixing sweat with grime and evenly distributing the mess. Great camouflage, if nothing else. What he wanted to do was get up and pace and fiddle with stuff and generally drive the natives nuts. Spread the joy. Given that the room measured about ten by ten feet and held two men, the pallet, a backpack, and one major, that was a bit of a no-no, even by his standards. The realization didn't diminish the urge.

While Carter and Teal'c had proved conclusively that they didn't need their CO's able assistance to dig themselves *into* a real deep hole, right now said CO had no idea of how to drag them *out* of said hole. He should have. That's what being in command meant, right? Right. It sure as hell didn't mean being terrified of hopping in any direction because whatever direction you chose to hop in might be dead wrong. Emphasis on *dead*.

"This isn't your fault, Jack."

Perversely, Dr. Jackson's ability to read minds—specifically Jack O'Neill's—remained unimpaired by smashed spectacles. Having had twice his annual allowance of confessions wormed out of him earlier, Jack was in no mood to share warm fuzzy feelings. Instead he stared at the walls; anything to avoid that blue drill bore gaze coming from Daniel's end. The faces on the wall stared back. The faces didn't give a damn. They stared back with their blank eyes and Buddha smiles, too pretty by half and effete enough to raise Jack's hackles. Apophis sprang to mind. And Ra, for that matter.

"What are you going to do about Sam?" Typical Daniel. If subtle doesn't work straightaway, switch to frontal attack. "I checked her medikit, Jack. She never used the morphine. She knows what's coming. So do I, and we can't afford to wait much longer. If we do nothing, she'll go into septic shock in a day, two at the most."

Jack knew perfectly well and didn't need to hear it. Didn't *want* to hear it. "Daniel—"

"I'll do it."

The look on Daniel's face made Jack swallow his reply.

"There was this kid on Abydos. Crazy about digging up artifacts. Care to guess who he got it from?" Daniel gave a bleak little laugh. "A chamber caved in, and a stone block landed on his arm. We didn't find him until three days later. By then the infection had set in. I was the only one who had a rough idea of what to do."

"You never told me."

"It's not a fun story." Daniel shrugged. "If I hadn't put a bee in his bonnet, the kid wouldn't have been there. I always blamed myself."

"I know the feeling," muttered Jack. A shaft of sunlight pouring through the hole in the ceiling had crawled up the wall and illuminated three of the smirking poster boys, cozily grouped together. If he had a hammer and chisel, he'd give them a nose job. Make them look like the Andrews Sisters. "Who are these guys, anyway?"

Abruptly hauled back from the sands of Abydos, Daniel blinked. "What?"

"Not *what*. Who. They." Jack pointed at the relief.

"Oh." Daniel scrambled to his feet and walked closer to the wall, until he actually could see what he was talking about. "They're the original *Rakshasas*. Bhaya, Mahabhaya, and Mrityu."

"Of course they're the Rickshaws. Popular vocal group in the fifties. Why did I ask?"

Dr. Jackson grinned, which did interesting things to the left side of his face. "The *Rakshasas* are demons. Their names mean Fear,

Terror, and Death."

"Charming. Aren't they a bit girlie for the job?"

"Depends on the job. They're shape shifters. According to legend they're the children of the Vedic goddess of death, deceit, and destruction, Danu. She's said to have…" The sentence petered out, and Daniel stared at the relief, open-mouthed. "Uh-oh."

"Daniel?"

"The lady traveled under several aliases. Dhumavati's one of them. And so, by the way, is Nirrti. What did Sam say Macdonald's tattoo looked like?"

"A dove." Jack didn't like where this was going.

"Or a pigeon. The pigeon's supposed to be Nirrti's messenger. Messenger of doom, obviously. The *Atharva Veda* even lists charms to ward off pigeons." Daniel turned away from the wall and sat cross-legged on the floor. "*Upon those persons yonder the winged missile shall fall! If the owl shrieks, futile shall this be, or if the pigeon takes his steps upon the fire! To thy two messengers, O Nirrti, who come here—*"

"Daniel! I get the idea. Where there are Jaffa, there usually is a Goa'uld."

"As far as we know Nirrti doesn't have that many Jaffa," Daniel offered.

"Yeah, well. Maybe she's started a recruitment drive," retorted Jack, but his heart wasn't in it. Something else had occurred to him. Something that might just— "What's the one thing no self-respecting Goa'uld would be caught without?"

"A makeup kit?" The quip was followed by a penetrating glance. "Jack, I know what's on your mind. But we've got no proof that she's here, and to go off on a wild goose chase to—"

"One day, Daniel. You said it yourself. We've got a day. And before I start chopping off bits of Carter, I intend to use that day to try and find Nirrti's sarcophagus."

CHAPTER ELEVEN

Teal'c had heard the Stargate activate, but by the time he had succeeded in scaling the cliff, the arrivals were long gone. Or perhaps, he mused, they had not been arrivals. Perhaps Dr. Fraiser, favored by the luck of children and madmen, had found the DHD and had indeed gone home.

The area beneath the Stargate was sunlit and deserted, unremarkable, and the gray walls of the ruins breathed a semblance of coolness. Even the jungle noises had returned, dispelling the silence, and he strode out into the clearing, confident that he would be safe for the time being. In a patch of mud, not far from the place where he himself had landed four days ago, he found two slim lengths of white plastic. Teal'c recognized the strips—flex-cuffs—and squatted to examine them more closely.

They were torn, their ends frayed and showing teeth marks. It indicated several things; two prisoners had been brought here— No, they had been *sent* here. Had they been escorted, their escape would have been foiled. And whoever had sent them, surely wished for them to die. Cuffed, and therefore most likely unarmed, they would not have stood the slightest chance against the beasts.

Except... He slowly swiveled on the balls of his feet, surveying the clearing once more. This time the beasts had not attacked. The prisoners' boot prints told their own tale. Once they had freed themselves, the two men—the size of their boots made them men—had risen and walked off in different directions, though well within sight of each other. Teal'c recognized the pattern. He himself had followed it a hundred times and more; they had been exploring. Which suggested they were new to the territory. If they—

A ponderous rumble rolled across the glade, familiar and startling at the same time.

"*Hasshak,*" Teal'c muttered under his breath. Foolishly, he had allowed himself to neglect that particular source of danger.

He rose, loped back toward the cliff, and climbed the nearest tree

to a nest of broad branches, some ten meters above ground. By the
time he had settled into this aerie, the fourth chevron was locked.
He sat virtually at eyelevel with the face in the wall and, for the first
time, found occasion to study it. Almond-shaped, heavy-lidded eyes,
that stared at him with the peculiar blank look of carved stone; a
strong, straight nose; sensuously curved lips that gaped to reveal a
row of sharp teeth; a long, pointed tongue, lolling like a ramp from
the cavern of the mouth out onto the clearing. For reasons he could
not clearly define, Teal'c found the sight profoundly disturbing.

The *Chappa'ai* was set in the idol's forehead, a massive spinning jewel, its outer ring now dotted with five amber lights. Six. The
seventh light all but paled under the mighty rush of the wormhole
exploding across half the glade. Then the event horizon retracted and
stilled. In these few moments of deceptive peace, Teal'c sensed rather
than saw movement.

Scanning the huge face, his gaze finally caught on the dark recess
of the mouth. There. Behind the points of the teeth flitted shadows,
nervous yet eager, as if they wished to emerge but did not quite dare
yet. Curious… His attention was distracted by four figures tumbling
from the Stargate, flailing and screaming and all too reminiscent of
Teal'c's own arrival on the planet. Fleetingly he recalled the excruci-
ating wrongness of that journey and asked himself if it was the same
for these men, or if they had too little basis for comparison.

They were young and fit and clean-shaven, in smart uniforms,
and all had been part of the unit that had journeyed to M3D 335 on
the same day as Major Carter, Dr. Fraiser, and Teal'c; the unit that
had been goaded into a pointless race by Colonel Norris. They struck
the ground in an ungainly jumble of limbs and equipment and spent
several minutes shaking off the shock and the effects of the impact.
Eventually, one of them struggled to his feet.

"This ain't like they told us," he observed and added, "Can't see
that PhD thingy either."

"The *what* thingy?" asked another.

"That phone-home-device or whatever it's called."

"*D*HD! *Dial*-home-device, you ass!"

"Who cares?"

"Shut up!" The speaker was the young corporal who had assisted

Major Carter at the Marine camp. "You hear that?"

"Hear what? It's dead silent."

It was true. Like a tape recording that had stopped abruptly, the jungle noises had ceased again, almost as if the forest were holding its breath in anticipation. The quiet chafed at Teal'c's awareness like a rough shirt on tender skin.

Into the silence one of the men said, "Oh boy."

Pouring out from the mouth and coiling down the tongue came the beasts, two dozen of them, jostling and pushing and flooding the glade. What had restrained them until now? At the back of Teal'c's mind a vague recollection began to congeal into realization, but before it could take shape the events unfolding below demanded his full attention. The Marines had formed a protective circle, their backs to each other, firing at the heaving mass of black bristles and fangs and making the same discovery Major Carter had made, namely that projectile weapons were ineffectual against these brutes' armor. The Marines would not prevail. He knew it for a fact, and they would find out soon enough.

Teal'c felt torn. Although he had every reason to suspect their intentions, to stand by and watch these men being ripped apart was impossible. With sudden resolve he slung the staff weapon from his back where he had strapped it for the climb up the cliff, aimed, and loosed a series of rapid blasts at the beasts, killing one and wounding several others. The rest paused, shuffling uncertainly, then retreated a few meters, giving the prey a fraction of breathing space. The Marines saw their chance and took it.

"Now!" bellowed Major Carter's corporal. "Go, go, go!"

His comrades lowered their weapons and sprinted across the glade toward the edge of the forest. In a reckless act of bravery, the corporal himself held his position, determined to cover his friends. A swift glance over his shoulder assured him that the men had almost reached the presumed safety of the tree line. He fired a last burst at the creatures, wheeled around, and ran. As though they had been waiting for that moment, the brutes attacked, flanking him on both sides. He hooked and feinted like a hare, but they inexorably drove him off course and cut off his escape route. Instead of joining his comrades, he came racing directly toward Teal'c's tree and the dead end behind.

A mere twenty meters further were the cliff and nothing but thin air.

Without even thinking about it, Teal'c set aside his staff weapon, tore free a vine and lowered it. "Jump, Corporal Wilkins!"

The man's head snapped up. He tripped, staggered, regained his balance, and bounded for the vine. Teal'c no sooner felt the corporal's weight yank against his grip than he began to haul in the makeshift rope, ignoring the pain in his barely healed shoulder to pull even faster. For all he knew the brutes were capable of leaping and might still bring down their victim. And leap they did, snapping and snarling, but to no avail. Seconds later, Teal'c dragged Corporal Wilkins onto the branch beside him. The corporal's eyes went wide when he recognized his rescuer, but he did not comment. Instead he glanced past Teal'c and back down to the ground. Below, the beasts had abandoned their futile hunt, swarmed into a turn, and set off after the Marines who had fled into the forest.

Fingers still cramped around the vine, Corporal Wilkins fought to bring his breathing under control. "Uh, thanks. Nice shooting. That's one hell of a gun you've got there, Mr. Murray," he gasped. "Sorry, sir, I don't even know your rank. What are you, sir?"

"I was First Prime to the false god Apophis. I have renounced my service."

"Ah," said Corporal Wilkins, obviously deciding not to pursue the subject. Suddenly his expression darkened. "I gotta get down, go after the guys. They might need—"

"That is inadvisable."

"Well, that's just too bad, sir." The young man began to ease himself off the branch. "I don't know how you First What's-Its do stuff, but in the Corps we don't leave our guys in the lurch."

Teal'c grabbed a fistful of uniform and hauled the struggling, swearing man back to his side. "We do not leave behind our people either, Corporal Wilkins. However, all you would accomplish by searching for them now is your own demise. Your weapons are useless against these beasts. If your comrades are lucky and smart, they will not fight but outrun the creatures. You have risked your own life to give them an opportunity for escape. You have done enough."

The corporal's face plainly stated that he begged to differ, but in the end he acquiesced as there were indeed no shots being fired in the jungle. "Sounds like you're right, sir. They're running."

Too fast to even look back and ascertain your whereabouts, Teal'c did not reply. Life had taught him that idealism was a precious commodity, and he had no desire to quash it where he found it.

For a while they sat quietly, watching the glade below. At length, his voice still a little unsteady, Corporal Wilkins declared, "I suppose I should go back and report to Sergeant van Leyden, tell him what happened, bring reinforcements." He scanned the clearing. "Except... You know where that DHD thing is, sir?"

"I do not."

"But they told us it's always by the gate."

"Mostly, but not always," Teal'c answered. "It may have been hidden on purpose. Or it may not exist at all."

"*Not exist?*" The young man parroted, his face draining of blood. "So what are we—"

In the foliage above a bird began to screech, and at the same time Teal'c felt a diminishing of the vague sense of discomfort the unnatural silence of the forest had caused. Again realization hovered just beneath the threshold of conscious thought, again events dispelled it. A second bird answered the screech, then other animals chimed in, until the normal cacophony of the jungle was restored. Little later a bulky black shape appeared across the glade, not far from where the three Marines had vanished. The beast moved sluggishly, uncertainly, as though it had woken from drugged sleep in a location it had not expected to find itself in. Behind it and at its side, others broke from the forest, all in a similar state, until the whole pack was staggering up the stone tongue and back into their lair under the walls of the ruins.

"I'll be damned," muttered Corporal Wilkins. "They suddenly feel like a nap or something?"

"I do not know, Corporal Wilkins," Teal'c answered truthfully. "However, it appears that now would be a good time to leave."

Within minutes they were back on solid ground. His sidearm drawn and raised, Corporal Wilkins cautiously approached the beast Teal'c had slain. Even in death it seemed gigantic, its body covered in spikes a quarter of an inch thick, its stubby trotters ending in claws. Its snout was pointed and from under slack flews protruded a set of razor fangs stained with old blood.

"That is one danged ugly critter," the corporal declared. Then he holstered his weapon and glanced toward the edge of the jungle. "No good going after the guys, I suppose. Might end up walking in circles for days."

"Indeed," confirmed Teal'c, only too aware of his own experiences.

"So what do you suggest we do, Mr, uh, First Prime, sir?"

"I shall continue to follow the trail of Dr. Fraiser. She is… unwell, and it is imperative that I—"

"Dr. Fraiser's here? And Major Carter, sir?" At Teal'c's nod, Corporal Wilkins swallowed. "Sir, are you trying to tell me you've never been back to Earth?"

"We have not. The Stargate malfunctioned."

"I don't think so."

"Why do you say that, Corporal Wilkins?"

"Colonel O'Neill and Dr. Jackson came looking for you, sir. They…" The young man blushed, clearly uncomfortable. "I think—I *know*—Colonel Norris lied to them. I spoke to them briefly. Then they disappeared. We were told they'd gone back to Earth. Like you, sir."

Driven by a sudden, sickening certainty about who the two prisoners had been, Teal'c's gaze arrested on the spot where the flex-cuffs had lain. They were gone now, trampled under by hundreds of claws.

The cab they'd taken from Sea-Tac International stuttered to a halt at a street corner in one of the least savory areas of suburban Seattle.

"That's forty-five bucks," said the driver.

George Hammond stared at his travel companion who smiled innocently and turned up empty palms so as to indicate penury.

"You gonna pay me today or what?" the cabby snarled.

Clearly the US Air Force was going cover the cab fare as well. Hammond pulled a fifty dollar note from his wallet and handed it to the driver. "Keep the change."

"Ain't takin' nothin' bigger than twenty dollar notes."

Snapping forward in the seat, Maybourne poked his head through the open partition. "Take it," he hissed. "And we want the change back. All twenty bucks of it."

The tone was steel-edged, suggesting that refusal would be a bad mistake, and the driver knew better than disputing the math. Without another word he gave Maybourne two tens, then growled, "Out!"

Hammond slipped from the cab and watched as it drove off, tires smoking. Obviously the cabby wanted to get the hell out of here, and who could blame him? The street was lined with shops that had gone bust, windows boarded over and signs faded or dangling. The only establishments still in business were a drinking hole, a heavily barred liquor store, and a hot dog stand at the corner of the next block. A wino had occupied a stretch of curb and was ranting at a hydrant. In an alley opposite, two shadowy figures abruptly ducked behind a dumpster when they noted Hammond's interest. A trio of teens, in low-slung jeans wide enough to accommodate a small country, swaggered out of the liquor store, clutching paper bags and giving him the hard man stare.

He turned, expecting to find Maybourne right behind him. Instead, the ex-colonel had made a beeline for the hot dog stand. He'd also pocketed the change from the cab fare. Beginning to appreciate Jack O'Neill's recurring itch to shoot the man, Hammond headed after him. Given time of year and latitude, the night was surprisingly muggy, and he wanted to unzip the windbreaker. Fingers already on the tab, he reconsidered. Presumably the idea was to remain *in*conspicuous. The Aloha shirt had parrots on it.

At the hot dog stand, Maybourne was squirting relish on a dog that, by Texan standards, was a Chihuahua. A runt at that. The less than sanitary individual manning the stand demanded an extortionate six bucks for the feast, and Maybourne forked over one of the ten dollar bills and grinned at Hammond.

"Want one, George? My treat."

"You could have eaten on the plane," groused Hammond, deciding not to point out the obvious.

"And poison myself with the junk they serve?" Maybourne demanded around a mouthful of hot dog. A glob of relish escaped and left a green trail down his front. Two bites later the dog had disappeared. He scrunched the napkin into a ball and lobbed it into the gutter. "Let's go."

He briskly strode across the street and into the alley, deserted now, apart from a few rats. At its end, Maybourne took a left, crossed another street, found another alley, until they emerged on an avenue that looked somewhat more reputable than the area where they'd started out. Directly opposite rose a tall, institutional gray façade. George Hammond recognized it without ever having been here.

"St. Christina's Hospital. That's where Conrad held Major—"

"No names." Grinning faintly, Maybourne checked up and down the street. "Doesn't look like we've got company yet, but you can bet your two-star derriere that the NID will pick up our trail. We don't have much time."

"Time for what?"

"Getting inside."

Next to the former hospital stood a tenement building. Maybourne headed for the entrance, bounded up the stairs, nudged the front door. It clicked open. "Lucky the landlord's too stingy to fix it. Fire escape would have been a bit too public for my liking. After you, Huggy."

"Don't push it!" Hammond ducked into the building.

The stairwell was dark, smelled of damp newspapers and floor polish, and served six floors. They climbed every single one of them, plus an additional set of steps onto the roof. Sodium streetlight poured over the cars parked below, a few lit windows adding brightness; somewhere nearby wailed an ambulance, its horn drowning out a mix of TV shows and the rattle of cheap air conditioning units. Up the block, a black SUV pulled into the street, crawled past the hospital, and disappeared again.

"Company," muttered Maybourne. "Won't take long till someone decides to see if we're home already. We've got maybe ten minutes, fifteen at the most."

Hammond felt himself shoved along the parapet and out onto a metal catwalk that connected the tenement to the hospital. The hand-painted sign *Warning! Condemned!* wasn't half as forbidding as the notion of jumping the gap between the buildings, so he didn't argue.

Over on the other side Maybourne pushed past him, flung open a hatch and plunged down a dark flight of stairs. "Move it, General! ORs and offices are on the third floor. You don't want to meet the boys from the SUV, I guarantee you."

Guided only by the meager light filtering in from the street, they clattered down the staircase, one floor, two, three, their footfalls echoing through empty corridors and ricocheting from tiled walls. Maybourne shot from the stairwell, barreled down a hallway, scanning room numbers as he went, and stopped outside a closed door. A few seconds later Hammond caught up with him, panting and wishing he were thirty years younger, thirty pounds lighter. By the time he could breathe again, Maybourne had forced the lock.

"It was a real sweet deal. Instead of dismantling the facility, the NID said a silent prayer of thanks and took it over the way Conrad's people had left it." He hit the light switch, illuminating what looked like a cross between a lab and a control room.

The banks of surveillance monitors, the computers, a couple of electron microscopes were easily identifiable, but most of the scientific equipment was Greek to Hammond. Either side of the monitor banks, a large window opened onto an operating theatre. Along one wall stood several empty glass containers. Fish tanks? Hardly. The opposite wall housed nine large steel drawers. Morgue drawers. His gaze drifted back to the OR below, the gurneys there, the operating table.

"This isn't where they held Carter," said Maybourne, as though he'd read Hammond's mind. "She was a couple doors down. If there's time, I'll show you."

"Thanks. I'll pass."

"Suit yourself. So, let's see what we've got." Maybourne walked over to the wall with the drawers, pulled the nearest one, and grimaced at the body inside. "Oh boy!"

George Hammond felt grateful that the corpse was frozen. If he'd had to contend with the smell, too, he might have thrown up. The pale torso looked like something had eaten its stomach from the inside out. "What in God's name is this?" he croaked. "Some Level IV virus? Hemorrhagic fever?"

"No. Even the NID aren't crazy enough for that. Besides, this isn't a containment lab." For once the slick façade had crumpled, and Harry Maybourne actually looked troubled. "Whatever they're doing, it's definitely not healthy."

"Obviously not, but I don't see what that's got to do with the Marine base on '335"

"Check his dog tags."

He was right. The dead man was a Marine. "What the hell?" whispered Hammond.

"Yeah. Two months ago nine Marines dropped off the planet. Nobody knows what happened to them. Looks like we just got a pointer." Maybourne closed the drawer, flung himself into a chair, and switched on a computer. When the machine started to boot, he hit F8, switched into DOS mode, and entered some kind of code, fingers flying over the keyboard. "It's a backdoor I made for myself when I was still a member of the club. Bypasses the security program."

Moments later a list of folders popped up. Lots of folders. He dipped in and out of them, randomly opening files, skimming over information, moving on to the next.

"What are you looking for?" Hammond asked.

"I'll know when I find it."

"How about this one?"

The folder was called *Series 3.7*. Shrugging, Maybourne opened it. Nine subfolders. Nine names, one of them identical to the name on the dead man's dog tag. They'd found the vanished Marines alright. "Good guess. You play the lottery? You should, you know."

Somewhere on the lower floors a door slammed, putting paid to any further search for information. Maybourne slipped a DVD from his pocket, placed it into the RW drive, and began downloading the files. The burn seemed to take forever. As soon as drive stopped whirring, he snatched the disc, put it back into its jewel case, and shut down the computer. "Let's hope the stuff copied alright. We don't have time to check."

Out in the corridor they could hear voices, hurried footfalls — three men at least, probably more. As quietly as they could, they raced along the hall, back the way they'd come. It wasn't quietly enough.

"Third floor!" somebody shouted.

Seconds later a tall, bulky figure emerged from the stairwell, cutting off their escape route. Skidding to a halt, George Hammond longed for his sidearm, securely stowed in a Washington hotel safe. Nostalgia was nipped in the bud when he recognized the man. Wrong time for wishful thinking.

"Drat!" He turned on his heel, retracing his steps, Harry Maybourne right beside him.

At their six, Adrian Conrad was gaining, and there was no staircase at the upper end of the corridor. Maybourne hung a right, hared into a nurses' station and through a door opposite into an equipment store. Dead end, and Conrad had reached the station. For want of any other bright ideas Hammond slammed the storeroom door, wedged the backrest of a chair under the knob. It'd last five minutes, if that.

Inside the storeroom were three rows of metal shelves, holding linen, the world's most comprehensive collection of bedpans, and nothing even remotely resembling a weapon. Outside, Conrad was working on turning the door into matchsticks.

"Now what?" gasped Hammond.

By ways of a reply, Maybourne took three steps to the rear wall and yanked open a flap. "Laundry chute."

"You gotta be kidding!"

"Wanna wait for him instead?"

As if on cue a door panel cracked under Conrad's onslaught. Hammond dived into the chute head first, hurtling down three floors and landing on a pile of dirty linen in a laundry cart, without time to reflect on the synchronicity of his and Jack O'Neill's luck. A rumble above announced that somebody was on his way. He scrambled from the cart, clearing the landing zone. Seconds later Maybourne arrived, followed by a roar of fury.

The ex-colonel disembarked and pushed the cart out from under the chute. "That should slow him down," he stated. "Talk about anger management issues."

"Oh, he has. And I'm sure he'll make his feelings known when I hand you over to him, gentlemen."

The disembodied voice came from a swirl of steam that obscured the ill-lit maintenance tunnel, but Hammond didn't need visuals to recognize the owner of that lazy drawl. "Playing with the rats, Colonel?"

"Given the company you keep, General, I suppose I should be the one asking that question." Simmons materialized from the steam cloud, aiming a Glock 17 at them. "Now, if you'd please raise your hands and step out from behind that cart. You, too, Maybourne."

"About to graduate to murder, Simmons?"

"What murder, General? SG-1 has tragically disappeared, and you've been abducted, probably killed, in DC. So who's to—"

The report of the shot hammered from walls and pipes and seemed to compress the steam. A gun tumbled through the air, and Hammond, half deafened, saw rather than heard Simmons's shout. Clutching his right arm, the colonel broke to his knees.

"Jack sends his regards," said Maybourne, holding a Beretta whose existence he'd previously neglected to mention. "Shame your back wasn't turned." Still keeping his bead on Simmons, he picked up the Glock, tossed it at his companion. "You may want this, General."

Hammond caught the gun, shook his head. "So help me, Harry, you're starting to grow on me."

"Don't panic. It won't last." Grinning, Maybourne pointed down the tunnel. "Exit's that way."

It happened so fast, the skin seemed to slough while it lost its glow and turned dull and yellow. Angry black moles appeared where cells broke down, always in the same places; in the middle of the left cheek and on the chin, growing voraciously. Unless treated in time, he—the real one—would die from skin cancer. Lines and wrinkles crawled like cobwebs, scoring deeper and deeper, until the face looked like an ancient, leathery apple, dry and waxy to the touch—if she could touch it. She wanted to, wanted a way to beg forgiveness, offer comfort, warmth, make it easier for him. And him. And him…

She'd lost count, couldn't remember how many.

I can tell you, healer. I even can show you, if I choose to do so. I can show you all of them again. Every single one of them.

"No!" Janet's teeth were rattling so hard, she could barely talk. "Please… It isn't necessary."

Why bother talking? There is no need. I know. I always know.

"I'm human. Talk is what we do."

But, human, you keep telling yourself how inhuman your actions are. Why pretend?

Janet couldn't remember, was too cold and too tired to remember anything, and Nirrti's laughter hammered through her skull and seemed to crush the breath in her lungs. At last the pressure eased, though never enough to feel free or forget the presence in her mind.

Inside the tube muscles atrophied, joints thickened with gout and arthritis, the spine curved and vertebrae fused as discs shrank and were resorbed. His eyes were staring at her—they always did. First with the innocent curiosity of a young animal, then, though there was no rational thought and never would be now, with a visceral awareness and terror of what was happening to his body.

She reached out, touched the glassy surface of the tube; a gesture as ineffectual as anything else she could have done. She still couldn't help it, because she knew what was coming.

The eyes, blue and staring, turned milky with glaucoma, and like a child alone in the dark he began to sob, toothless gums bared, gnarled and shriveled hands groping the inside of the tube. It lasted a minute, two, three—too long, however long. Then the movements stilled, slowly, almost gently, and the ancient body died cell by cell. The amniotic fluid—Janet had no idea what else to call it—inside the tube darkened to purple as its molecular structure and properties changed and it began to break down dead flesh and bone into their component proteins.

It will feed those worthy of survival.

It made sense.

The thought had come unbidden, and Janet tried to push it away, knowing it wasn't hers, couldn't be hers. But the others had to survive. Survival was important. Survival meant lives saved. She was a doctor. She saved lives. She was saving lives.

Very good. You are beginning to understand. I am proud of you.

She could feel it. It felt warm, soothing, soft like a down blanket, and it somehow eased the terrible coldness of the lab. The need to hang on to the feeling became overwhelming. That and saving lives. No time to lose. She moved on to the next tube, found the crystal that would trigger the aging process, pushed it deep into its socket.

The clone inside the tube began to alter, decaying before her eyes, silently and rapidly. All of a sudden she was trapped in a flutter of a memory. She'd seen this before. The face in front of her was overlaid by another, familiar somehow. The process then had been slower, not as efficient, and it had enabled her to win that race against time.

She'd found out how this worked. Or something very much like it. Nanites?

Somewhere inside her mind Nirrti gave a chuckle of surprise, and the sensation was pleasant. She also sensed something else, swirling red and violent and entirely unashamed of its greed. Nirrti wanted him. The other one. The one familiar, the one who hadn't died.

It seems I am indebted to you. It would have been such a waste, and I have plans for him.

"It was none of my merit. The process was flawed." There was something else, Janet recalled. Someone else. Someone who'd helped. But she didn't mention it. If she did, the glow of pleasure surrounding her might diminish and she couldn't bear that. It was too cold to risk that little bit of warmth.

Luckily, Nirrti didn't seem to have noticed, still preoccupied with the revelation. A wave of scorn trawled through Janet's awareness.

The process was flawed indeed. Pelops was a fool who accepted boundaries without testing them. His method took a hundred days to induce death of old age, and he was happy with it. I can gestate life in hours, destroy it in minutes.

"You are a goddess, Lady Nirrti." Janet hadn't meant to say it, but in retrospect there didn't seem to be a reason why she shouldn't. It was true, after all, wasn't it?

Laughter flooded her mind, not the mocking onslaught she had learned to dread but a more intense burst of the delight she'd sensed earlier. Then it gradually ebbed and flattened, until Janet was alone again. Alone but not unobserved. She knew that now. The goddess was all-seeing.

Another tube, another crystal activated, another clone shriveled and died. Gestate life in hours, destroy it in minutes. Janet smiled. She was aiding the goddess.

From far down the endless row of tubes came the dry scrape of a door sliding open. She ignored it, not permitting herself to be distracted. Footsteps approached, halting and diffident, and finally slowed to a stop behind her. When she turned at last, she found herself facing the… What was he? Father, brother, *alter ego*—all of the above—to the things she was ordered to obliterate?

It appeared to perturb him. Pale as death, he watched himself wizen until he was ancient beyond recognition and incapable of sustaining life. In a flash she understood that this was the fate that awaited those who displeased Lady Nirrti; they died a hundred deaths.

The freezing air in the lab became more tangible again and seeped into Janet's bones. Shivering, she crossed her arms, hugged herself. "What do you want?" she asked, if only so as not to think the unthinkable any longer.

"Lady Nirrti wishes to see you," he hissed, his voice harsh with a hatred that begged for punishment.

"Will you take me to her? I don't know where she is."

"The Jaffa"—the word dripped boundless rancor—"waiting by the door will take you." His gaze rose at last, edged to the nearest tube and its contents, arrested there. "According to her I'm the one who has made them deficient, so I've been ordered to finish this task."

The giggle broke free without her volition, but she made no attempt to stifle it. The irony of the punishment was sublime, biblical even. *And if thy right eye offend thee, pluck it out.* The offender commanded to eradicate himself.

She giggled again, turned, and quickly walked along now empty tubes and toward the door. The instant it slid open, she was wrapped in deliciously warm, moist air. As promised, two Jaffa were waiting for her, the same clones she had found so abhorrent earlier. She couldn't remember why now. They were quite beautiful, tall and broad-shouldered and dark-haired, with deep green eyes. Lady Nirrti was right. You couldn't have too many of a good thing. Janet burst out laughing.

Tentatively at first, then more boldly, she stroked the chest of one of the men and suddenly realized that she had been too wrapped up in work and caring for her daughter to—

She had no daughter. She'd never had a daughter. She'd stolen an alien child, the rightful property of Lady Nirrti, and had withheld that child and— A sequence of images flashed through her mind, one more vile than the other, until her whole body tingled with shame. The cold seemed to creep back, and she grasped that it had nothing to do with the temperatures in the lab. It was inside of her, a legacy of her transgression.

Trying to control a shudder, she nodded at the Jaffa. "Let's go.

Lady Nirrti is waiting."

They led her down into the vault. From there, the ring transporter took her to the roof of the building; a terrace high above the jungle. Below stretched an endless sea of green, bleeding into a scarlet sky. A huge sun was setting, cupping half the horizon, and now and again brilliantly colored birds burst from the canopy as if to take one last look before dusk fell.

"Pretty, is it not?"

Janet spun around, again aware of the icy lump of guilt within her. She dropped to her knees. "Lady Nirrti, I—"

"Quiet." Under a red and gold sunshade fluttering gently in the breeze stood the goddess, looking at her sternly but not unkindly. Willing to forgive? "You wish for my forgiveness, yes? You wish to prove yourself to me?"

"Yes, Lady Nirrti. I beg you." Janet was shaking with cold, felt tears streaming down her face. "Please," she whispered.

The goddess moved toward her, touched her shoulder. Under the heat of Lady Nirrti's touch, the ice began to melt at last. Radiant warmth spread from her hands, burning and soothing at once. "Rise, child. What is your name?"

"I have no name, mistress. You haven't seen fit to bestow one on me yet." The answer pleased the goddess; she could tell from the warmth leaking into her, and she rose toward its source like a flower toward the sun.

A delicate hand, framed by a ribbon device, cupped her face. "I shall name you." Lady Nirrti smiled. "You shall be called Mrityu, my daughter."

She rolled the sounds through her mouth and mind and decided they tasted good. Strong. "Thank you, mistress," whispered Mrityu. "But I still wish to prove myself to you."

"You shall. Oh, you shall." Lady Nirrti's laughter danced on the evening air like sparks of light and sunshine. "Come with me. I will show you your task." The goddess led the way under the sunshade, casually flicking a hand at the mounds of silk-covered cushions strewn across the stone floor. "Sit."

Despite the invitation, it struck Mrityu as disrespectful to seek her own comfort before the goddess was seated. So she waited until Lady

Nirrti had settled on a pillow and only then sat down herself. "Please show me, mistress."

A recess in the floor released a dull gray orb, which slowly ascended until it hovered at Mrityu's eyelevel. She recognized the device; a communication globe. The grayness under its surface began to boil and swirled apart on the image of two people, a man and a woman. The woman was injured, and the man was attending to her.

"Do you remember them?" asked the goddess.

Somewhere beneath the warm mists that filled Mrityu's mind a memory stirred, faint and shapeless. "I do… I think."

"Good. You are to bring them to me."

CHAPTER TWELVE

Character Displacement: Artificial divergence of characters in related species whose territories overlap.

If you thought about it, the method of lighting was ingenious, not to mention environmentally friendly. Nothing necessarily new—archeologists had hit upon the same trick sometime in the late eighteen hundreds—but this had to be older by several centuries, perhaps millennia. While his fingertips stroked the shiny silver disk, Dr. Jackson studiously avoided actually looking into it. His reflection was a bit of a shocker right now. Besides, the principle of the thing was far more interesting. There were dozens and dozens of these mirrors mounted in strategic places and refracting the surface light all throughout the maze beneath the ruins.

"Daniel!"

He whirled around, blinking into the gloom behind him. It'd been growing steadily dimmer for a while now, which meant that it had to be late afternoon at least, perhaps evening already. They'd left the wardroom two hours ago, and he'd been on point ever since—a classic case of the blind leading the maimed. Or, as Jack had put it, Daniel might not be able to see where he the hell was going, but at least he could run there if necessary.

At the end of the corridor, two blurry figures emerged from the shadows; Jack all but carrying Sam, and never mind that it had to be murder on his ribs. "Daniel!" he called again. "Wait up!"

"I can go faster, sir," Sam chimed in immediately.

"I don't recall anybody asking your opinion, Carter."

"Sorry, sir."

Daniel could hear the forced cheeriness in her voice, didn't like it. She was holding on too hard, wasting strength she didn't have on reassuring him, herself, and first and foremost Jack. Who, by Daniel's estimate, was about nine tenths along the way of blaming himself for the entropy of the known universe.

At least he'd agreed to scrapping Plan A, which had been Jack going off on his own to find a sarcophagus that might not even exist or, if it did exist, might be on the other side of this godforsaken planet, while Daniel and Sam sat tight in the wardroom. The prospect of getting killed and/or eaten in the process hadn't seemed to deter him—there was a surprise!—but what had clinched the argument in the end was the question of whether Sam would still be mobile if he had to come all the way back and *then* take her to wherever that hypothetical sarcophagus lived.

"Any sign of the exit yet?" he asked when they caught up.

"Can't be far now. Up there." Daniel jerked his chin at a flight of stairs twenty yards down the corridor. "We're definitely on or near the upper levels. See how the halls are wider and more ornate? A floor down they didn't have those wooden pillars either, so—"

"Daniel."

"Sorry."

"Just… just get us to where we're going, okay?"

Daniel bit back the obvious reply; namely that he didn't have a clue *where* they were going. Or that the odds of his spotting an inscription saying *Sarcophagus This Way* with a little arrow underneath were negligible. Instead he simply nodded, turned around, and headed for the stairs, trying not to feel like Gandalf in the Mines of Moria. Everyone knew how that story went; Gandalf, consumed by a fire demon, ascends to a higher plane of existence. Not just yet, thanks all the same.

Halfway up Daniel realized that the quality of the light had changed to something more… immediate, for want of a better word. And it was brighter, not by much but enough to be noticeable. Instinct and habit made him want to run up the steps. He curbed the impulse and checked his six.

"Keep moving! We're okay."

Jack's definition of *okay* had to be the most elastic of any word in the history of linguistics, but now probably wasn't the time to discuss it. Daniel kept moving, as ordered. About to crest the top of the steps he slowed, listening past the soft shuffles and gasps on the stairwell behind him. It was quiet, no voices, no noises of any kind. Suddenly something brushed his face. He recoiled, winced in embarrassment a second later. A draft. Seemed his nerves were stretched a little more taut than he liked to admit.

The draft picked up, turned into a breeze, warm and heavy with the scent of flowers. He inched out into a vast room. Like everywhere else, it was decaying; wooden carvings rotting in humid air, friezes suffocating under lichen and creepers, masonry crumbling and inviting in its own destruction. Still, you could tell that the room—maybe a covered market—would have been grand once. And in one respect it was very different from the endless succession of chambers they'd passed since leaving the wardroom.

"Looks like a parking lot," offered Jack, lifting Sam over the last couple of steps. "Where do I pay?"

"At the exit." Pointing across the room, Daniel grinned.

One wall was missing, replaced by a row of wooden pillars. Between them, sunlight splashed onto marble tiles, painting the floor a deep red. Past the pillars, grass and foliage and the gray frontage of the buildings opposite.

"Cool. Now where?" Jack asked.

Daniel gave a small shrug. "If they built this along the same lines as the temples in Angkor, the center of the complex is right at the top of the mountain. So we keep going up."

"Fine."

"Sir, this is pointless," Sam murmured, eyes closed, propped up between that staff weapon and Jack's arm around her waist. All pretense at reassurance gone, she sounded like she didn't care anymore. Like it didn't matter anymore. "You can't—"

"You're tired, Carter." Jack didn't look at her when he said it. "We'll check what's up the road there and then take a break."

His tone, as falsely upbeat as Sam's had been earlier, precluded any argument. Daniel took it as a command to move out, started walking again, through the market hall and out into the open.

It was more than a temple precinct, he thought, desperate for something, anything, to distract himself. This had been a city once. The so-called road was a narrow stretch of lawn lined with statues, and it branched out into numerous smaller side streets. The roofs peaked into a myriad spires and pagodas, and above them rose the canopy of the forest and a lavender evening sky. Birdcalls here and there, and an overwhelming sensation of peace he'd known to be deceptive ever since he and Jack had discovered the mangled corpse on the temple wall. Still, it would do for now. There even was the far-off whisper of a waterfall, just to up the Zen factor.

As they drew closer to the massive structure at the top of the grass road, the whisper gradually turned into splashing. The road funneled into what might have been an audience hall. Soaring ceilings, tall columns, more statues, and at the far end some kind of dais that would have held an altar or throne. Opposite the dais, pink light streamed in through an archway screened by a cascade of water. Daniel had found his waterfall.

"Might as well rest here," Jack announced and steered Sam over into a corner that would cover their backs while still allowing a clear view of almost the entire room. Once there, he carefully eased her to the ground and nodded at the staff weapon. "Mind if I borrow this, just in case? I'm gonna go find some fire wood. Your teeth are rattling."

"Sir—"

"Thanks, Carter." He picked up the staff and rose. "Daniel, stay with her. If I'm not back in thirty, clear out and find that goddamn sarcophagus."

Daniel watched him disappear among the pillars and turned to Sam. She was beyond pale, and fever and exhaustion had punched olive smudges under eyes that looked too big for her face. "On a scale of one to ten, how bad is it?"

"Twelve point three," she rasped, tried to shift to a position that didn't hurt and eventually gave up. "You've got to talk to him, Daniel."

"*I've* got to talk to him? What makes you think he'll listen? He hasn't listened to you, has he?" Daniel squatted and offered Sam his canteen. She took it, drank greedily, handed it back.

"Thanks. And no, he hasn't. Last time I tried, he started talking about hockey and some highly involved maneuver he called a *fishhook*. I lost track after the third preparatory pass."

It coaxed a chuckle from Daniel. "I can explain it to you if you're interested. Side-effect of watching one too many hockey games with Jack." His amusement faded, as if evaporating in the jungle heat.

"Right now he's about as amenable to reason as Colonel Kurtz. Actually, I don't think I've ever seen him like this."

"I have," Sam said quietly.

Daniel shot her a sharp look. He couldn't be sure because he hadn't been there, but he could guess, and he suddenly understood the origins of his own certainty that he wouldn't die out here as long as Jack was around. Jack would flatly refuse to *let* him die. Of course, there were limits even to Jack's powers of refusal. Right now Daniel was staring at one of them.

Sam had unwrapped the bandage to reveal a wound looking twice as bad as it had a few hours ago. Around the edges blisters had formed, filled with brownish fluid, and she inspected them, sick fascination on her face. "I guess that clinches it," she muttered, one finger carefully pressing down on the swollen tissue. Gas escaped, crackling softly, and she flinched. "Think he'd listen to that?"

With sudden determination, she angled for her backpack, fished out the medikit, removed an ampoule of morphine and a syringe.

"Sam, what are you doing?"

By ways of an answer, she snapped the top off the ampoule, dipped in the needle, pulled back the plunger, popped the cap back over the needle and dropped the syringe in her lap. Then she fumbled for her belt, dragged it from the loops, and cinched it around her thigh.

Finally, she gazed up at him. "I could do with a hand, Daniel. For starters, that tourniquet's nowhere near tight enough."

The sudden lump in his throat got in the way of replying. Of course she was right. Thirty seconds ago he'd have said it was the only sensible thing to do. But being faced with it somehow put a different complexion on the issue. He could hear the wails of a child on Abydos, and his stomach flipped. "Sam, are you absolutely sure?" he croaked. All of a sudden Jack's crazy notion of looking for a sarcophagus seemed entirely logical. "What if... What about your career?"

God, Jackson! You're really clutching at straws, aren't you?

"Medical separation. Are you going to help me or what?" She cocked her head, studied him for a moment. "Look, Daniel, I know this isn't fair. But I don't want the Colonel to have to do it."

Which, fair or not, precisely coincided with Daniel's own sentiments. He took a deep breath, willed his hands to stop shaking.

"Okay. Where's your knife?"

"Sorry, Mr. Conrad." Outside the ambulance, the detective apologized for the tenth time. Next the obsequious creep would offer to lick Conrad's boots. "We, uh... There were rumors that you'd, uh, passed away, sir."

"Do I look like a ghost to you, detective?" Conrad laughed, a perfect mock-up of the real item, and slapped the man's shoulder for emphasis.

"No, sir." Dutifully, the detective chortled. Then he slid another withering glare at the two beat cops who'd been summoned to the scene by a neighbor with acute hearing and had proceeded to arrest Simmons and his pet Goa'uld.

Simmons devoutly hoped that the pair would end up directing traffic for the rest of their natural lives. He shifted on the gurney, just as the paramedic inserted a probe into the wound canal. "Ow! Goddammit, watch what you're doing!"

"Sorry, sir." Blushing, the woman steadied his arm. "The lidocaine should be working by now. I can give you another shot, but you really ought to let us take you to the ER."

"No! I haven't got time for that. Just get the hell on with it."

The only glimmer of satisfaction Simmons could wring from the situation was the fact that Maybourne, son of a bitch that he was, had managed a clean shot. The bullet had gone in and out, missing the bone, and CSI had found the damn thing embedded in the tunnel wall. What they hadn't found, thankfully, was his own Glock. The gun might have detracted a little from the surprisingly convincing tale Conrad had spun to the police.

Speaking of... Through the open doors of the ambulance, Simmons had been able to admire the red and blue lightshow the police cruisers projected onto the façade of St. Christina's. Now the detective's stocky shape interposed itself between him and the vista.

"You alright, sir?" The detective, clearly one of Seattle's finest, screwed on a solicitous face.

"I got shot in the arm! How do you think I am?"

"Uh, sir?" The man climbed aboard. "Mr. Conrad has cleared up the, uh, misunderstanding and filled us in on what happened, but I'll need a statement from you, too, sir."

"Fine. Whatever." Just as long as it took his mind off the paramedic's clumsy ministrations. A flash from somewhere beyond the police cordon exploded in his eyes, and Simmons swore. His portrait plastered all over the six o'clock news was the last thing he needed. At least they hadn't spotted Conrad. Yet. "For God's sake, get those vultures out of here! Now!"

At the detective's nod a bunch of his minions descended on the representatives of the media and drove them from sight and earshot. "Alright then." He perched on the gurney opposite. "So you're Mr. Simmons. Mr. Frank Simmons?"

"Colonel."

"Sorry, sir?"

"Colonel Frank Simmons. And no, I'm not in uniform, but then I don't usually wear it to bed either."

"Ah. Sorry. And your employer is…?

"A government agency."

The detective was starting to look pleasantly pained. "Which agency would that be, sir? There were a few dozen of them last time I checked."

"That's classified."

"Excuse me?"

"What I do and who I work for is classified, Detective. Can we leave it at that?"

"For now, sir." Head bent, the man scribbled something on his notepad. The overhead light illuminated flakes of dandruff sprinkled over greased-back black hair. "So, tell me, Colonel. What were you doing in the old hospital?"

"Mr. Conrad was giving me a tour of the premises. You do realize that the hospital is his property?"

"Yeah, we know that. Still doesn't explain what you were doing there, sir. Not at that time of the night and in the basement of all places." Apparently Mr. Detective was smarter than he looked.

Fine. Simmons made a show of waving away the paramedic who'd just put the finishing touches to the bandage around his arm. Then he sat up and leaned forward until his face was inches from the policeman's and he could smell breath laced with coffee, donuts, and pepperoni pizza. "Detective," he whispered. "I'm not supposed to divulge this to you or anybody else, but in the interest of clearing up this matter I'm willing to reveal certain information that is highly classified. Can I trust you to keep this information to yourself?"

The detective returned a slow, bovine stare and finally nodded.

"Mr. Conrad's company is carrying out some research and development for the Pentagon. Part of this research is being conducted at St. Christina's Hospital."

"In the basement?"

"Mr. Conrad was showing me the ventilation system that serves two of the laboratories. And that's all I can tell you I'm afraid."

This time it seemed to have worked. No more probing in that direction. Instead the detective scratched an old pockmark on his cheek and said, "Fair enough. But see, it still doesn't add up, Colonel. Mr. Conrad thinks the two men who attacked you in the basement were addicts looking for prescription drugs. Now, if I were in those guys' shoes, the basement'd be the last place I look."

Simmons gathered his injured arm and placed the hand in his lap. Hopefully the local anesthetic would wear off soon. He'd rather deal with the pain than with a limb that felt dead like a prosthesis and wouldn't move unless he manipulated it. Pushing aside his discomfort, he dredged up a smile, finely judged, midway between understanding and condescension. "Look, Detective, don't get me wrong. I have the highest respect for Mr. Conrad. In his field he's a genius, no doubt about it. However, he's also a recluse. Which means that he can be a little naïve when it comes to the kind of thing you and I deal with on a daily basis. Those men weren't junkies. For starters they were well outside the usual age bracket." Simmons blew out a breath for effect. "I also recognized one of them."

"Come again?" The detective snapped upright on the gurney, all but shivering with excitement.

"The man who shot me is a former colonel in the US Air Force, convicted on high treason and espionage charges. About two years ago he managed to escape from Leavenworth. His name is Harry Maybourne, but he also goes by Charles Bliss and a string of other aliases. Odds are he was trying to find out about the research Conrad is doing for us."

"What about the other one?"

"Never seen him before, but you may safely assume that he's no choirboy. Somebody like Maybourne doesn't waste his time with amateurs."

"Yeah. Reckon you're right on that one, sir. We'll send out an APB."

"Well, if there's nothing else…" Simmons's tone left no doubt that there was to be nothing else. He eased himself off the gurney, grateful to find that standing up posed less of a problem than he'd imagined.

Pocketing his notebook and other paraphernalia, the detective got up too. "I'll get a car to take you and Mr. Conrad wherever you're going."

"That will not be necessary. I have a driver on standby." The voice sounded relaxed and came from the rear of the ambulance. Conrad stood leaning against the door, one hand extended. "Here, Colonel. Let me help you."

The Goa'uld grabbed Simmons's left biceps, harder than necessary and smiling in the knowledge that there would be no protest in front of witnesses. He was playing mind games again. Driven by a brief surge of panic, Simmons meant to reach for the remote that controlled the naquadah collar, then it dawned on him that he was defenseless. The remote was in his right pocket, to be activated by a right arm that currently dangled from his shoulder like a lump of cold flesh.

Conrad's smile broadened. "Mind your step," he said, guiding Simmons down from the ambulance. "Do not worry, we shall not have to go far. The vehicle is waiting at the next corner."

One piece of good news. Simmons's NID agents had had the smarts to clear out and wait on the sidelines as soon as they'd heard the police sirens. The only ones to get caught had been he and Conrad, who'd come to look for him in the basement.

Simmons and his escort passed the police cordon. As soon as they were out of earshot, he yanked his arm free. "Don't ever dare to touch me again!"

In the red light strobing from the cruisers, Conrad's face looked truly alien. "As you wish," he whispered, still smiling.

"And you'd better remember it!" Simmons headed for the SUV

at the corner, forcing himself not to run. Behind him he could hear Conrad's footfalls, their steadiness seeming to mock him.

As he approached the car, one of the agents got out and opened the passenger door. "You okay, Colonel?"

"I'll survive." Cradling his arm, Simmons sidled into the seat. "Phone our hacker back in DC. Seattle PD are bound to find Hammond's fingerprints somewhere in that barn." He jerked his chin at the hospital. "When they run the prints through AFIS, I want them to get back Hammond's picture and vital stats together with the record of a likely heavy."

"Yessir."

Conrad had arrived and was folding his tall frame onto the rear bench. Simmons resisted the urge to turn around to keep an eye on him. Instead he squinted at the agent. "Actually, let's get them the record of a cop killer. Increases the chances of some state trooper doing us a favor and shooting Hammond on sight."

The man grinned, closed the door, and climbed into the rear. Simmons could hear the soft beep of his cell phone keys. He had perfect pitch, could tell the number just by listening to the sounds: 555-377-8008.

"Where're we going, sir?" asked the driver.

"Cheyenne Mountain. Hammond and Maybourne are bound to try and run home to momma. In the unlikely event that they get there, I want to make sure we've got a welcoming committee in place."

Indigo shadows crawled in, claustrophobic like cobwebs on your face, and Jack turned full circle, surrounded by stone walls, teeming plant-life, smirking statues. God, he hated those things! Couldn't really say why. Maybe he just hated them for the sake of hating *something*. Shivering, Jack let out a deep breath. This place was getting to him, was all. Too damn quiet for starters. And who was mowing the lawn, anyway?

The grass under his boots was short, evenly clipped, and the odds of the groundkeeper driving a John Deere through here on a regular basis struck him as slim. He remembered, ages ago, reading some science fiction novel where lawn care was handled by tall green things with mouths in their paws. They jumped real well, and when they weren't grazing they sucked unsuspecting tourists dry. Not a good thought.

On the upside and going by the pristine state of the turf, those monster hogs Carter had mentioned probably didn't come to play in this particular circle of hell. Jack checked his watch. Twenty minutes left. He'd better find that firewood. Ahead was an archway, muffled by shadows. Either side of it, more statues, peering from the gloom with a greediness that made him squirm and broadcasted a recommendation to stay out. Yeah, well. Maybe next time. Ignoring the faces, the stares, he moved through the archway into some kind of temple.

The darkness drooping beneath the vaulted ceiling seemed rancid, ancient, as if it'd been hanging there since the day this bastard of a planet had congealed from primordial soup to whatever it purported to be now. Evening twilight trickled through a high, narrow window, lifting charcoal to medium gray and outlining an array of wooden screens, not unlike the kind you'd find in an old Catholic church. Except for the artwork, of course. That was about as far removed from Catholic statuary as you could get. And the sense of being watched hadn't lessened. On the contrary. It was almost physical, stroked his neck, his back, a congregation of popsicle millipedes boogieing up and down his spine.

Pulse thudding in his throat, he did another slow three-sixty, staff weapon raised and primed this time. Nothing. But the creepy sensation of being touched by a ghost had ceased. For now. Jack struggled to control his breathing and slipped between two screens, in the hopes of finding something wooden and portable back there. Zip. Not even a chair. Carter was dying, and all they had on offer were goddamn screens and prying eyes!

Fury, blinding and irrational, sloshed over him in a red-hot wave. He smashed the staff into a screen, sent splinters flying, threw the weapon after them. The *Rakshasas* again, Fear, Terror, and Death, and that was just fine by him; he'd take them apart chip by chip and with his bare hands if he had to, punch holes in their grinning faces. His fists crashed into the panel, leaving smears of blood, kept pounding regardless, needing the pain to numb a different kind of agony, again and again and—

"Don't move!" Though cold beyond freezing the voice sounded vaguely familiar.

Notwithstanding, hanging around for the reunion didn't seem advisable. Adrenaline still fizzing through his body, Jack dropped, rolled under a screen just ahead of the track of bullets that hammered dust and stone flakes from the floor. Damn! So he'd felt watched for a reason. Another round tore through the screen, whisked past his head. Slugs, not energy bolts. The shooter—a woman, incidentally—probably wasn't Jaffa, but she had X-ray vision anyway. The next round was half an inch closer.

You're a shrub, O'Neill! What the hell made you think this was a safe place to throw a tantrum?

His opponent was on the move, slowly edging her way around the wooden partition. Butted up against another screen four meters away lay his staff weapon, and the lighting or absence thereof would work to his advantage. Maybe. Disregarding the protests from assorted parts of his anatomy, Jack burst from cover, dived for the staff weapon—with catlike grace, he would have liked to think, though reality was more along the lines of a startled bullfrog—grabbed it, brought it up rolling onto his back, and fired. Some pals of Fear, Terror, and Death flew apart in a shower of shards and smoke, and then a shadowy figure gradually straightened up behind what was left of the screen. Along the handle of the weapon Jack was staring at the shell-shocked face of Dr. Janet Fraiser.

"Colonel O'Neill! What in God's name are you doing here?"

"For cryin' out loud! What is this? The local feminist association trying to eradicate me? First Carter and now you!"

"Sam? You've found Sam?"

"Let's just say she found me. Mind pointing that gun someplace else? If it goes off now, it'll take out equipment I'd hate to lose."

"I'm sorry, Colonel. I'm so sorry." Hands trembling, Fraiser lowered her weapon. She had a nasty gash on the side of her head and a starved look about her, but otherwise she seemed to be in full working order. Thank God for that. "I could have—"

"Save it." Oscillating between irritation and giddy relief, Jack skipped the sideways shuffle and heave that would have allowed him to get to his feet relatively pain-free and hauled himself up the staff weapon instead.

She watched his performance with an air of solemn curiosity and stated, "You're injured."

"Yeah. Must have forgotten to read the health warning on the label before I let myself be dumped in this place. Where's Teal'c?"

An odd flicker of uncertainty and something else—indefinably wrong—raced through her eyes. It could be shock, grief, the twilight in this ghost train of a room, any of a hundred things, including Jack's own paranoia. "We were separated. I've spent days searching, but…" She gave a small shrug and nodded at the jungle vista outside the window, now rapidly changing from green to black.

"Crap," Jack muttered softly. Then again, it probably would have been too much to hope for to get back Fraiser *and* Teal'c in one handy package and, admittedly, he was worried a little less about the big guy than he had been about the doc. "It's alright. We'll find him. Meanwhile, you ready to make a house call?"

Shaking off whatever it was that had rooted her in place, she picked her way through the wreckage. "What did you do now?"

"Not me! Carter. Here, take as much of this stuff as you can carry." He gathered some chunks of wood, piled them into her arms.

Over bits of splintered screen, she gazed at him wide-eyed. "Sam? What's wrong with her? Where is she?"

"I left her and Daniel in some lobby with a waterfall. Very feng shui."

"I've been there. Reminded me of *The King and I*. What about Sam, sir?"

"She isn't doing so good." He picked up some more shards, stacked them atop the pile she was holding.

"Colonel?" Okay, that was more like Fraiser, complete with her best *Don't hold out on me or it'll hurt* look.

"It's gangrene, Doc."

Fraiser damn near dropped the wood. "You're sure, sir?"

"Positive." That impotent rage threatened to surge back, and he put a boot through what was left of the screen, scooped up the fragments, grabbed the staff weapon. "Let's go."

Outside a lilac moon had begun to crawl over the treetops, casting dishwater light on forest and buildings and flattening perspectives until the statues looked like old black-and-white photographs. Fraiser headed for a narrow alley between two buildings. It was pitch-dark but seemed to have the advantage of being statue-free.

"Hey, Doc? Where're you going?"

"It's a shortcut." Sensing his hesitation, she stopped and turned. The moonlight made her face appear bloodless. "I've been spending nights here ever since I lost Teal'c, sir. I know my way around."

"Fair enough. Lead on."

He followed her through oppressive silence. The grass swallowed any sound of their footfalls, and the only noises, barely audible, were Fraiser's soft breaths and his own and, faintly, the splashing of the waterfall. It quickly grew louder, and when Janet led him from another alley out onto a broader thoroughfare, he could make out the pillared front of the hall.

Somewhere behind the pillars hovered a dull gleam of brightness. Probably a flashlight, probably a lousy idea, and both Carter and Daniel ought to know better, but he was grateful to see it. Picking up his pace, he half-ran past Fraiser, past the outer line of columns, and across the hall.

"Hey, kids! Look who—"

Stopping hadn't been a conscious decision. It'd been more like slamming into a wall. Daniel knelt by the prone figure on the ground, diving knife in hand—had to be Carter's, Jack thought absently—and looked up at him with an odd mix of anguish and pity in his eyes. A tourniquet around Carter's leg, on the floor a discarded syringe, empty, glinting in the beam of the flashlight.

"Daniel?" Jack's voice sounded alien, even to him.

"We can't wait any longer," said Daniel, visibly bracing for an argument, a hint of accusation in his tone. "I just wish you'd— You're early. The morphine took a while to kick in."

"Yeah." There would be no argument. Because there was no sarcophagus, was there? There never would be. Half tempted to turn and see if the fight draining from him had left a trail, Jack inched closer.

Carter was gazing at him with a doe-eyed alertness belied by the pin-prick pupils. "'s okay, sir," she slurred. "Won't hurt a bit."

Let her believe that. But Daniel was right. It had to happen now. Unable to look away from the hellish mess that was Carter's injury,

Jack crouched. "Need a hand?"

Surprise or misery or both nudged Daniel into a shudder. "Fire would be good," he murmured. "Hot water. Sam's got cooking gear in her pack, so—"

"How about you let me check her out first?" said an indignant voice behind them.

Daniel's head snapped up, and he blinked into the direction of the speaker. "Janet? My God, where—"

"Let's save the welcome home party for later." With a brusqueness out of character for her, Fraiser shouldered Daniel aside, squatted next to Carter, and nodded at the flashlight sitting on the floor. "Somebody hold this for me."

"Sure." Sounding a little uncertain, Daniel picked up the light. "Like this?"

"Higher! And more of an angle! I can't see a thing. Yeah, that'll do." Seconds dragged into minutes dragged into an eternity filled with Carter's soft moans as the doctor probed the wound. Eventually Fraiser glanced up and straight at Jack. "Why did you wait this long? I can try, but whatever I do, I doubt she'll make it."

Daniel flinched, stung. "For God's sake, Doc, *she* can hear you!"

Ignoring him, Fraiser kept staring at Jack, her eyes near-black and utterly cold. "If she dies, you're to blame."

"I know." He wasn't quite sure how he'd managed to talk around the swirl of nausea rising in his throat. Nausea and an overwhelming sense of wrongness.

The flashlight jerked, then clattered to the floor, its beam briefly shooting upward as it flipped. Mercifully, Fraiser's eyes sank into shadow. Daniel had grabbed her shoulders and shook her roughly. "What the hell is the matter with you? Jack's no more to blame than—"

"Daniel!" Jack struggled to school his expression into something between neutral and dead. "This isn't helping. Let her go."

A hint of bewilderment and panic flashed across Fraiser's face, and she came to her feet, avoiding anyone's gaze now. "I'm sorry, Colonel. That was out of line. She… Sam is a friend." For a moment she seemed to listen inward, then said, "I can't do much here. Bring her to where I'm staying. It's safer, and I've got a small surgical kit in my pack. I'll need it."

Wordlessly Daniel made to pick up Carter. With a swift pat to the back, Jack stopped him. "I'll carry her."

Daniel acknowledged it with a nod, moved aside. "Jack?"

"I can handle it." Barely, but that wasn't what Daniel's question had been about anyway. His knees vigorously disagreed with the undertaking, and he found out the hard way why Fraiser had advised against heavy lifting when she'd first examined his ribs—a lifetime ago. Though Carter wasn't heavy. Not exactly huge to start with, she'd lost a dramatic amount of weight.

Now, dopey from the morphine, she nestled her head against his shoulder, smiled at him, and muttered, "Nice."

"We aim to please, Major." He tried to smile back, didn't quite make it. His gaze settled on Fraiser, who was watching them with the look of a scientist studying a pair of lab rats. "Which way?"

CHAPTER THIRTEEN

"But the others did get back. So there has to be a way off this planet," Corporal Wilkins said for the eighteenth time since their encounter, and he was sounding anxious. "If it's all the same to you, sir, I don't wanna end up like Gonzo, poor bastard."

'Gonzo' was the man whose body they had discovered at some distance from the Stargate, hanging off a lintel in the perimeter wall. The corporal had served with him, and he had insisted on cutting down the flyblown corpse of Private Joe Gonzales. The beasts had inflicted terrible injuries, but Private Gonzales had died from a single shot to his head. Someone had possessed the mercy to spare him further suffering.

Once they had buried him, they had continued in a south-easterly direction. Just after nightfall they had come upon a ruined guardhouse and set up camp for the night. Approximately two hundred meters further on, across open terrain, was a large gate in the city walls, now swallowed by shadows. Had they arrived earlier, Teal'c might have proceeded inside, although some indefinable instinct warned him against any such foray. However, instincts or no, tomorrow at first light they would have to explore what lay beyond the gate.

"I was wrong. We should have gone looking for White, Lambert, and Ryder."

The corporal was referring to the soldiers who had arrived with him. His petulance was beginning to tax Teal'c's patience. Or perhaps it was merely a combination of the relentless heat and humidity and the renewed silence of the forest. A nub of masonry was pressing against his still aching shoulder, and Teal'c noiselessly shifted his position, wishing he could afford the peace of *kelno'reem*. He had seated himself by the doorway, observing a jungle and ruins bathed in pale starlight. It imbued the world with a ghostlike quality, enhancing the now familiar sense of foreboding that had befallen him as soon as the silence settled over the trees once more.

From behind came a soft rustle. Corporal Wilkins had risen and crawled closer on all fours to peer out the door. "I gotta go find those clowns," he muttered and, with the next breath, "Got a stinking headache, though."

Unable to discern any smell and struggling to keep his tone civil, Teal'c replied, "I recommend you ingest appropriate medication and try to sleep. I shall wake you for your watch."

"Been popping aspirin for the past three hours, sir. It's a miracle if I've got any stomach lining left after this." More rustling. The corporal had retreated to the back of the room and was rummaging through his backpack. Then he returned, carrying his weapon. "Gotta go find them," he said again.

Teal'c grabbed a fistful of his sleeve. "Corporal Wilkins, we have discussed this repeatedly. It would not be wise for you to attempt a search. Not on your own, and especially not in darkness."

"Let go of me!" The corporal yanked his arm free and only barely seemed to curb the impulse to train his weapon on Teal'c. "I've got my orders, and you're not authorized to stop me. Sir!"

The address was made to sound like an insult, and Teal'c felt his blood boil. "What orders, *hasshak*?" he hissed. "Not long ago you were attempting to run back to M3D 335 like a frightened boy!"

The weapon snapped up, but Teal'c was faster. On his feet in the blink of an eye, one hand clamped around the barrel, he wrenched the submachine gun from the corporal and jabbed its stock into the man's midriff. For a moment Corporal Wilkins sagged back, winded, then he collected himself and was about to attack again.

A sound from outside, a stone accidentally loosened and kicked by a boot perhaps, penetrated the scrabbling noises of their fight.

"Quiet!" Teal'c barely breathed the command and his hand shot up in warning.

The corporal's training reasserted itself. Slowly and carefully, he recovered his submachine gun and moved in behind Teal'c who had retrieved his staff weapon. Directly south of them a dark shape oozed from the tree line like a thing spawned and bred in the jungle. Curled into a crouch, it approached the guardhouse, its silhouette broken up only by the black protrusion of the gun barrel. A Marine then, or perhaps—

The half-formed hope was smashed by a shot tearing through the window at the far end of the room. Corporal Wilkins cried out, and Teal'c whirled around. The flare from his staff weapon briefly illuminated a blackened human face. It dropped from sight in a shower of dust and crumbling masonry. The corporal had been hit, but not grievously. Sprawled on the ground he opened fire on the man approaching from the trees. None of the rounds struck its target. But it could only be a matter of time.

Teal'c did not feel the curious tingle that would have announced the presence of a Goa'uld symbiote. "Hold your fire!" he shouted. "We are friends!"

The answer was a barrage of shots from the window. Flattened against the doorjamb, he loosed another staff blast. This time there was a scream and the thuds of a body dropping limply behind the casement. Teal'c cursed softly, hoping the man was wounded rather than dead. Barring Dr. Fraiser's assault on him, this was the first instance of human aggression he had encountered, and it almost came as a relief. Because, unlike the other dangers on this planet, it was comprehensible and meant that questions might be answered—provided he could take at least one of the attackers alive. He needed information, and in his experience dead men spoke very little.

"No friends in this game, Mr. First Prime," the corporal snarled. "It's either them or us, so save the negotiations for when they're dead."

"I was not aware that this was a game," grunted Teal'c, keeping a close eye on the other hostile who had dropped in a patch of ferns and was almost invisible now. "We need to—"

The ferns twitched. Their movement provoked an extended burst from Corporal Wilkins's gun. Stalks and fronds ripped apart, and the man hiding in the clearing returned fire briefly, then leaped up and scurried toward the tree line. Without Teal'c's volition, the tip of his staff weapon swiveled after the fleeing figure, blossomed orange in the night, ready to unleash death. His fingers were tightening on the weapon's grip, nearing the pressure required to trigger the blast. He heard the bellow of blood in his ears and, faint but clear, a voice commanding him to kill lest he be the one killed.

"What are you waiting for?" Corporal Wilkins screamed. "Shoot him!"

With supreme effort Teal'c forced his hands to unclench and was rewarded by a sharp bolt of pain that ripped through his skull and scattered his confusion. Howling with fury, the corporal brought up his gun, fired. A reckless sprint spirited the attacker to the relative safety of the jungle. But there might be a second enemy yet hiding behind the guardhouse. Teal'c ran out the door and around the building, Corporal Wilkins in close pursuit.

The man was still there. Even in the pallid starlight his wounds seemed horrid, his face melted away by the staff blast. But he was alive and, though blind and undoubtedly in agony, he would not desist. Clutching a K-bar knife in his right, he had pushed himself to his knees and was listening intently for any sound that might betray his opponents' position.

Knowing that it was a half-truth at best and would be to no avail, Teal'c said, "Put down your weapon. We have no wish to kill you."

The knife slashed at Teal'c's leg, and only a jump back saved him from injury. The man opened what had been his mouth and emitted a gurgling noise. It could have meant anything; a plea for mercy or a pledge to fight to the death. Teal'c never found out. Corporal Wilkins had arrived, weapon raised, but before he could fire or Teal'c could intercede, the wounded soldier gave a keening wail. The knife slid from his fingers, and he fell forward, his whole body racked with spasms that gradually eased until he remained perfectly still.

Plagued by regret Teal'c crouched, reached for a neck slick with blood, hoping to find a pulse. He did not succeed. The man was dead, and perhaps it was kinder this way. About to remove one of the man's dog tags, Teal'c heard a soft metallic click and forced himself not to show any reaction. He had expected this.

"Sorry, Mr. First Prime," the corporal said. "Nothing personal."

"If it is not personal, what are your reasons?" Teal'c enquired calmly, his right hand furtively digging into a pile of rubble and mortar dust.

"No more than one winner in this game, Mr. First Prime. You're good, but you ain't good enough. Or maybe you are, but we're not gonna find out. 'Cos if you're dead you're not gonna be chosen."

Teal'c's fingers closed around a fistful of debris. "And only the best survive the challenge and are worthy to serve their god."

"That's right."

Starlight reflected in the corporal's eyes, making them seem drained of color, drained of soul. This latter notion, Teal'c believed, was none too far from the truth. He himself had survived a Jaffa training camp, survived the final selection. He had killed to survive. But not in cold blood. Not a warrior of his own team. So what was happening? He could not afford to think it through now. He had to act, else he would have mere seconds to live.

"I see," he said, allowing his left hand to slide along the grip of his staff weapon.

The movement was minute, but it was enough for Corporal Wilkins to notice and be distracted. His gaze shifted. "Don't even—"

Teal'c's right shot up, flinging a handful of dust and broken stone at the man's face. Corporal Wilkins cried out, controlled the reflex to claw at his eyes, fired, and missed. In throwing the rubble, Teal'c had dropped sideways. Now he bounded to his feet and was on the disoriented man in one leap. For the briefest of moments, he felt a craving to kill and attain the glory of selection. He forced it away, knowing it was not his own mind speaking to him, twisted the weapon from his opponent's hands, and knocked the corporal out cold.

Patting down Corporal Wilkins, he found a sidearm and a combat knife, which he pocketed. The sidearm he unsafed, taking a deep breath. His theory might be flawed, but putting it to test was the only option. The damage inflicted would be temporary after all. He placed the gun next to the corporal's ear and fired. Then he turned the man's head and repeated the process.

Roused by the noise and pain, Corporal Wilkins gave a yelp and his eyes snapped open. Wary of a renewed attack, Teal'c sat back on his haunches, watching his patient. The corporal blinked several times, awkwardly pushed himself to a sitting position, and squinted around in some confusion. Finally his gaze lighted on the dead soldier, and his eyes darkened with anguish. Teal'c knew then that both his suspicion and his treatment had been correct.

"Ryder!" the corporal croaked, evidently recognizing something other than the soldier's face. "Ryder. How—" It was then that he became aware of his deafness. Staring in panic, he fingered his ears, brought his hands away smeared with a trickle of blood. "What happened to me, sir?" He all but screamed.

"Do not be afraid," Teal'c said. "It will pass in time."

Hearing himself speak, he grasped that his method of curing the madness, while successful, had one fundamental flaw.

For the first time in days Sam Carter wasn't in pain or immediate fear for her life, and the morphine was trying to suck her into a blurry, wooly headspace. Maybe she should have taken the stuff from the start. Things really were a lot more pleasant this way. She refused to concede that this absurd sense of wellbeing had anything to do with her current mode of transport.

No way.

"Stop fidgeting, Carter," he muttered. "You're not helping."

"How about piggyback?" she offered and tried to straighten up.

"Major! If you don't keep still, I'll sling you over my shoulder, caveman-fashion, I swear!"

Worth thinking about. She'd have a nice view of his ass. And he did have a great ass. For a commanding officer. Sam giggled.

"For cryin' out loud!"

"You okay, Jack?" Soft and concerned, Daniel's voice came drifting through the halo of his flashlight.

"Yeah. Except Carter's contracted ADD on top of everything else."

The beam of the flashlight froze in place, allowing them to catch up. "Want me to carry her for a while?" asked Daniel.

No.

"No. I'm fine."

Thanks, sir. Not that Daniel doesn't have a cute butt, but—

"We need to keep moving." Janet, cold and impatient, not like Janet at all.

Sam remembered now. This was why she had to stay alert. "Something's wrong," she murmured.

"Everything's okay, Carter," the Colonel said immediately. "Doc's gonna look after you."

The way she'd done earlier? With cold hands, colder eyes, unaware or uncaring that she didn't heal but hurt? Not like Janet at all.

"No," Sam rasped.

He wasn't listening. "How much further?"

"About five minutes, tops," the Dr. Fraiser dybbuk replied, trying to sound soothing.

"You gave us the *five minutes* spiel half an hour ago," snapped Colonel O'Neill. "Mind telling me where we're going, Fraiser?"

Janet pointed up. Same walls, same statues, same treetops silhouetted against an indigo sky full of alien stars. The stars looked cool and clean, as far away from this planet as you could get, and Sam wanted to be there. Maybe it was she who was wrong, not Janet. Couldn't tell anything for sure, not with that goddamn drug in her system. Next time she'd do it the way people did in the movies — bite down on a leather strap.

They climbed an alley of stairs and the ruins below fell away into darkness. No animal calls, and it felt like the forest was brooding, hatching something. Whatever it was, you could bet your six that it wouldn't be good for either your health or your sanity. After all, just look at them. Her. Janet. And what about Teal'c? Where—

Tripping on a step, Colonel O'Neill nearly lost his balance. After that there was a distinct seesaw to his step. Sam looked up, saw his mouth compressed to a tight line, muscles in his jaw working.

"Sir, I could try to—"

"Don't say it, Carter," he gasped.

"Levitate?"

He barked a brief laugh. "You're high, but you're not that high, Major." Up ahead, the flashlight had stopped rising. "Keep going, Daniel!"

"Wouldn't know where. I'm at the top."

"Jacob's Ladder has an end?"

By the time they reached the paved plateau at the top of the stairs, Sam was still trying to figure out how her dad came into this and what he needed a ladder for. Daniel was waiting for them, caught on to the limp.

"Dammit, Jack—"

"Save it, Daniel. Where now?"

"It's through there, sir." Janet, hovering like a gloomy ghost.

Obediently Daniel's light illuminated *through there*. It was a passageway barely wide enough for two people to walk side by side.

Wreathed around the entrance was a trio of figures.

"Great," murmured the Colonel. "Fear, Terror, and Death."

"Bhaya, Mahabhaya, and Mrityu." Daniel yanked the flashlight away from the statues.

For the briefest of moments the beam brushed Janet's face and the inhuman anticipation written there. This wasn't right. Sam had known Janet Fraiser for five years, they were friends, close friends, and this wasn't Janet. This was a shell filled with something unspeakable.

"Don't go in there, sir," Sam whispered. "It's wrong. It's all wrong."

"What's wrong, Carter?" he asked back quietly. "Goa'uld?"

"No. No, not that." How was she going to explain? There was nothing she could put her finger on, and her brain wasn't working.

Janet edged closer, placed an icy hand on Sam's forehead. "Fever's spiking, Colonel. She's probably getting delirious. We can't afford to wait."

Perhaps it was true. This was Janet, after all. Carried into the building, Sam clung to that thought for dear life. It didn't help. Shadows threatened to smother her, and the wrongness exploded out of all proportion. She fought an impulse to curl up, claw Colonel O'Neill's shirt like a startled cat. Wouldn't do. Wouldn't do at all.

Sounds were reduced to boot falls that drowned out the patter of Janet's bare feet—how come she was barefoot?—and the steady plinking of condensation from the walls and ceiling. The gleam of Daniel's lamp ghosted ahead over moss-coated masonry, until it tumbled out into a chamber and refracted into dazzling brightness. All around the room gilt friezes flickered to life as the beam of the flashlight danced over them.

Daniel sighed softly, enthralled, his reaction as unalterably out of place as it was normal and reassuring. Everything would be okay. Wouldn't it?

"Give me a hand, Daniel," the Colonel said.

"What? Oh."

"Here, let me hold this." Smiling, Janet reached out for the flashlight and staff weapon Daniel was carrying.

No.

"Sure, thanks."

"No," croaked Sam.

Or maybe it had been a shout rather than a croak. Colonel O'Neill's face tightened, all hard angles, the way it did when he was trying his damnedest to keep a lid on his feelings. Had he ever realized that they knew him far too well to buy it anymore?

"It's gotta be done, Carter," he murmured. "I'm sorry."

What was he talking about? Oh. Her leg. With an air of detachment she stared down at the festering mess. Right now it was easy to pretend this didn't belong to her. She didn't care. Much. She cared about the staff weapon. Which was changing hands.

No. Sir, can't you see it's wrong?

Daniel's arm, warm and strong, slipped under her back, and together he and Colonel O'Neill eased her to the ground. Stone tiles, and when she turned her head they felt cool under her cheek. Past Daniel's back she watched as Janet carried the weapon across the small room and placed it on the floor along the wall.

The doctor turned, shining the flashlight directly at Sam, blinding her. "See?" Janet asked. "Nothing to worry about."

"Uhm, Janet?" Going by the tone of Daniel's voice there was everything to worry about. "I don't see any—"

"Surgical kit," completed the Colonel. "What the hell is going on, Fraiser?"

By ways of a response, the light receded. Sam squinted against the glare, but all she could make out were a pair of bare feet walking backwards.

Suddenly Colonel O'Neill leaped from his crouch. "Don't! Don't do—"

"Unless you want to be cut in half, stay where you are!" The voice was glacial. Not Janet's. Not Janet's at all.

The rings shot from the ground. Daniel grabbed the Colonel's arm, yanking him away from the periphery, yelling something Sam couldn't understand under the hum of the ring transporter. Around them the room disintegrated in a brilliant flash of light.

A heartbeat later, she found herself lying on a different floor.

"—trying to kill yourself, Jack?" Daniel finished hollering. Then his jaw dropped, and he took in their new location still hanging on to the Colonel.

They'd landed in a basement vault—surrounded, from Sam's perspective, by a picket fence of armor-clad shins. Her gaze traveled up the shin plates, thighs, bellies, chests, to the faces... face. One face, times six.

"*Kumtraya*," she whispered.

"If that's Harlan's idea of a joke, so help me, this time I shoot the fat old bastard!"

"With what, Jack?" Daniel slid a pointed glance at his friend's empty hands. Janet had seen to it that their staff weapon wouldn't make the trip.

"Good point. Make that *throttle*."

"Besides, I don't think they're robots," Daniel added. "I think they're real."

"That's what you thought last time." The Colonel freed himself from Daniel's grip and took a couple of steps toward the nearest Jaffa, regarding him as if he were mustering the troops. "I remember this guy from the exercise. He's one of Norris's surprise mob."

With peculiar grace, almost as if he were performing a dance, he spun on the man to his left. His elbow slammed into an unprotected midriff, and the Jaffa recoiled, startled. Colonel O'Neill tried to follow up with a right hook, but the man had regained his wits, blocked the punch, and delivered two hard, rapid jabs to the Colonel's chest. Smiling, he watched as Jack O'Neill doubled over, fighting for air.

The Jaffa raised his staff weapon for a blow. His doppelgangers cheered him on. "Let's see how this feels. Maybe—"

He didn't get any further. Daniel had grabbed the nearest thing remotely looking like a weapon and flung it at him. The staff missed its target as the backpack hit the Jaffa in the face, exploding into a shower of field rations and cooking gear, and two of the man's doubles piled on top of Daniel to inflict an etiquette lesson. The remaining threesome looked on unconcerned.

Between their legs Sam could see movement. Somebody else had entered the vault. Delicate feet, golden toe rings and anklets, sheer, flowing fabric. A woman. Jaffa?

"Enough!" The metallic resonance of the voice gave it away. A Goa'uld.

Fighting a bout of dizziness, Sam watched as Colonel O'Neill and Daniel were dragged next to her and pushed to their knees.

"Kneel before your goddess," one of the Jaffa intoned, while the others shuffled aside to clear a path for the Goa'uld.

"You were right," the Colonel muttered at Daniel, eyes narrow. "Did I mention that I hate it when you're right?"

"Sorry."

Sam had no idea who or what they were talking about, until the Goa'uld casually strolled into her field of vision. Nirrti. Could this day get any worse? Probably yes. Her interest in the prisoners seemed to be strictly confined to one person only, and the look on her face was predatory. Great.

"We meet again, O'Neill," observed Nirrti.

"Thrilled. Can we go now?"

"If you wish." Nirrti stepped closer and nudged Sam's side with her foot. "Naturally, if you leave, she dies."

"So?"

"I believe it would distress you."

"You believe wrong." To anyone who didn't know him well, the Colonel's show of indifference should have been convincing. The only giveaway was a white stress line around his mouth, always there when he was holding on too hard.

Nirrti's fist closed in his hair, and she pulled his head back, forcing him to look at her. "And you are lying. You persuaded your superior to free me in order to save the Hankan girl. Because the thought of her death distressed you."

"We all make mistakes."

"Indeed." Nirrti smiled. "Some greater than others."

His control began to slip. "What do you want?"

"You."

"Fine." The answer came too rapidly, flagging up his relief. "You can have me, but you let Daniel and Carter go."

"You are hardly in a position to make demands, Tauri." To underline her point, Nirrti forced his head back further. "That is what you told me not so long ago, is it not? Count yourself lucky that I do not hold grudges. I shall grant your wish. Some of it at least." She abruptly released the Colonel and addressed the Jaffa guarding Daniel. "Take this one back to the shrine and set him free. I have no use for him."

"No!" Colonel O'Neill tried to get up, but a pair of beefy hands held him in place. "He's injured and unarmed. It's a death sentence."

"It is what you asked for."

"You damn well know it isn't. I—"

"Can't wait to get a bit of fresh air." Through a bruised and swollen face, Daniel tried to grin. "Hate to tell you, Jack, but you could do with a shower. Don't get into any trouble while I'm gone. I'll be back and—"

"Enough! Take him away!"

The Jaffa hauled Daniel to the center of the vault. From the cage of the transporter rings he kept smiling at Sam and the Colonel until he disappeared in a pillar of white light.

CHAPTER FOURTEEN

Missing Link: Absent member required to complete a developmental chain.

"I am hurrying up!" hissed Maybourne and inserted the fifth skeleton key in as many minutes into the door lock. "Don't know what he thinks he's keeping in there. Last time I saw something like this, I was in Leavenworth."

Probably a hyperbole, but still not exactly encouraging, given the fact that Harry's lock-picking talent wasn't what had busted him out of jail. That particular miracle had been wrought by Jack O'Neill calling in a lifetime collection of chits.

Not for the first time tonight George Hammond wished they could have hidden out at Jack's place. It would have made things easier all round. But Colonel O'Neill very likely headed the NID's list of People To Be Put Under Surveillance. Hammond sighed and checked over his shoulder. The orange-pop glow of streetlamps bounced off low clouds and trickled into this backyard in suburban Colorado Springs; a timid soul in one of the neighboring houses had left on a nightlight, and three or four yards over a lovesick tomcat yowled his misery. Otherwise everything was quiet. Question was for how long.

"Hurry up," Hammond whispered. Again.

"For the—" A gentle click cut off the tirade, then the lock gave. Maybourne straightened up and eased a kink from his neck. "See?"

He nudged the crack in the door wider and slipped inside. A fraction of a second later Hammond heard muffled cussing, followed by a series of dull thuds. Damn. "Stand down, Sergeant!"

There was a pause. Next the lights came on and the door flew all the way open. In the frame stood Sergeant Siler, wielding the great-grandmother of all wrenches. If Harry had been given a center parting with that thing, he probably needed a neurosurgeon.

Behind the wire-frame glasses, the sergeant's eyes were wide as saucers. "General! I... You..." The wrench gave a diffident wiggle that made Hammond want to duck. Siler swallowed. "Uh, sorry, sir. Please, uh… come on in."

"Thanks." Hammond stepped into a small, well-appointed kitchen that was twice as clean as his own and outed the unassuming sergeant as either a neat-freak or a hobby cook. A groan from behind the door made him turn.

Maybourne was coming to, gingerly probing what promised to become the goose-egg to end them all. "I'm okay. Thanks for the concern."

Siler's eyes went even wider. "Sir, that's Colonel Maybourne!"

"I noticed. You won't be needing the wrench, though."

"Yessir." Siler closed the door, locked it, and deposited the tool on the kitchen table. "Was it him who kidnapped you?"

Evidently the NID had stuck with the abduction tale, the easier to explain his planned demise, no doubt. Hammond shrugged. "In a manner of speaking."

"Want me to call the police, sir?"

"No," said Hammond.

"No!" yelped Maybourne, picking himself up from the linoleum. His gaze arrested on Siler, and his jaw dropped. "On second thought, maybe you should. I'm not sure that's legal."

The sergeant's pajamas displayed scenes from the marital life of Marge and Homer Simpson you didn't get to see on any television network Hammond had ever heard of. Siler blushed furiously and cleared his throat. "Present from Colonel O'Neill. Sir. He dropped it off last time he put me in the infirmary."

Taking in the nightwear, Harry Maybourne looked like a man about to weep for joy. "That's Jack for you. Thoughtful to a fault."

"Uh, yessir," the sergeant muttered a little uncertainly. Then he decided it might be safer to opt for a change of topic. "General, it's not that I'm not pleased to see you, but, with respect, sir, what are you doing here?"

Excellent question—and kind of a long story. Luckily, when he'd set out to elope with a USAF general, Harry had come prepared. For the first time in his life, George Hammond had traveled on a false passport. Harry also had demonstrated how to hotwire a car. Assuming—correctly—that there would be no NID goons posted across the border, they'd evaded several roadblocks, driven from Seattle to Vancouver and flown back to Denver from there. After that they'd hitched a ride down the I-25 to Colorado Springs. The truck had dropped them off ten minutes' walk from George Hammond's house—and a black sedan waiting for them outside. They'd turned around and crept away, desperate for a bolt hole now.

"I apologize for the break-in, Sergeant," Hammond said. "When we didn't see a car in the driveway and nobody answered the door I figured you were on night-duty. We had to get off the street before they caught us."

"Car's at the workshop. Needs a new transmission," Technical Sergeant Siler admitted, clearly dismayed about having to resort to the services of a car mechanic. "Who are *they*?"

"NID."

"Should have guessed," muttered the Sergeant. "Cheyenne Mountain's crawling with them. And Colonel Simmons pretends he's been put in command of the SGC."

"Simmons is on my base?"

"Does his arm bother him?" Apparently the blow to head had affected Maybourne's sense of relevance.

Hammond shot him an angry look. "Since when have they been there?"

"They got there first thing this— yesterday morning. Seems like they're keeping an eye on everybody. Sir, what's going on?"

"That's what we're trying to find out. I need your help, Sergeant."

"Sure thing." Siler nodded solemnly, the sentiment somewhat at odds with Homer and Marge's frolics. "How about I make us some coffee? No offense, but you look like you could use some."

"Sounds good." Maybourne craned his neck to sneak a peek into what presumably was a living room. "You got a computer?"

"Yep." Going by the mulish expression he adopted, Siler was less willing to render assistance to rogue colonels. The precise whereabouts of the machine or permission for Harry to use it weren't forthcoming.

"It's alright, Sergeant. He's playing on our team for a change," interceded Hammond.

Siler grudgingly pointed at an archway that divided the kitchen from the den. "Through there."

Nodding his thanks, Maybourne made a beeline for it, George Hammond on his heels. The computer wasn't quite state-of-the-art, but it would do. Besides, they didn't exactly have a choice. The usual IT ritual of startup and boot seemed maddeningly slow. Maybourne dropped into a chair, slapped the DVD into the drive, waited for it to load, clicked the first file open.

A video clip started to play, picture fuzzy, sound dull and bubbling with static. The image showed the OR Hammond had seen at St. Christina's. Only now it was in use. A man—PFC Thomas J Corbett, according to the file label—was strapped to the operating table, intubated, eyes taped shut, his midriff iodine red from disinfectant. Arranged around the table was a group of doctors and nurses, their identities hidden behind green masks. The meticulous choreography of a surgical procedure played out, though what exactly they were doing beat Hammond. Best he could tell, it wasn't a tonsillectomy.

"We need to show this to Dr. Fraiser. She might—" He cut himself off. They wouldn't be showing this to his CMO any time soon. Janet Fraiser was missing, so were Major Carter and Teal'c.

"Oh hello," murmured Maybourne, never glancing up from the screen.

One of the OR team had opened the lid of a sterile container and lifted out a pale, limp sac, riddled with veins and glistening with some sort of clear, moist coating. The surgeon shoved the sac into the incision in the man's stomach, then began suturing the edges to the peritoneum.

"What on Earth are they doing?"

"Looks to me like they're making a Jaffa, sir." Siler had noiselessly padded into the den and was peering over their shoulders at the monitor.

The unexpected reply made Hammond jump; a reaction he resented. "Impossible," he snapped. "That's—"

"—precisely what they're doing. Well spotted, Sergeant." Maybourne had paused the recording and swiveled the chair around to face them. "Talk about not seeing the wood for the trees. This is nothing new. A few years ago, when I was running Area 51, we were toying with the idea. One of the reasons I was so keen to get my hands on Teal'c." He made a faintly apologetic noise and dodged Hammond's glare. "I scrubbed the project. It didn't work. We had pouch cell cultures harvested from a bunch of injured Jaffa, but we never got beyond testing it *in vitro*. No matter what we tried—and believe me, we tried everything on the market and a few things the FDA doesn't even dream of—the human immune reaction was so massive, the cell cultures practically self-destructed."

"What would you gain by turning people into Jaffa?" Hammond had trouble wrapping his head around a concept so Frankensteinesque.

"Are you kidding, General?" Maybourne snorted. "Vastly improved combat skills—strength, speed, reaction time, stamina, you name it—plus self-healing powers that could reduce casualties by a factor of ten. The strategic advantages are incalculable, and I bet you dollars to donuts that's why the NID is trying it again."

"But you already proved that it doesn't work."

"*Did*n't work. Like I said, it was a few years back. Since then, bio-genetics have taken another quantum leap. Those guys"—he jerked his chin at the image on the monitor—"may have got the solution."

"Not for him, they haven't." Staring at the screen, Hammond fought down a bout of nausea. "We found him in one of those morgue drawers."

"True. How about this: PFC Corbett and the other poor bastards stubbornly insist on biting the dust, whereupon silver-tongued Simmons wheedles his pet Goa'uld into lending a helping hand? Ask yourself. What was Conrad doing at the hospital?"

The million dollar question. And it made perfect sense. Talk about a deal with the devil. They still didn't have all the pieces of the puzzle, and Hammond still didn't know how the exercise and the Marine camp on M3D 335 came into it, but he was convinced they were connected somehow. Simmons's involvement in both, the Marines' involvement in both, was too much of coincidence. He thought of the corpses in the lab at St. Christina's. Fine young men, and no doubt they'd volunteered for the job. But with equal certainty they'd never been told the truth about what it really entailed. And what was happening to the dozens of others who'd been sent to Parris Island? What had happened to his own people? For a brief moment he indulged in a fantasy about locking the NID colonel in a room together with Siler and his wrench. It might clear up matters pretty damn quick.

Realizing that his fists were clenched, George Hammond slowly uncurled his fingers and let out a deep breath. It all came back to the moon and what was going on there. They needed intel, simple as that. They also needed an expert, but first things first.

"When are you on duty, Sergeant?" he asked Siler.

The sergeant finally set down a couple of coffee mugs that had stopped steaming quite some time ago. "Zero seven hundred, sir."

"Good. We can't risk making phone calls, because the lines probably are bugged, but I want you to find a pretext to talk to Colonel O'Neill. Tell him—"

"Sir?" Siler wore the same ominously puzzled expression Hammond had seen on Major Warren's face, eons ago or so it seemed. "Colonel O'Neill and Dr. Jackson are on Parris— I mean, M3D 335."

Maybourne cussed. "When was Jack supposed to come back?"

"Yesterday." Feeling himself go cold, Hammond asked, "I take it he hasn't made contact since gating out?"

"No, sir. Not as far as I'm aware," mumbled Siler, his face falling as he realized what it meant. "Maybe I just didn't hear about it," he offered.

And pigs could fly. The sergeant, in his unobtrusive way, managed to be one of the best-informed people at the SGC. Occasionally he seemed to catch the latest news before the base commander did. Hammond found a chair, slumped in it heavily.

"Not your fault, George," said Maybourne.

"The hell it isn't! *I* gave him permission to go. I sent Dr. Jackson along for good measure. Without having a clue about what's happening on that moon—apart from the fact that three of my people disappeared there. And now two more have vanished, thanks to me."

"How were you going to find out, *unless* you sent someone to investigate? And don't tell me that Jack didn't give you an earache and a half about going."

Wrong. George Hammond had been too damn clever for his own good and jumped at the opportunity of getting back his best unit commander. Christ, he'd practically pushed Jack into it! And none of these profound insights was going to change a thing—as Major General Hammond would have been the first to point out to Colonel O'Neill if positions were reversed. He'd find out alright, and then he'd bring Jack and the rest of SG-1 and Dr. Fraiser home.

"Siler!"

Jolted from his contemplation of a mug of coffee, the sergeant flinched. "Yessir."

"Can you get me into the mountain and through the gate without anyone noticing?"

"Come again, sir?"

"Can you get me—"

"And me," Harry piped up.

"Out of the question," Hammond said mechanically. "Apart from anything else, it's too risky."

"I knew this gig was dangerous when I signed up for it, General. Same as Jack, I would imagine." Turning to Siler, Maybourne added, "Anyway, whaddya say, Sergeant? Two men into the mountain and through the gate without anyone noticing?"

Scratching the back of his head, the sergeant muttered, "Maybe. I'm gonna have to figure out a couple things, though."

Daniel stared up at a strip of sky, which had begun to turn a watery predawn green. Maybe the revolting color scheme was down to his one functioning eye having decided to get its own back. Or maybe it was just the budding migraine. That at least was no great surprise, not if you spent half the night draped head-down over a staircase. He had a vague recollection of being forcefully catapulted over the top of the stairs. The fall must have knocked him out.

A flock of birds barreled from the treetops, screeching but offering no further clues. His legs still pointed uphill, and he studied them briefly. Trying to get the right way up might be a start. It would hurt. Then again, that was fast becoming a habit. Oh yeah. He tentatively wiggled one foot, then the other. It hurt alright, but he didn't think anything was seriously damaged. Given his track record lately, that alone was reason to break out the champagne. Well, okay, he'd settle for water. Pushing himself up, he looked around for his backpack. Nothing. What the...?

Suddenly he remembered. He'd hurled it at some Jaffa who'd been about to break Jack's back. After that things got a tad hazy. Something to do with a pair of outsize twins pounding him into the floor tiles. *Twins*? There'd been six of them, perfect look-alikes. *Congratulations, Mrs. Jaffa! It's identical sextuplets.* Probably not what had happened. After all, Jack had identified the guy as one of Norris's boys... six of Norris's boys. Jesus!

So what *had* happened?

Maybe it was better to postpone the problem until his skull had stopped throbbing and he was capable of gathering at least one clear thought. He looked up at the sky again. The sun was rising fast. You could feel it; air temperature and humidity already racing toward another record high. The steps were still cool, though, and so was the wall Daniel used as a prop to push himself to his feet. Shivering a little, he closed his eyes... eye and waited for the world to stop spinning. It did. Eventually.

Fifteen or so steps up was the top of the staircase. He recognized the place. They'd followed Janet up there last night. Just before she'd sold them out to... *Nirrti*. A bolt of panic knocked the breath from his lungs. Nirrti had Sam. And Jack. And Daniel had been thrown out like a drunken gatecrasher, because she had no use for him. She wanted Jack, that much had been clear.

Why? What made Jack so different? Apart from the obvious, of course.

At this juncture, the answer to that question wouldn't be of any help. A little wobbly at first, Daniel began to scale the stairs. Halfway up, he stopped. What was he going to do? Return to the shrine, in the hope of finding somebody who'd show him the transporter controls? And then? Storm Nirrti's stronghold, nibble his way through force shields, bombard Jaffa with backpacks, and single-handedly free his team mates?

Not damn likely.

Nirrti hadn't sent him back out here from the goodness of her heart. She'd sent him out here to spare herself the trouble of killing him personally.

Keep this up, and you'll have accommodated her plans inside the next two hours, Jackson.

An insistent little voice told him to try and find Teal'c, but this idea was nearly as crazy. Teal'c was the proverbial needle in a planet-size haystack—if he was still alive. In light of last night's events, Janet's admission that she had lost him could be interpreted in any number of ways. The only sensible choice was to get back to the Stargate, find the DHD, bring help. Sometimes he hated sensible choices.

Slowly he turned and squinted at the blur of the ruined city spread out below; a sea of stone, unmoving and unmoved. Far in the east stone seemed to butt onto thin air. It had to be the temple where the Stargate was; it stood on a cliff rearing over the forest. To the north the terrain rose steeply, its highest point occupied by a fuzzy gray blob. If he were Nirrti, he'd camp out up there. Daniel filed the thought away for further examination. Southward, the gaps between buildings seemed to widen until they opened into one large space, lined by the city wall and the jungle beyond. Inset into the wall was what had to be a gate. Of course, at that distance, he was unable to tell a trolley from a trampoline, though on the whole a gate made more sense than either of the other two items.

Daniel decided to head south.

By the time he'd reached the bottom of the staircase, the sun had climbed above the rooftops and was teasing the back of his head. Flies started buzzing in the warm air, and somewhere to his right he heard the faint murmur of the waterfall. He turned left, out of the sun and into a narrow alley that, two corners on, began to meander wildly until he could no longer tell which way he was going or whether he'd doubled back on himself. Great. So when was this wide-open-space thing going to happen?

Ahead was a building that once might have been an inn of some sort. Behind a crumbling archway lay an inner court seamed by two tiers of galleries. Bamboo ladders connected the galleries to the ground and led up to a roof terrace, maybe high enough to overlook the area and recover his bearings.

Rungs creaking under his boots, small plumes of dust billowing from the twine that tied the ladders, he climbed to the top. The terrace was dotted with holes where joists had given and the ceiling collapsed into the rooms below. Carefully, Daniel picked a path to the parapet. He hadn't gone back on himself. Not quite, anyway. He'd just ended up a lot further east than planned. His best option was to make it to the city wall and follow that to the gate.

"Turn tail and run," he whispered bitterly. Knowing that it wasn't true, that getting himself killed wouldn't save Jack and Sam, didn't help. It sure as hell *felt* like he was running—leaving them behind. And nothing to be—

The shot missed him by a whisker, passing close enough for a whiff of displaced air to brush his skin. Swearing, he dropped flat behind the parapet just as a second round tore past. This one would have hit him. Daniel crawled a couple of meters along the wall and cautiously inched his head over the edge. Number three grazed his ear, and he ducked with a gasp, dabbing at the trickle of blood on his neck. The shooter definitely was getting warm—and whatever else he or she might be, it wasn't Jaffa. After five years of playing with the things against his better judgment, Daniel recognized the bark of a submachine gun when he heard it. He wouldn't stake his life on the make and model, but that was beside the point. Jaffa didn't use submachine guns—not even K'tano's former mob, not anymore; Jack had repossessed the P90s.

Keeping his head down, Daniel shouted, "You're shooting at a friendly! My name is Daniel Jackson. I'm a civilian advisor, US Air Force, but I don't expect you to take my word for it. So I'm going to get up for you to take a look. I'd be grateful if you could suspend target practice for the time being."

No reply. But no more potshots either. Hands raised, Daniel slowly came to a stand, expecting the shooter to show himself, too. Nope. Empty casements stared back at him from the building opposite, and the alley below was deserted.

"Hey! Where are you?"

It was instinct more than anything else. He spun around just in time to see a figure dashing from one doorway to the next. A split-second later another shot rang out, Daniel hit the deck, and the attacker scrambled for the entrance to the inn.

"Oh crap," muttered Daniel. "Slick move, Jackson."

The guy, whoever he was, meant business and didn't give a damn about civilian advisors. For reasons best known to himself, he'd declared open season on archeologists. By now he also would have realized that his prey was unarmed. Not even a backpack to toss, Daniel thought ruefully.

He darted back to the roof hatch and froze at the creaking and groaning of bamboo on stone. Someone was coming up the ladder.

"Crap," he muttered again. His only escape route had just been cut off.

Darting precariously between the voids in the terrace floor, counting off seconds in his head, he ran for the far side of the roof. Okay, now or never. If he left it too late, he'd be toast. Daniel dropped to his knees, slid toward one of the holes. From the edges jutted the remnants of beams, and here was hoping they weren't too rotten to take his weight. He grabbed hold of the end of a joist and eased himself into the opening, legs dangling. Holding his breath, he let go.

And crashed hard onto the wooden floor. The drop had only been about four feet. Daniel had figured it'd be more, which skewed his landing and sent him staggering against the mildewed remains of a bed. In a cloud of dust and clatter, the bed frame collapsed under the impact. A heartbeat later the rapid thud of booted feet came from above, closing fast.

Daniel scrambled for the door, knowing the dust would settle, but not in time to conceal the recent upheaval. Out on the gallery he started running, not caring whether he could be heard now. It didn't matter anymore. His trigger-happy playfellow would guess where he'd gone and could come bursting from any of these rooms at any moment.

The thought had barely formed when, in a shower of splintering wood, the shooter slammed through a door panel. In front of Daniel, not behind. For a startled second they looked at each other, then the man smiled. He was a Marine. A goddamn US Marine, so what the hell had happened to *posse comitatus* and all that? Of course, this wasn't exactly US soil. And maybe this was the wrong moment to ask for clarification.

The muzzle of the submachine gun—an MP5, incidentally—lowered to point at Daniel's chest, and the Marine chuckled. "Run, Mr. Civilian Advisor. Run."

Daniel had no moral qualms about being shot in the back. Presenting the honorable front got you just as dead and quicker. He turned on his heel and hared back the way he'd come, the Marine's laughter driving him like a gust. A hailstorm of rounds exploded around his feet. The son of a bitch was toying with him. Or not. The next burst went over Daniel's head, too close to tell if it'd missed by accident or design. He kept running, bent low, arms curled over his head.

Idiot! Like that's going to protect you!

As if to prove the point, two rounds in quick succession scraped his arms. Yelling, in rage rather than pain, he flung himself sideways through the nearest door. Mercifully, it led into a corridor rather than a guestroom. Maybe there was another wing. Preferably with an exit.

Daniel straightened up and sprinted down the gloomy hallway. More shots rang out from the gallery, and there was shouting, words drowned out by the cackle of the gun. Too bad, but if he was honest, he didn't much feel like making conversation. Ahead loomed a set of three doorways. He ducked through the last one, almost sobbing with relief when it opened onto a dark, narrow staircase. There was a way out after all.

Two steps at a time, he hurtled down the stairs into a soot-blackened, windowless kitchen—and stuttered to a dead halt. If there had been a backdoor once, it was buried under a mountain of debris where the rear half of the room had collapsed. The only exit from the kitchen was the staircase. He fought down a rising tide of panic, tiptoed back to the bottom of the stairs. Maybe he'd have enough time to— No. His pal was coming.

Across the room lay the upturned husk of a clay stove. When he pushed the door open a half dozen shiny eyes stared at him maliciously and three rats—or what passed for rats in this place—scurried past him. Suppressing a shudder, Daniel backed into the oven on all fours and pulled the door shut behind him. The fit was claustrophobic, the stench sickening, his whole body ached, and he'd probably die in this hellhole. In about sixty seconds or so.

Heart racing, he tried to listen to the noises outside. A few squeals from the rats voicing their protest and then the creak of a loose floorboard on the stairs. His pal was coming alright. The footsteps were quiet, measured, made by someone in total control of the situation. All the guy had to do was rip open the oven door and turn Dr. Jackson into shish kebab.

The footsteps stopped. Daniel gritted his teeth. Under his right hand he felt something hard and jagged. An old bone perhaps, or a shard. His fingers closed around it. He'd gut the bastard or at least go out trying.

Sorry, Jack. Seems I was wrong. Or maybe it means that you're—

The door flew open. His hand shot up and instantly was clamped in an iron grip. The owner of those relentless fingers crouched, peered into the oven.

"Daniel Jackson. I am most grateful to find you alive." Teal'c's face lit up in a rare, broad smile.

He looked like a caged animal, Mrityu thought, poised to strike and devious. He *was* a caged animal, without discipline, without the sense to save his strength, without the wisdom to submit to his goddess. After endlessly pacing its cage until its energy was spent and reduced to helpless inertia, the animal had retreated into silence, sitting on the floor, back pushed against the wall, refusing to accept any kind of hospitality. He would be brooding, scheming, underneath.

Mrityu deactivated the force shield and quietly slipped into the room, waiting until he took notice of her. When he did, the anger simmering in his eyes crumbled to incomprehension and the profound hurt of betrayal. The look haunted her more than she cared to admit, spoke to something—someone—she did not dare to reawaken. Though she was on her own for the moment, free of the radiant pressure in her mind, she knew that even the contemplation of misconduct might bring punishment.

And when has that ever stopped you before?

Not Lady Nirrti's thoughts but a voice from deep within Mrityu herself. Frantically, she silenced it, wishing she could erase it, wishing she could avoid those dark, probing eyes. Why was he staring at her like that?

"Lady Nirrti wants to see you," she said, hoping he would look away.

He didn't.

"What did I do, Fraiser?" he asked. "I mean, I must have pissed you off somehow. It's the only explanation I can come up with. So what was it? Cholesterol levels too high? Blood count off? What? I'd just like to know."

She didn't understand his questions. Wasn't Lady Nirrti instructing him? Or perhaps he was slow to listen. Mrityu recalled that she herself had not truly grasped the meaning of the voice at first.

"Give it time," she said, trying to sound encouraging. After all it wasn't his fault. That look in his eyes made encouragement difficult, though. She dropped her gaze, noted that the bed hadn't been slept in. "You should have rested."

"*Sir.*"

"Excuse me?" Mrityu blinked.

"I still outrank you, *Major.* So it's *sir* or *Colonel* or *Colonel O'Neill* to you. Any of the above'll do nicely. Are we clear?"

"You'll soon be given a new name."

"Can't wait," he muttered. Eyes narrowing a fraction, he pushed himself up from the floor, slowly and clumsily. When he stood at last, he remained slightly stooped, arms crossed protectively in front of his chest. "What's your name?"

"Mrityu," she replied.

"Death." His face twisted, whether in shock or anger she couldn't tell. Struggling to keep his voice even, he asked, "She told you that's what it means, right? Mrityu? Death."

"You're lying." But the creature within wailed, because it recognized the truth in this—so many deaths. A silken drape brushed her shoulder as she backed away, and she flinched, ducked behind the flimsy fabric as though it could shield her. "You're lying."

"I think we both know who's lying." He took a step closer, swiped at a barrier of silk. "You and Teal'c got separated? *Separated* as in: you killed him?"

"No!" Another step, and she was holding on to the drape as if to steady herself. "I disobeyed. I couldn't… I—"

"And Sam? She trusted you to help her."

"Carter is fine!"

"Her name is Samantha. You call her Sam. She's your friend. Your best friend."

"No." Her shoulders struck the wall. No more room to back off, and he still kept coming, and that buried thing, creature, in her mind was fighting her tooth and nail. *Please, mistress, help!* Silence. Only silence. Mrityu was beginning to feel cold, rime chilling her body from the inside out. "Don't! Don't come any closer!"

Two more steps. He wasn't listening. "You missed the main event last night. Did you know Nirrti has ways of using a healing device that will hurt the other person? Sam eventually passed out. Before that she screamed a lot, though. First, do no harm. Is that what you were thinking of when you sold her out? And Daniel? And Teal'c? First do no harm. You swore an oath, Janet. That's your name, by the way. Janet. Janet Fraiser and—"

"Stop it!" She flung herself against him with everything she had.

He staggered back against a low table, fought to regain his balance, lost, and slowly crumpled to his knees. For a while the only sound in the room were his gasps, low and shallow and never drawing enough air.

First, do no harm. First, do no harm. First…

"I warned you," she whispered, shivering. "Why can't you ever listen, sir?"

Waves of cold coursing through her, she edged closer, crouched beside him. He'd gone chalky white, sweat beading on his forehead, and she didn't like what his breathing was doing. The bruised ribs shouldn't cause him so much trouble, not after all this time. How did she know that? An exercise gone wrong. And he'd blamed himself. He was a friend, too. She gently clasped his shoulders.

"Your hands," he panted. "Freezing."

"Don't talk. You think you can straighten up a little? I want to take a look at you."

"I'm—"

"Peachy. Yes."

"What?" His eyes flew open, and he caught her in that disconcerting gaze again. "Janet?"

It was easier to bear now. And harder in some ways, because she couldn't be sure whether she'd be telling him the truth. "I don't know, Colonel. And I don't know how long it'll last, so—"

"What did she do to you? Tell me, Janet. You've got to."

"Don't, sir. Please. Don't say anything."

"She's nowhere in sight." Of course he wouldn't let it rest. He never did, did he?

"She doesn't have to be. She can make me do things." When she lifted his shirt and touched his bare skin, he flinched. Because her hands were cold. Or because he didn't trust her any longer—and why should he? "I'm sorry, sir."

"I'm starting to think it's not your fault, Doc."

The bruising was worse than she recalled. Maybe ribs were broken. No wonder he—

What are you doing? I asked you to bring him to me!

It cut into her like shards of ice, tightened around her mind, made her want to curl up and whimper. "Forgive me, mistress. I did not mean to—"

"Janet? Who are you talking to?" The Tauri's eyes were on her, they hadn't left, as though he thought he could keep the creature rampant just by staring at her.

There is no need for words! I told you this before. Do it again and you shall be punished.

I forgot, mistress, Mrityu stammered. *I forgot.*

What did you tell him?

Nothing. Nothing, mistress.

A lie. It was a lie. The creature had broken free. The creature had talked to the Tauri. She knew him. And if Lady Nirrti found out... Distract her. Distract her now.

The Tauri is injured, mistress. He requires healing, else the injury will worsen.

The silence that followed was intolerable. The Tauri kept saying things, but Mrityu barely heard him. At last the cold eased a fraction.

Bring him.

Yes, mistress. Yes.

"Janet? Don't listen to her, Janet." The Tauri's hands were clasping her face, freezing her skin and the flesh underneath, holding her in place so that his eyes could haunt her at leisure. "Stay with me. Come on, Janet."

"Let go of me!" she hissed.

"No. I need you, Janet. I need your help. Sam needs your help. If you help us, we can all get out—"

"Don't ever touch me again!" She slapped his hands aside, wishing she could do the same to his gaze. Why didn't she look away? Why? "Guards!"

The two Jaffa had been posted outside the room and arrived within seconds, and the Tauri finally found something other than her to hold his interest.

"Lady Nirrti wishes to see him. Bring him." Mystified, Mrityu heard herself add, "But be careful. He is injured."

CHAPTER FIFTEEN

"**S**top clucking, Teal'c. I'll be fine." To demonstrate the veracity of this statement, Daniel Jackson flexed both arms. "Well, fine-ish," he grumbled, and the grin he had attempted wavered a fraction.

At first, Teal'c had taken the facial contortions for a rictus of pain. An easy mistake, considering the general state of Daniel Jackson's features. Several bruises and lacerations had been added to the existing damage. The young man also looked worn out and dejected, which was unsurprising in light of the news he had brought. O'Neill, Major Carter, and Dr. Fraiser were in the hands of Nirrti. Teal'c intended to rectify that situation as soon as possible. He had not developed a plan yet, but he would cross that bridge when he came to it.

"Your range of motion seems to be adequate," he said.

"I told you I was fine. The bullets took along a bit of skin, that's all. Rambo over there was saving the fun part for later." Daniel Jackson cast a sidelong glance at his attacker who lay tied up in a corner of the gallery and entertained himself by ranting at Corporal Wilkins. "How did you find me, anyway?"

It seemed a curiously irrelevant question. Was it not enough that Daniel Jackson *had* been found? Perhaps not. Teal'c carefully rolled up an unused end of gauze and stashed it in his medikit. "Corporal Wilkins and I had entered the city at first light to explore the ruins. We heard the shots and followed them. It was fortuitous that we arrived here in time to see you take cover in the corridor."

"Yeah. Maybe I wasn't wrong."

"Wrong about what?"

"Uh." Daniel Jackson blushed. "It's something to do with my personal belief system. Kinda difficult to explain."

"It would appear that way."

Whatever Daniel Jackson had meant to say, he did not finish the thought. Instead he leaned forward and placed a hand on Teal'c's arm. "I don't think I've ever been so glad to see anyone."

"Nor have I, my friend."

It was true. When he had discovered Daniel Jackson in his hideout, Teal'c's knees had threatened to buckle with relief. A kind of weakness, he decided, that was entirely acceptable. He smiled at the memory, grateful that, for the first time in weeks, he truly had something to smile about. His pleasure faded as he retrieved the handgun he had used on Corporal Wilkins the night before.

"Uhm, Teal'c?"

"Yes, Daniel Jackson?"

His friend wore a troubled frown and wordlessly pointed at the weapon.

"It is purely for medicinal purposes." Teal'c rose and walked over to the two Marines.

As he approached, Corporal Wilkins looked up, grinning. "Can't really tell what Lambert's saying, sir, but I think he's pissed."

"Hopefully we shall be able to remedy his disaffection."

"I'm gonna remedy you, you son of a bitch! Cut me loose or I'll kill you!" The execution of Sergeant Lambert's threat seemed to pose certain logistic problems.

"I shall release you shortly." Impervious to the man's rage, Teal'c squatted in front of him and raised the gun. "However, I must ask you to hold very still now. I do not wish to cause more damage than absolutely necessary."

"What the hell?" The sergeant's eyes went wide. "You keep that thing the hell away from me! You hear—"

"Hold still!"

In fact, it would be considerably easier to knock the man unconscious, much as he had done with Corporal Wilkins, but Teal'c was not above petty retaliation. Sergeant Lambert had injured Daniel Jackson. Given the chance, he would have killed the young man. Teal'c saw no reason to spare him any discomfort and pulled the trigger. As the report of the gunshot shredded his eardrum, the sergeant cast into doubt Teal'c's intellectual capacity, manhood, and parentage.

"Teal'c!" Alerted by the noise, Daniel Jackson had joined them. "What are you doing?"

"What is necessary."

The stream of invective reached a crescendo and abruptly ceased when Teal'c fired again and destroyed the second eardrum. Sergeant Lambert drew a harsh breath, shuddered, and turned very pale. His gaze fixed on Daniel Jackson. Eventually he stammered, "Jesus, Mr. Jackson…" He paused, shook his head, momentarily thrown by the fact that his own voice had disappeared. "I don't know what to say. I'm so sorry. I've no idea why—"

"It's alright." Realizing that the sergeant couldn't hear him, Daniel Jackson winced and, somewhat reluctantly, patted the man's shoulder. "It's alright," he shouted again. Then he turned to Teal'c. "Don't tell me. This is some sort of weird Jaffa ritual you've neglected to mention so far."

"It is not." Teal'c tucked the handgun into his belt and gestured at Corporal Wilkins to untie his comrade. "It is the only method I could devise to protect these men."

"*Men*? Plural? And protect them from—"

"Corporal Wilkins was in the same predicament as Sergeant Lambert. Last night he attempted to kill me."

"He *what*?"

"Daniel Jackson, do you recall the events of PJ2 445?"

"Like yesterday." The young man stared at Teal'c for a long moment. Then he sighed. "Can we please not play Guess The Planet? My head hurts bad enough as it is. Does the place have a name?"

"It does not. Although I presume that some of the sounds the natives made might—"

"Oh, hang on. White naked plant guys, right?"

"Indeed."

"Yeah, I do remember. My head felt pretty much the same then." Daniel Jackson eased himself down the wall and into a sitting position. "So what does that have to do with Marines going on the rampage on P-whatever-this-is."

"Do you also recall what caused our discomfort?"

"Sure. It was those plants."

"How?"

"You know, the last time I had this type of conversation I was in grade school."

"Humor me, Daniel Jackson."

"The plants emitted some sort of infrasound that gave everybody a migraine and made them cranky. Especially Jack. You're saying the same thing's happening here? Low frequencies causing uncontrollable aggression?"

"In general, yes."

"And in particular?"

Teal'c slowly inclined his head. "This is not a natural phenomenon, and it affects carefully selected areas of the brain. It is a toy."

"A *toy*?"

"A form of entertainment," he corrected himself, unsure of how exactly to explain it. "On your television, do you not have programs where people allow themselves to be hypnotized for the amusement of others?"

"Yeah. Those bark-like-a-chicken-cluck-like-a-dog shows. Why?"

"The principle is not dissimilar. Some Goa'uld use this toy to achieve control over people and bend them to their will. Most often it is done for entertainment. However, I believe in this case it serves a different purpose. The victims appear to be forced into very specific behaviors."

"You mean mind control?" Glancing out across the courtyard below, Daniel Jackson frowned. "I don't know, Teal'c. Even in deep hypnosis you can't force a person to do something that goes completely against his or her character and convictions."

"This is more potent than hypnosis. I have seen mothers slay their newborn because a false god suggested the idea." The memory, as unwelcome as it was vivid, made Teal'c wince. He pushed it aside, carried on. "It also is potent enough to overcome these Marines' code of honor and force them to perceive each other as deadly rivals."

"Potent enough for Janet to betray us." This was a statement, not a question. Daniel Jackson's gaze strayed to the two Marines who seemed busy trying to communicate their mutual apologies. "And deafening a person negates the effect?"

"Apparently."

"I'm not deaf. Neither are you. So why aren't we going berserk?"

"Because for us to attack one another would require a direct command from Nirrti. She has attempted to control my actions last night, but I believe that, to a degree, my symbiote protects me."

"In other words, I could snap at any moment. You'd better keep that gun handy." The young man frowned, then decided to pursue a more constructive thought. "If it is a signal of sorts, there has to be a transmitter somewhere."

"Indeed."

Abruptly, Daniel Jackson came to his feet. "I want to show you something," he announced and headed for the ladder to the roof.

Teal'c was less than thrilled at the prospect of venturing into a location as exposed as that, but he had recognized the look on his friend's face. There would be no stopping him.

Although the sun had not reached its zenith yet, heat beat down relentlessly and chased shimmering specters through the air above the rooftop. Shading his eyes with one hand, Daniel Jackson stood by the parapet and stared out across the abandoned city and at a steep hill that rose from the jungle north of them.

"I can't see well enough, but I think there's a building up there," he said.

He was correct. Invisible from beyond the city walls or the narrow alleys below, an elaborate stone edifice perched atop the hill. The glint of a reflection on the upper levels caught Teal'c's eye. It came and went, a small bright flash cast by polished metal—most likely a harness—that told him someone was keeping watch up there, patrolling the battlements.

"It seems to be a fortress," Teal'c observed.

"I think that's where Nirrti keeps Jack and Sam and Janet." Daniel Jackson's expression hardened, cold fury hovering just below the surface. "It's her hideout. Has to be. And it's higher than anything else around, right?"

"That is correct."

"Then that's where the transmitter is, too. And that's were we're going."

Even if Teal'c had wanted to argue with this decision, he knew he would not have prevailed.

Heckle and Jeckle were trotting along gamely, giving him the evil eye behind his back, but, as per Fraiser's order, they hadn't touched him. They hadn't even tied his hands. Still, now wasn't the time to try anything fancy: a) it might be useful to get an idea of what Nirrti was up to, and b) he stood a snowflake's chance in hell of taking out the twins, quintuplets, or however many there were of these guys. This despite the fact that he was only in about half as bad a shape as he'd led Fraiser to believe.

Jack pretended to study the flagstones and from under half-closed lids slid a glance at the doc. She—or whoever was running the show inside her head—had closed herself off completely, avoiding his gaze, not talking except to give orders. He knew enough about deprogramming to realize that there would be no getting through for the time being. But he'd seen what he'd wanted to see. Somewhere underneath it all, the essence of Janet Fraiser was still there, the healer was still there, and as long as that was the case, Carter had a chance of surviving. If she was still alive.

Yeah. Right. That's it. Think positive, O'Neill!

Tossing the thought into a mental compartment where he kept pointless dusty things—memories of Iraq, for instance—he forced his attention back on the here and now. Which, by a margin of about a millimeter, wasn't as bad as it could have been. If Janet had told him the truth—and he was pretty certain she had—then Teal'c might still be out there. And if Teal'c was still out there, then Daniel's odds of survival had improved a little. Always provided that Teal'c found him or he found Teal'c. After which happy reunion they'd hopefully develop enough sense between them to dig up that DHD and get the hell Earthside.

Uhuh.

Daniel wouldn't leave. Neither would Teal'c.

So you'd better come up with an escape scenario that includes one Jaffa and one archeologist turning up when you least expect them to.

Piece o' cake. Unlike mapping a way out of here. Currently they were marching along a corridor six minutes away from his deluxe quarters, and that was the precise extent to which he could pinpoint his location. The route had been carefully chosen to avoid any windows, any landmarks at all that would have allowed him to orient himself. Nirrti's idea or Fraiser's? The doc knew him better, was one of the few people who'd ever had the dubious privilege of reading the complete, annotated deeds of Jack O'Neill. She knew exactly what he could and couldn't do. Sweet.

How was he going to work around that?

The usual way. Do the craziest thing possible at the unlikeliest moment.

Sounded like a plan.

They reached a wide stone staircase that spiraled, floor after floor, around a massive hole in the ground. Unless there were two of the things in this place, he'd been herded through here on his way up from the vault last night. The staircase was busier now. Below and opposite, flocks of umpteentuplets came jogging from one of the numerous hallways and scurried up the steps, some staring and smirking, others ignoring him. One little piece of intel at last. Quarters had to be off that corridor, which made it a good place to avoid. Among the men falling out, Jack spotted several copies of Heckle and Jeckle, identical right down to the snagged teeth, a half dozen brawny blond beach bums with a birthmark on the left side of their collective jaw, and nine lean, wiry Hispanics. Those were the biggest groups. A few other types came in threes and fours. All were Jaffa.

Had the men Carter had seen on M3D 335 been copies or originals? And was Nirrti planning to liven up her collection of multiple Marines with a bunch of Air Force colonels? Make a few carbon copies of one Jack O'Neill, brainwash, and return to sender to wreak havoc — from 'I' for iris codes to 'S' for self-destruct. So not gonna happen. Back in the bad old days, he and his team mates had carried cyanide capsules on some missions. Jack briefly wondered if Fraiser knew that, too, and veered a little closer to the edge of the steps to peer down into the stairwell. Fifteen, twenty meters to the bottom. Just how dead did you have to be for a sarcophagus not to work anymore? Did it ever not —

"Colonel, don't!" A small hand, surprisingly strong, surprisingly cold, closed around his wrist. Fraiser's face had a drawn look, the kind you'd see on people who suffered from migraine, but her eyes were clear and focused — though he could tell what it cost her to keep them that way. "Don't," she whispered again.

"Janet —"

"I'll try to help you. You and Sam. I can't promise that I'll manage, but I'll try. Just don't."

"*Try* isn't good enough. If Nirrti does to me whatever she's done to you and then sends me back, I'll put the entire planet at risk, Doc. I—"

"She won't. Right now she's not interested in intelligence. She… I think she's got a crush on you, sir."

"She *what*?" If this was supposed to make him feel better, the technique needed refinement. Thanks to that queen bee drug, Jack remembered blessedly few of the more salacious moments with Hathor. The stuff he did remember had persuaded him to quit dating Goa'uld. "Look, Janet—"

The hand pulled, fingers steely all of a sudden. "Move, Tauri! Lady Nirrti does not like to be kept waiting."

Too damn bad.

Heckle and Jeckle evinced an interest, and Jack decided that he wasn't going to provoke a shove fest. Back to Plan A. Find out what Nirrti really wanted and hope it wasn't rugrats in Goa'uld suburbia. He moved.

The lower parts of the staircase were quieter. Right at the bottom would be the vault and the ring transporter, for all the good it did him. They didn't go all the way down anyway. Fraiser, back in robot-mode, led him into a corridor that was textbook early System Lord: gloomy, ostentatious, and golden. For some bizarre reason, the décor felt almost comforting; a known quantity.

As they approached, the double doors at the end of the hallway slid open, spilling a blast of frigid air from the room beyond. If nothing else, this probably explained Fraiser's chronic hypothermia. Jack pulled the tattered, filthy BDU shirt tighter around him. At least it wasn't Nirrti's boudoir. Too cold. Too public. From endless rows of glass cylinders—incubators—that radiated all around him stared countless eyes. One row was empty, but the others held bodies and perfectly identical faces, eerily reminiscent of the prying faces out in the ruins. Clones. Hundreds of them. Nirrti stood at the center of the lab or whatever this was, like a spider crouching at the center of her web.

"Some IVF clinic you got here," Jack said, if only to stem the wash of nausea that threatened to race up his throat.

No reply—except a poke in the back from Heckle or Jeckle, propelling him closer to Nirrti and the thing next to her. It looked like a surgical table, straight out of some alien abduction yarn in the *National Enquirer*, and he chose to ignore it. Better not to draw attention to the possibilities.

By the looks of her, Nirrti seemed disconcertingly aware of what was going through his mind. "Take off your shirt."

"Thanks. Never before happy hour."

Goa'uld really had no sense of humor. "Make him take it off," she said to Heckle and Jeckle, who'd painted on hopeful grins.

"Hey, why didn't you ask?" Jack unbuttoned his shirt and contrived to peel it off his shoulders without jarring his ribs too much. "Where is Carter?"

Ignoring him completely, she stepped closer to inspect the black-and-puce quilt work on his chest. Between the room temperature, the leering faces in the incubators, and the gleaming metal tips of the ribbon device on Nirrti's hand, Jack felt an involuntary rush of goose bumps skitter across his skin. Nausea bounced back, then the metal claws dug into a bruise. He managed not to flinch, but a gasp tore loose whether he liked it or not. Nirrti raised an eyebrow, smiled. If this was her idea of come hither, he was in trouble. On the upside, unless somebody decided to crank up the heating, she'd definitely be out of luck.

"Where is Carter?" he asked again, suppressing a shudder.

"Mrityu exaggerates."

The statement was accompanied by another dig of the claws, deeper and with more relish, and this time he did flinch. "How about just answering?" he yelped. "That's a process where I ask a question and you spit out the requested information. Let's try it again. Listen carefully. Where the hell is Carter?"

"Silence!" Seasoned with a pinch of glow-eye; normal Goa'uld behavior at last, in its own sick way as reassuring as the décor in the corridor. Nirrti swung on Fraiser. "You lied to me, child!"

Child?

"No! I wouldn't. The Tauri *is* injured!" Fraiser's teeth were rattling so hard she could barely speak, and she seemed a hair away from all-out panic. "He—"

"Shows no damage that would require intervention."

While Jack had to agree with the diagnosis, he didn't much like what was happening to Fraiser. She'd slumped to a heap on the floor, eyes rolling back, limbs graduating from shivers to convulsions.

"Stop it!" he barked at Nirrti. "Whatever you're doing to her, just stop it. I'll cooperate."

Heckle and Jeckle looked disappointed, and Nirrti smiled again, still staring at Fraiser. "Go! You are no longer needed."

"Mistress, please."

Something other than her own free will picked Fraiser up from the floor, her movements jerky and uncoordinated as those of a puppet. She was all but whimpering. Her eyes met Jack's, and he saw a strange replay of what she would have seen last night: confusion, rage, and hurt. Riding on the tail of it, a flash of understanding—maybe. Then she turned away and shambled for the door.

"Very impressive. You have come close to corrupting her, Tauri. She must be fond of you." Nirrti's voice made the temperature drop by another five degrees at least. "Lie down." She pointed at the steel table.

Hell, no! The thing looked about as cozy as a deep-frozen bale of barbed wire, and its charms paled to insignificance compared to the notion of what she'd do to him once he got up there. Next time he stood in line at the supermarket checkout he'd read one of the Who's-dating-whom-in-Hollywood rags—anything but the *National Enquirer*.

Stall, Jack. Stall.

"First I want to see Carter."

He clocked her nod a split-second too late. It wasn't for him anyway. It was for Heckle or Jeckle and a beefy fist that whacked a whole new color into the biggest bruise. The crack was audible, and he wondered if Fraiser would be pleased to know that at least one rib *was* broken now. The only positive thought that sprang to mind was that you needed air in order to scream, so he wasn't screaming. To make up for it, his knees buckled, but the twins were kind enough to catch him and slap him onto the table like a side of pork.

"Later," said Nirrti.

"You could have just said so," he gasped. The steel surface of the table was icy enough to numb some of the pain. Jack tried not to move. "For God's sake, what is it you want?"

Her face was inches away from his, the hand with the metal claws cupped over his forehead in mockery of a caress. "What I've always wanted, Tauri. A *hak'taur*."

Okay, it was official. He was in trouble. Bun-deep in raw sewage. Because one of them had to be nuts, utterly and completely crazy. "You should check the manual. For hak'tauring they generally recommend using someone slightly less decrepit. As in *freshly bred*."

"Age is no consideration. I can make you as young or as old as I choose. I can make as many of you as I choose."

"And we'll all be insolent and juvenile and leave a mess in the kitchen."

The metal tips trailed down the side of his face and traced his mouth. "Be silent."

Excellent advice, but Jack had a nasty suspicion that she might try to play tonsil hockey if he stopped talking. "Why me?"

Mercifully, she straightened up and the claws went away—question was whether that calculating gaze could count as improvement. "The Asgard have shown an inordinate interest in you."

Crap. "Oh, come on. You know what old Thor's like. Sucker for losers."

"The Asgard never do anything without cause. They are interested in you for a reason. I am curious to find that reason and use whatever it is that makes you so special, Tauri."

"Hey, I can tell you that. I know all the best fishing holes in—"

"Be silent!"

The beam of light shot from somewhere high up in the ceiling and slammed into his retinas like a white-hot piston.

"No way this is going to work." Harry Maybourne's defeatist mutterings somehow found their way from behind the crate where he was hiding, across a heap of netting, and around two pallets of MREs that concealed Major General Hammond. "They'll pull us out at the checkpoint."

"Shut up," Hammond muttered back. "Siler set this up. It'll work."

The truck hit a pothole and bounced any reply Maybourne might have made into oblivion. In fairness, Hammond did have his doubts, but even being found at the checkpoint beat sitting behind closed curtains in the living room of Siler's house and doing precisely nothing. Which was what they'd practiced for an entire day. Well, they'd fine-tuned the details of the plan. Around five in the afternoon, Siler had come back, bundled them into the back of his pickup, and driven them to a logging road halfway up Cheyenne Mountain. The supply truck had been waiting for them. Its driver was an old buddy of the sergeant's and had been instructed not to have any questions.

They were slowing down now, and the truck rolled to a stop. Voices from outside, some banter between the MPs at the gate and the driver, then they were moving again, and the echo of the engine noise changed into something more throaty. The truck was barreling down the access tunnel, creaking to its second and final halt a minute later. Commotion and more voices outside, the tarp snapped open, and the flap clanked down. A couple of airmen clambered into the back of the truck, just as Hammond stepped out from behind his MREs.

"Uh," said the man in front.

"You haven't seen me, son," Hammond advised conversationally. "And close your mouth. It's getting draughty in here."

As per orders, the airman took control of his jaw. "Seen who, sir?"

"Exactly."

"I suppose we haven't seen this guy either," his colleague asked, nodding in the direction of Maybourne's head, which had risen above the crate like a dyspeptic August moon.

"Especially not him."

"Christ," groaned Maybourne. "This is supposed to be the country's most secure air defense facility."

"It all depends on whom you know, Colonel. And don't go legit on us. It doesn't suit you." Hammond grinned and turned to the airmen. "How about you gentlemen tell us where to take those supplies?"

Half an hour later, Hammond and Maybourne wheeled a cart stacked with MREs out of the lift on Level 19. En route to the storage room they passed a brace of black-suited NID agents who never gave them a second glance, thus proving the smokescreen properties of olive drab fatigues. Siler was waiting for them in the storeroom. Lined up next to him sat three oil drums, two of them empty, the third filled with scrap metal and old rags.

"Planning to start up a steel band, Sergeant?"

"Uh… No, General." The owlish glance Siler cast at Hammond was accompanied by a blush. "I'm really sorry, sir. It's gonna be uncomfortable, but it was the only thing I could think of."

"You gotta be kidding!" Harry stared at the drums as if they were going to bite him.

Siler's shrug made clear that this wasn't a joke. George Hammond had his own qualms—something along the lines of being wedged into a metal tube and not leaving it again without the aid of a blow-torch—but unfortunately their options were limited. "I hope you know what you're doing."

By the time they were back in the lift, inside the oil drums and on the same cart that had carried the MREs, Harry had got over his initial shock. The barrel to Hammond's left hummed a Bob Marley number, muffled and off-key. The musical interlude was cut short by a clang, fist on steel, which advertised that Siler had no intention of getting together with Colonel Maybourne or feeling alright.

The lift bobbed to a halt. Hammond heard the doors slide open, then the cart rattled out into the corridor. Lots of activity, boots on concrete, voices. Some he recognized, others were unfamiliar. NID? If so, they had all but taken over his base. He felt a hot bolt of anger and pushed it down—there were few things more counterproductive than blowing one's stack while sitting in a barrel. Especially with the lid on.

A left turn came next, and Hammond, who could draw a map of the base with his eyes closed, knew that they'd entered the gate room. By the sounds of it, the place was packed to the rafters. What on Earth was going on?

Somebody else had the same question.

"Hey! You there! Sergeant! What the devil do you think you're doing?" The stuffed-up tones of Lieutenant General Crowley. It explained the crowd. Crowley was shipping out more Marines.

"Sorry, sir." Siler sounded anything but. "Monthly gate calibration test. Won't take a minute."

"Monthly *what*?" barked Crowley.

For once, Hammond shared the man's sentiments. *Monthly* what? The sudden urge to laugh was short-lived, though. From somewhere very close came another voice.

"I can't recall any such test being scheduled," Frank Simmons observed. "As a matter of fact, I can't recall any such test being in existence. I'd like to see what's in those drums."

"Sure, sir." Siler popped the lid of the dummy barrel. "Basically, it's just a pile of trash metal and stuff, to the weight of man. We check traveling speed, accuracy of reconstitution, that kind of thing."

"Test coordinates have been entered." Sergeant Harriman, obviously briefed by Siler, announced over the PA. "Ready to dial when you are, sirs."

"Where are you sending these?" asked Simmons.

"P5C-12," replied Harriman without missing a beat and hopefully not serious. The planet had a sulfur dioxide atmosphere. "With respect, sir, it's imperative that we conduct the test, particularly in light of the problems we've been experiencing in getting a lock to M3D 335."

"After we've checked the other barrels," Simmons said suavely.

This time there was no audible reply from Siler, and George Hammond's heartbeat raced for a new speed record. The frantic thudding probably set off the seismometers in the control room. Was it just him, or had the temperature inside the barrel jumped by about twenty degrees? He felt a trail of perspiration trickle down his back.

"Oh for God's sake! Sometimes your paranoia makes me wonder, Colonel!" Bless Crowley and his impatience. "Let's just get this over with. You can rewrite the rulebook later. Sergeant, carry on!"

"Yessir." Siler, somehow managing to keep the relief from seeping into his tone. "Uh, actually, General, if some of your men could give me a hand, it'd be a lot quicker."

Up in the control room, Harriman also had decided to speed up things. Under the whine of the klaxons, the Stargate began to dial. One by one, the chevrons locked, and Hammond could see the sequence in his mind; oddly shaped glyphs that represented Scorpio, Crater, Triangulum, Capricorn, Sextans, Sculptor, and Earth as the point of origin. The rainstorm noise of the establishing wormhole erupted, and he, Maybourne, and a barrel full of trash found themselves carried up the ramp by a crew of Marines and pushed through the event horizon.

If anything, the trip proved that negotiating Niagara Falls in an oak cask was a stupid idea. Hammond's drum exited the wormhole, collided with a stone dais, tipped over, bounced down a set of stairs, and rolled along some very bumpy ground. Until it came upon an obstacle that refused to be flattened.

"*Leaa! Kree no tel, Chappa'ai!*" said the obstacle.

Damn. They had a welcoming committee. Not necessarily cause for worry, but he would have preferred a quiet arrival, just in case. Several pairs of feet ran closer, the barrel began to move again, and Hammond counted his blessings. As it happened the folks out there were turning the oil drum the right way up. He worked his arms above his shoulders, placed palms against steel, and pushed. The lid popped off with a clang, provoking shouts of *Kree!* among his audience.

Hammond gratefully breathed in a lungful of fresh air, chilly as ever, and began to heave himself from the barrel. Literally the first thing he saw was a pockmarked face, crowned by a golden skullcap that reflected the pale cold light of the twin suns of Chulak. Okay, cancel the reservations about the welcoming committee. The need for negotiations and a search that might have taken days had just become null and void. Maybe their luck was turning.

The face split into a broad grin, black eyes glinting with delight. "*Tal ma'te*, Hammond of Texas! If you wish to thread the needle, I advise you do so in a glider. It is more comfortable."

"I'll take it into consideration. It's good to see you, Master Bra'tac. Mind giving me a hand?"

While Bra'tac extracted him from the barrel, three young Jaffa, students or bodyguards or—almost inevitably with Bra'tac—both, investigated the other two oil drums. The discovery of Hammond's companion resulted in raised eyebrows.

"He is not one of your men," Bra'tac observed.

"No, he isn't. Usually," Hammond added a bit uncertainly. "Bra'tac, meet Harry Maybourne."

Geniality disappeared under a flinty mask of hatred. Bra'tac straightened to his full height, and a subtle shift in stance flagged up the very real threat this old warrior still represented—even at a hundred and thirty-seven years of age. "Teal'c resigned his right to disembowel you, Colonel Maybourne. I did not."

Maybourne, framed by two Jaffa who immediately tightened their grip on him, went positively green around the gills. His attempts to use Teal'c as a guinea pig had made him *persona non grata* at the SGC, but somehow Hammond hadn't counted on the fact that Bra'tac knew. Now he wondered why not. Bra'tac was Teal'c's teacher, mentor, surrogate father. Of course Teal'c would have told him.

Calling himself a fool for missing the obvious, George Hammond adjusted the truth a little. "Don't, Master Bra'tac. He has… changed his ways. Teal'c is in danger, and I wouldn't have found out if it weren't for Colonel Maybourne. We need your help."

Luckily, Harry was smart—or conceited—enough not to contradict.

Bra'tac let go of a soft breath, but the tension in his eyes and body didn't ease. "Teal'c is in danger?"

"Teal'c and the rest of SG-1 and Dr. Fraiser. They've disappeared." Hammond squared his shoulders against a shiver, fully aware that it wasn't brought on by the glacier winds of Chulak. Even Bra'tac's woolen cloak would offer no protection against this kind of cold. "Can we go somewhere a little less exposed and talk?"

The only answer were a slight nod and an apparently telepathic order to the young Jaffa, who relented enough to allow Maybourne to walk. In a theatrical swirl of black wool, Bra'tac turned and started across the wasteland around the gate and into the forest. They hiked in silence for longer than Hammond's back considered tolerable, until they reached a small encampment, home to about twenty warriors and their families. At its center stood a large, colorful Jaffa tent. Bra'tac motioned for his guests to enter, while people in the camp looked on curiously. No one approached to greet them. Things were in the balance, undecided as yet.

Under a vent in the roof burned a fire, and piled around the hearth lay cushions and bolsters in the same vivid hues as the tent itself.

Finally, Bra'tac spoke. "Sit, Hammond of Texas." And, with a curt nod at Maybourne, "You, too."

As they eased themselves onto the cushions, a woman appeared, carrying a tray of food. Bra'tac waved her away, and the meaning of the gesture was clear: he was not going to break bread with Harry Maybourne just yet. Eventually he said, "Tell me what happened."

He listened impassively, while Hammond outlined the bare bones of SG-1's vanishing act. The tale finished, and Bra'tac frowned. "Why do you request my help? Do you not have men enough to search for them?"

"If I may, Master Bra'tac?" Harry damn near bowed into the cushions.

Ludicrous as it might have looked, the show of respect had the desired effect. Bra'tac snatched a quick glance at Hammond, as if to reassure himself that this was acceptable, then he snapped, "Speak."

"We need an expert," Maybourne announced. "That's why we've come to you."

"An expert in what?"

"Jaffa." It got him a briskly raised eyebrow by ways of permission to continue. Harry did just that, explaining their find in Seattle and its ramifications and wisely omitting his own involvement of bygone years.

"So you think that someone is trying to turn your Marines into Jaffa?" Bra'tac tossed a fresh log onto the fire. "It is impossible. Unless—"

"Unless?"

"Unless the Tauri who are behind this have acquired the assistance of a Goa'uld."

"Conrad."

Bra'tac shook his head emphatically. "No. It would require a great degree of scientific and medical knowledge."

There was one Goa'uld who fit the bill, but George Hammond was in no mood to contemplate that possibility. It was a little too ugly for comfort. Besides, all of this was pure speculation, at least until they managed to dig up a fact or two. "Master Bra'tac," he said. "We believe the key to all this is on the moon, M3D 335. Will you and your men accompany us there?"

Only the soft crackle of the fire filled the silence. Barely daring to breathe, Hammond watched the shine of the flames play in Bra'tac's eyes. Just as he was at the brink of gritting his teeth—or putting his fist through a cushion—a wolfish smile stole across the old warrior's face.

"Very well, Hammond of Texas," said Bra'tac. "I never could resist a good mystery. We shall fight together once more."

CHAPTER SIXTEEN

Apoptosis: Genetically programmed cell death.

God, this place was a dump! Frank Simmons cast another glance at the moon above his head. The pregnant misery wasn't a moon, of course. It was the planet around which this dust ball revolved. Funny how, even centuries after Galilei and light-years across the galaxy, you still couldn't help thinking in geocentric terms.

He'd already decided that gate travel was overrated and wished he'd stayed Earthside, especially given his injury. If he ever got his hands on Maybourne, he'd kill the bastard. Unfortunately, Maybourne and Hammond seemed to have dropped off the face of the moon, pun intended. The NID's best guess was that they'd slipped across the border into Canada—like a pair of draft dodgers. The thought brought a sour grin. Not that Simmons believed for a moment this would be the end of it. Hammond wasn't the guy to let things go, and Maybourne was a pain in the ass on principle.

While the golf cart supplied for people who couldn't be expected to walk—himself, Crowley, and a couple of xenophysicians from Area 51—crawled from between the walls of the canyon and out into an arid plain that made North Dakota look alpine, Simmons's mind flipped back to the so-called calibration test. Something about it had smelled fishy, if only because he knew the tech sergeant who'd shown up with the barrels. He'd interviewed the man, one of Hammond's special cronies. Hell, what was he thinking? They all were. Including the meek-looking nerd at the dialing computer who'd provided information on P5C-12—some piece of rock with an unbreathable atmosphere that wobbled around in the general direction of Alpha Centauri. Very plausible and well-documented, except there was no way of proving that P5C-12 had in fact been the destination of the oil drums.

Anyhow, it was a moot point now, wherever the damn barrels had gone. If Hammond stayed out of the picture—and Frank Simmons fully intended to ensure that the he did—the days of the sergeant and the nerd and the entire herd of Hammond fans at the SGC would be numbered. With SG-1 and the good General having disappeared so tragically, there was nothing to stand in the way of progress. Fate was a funny thing, Simmons reflected. The rigged USMC/Air Force exercise—originally intended as a springboard for shoehorning the Marines past Stargate Command and into a place where they could operate according to NID requirements—had snowballed in ways nobody had ever dreamed of. One of the advantages was that the problem of communicating with M3D 335 was a thing of the past—though, admittedly, Simmons's presence on the moon now was down to curiosity more than anything else. He wanted to see his Jaffa.

Ahead, a cluster of miniature huts and fences that formed the camp grew steadily larger. One of the Area 51 scientists perched in the back of the golf cart peered at it and offered his expert opinion. "Bit unprotected, isn't it?"

Crowley, who was driving, gave a snort and cast a quick glance over his shoulder. "It's perfectly protected. Visibility works both ways. In the unlikely event that anyone actually gets past security at the Stargate, the guys in camp'll see them coming from the literal mile off. The only way of dropping in unannounced is from the air, and that isn't going to happen here. The Marine Corps owns this moon."

The xenodoc sniffed, unconvinced, but he didn't offer any further strategic insights. His colleague, a hatchet-faced brunette, sighed in ennui. Simmons half expected her to chant *Are we there yet?*

Ten minutes later they were there, and Crowley displayed the good sense to nip Norris's welcoming ceremony in the bud. "Take it as read, Colonel," he barked when Norris threatened to protest. "We want to see the men who have completed survival training."

He should have said *successfully*, Simmons thought. They'd all completed it. Some were just deader than others.

"Yessir!" Norris snapped, bright red in the face. Then he turned to the sixty or so Marines lined up on the square. "Everyone fall out, except Alpha platoon."

Men started to scramble, scaring up a cloud of dust. Some headed for the mess barrack to gossip over coffee; others hung around the fringes of the square to watch, probably jealous of the men who'd been singled out. His Jaffa, the first step toward assuring Earth's safety and the continuation of the American way of life.

There were twenty of them, plus an additional four on guard duty at the gate. Better than projected. The way this was going, they could start assembling Beta platoon before the week was out. Still, the twenty men who made up most of Alpha seemed adrift in the vast central square of the camp. Simmons knew damn well that he'd been entertaining visions of an army and that visions rarely corresponded to reality, but the frustration was there and nagging. So far they'd sent out almost a hundred Marines and lost most of them. But, as he'd repeatedly tried to persuade himself, a twenty-five percent success rate wasn't to be sneezed at. Well, nearer thirty percent, if you figured in Nirrti's share. And the fact of the matter was, before Nirrti had come on the plan, they'd had a *failure* rate of one hundred percent. Those were figures you couldn't argue with.

Van Leyden, the NID agent in charge on the moon, slipped in behind him. "Nice of you to stop by, Colonel. Looking good, aren't they?"

Superficially the men looked no different, except perhaps for the fact that they were glowing with health. Even the three who had returned from 'survival training' only yesterday. After what they'd been through, they should at least show a few scrapes and bruises, but none had so much as a hangnail.

"Yeah," Simmons agreed. What else was he supposed to say? That he wished they wouldn't have to pay in Jaffa? "Any complaints from our good friend, Lady Nirrti, regarding her reimbursement?"

"According to the reports she haggled like a bazaar dealer, but in the end she agreed to twenty percent. No histrionics since."

That was a surprise. From what Simmons had witnessed, Nirrti would give up her lifeblood rather than her histrionics. And a Goa'uld actually honoring a bargain? Rare, by all accounts. The rarity being one of the reasons why Conrad was back in his cage—throwing straw from it, for all Simmons cared. "You're sure?"

"Yep. Master Sergeant Macdonald is our liaison at the other end, and he's in charge of seeing that she sticks to the deal. Macdonald says she kept six of the guys. I can give you their names, if you like. I can also give you the casualty list. It's long, but that was to be expected. Only the very best made the cut. These guys are good to start with, and in order to make it they had to go up against each other."

With a little persuasion courtesy of Nirrti's technical expertise. Which meant she could have tried her hand at persuading subjects other than those designated. Simmons had a fleeting memory of an infatuated young farm boy. "Is Macdonald aboveboard?" he asked.

It got a laugh from van Leyden. "You mean did she turn him? No way, Colonel. Macdonald's third generation USMC. His old man's sergeant major to the Commandant. Nobody turns Macdonald. Besides, I'm in regular contact with him. I'd have noticed if something were off."

"Let's hope so." Simmons still wasn't entirely convinced. Then again, why waste time questioning things that actually worked out? He directed his attention back to the square.

Crowley was holding forth about what an honor this was and how Alpha platoon would perform to the greater glory of God and country. The men seemed to believe it. Just as well. Once Crowley had finished pontificating, Norris took over to handle the mundane. Alpha platoon was to report to sickbay for medicals. The doctors were expecting them. Simmons wondered briefly what Norris would say if he knew the real specialty of the doctors newly arrived from Area 51.

"Norris is developing a spine," van Leyden whispered. "He's been giving me hell over that incident with O'Neill and Jackson."

"He knows they never made it back Earthside?"

"No. Not yet, anyway. But he was pretty shocked when things got rougher than absolutely necessary. Our boys still have problems gauging their own strength. Anyway, he could cause trouble down the line."

"Well, in that case I'd suggest another unfortunate gate malfunction."

A warm breeze chased dust devils across the square, playing around the men's feet as Alpha platoon fell out in the direction of the shack that housed the sickbay. Crowley ambled over to Simmons and van Leyden.

"Pleased with what you've seen, Colonel?"

"Yeah," Simmons grunted, unwilling to engage in a back-patting fest just yet.

"So what are your plans? Staying around for a while?"

"General, my urge to sleep in tents is something I learned to control years ago. First time at summer camp, if I remember correctly. So, no, I won't be staying. I'll wait for the preliminary results of the medicals and then head back to the SGC."

"Suit yourself." Crowley gave a shrug and pointed in the direction of the mess. "How about a coffee while you're waiting?"

Simmons's preferred blend was dark-roasted Sumatra, freshly ground, which the mess probably didn't serve. On the other hand, accepting the invitation definitely beat standing out here and admiring the orange-bulge-set. "Thanks." He started heading for the mess building. "By the way, General?"

"Yes?"

"That idea we discussed?"

"And which one of your many ideas would that be, Colonel?" Crowley chuckled and sneaked a glance at van Leyden, inviting applause. Van Leyden knew better than doing him the favor.

"The one that'll take care of the little problem that's been accumulating at the training site."

"Would that be the problem that's been aggravated since your boy van Leyden here had the snot beaten out of an Air Force officer and a civilian before marooning them on our playground?" Apparently, the general didn't take kindly to his jokes being ignored.

"Look, General, let's not get into a pissing contest, shall we? Otherwise I'd see myself forced to remind you how this mess started." Simmons smiled. "We've got to test the men one way or another, so they might as well do something productive instead of setting new records for one-armed pushups."

"Alright, alright!" Some of the Marines still loitering on the square were stealing curious looks. Realizing that he had an audience, Crowley lowered his voice. "I never said I didn't agree with you. Better not to leave any loose ends. When do you want to stage it?"

"The sooner, the better. Tonight. And General?"

"What?"

"If Alpha comes across the SGC's Jaffa, they're to take him alive. We may need him."

"Daniel Jackson. I insist that you take a rest!" This time Teal'c seemed to mean it. He caught a fistful of Daniel's shirt and yanked hard. "We cannot afford to lose our way because you are ailing. You shall rest and you shall eat."

"We cannot afford to waste time on lunch breaks!" Admittedly, his protest would have had more impact if Daniel hadn't listed in the direction of that fistful of shirt.

Teal'c caught him and safely deposited him on the ground. "It will be dinner break."

"That wasn't fair," muttered Daniel, wondering if the hallway would stop bobbing any time soon. It felt like getting back on dry land after a round-the-world sailing trip. Maybe sitting down wasn't such a bad move after all. The two gunshot wounds didn't trouble him; they were mere scratches. His head was different matter. It hurt to the point of Daniel occasionally losing what was left of his vision. The latest such incident had prompted Teal'c's little attack, which was pointless anyway. Daniel had no appetite whatsoever. He closed his eyes instead, knowing he couldn't risk falling asleep.

The echo of soft footsteps told him that the two Marines had caught up, but he didn't bother to look. Instead he listened to a rustle, pop, rattle, and glug—at least until somebody nudged his shoulder too insistently to ignore. Daniel looked.

Sergeant Lambert was crouched in front of him, holding out a canteen and a couple of ten-megaton Tylenol to his erstwhile victim. "Take those. They should work. I'm real sorry, Dr. Jackson."

"Thanks, Sergeant. And quit apologizing."

Not having a clue of what Daniel had said, Lambert nodded. "Sorry, sir. I mean it."

"Oh for God's sake!" Daniel swallowed the Tylenol and grabbed Lambert's sleeve.

"What, sir?"

Using the canteen like a gavel, Daniel started tapping the man's arm: -.-• •- -• •• - •- •-•• •-• • •- -•• -•-- •-•-•- •• - ••• --- -•-

"c-a-n i-t a-l-r-e-a-d-y. i-t s o-k," Lambert spelled out. Then he grinned. "Not bad. When did you learn that?"

At age seven in the Valley of the Kings, because the second-hand radios mom and dad had didn't work worth a damn underground. The prospect of having to tap this out in Morse code sent the hallway bobbing again, so Daniel simply shrugged and smiled. It probably made him look enigmatic.

Corporal Wilkins had dug four MREs from his pack. Now he peeled out the candy bars and thrust them at Daniel, who accepted despite his lack of appetite. Sugar always worked. It might actually keep him going for another twenty minutes or so. Munching chocolate, he studied the corridor.

They'd all agreed that approaching the fortress out in the open would be a very bad idea, so he'd led Teal'c and the two Marines back into the maze of rooms, hallways, and subterranean passages he'd found yesterday. Had it only been yesterday? He was losing track of time. Another bad idea.

For about six hours they'd been heading steadily north, slowed down by dead ends that forced them into an endless succession of detours. Currently they sat in what looked like another cul-de-sac, which was lousy news. They were fast running out of options on this level, and doubling back to try their luck on the floor above held little appeal—or hope.

Like everywhere, the walls were crumbling. Dislodged by gigantic roots that had squeezed their way into the corridor, masonry had fallen and lay in moss covered heaps on the ground, creating an obstacle course—not improved by the darkness. This far in, there were no more mirrors to channel daylight, and they were dependent on the Marines' flashlights. The batteries wouldn't last forever, though. Unless they found an entrance to the fortress soon, they'd have to fashion torches—but maybe not just yet.

Staring at the roots, something struck Daniel as odd. He wolfed down the remainder of the second candy bar, scrunched up the wrapper, and groped his way up the wall and to his feet. The Tylenol seemed to have kicked in, but the hallway was still bobbing. Never mind. He'd marched through earthquakes before. Navigating from root to root, he stumbled the five yards to the end of the corridor.

"Daniel Jackson. What are you doing?" Teal'c used the exquisitely cautious tones of someone dealing with a raving lunatic.

"Come have a look at this!" Knowing what it would do to his head, Daniel resisted the temptation to laugh. "I should have seen it right away!"

It being the conspicuous absence of roots drilling though the wall that closed off the tunnel. More importantly, either side of the blockage was a figure carved in the stone.

"What is it?" asked Teal'c from behind, still sounding therapeutic—possibly to do with the fact that there was nothing to look at. Though that, very likely, had been the point.

"*Speak friend and enter.*" Daniel whispered ecstatically. Gandalf in the Mines of Moria, indeed.

"I do not understand." Teal'c's tone was graduating from therapy to Diazepam.

"It's from a book, Teal'c. These people are trying to open a closed gate, and *Speak friend and enter* is the only clue they've got toward the password."

"I see. Unless I am mistaken, the password was *mellon*, meaning *friend*." At Daniel's one-eyed stare of disbelief, Teal'c looked just about as smug as he could manage. Very, in other words. "I have seen the movie."

"Uhuh."

"You believe that this is a similar mechanism?"

"I believe it's a door," Daniel replied. "See those two figures. They're *dikpals*." Possessed by the sudden, inescapable notion of what Jack would make of that name, he brought his face back under control and pointed at the carvings. "It means *guardians* or *gatekeepers*—and they wouldn't guard just nothing. There's got to be an entrance here. Between you and our friends, we should be able to open it."

Like rubberneckers who'd arrived at an accident site too late, the Marines had joined them without understanding what all the excitement was about. Wilkins was the first to twig on. When Teal'c leveled his staff weapon at the wall, the corporal placed a restraining hand on his arm.

"Hang on. I'm thinking we don't wanna raise a whole lot of noise unless it's unavoidable. See this?"

"There's a crack there?" And no, Daniel couldn't see it, though that wasn't entirely surprising. He watched Wilkins's fingers outline a six by six foot square on the wall.

"Might as well try pushing," the corporal suggested.

They did. Two United States Marines and one Jaffa were pushing that wall to within an inch of its life, and nothing moved. Teal'c longingly eyed his staff weapon. Not yet. Daniel reached for the nearest piece of metal, which happened to be Lambert's canteen again, unclipped it from the sergeant's belt, and started knocking along the invisible square Wilson had drawn. Down the left vertical, the sound changed pitch. The wall was thinner there, which only made sense—unless it had some kind of bevel, the door couldn't open. Never underestimate a sugar high.

"It's got a central hinge," Daniel guessed. "Push on the right."

Three brawny men applied their combined weight to the right half of the panel. Without so much as a creak, the massive stone slab began to pivot until it stood parallel to the corridor walls, leaving a two-and-a-half foot gap on either side.

"Open Sesame," said Sergeant Lambert.

"Wrong story," Daniel remarked under his breath and turned to Teal'c. "We've got to leave Wilkins and Lambert here. In there they'll be at too much of a disadvantage—besides, we need somebody to keep the door open."

It took a while to persuade the Marines that it wasn't an issue of trust, but eventually they bowed to common sense. Lambert even went as far as offering Daniel his sidearm. The offer was declined in Morse, complete with an explanation of how Teal'c's staff weapon and *zat* would be quite sufficient. The two men, still grumbling, settled in behind the door, and Daniel and Teal'c slipped through one of the gaps into what Daniel hoped was Nirrti's fortress.

At first glance it was a dead ringer for what they'd encountered on the other side; walls in need of repointing, rubble-strewn corridors, tree roots in search of space. But the tunnel was leading steadily uphill now, there was less water damage, and at last the roots gave up, too. After about an hour of silently creeping up the passage, Teal'c froze and snapped off the flashlight. Darkness dropped like a lead weight, but once his vision had adjusted, Daniel could make out a faint bright glimmer—miles away it seemed.

"Someone is ahead," whispered Teal'c. "I can hear footsteps and voices."

Daniel had long given up on jumping at this type of announcement from Teal'c. Jaffa hearing was at least twice as acute as anything mere humans had to offer. "Any idea how many?"

"Not yet. We are too far away still. How do you wish to proceed?"

How do *I* wish to proceed? It was too dark to see Teal'c's face and determine if, maybe, this was a Jaffa joke.

"Daniel Jackson?"

Okay. No joke. So who had died and put Dr. Jackson in command? And that was a very nasty thought. Having decisions forced on him wasn't a happy thing either—probably dreamed up by some cosmic force that wanted to have fun at Daniel's expense. Something about the shoe being on the other foot. What was it Jack had said apropos of bad calls?

Of course Daniel had done it before. Digs with SG-11, meet-and-greets with SG-9, he'd gone undercover—hell, to all intents and purposes he'd led the Abydonians. But that didn't mean he had to like treading that fine line between reason and instinct or embrace this *other lives depend on my every move* tactical stuff. The kind of stuff Jack did every day of his life. The kind of stuff Teal'c had done. And look what it did to them. So, unless it was to teach him a redundant object lesson at the worst possible time, why would Teal'c—

"It is merely expedient, Daniel Jackson. Under the circumstances we both shall fare better if I supply the brawn to your brain."

"It's not like you're stupid, Teal'c."

"I am not. You, however, are not very brawny at this moment in time."

"Point taken. Though I'm sure if you thought about it, you could put it little more bluntly."

"Without doubt. How do you wish to proceed?"

Ah, yes. The million dollar question hadn't gone away, had it? Dr. Jackson, how do you wish to proceed? Apart from sauntering into a Goa'uld Shangri-La overrun with Jaffa clones and asking politely if they minded handing back your team mates, washed and pressed if it wasn't too much trouble.

Daniel's instinct was to charge in and free Jack, thus putting someone with the necessary training and experience back in charge. Reason told him it was a crap idea—and yes, he did hate treading that fine line. Jack was the one Nirrti wanted, which meant two things. First, he'd be under heavy guard—too heavy for two lightly armed men—and, second, he probably was safe for the time being. Probably.

Other lives depend on my every move.

It was a hell of a choice. "We try and find Sam," Daniel said softly and then, driven by some weird urge to justify himself, rattled on, "She's the technical wiz. So if I'm right about that transmitter, and if we're going to put that thing out of commission, we'll need her expertise. Besides, she's—"

"I believe it is a wise decision, Daniel Jackson."

"So what are we waiting for?"

And that was that.

Neon-bright streaks—stars stretched to infinity in hyperspace—rushed past the *tel'tac*'s cockpit window. Hammond watched them with something that bordered on a five-year-old's sense of awe and a good deal of humility. Only a handful of Earthlings, for want of a better word, had ever seen this. But it didn't stop man from using pilfered technology he couldn't even begin to comprehend to build a vessel capable of these speeds. Hubris? Or the desire to defend a planet that, polluted and overpopulated, still was the only home he had? Maybe a little bit of both. And if that was the case, did George Hammond really have a right to judge Simmons and the NID?

The hell he didn't. He wasn't quite that humble.

"We shall be leaving hyperspace soon." Bra'tac glanced up at him, hands cupped around the navigational controls of the *tel'tac*. It looked like he was cradling a glowing basketball. "You may wish to sit, Hammond of Texas."

"Why?" Maybourne asked suspiciously, white-knuckled fingers clutching the armrests of his seat. He wasn't really taking to this deep space thing and had been subdued ever since he'd first clapped eyes on the small transport ship.

Hammond made it to a seat with less than a second to spare. Engines roaring in protest, the *tel'tac* gave a sharp lurch, and the bright streaks outside the window abruptly contracted into shiny pinpricks. Harry gave a soft groan and closed his eyes.

"That is why," Bra'tac replied after the fact and in a tone that suggested smugness lessons were an integral part of Jaffa training. Teal'c had it down to a fine art, too.

Seemingly ponderous at sub-light speed, the *tel'tac* entered the system that was their destination. The second planet was a gas giant and, like Jupiter, had trapped more than its fair share of moons. The sixth of those moons was M3D 335, and it was rising; a small beige crescent that peeked over the orange and purple striations of its primary's atmosphere and slowly rounded into a disc, still beige and still unremarkable—but for what had happened there.

What had happened there—or what Hammond thought had happened—was the reason that he and Bra'tac had agreed not to use the Stargate. The trip in the *tel'tac* might take longer, but the fact that they could drop in unannounced and—thanks to the cloaking device—unobserved more than made up for the delay.

"Do you wish me to approach the moon's *Chappa'ai*, Hammond of Texas?"

"Yes, Master Bra'tac. It's as good a place as any to start looking."

"Indeed."

Bra'tac slipped the little ship into a retrograde orbit around M3D 335, and they slowly spiraled toward the surface and the night side of the moon. There was no cloud cover, only a fine haze that softened what few contours the landscape showed. This was one heck of a boring piece of rock, Hammond decided and watched the holographic display in front of Bra'tac instead. Not that he could make any sense of the Goa'uld glyphs that flicked through thin air. His best guess was that the *tel'tac*'s sensors were scanning for naquadah. Given that a Stargate's rings were made entirely of the metal, it was one sure-fire way of locating the gate.

Up ahead the endless plains suddenly were broken up by some sort of elevation, craggy, black enough to make the evening gloom seem bright, and jutting from the ground like Ayers Rock—only much,

much larger. At some distance to the east of it, between the ship and the range of cliffs, twinkled lights.

"There's the camp," Hammond said, rising from his seat again.

The *tel'tac* banked south to bring them in directly above the scattered collection of huts and tents.

"Looks quiet enough," offered Maybourne. Now that *terra firma* was in sight, he obviously felt that it was safe to leave his chair and had stepped up to the window.

"Yeah," Hammond muttered. Nothing seemed out of the ordinary. He wasn't quite sure what he'd expected—Goa'uld motherships, factory-size labs, the island of Dr Moreau—but all he saw was a thoroughly average training camp. "Let's find the gate."

Bra'tac didn't acknowledge, but the camp fell away beneath them and the *tel'tac* sped for the cliffs, sniffing after naquadah. Within moments the rock face had grown into a humungous obsidian wall.

"Dead end," Maybourne said dryly.

"It is not." Bra'tac launched a pitying glance in his direction. "Observe, Maybourne."

Presumably Sam Carter could have explained how this worked. George Hammond, on the other hand, didn't have the first idea—not that it bothered him too much, above and beyond the sudden covetous realization of how useful this gadget would be for long-range reconnaissance. The view from the window was replaced by a three-dimensional topographic skeleton of the area ahead. Tightly packed contour lines shone bright green and, about a klick north of their current position, retracted sharply into a gorge that sliced the cliffs in half.

"Very nice." As the map winked out, Harry gave a grin. "Listen, Master, if you got any of these to spare, I know some people who'd be happy to—"

"Cut it out," snapped Hammond.

It got him a sour stare, but Maybourne stopped wheeler-dealing for the time being. Without comment, Bra'tac shifted his hands over the surface of the basketball. The ship banked again and headed for the mouth of the gorge, climbing all the way to hug the top of the cliffs and turn east, following the canyon below. Seconds later, the *tel'tac* swept out over a sizeable crater and hovered, silently and invisibly, some fifty meters above the gate.

Beneath, a platoon-strength group of Marines stood lined up in orderly rows of two, clearly waiting to embark and clearly not expecting a free ride. In addition to Spaz-12s and rifles, each pair carried a grenade launcher. One of four men who seemed to constitute the guard force at the gate stepped in front of the DHD and began to dial.

"Where the hell are they off to?" asked Maybourne. "Kabul?"

"Unlikely," Hammond murmured absently, squinting at the DHD. "I can't see a damn thing."

Bra'tac's fingers slid over the controls, and the image in the window jumped closer—or so it seemed. Trying to ignore the knot of worry in his gut, Hammond stared at the brightly lit glyphs around the red centerpiece. "Earth," he said softly. "They're going back to the SGC."

"With that kind of gear? Are they planning to stage a palace revolution? I mean—"

"Hammond of Texas," Bra'tac interrupted, sounding a little vague. "You may wish to look at the *Chappa'ai*."

Vagueness in Bra'tac was enough of a novelty to make Hammond take up the suggestion. At first it didn't register, but when it did, he let out a low, slow whistle. "I'll be damned," he murmured under his breath.

The gate was spinning for its third lock. The second one, the one Hammond had just about caught, had been Auriga. It should have been Cetus. The third chevron engaged—on Lynx instead of Centaurus. Although the DHD showed the coordinates for Earth, the gate itself was dialing somewhere else entirely. The Marines below were either blissfully unaware of the situation—or fully aware of circumstances General Hammond had never been briefed on; they embarked briskly and without hesitation, pair after pair stepping into the event horizon and traveling—where?

"Carter was right," Harry said. "It's malfunctioning."

"I do not believe it is." Bra'tac didn't offer any further insights, and it was impossible to tell whether he contradicted Maybourne for the heck of it or whether there was something else on his mind.

Below, the last pair of Marines mounted the dais. George

Hammond was staring at the gate with the kind of desperate intensity that made your eyes water. Then the men disappeared, the wormhole collapsed, and the chevrons winked out.

"I didn't catch the first glyph, but I've got the rest of the address," Hammond announced.

"Indeed, so have I." Bra'tac flashed a sly smile, fingers gliding across the controls again. The *tel'tac*'s onboard systems played back a holographic image of *seven* glyphs.

Hammond wrestled down a growl and checked if Harry was entertaining any further notions of acquiring contraband technology. In fact, the ex-colonel wasn't. He was studying the gate and the surrounding area.

As if he'd noticed Hammond's stare, he suddenly turned. "Four guards at the gate. That's a bit light. Unless—"

"—the guards are Jaffa," Hammond finished for him.

"These men are not Jaffa." Bra'tac's dark eyes glittered with a mix of pride and righteous indignation. "You are Jaffa here and here"—gnarled fingers tapped the old warrior's head and heart—"and it takes years upon years of training to truly understand this. You may become Jaffa without a symbiote, but a symbiote alone will not make you Jaffa.

"However, I should not indulge myself. At one hundred and thirty-seven years of age and with these old bones aching, teaching sometimes seems more attractive than fighting." The shrewd glance he threw at Hammond gave the lie to that confession—Bra'tac could be as coy as a maiden aunt and obviously enjoyed the effect. Even when it was slightly marred by an agile leap from the pilot's seat. "*Jaffa! Kree!*"

The door to the cargo compartment slid open with a promptitude that suggested Bra'tac's men had been standing right behind it, rigidly at attention, shin guards spit-shined to a luster. Contemplating his disembowelment, no doubt, Harry retreated to the farthest corner of the cockpit. Bra'tac pretended not to notice and began to issue a clipped string of orders in Goa'uld.

Hammond felt a momentary twinge of sympathy for Harry. It passed when he remembered Teal'c, stolidly submitting to Maybourne's threat of using him as a lab rat. Had he considered it just punishment for his betrayal of Apophis? Or had he known it would never happen, because his trust in Jack O'Neill had been complete even then?

The memories spun away, scattered by a hard hand slapping Hammond's back. "Observe," Bra'tac said and turned him back to the window.

The glass—no, it couldn't be glass, Hammond reminded himself—the clear pane darkened to the charcoal tint of a celebrity limo's passenger windows, and from the cargo hold came an oddly rhythmic hum and a surge of light. He would have looked had Bra'tac's hand on his shoulder not stopped him. In front of the gate five metal circles—like miniature Stargates—seemed to pop from the ground, stacking on top of each other and infusing with sudden radiance. A ring transporter. Hammond was aware of the technology, of course, but he'd never seen it for himself.

The cloverleaf of Marines had sprung apart, diving into cover behind the DHD and the dais. As the rings whapped out of existence again, apprehensive faces, MP5s glued to cheeks, peered from the respective hideouts. The weapons were trained on the object the transporter had delivered, a small silvery sphere sitting harmlessly in the dust. George Hammond could relate to silver-sphere-o-phobia. A similar globe, inhabited by sentient bacteria of all things, had nailed Jack to the gate room wall and just about killed him. Though this one seemed to be of a different variety, and if he was right, it—

The little ball exploded into brutal brilliance—even the tinted window couldn't dim it completely—and if such nuclear brightness had an acoustic equivalent, Hammond was hearing it now, though tamped by distance and the *tel'tac*'s hull. If it felt like this inside the ship, just how bad would it be it out there? Legends claimed a banshee's shriek could kill a person. Hammond decided he believed it.

Outside, the Marines were reeling, eyes scrunched shut, hands clapped over ears, weapons discarded, mouths gaping in screams that remained inaudible under the noise. Within moments the men collapsed, crumpling like rag dolls while the light faded and the shrieking stilled.

"Are they dead?" Hammond asked in a dry-throated rasp, suspecting the answer but needing to make sure nonetheless.

"They are not," replied Bra'tac. "It was a stun grenade."

"Flash-bang for grownups." Harry's enthusiastic tone was at odds with the wistful look he shot Hammond, correctly assuming that the grenades were off-limits, too.

"Come quickly. We cannot wait until they revive or reinforcements arrive."

Bra'tac shooed them into the cargo hold and, together with four of his Jaffa, into position for the ring transporter. It was a snug fit, and the air buzzed with the smell of men sweating pre-battle adrenaline—though, if they were lucky, there would be no battle. Not yet, at any rate.

Men and smell and anticipation fractured to nothing. A ring transporter worked along the same principles as the Stargate, Sam Carter had said. Sounded about right, except the experience was a little less disorientating, a little less chilly. Like pictures changing in a slideshow, the stuffy cargo hold morphed into the crater around the gate and tepid air, with only a brief moment of blackness in between.

The Marines were out cold, draped around the dais and the DHD. Bra'tac crouched by the nearest man, a faintly Mediterranean looking hulk. Two quick slices with a knife exposed the Marine's midriff, and for a second Bra'tac recoiled, shoulders stiffening. Then he slipped his fingers into the pouch and teased the symbiote from its womb. Blindly searching for something—a host?—the black, spiky head undulated over the Marine's stomach, sniffing the air until it withdrew again—not soon enough for Hammond's liking.

"Jeez," groaned Harry, voice strangled with revulsion.

Bra'tac rose with an awkwardness that, for once, betrayed his age and rapped out a command, sending his troops into a flurry of activity. "This man is weak," he remarked grimly, turning to Hammond. "We must make haste. Come."

While his Jaffa began to tie up the unconscious Marines, Bra'tac headed for the DHD in a whirl of black wool and worry. Reaching the device, he dropped to his knees and opened an inspection hatch under the dialing table. "See?" he asked curtly.

George Hammond didn't. "What am I looking at?"

"These"—Bra'tac pointed at an array of colored crystals that gleamed dismally in the jaundiced light of the planet—"have been switched. That is why the symbols do no longer correspond."

"Can you fix it?"

"Worst thing you could do." Harry shook his head, heading off the reply. "Four missing guards will leave them guessing, but if you fix that they'll know that we know."

"Your *shol'va* is right, Hammond of Texas." You had to look twice to spot it, but Bra'tac was actually grinning a little. "Undoing the damage would reveal more than we want to reveal. By dialing the address for the Tauri, we can follow those warriors. If your information is correct, we shall find your people and Teal'c there."

"Alright." Hammond nodded slowly, then jerked his chin at the Marines who, bound and gagged and hovered over by Bra'tac's men, now lay side by side like a row of corncobs in a produce stall. "What about them?"

"They will be brought aboard the *tel'tac*. Two of my men will guard them."

Which left Hammond with Bra'tac, four Jaffa, and Harry Maybourne whose support was capricious, to say the least. Not exactly the stuff of conquests, but it would have to be enough. Without another word, George Hammond stepped to the DHD and dialed the coordinates for Earth.

CHAPTER SEVENTEEN

The last thing Sam remembered, though she couldn't recall how or why, was drowning in pain, and she gathered that memory and put it where she couldn't see it. She'd take it out, dust it off, and analyze it later, but right now other stuff probably was higher up on the agenda.

Like where the hell she was.

Unwilling to move just yet, she patted around and, much to her surprise, found soft, dry surfaces. That ruled out the jungle, which had a habit of being either hard and damp or squishy and sodden. It also was notable for a shortage of beds, and she was lying in a bed. Plus, she no longer reeked of bacterial rot, hell hog dung, and God knew what else. Somebody had bathed her, put her into clean clothes—clean sheets at the very least.

None of which explained where the hell she was.

Her eyes had drifted shut again while she wasn't paying attention, and now she forced herself into another effort to open them. Lids scraped over eyeballs coated with ground glass, but aside from that she was feeling better than she had in days. Less feverish, less woozy. Her leg didn't hurt, and that was very welcome news.

Of course it still didn't explain where the hell she was.

The room was on the smallish side, filled with the spicy, resiny scent of wooden wall panels and ceilings. No windows, though light filtered in through an open door and a couple of carved screens, inset into the wall and separating the chamber from the hallway outside. The carvings looked familiar. Figures. Daniel had called them Baklava, Balaclava, and Meyer. Or something. She probably was hanging around Colonel O'Neill too much.

The Colonel.

Daniel.

Events crashed in on her like a collapsing roof and yanked her up from the bed, bolt-upright amid a swirling cloud of fear and panic. No, not panic. You can't afford panic, Major! Concentrate on the situation.

She was the sole occupant of the room—no more than she'd expected—and the hallway seemed deserted. Okay, this could officially be declared weird. Unless she'd skipped a page, she should be held prisoner, in some state-of-the-art Goa'uld facility with a bunch of Jaffa (identical or otherwise) clomping up and down outside the cell. Instead, open doors and a bed. The latter had been a godsend, and the former she wasn't going to quibble with. High time to check out the neighborhood.

The sit-up had caused no side-effects, so she probably was alright to get up. Sam flung back the cover, a wispy sheet of silk and merely perfunctory in the heat, stood and toppled over, pole-axed too suddenly to break the fall. Her shoulder and hip took the brunt, slamming into an unforgiving stone floor with enough force to make her teeth rattle.

For a few seconds she just lay there, dazed, then she contracted into a curl, whimpering softly when the movement jarred parts of her body that didn't want to be jarred ever again. Cheek pressed against the coolness of the tiles, she groped through the fog in her brain, trying to think, because that at least didn't require any form of motion. What had happened just now?

… gravity will win, because that's what gravity does…

Physics 101.

But gravity can only win when the system's out of balance. She hadn't been out of balance, had she? Sat up straight, both feet firmly on the ground, both—

Both?

She couldn't remember because, once you'd learned to walk, it was just one of the things you did without giving it a second thought, like breathing. Of course breathing was different in that it was a reflex and didn't have to be learned, so—

Quit stalling.

One palm pressed against cool stone, Sam eased herself over, the skin on her back spiking into goose-bumps where it touched the floor. T-shirt shrunk in the wash? She slid her hands over her chest and realized that she was wearing some kind of crop-top, tight-fitting and embroidered. Last time she'd worn something along those lines, she'd ended up in a harem. Fingers glided on across a bare midriff, feeling warm and little sweaty, but no longer fever-hot. Just below the waist, more fabric, light and loose and silky. A sari. Cute. She'd blend right in with Nirrti's cronies.

Nirrti.

Time to get going.

Deciding to ignore the order, her hands kept exploring, and her right leg was in collusion. The knee bent, pulled up, for her fingers to feel taut muscle under the silk. All present and correct, and it really didn't seem necessary to continue the study, but her body was determined to do its own thing. Left leg. The bad leg. Better not to do anything too wild. Gently. Gently now. Her hand brushed a hip, reached down, found a thigh, angled for the knee, clutched a fistful of empty silk.

"No."

The terror that had been spinning in shiny whorls ever since the fall—from grace, from all that defined her life—cascaded up her throat, stifling a need to howl, turning it into soft keening, the sound of an animal trapped. She'd known, of course, from the instant she'd lost her balance; just as she'd known that it would have to come to this. But she'd wanted it to happen on her terms, be there, be awake when it happened, so she could find a way of dealing with it. Nirrti had taken that from her, too, like she'd taken everything else—Janet, Teal'c, Daniel, the Colonel.

No wonder the room had been left unlocked and unguarded. Dr. Samantha Carter, Major, USAF, wasn't going anywhere. The thought brought a laugh that sounded like a death rattle to her. Then the need to howl came back, kept in check only by her resolve not to give anyone that satisfaction—not Nirrti, not anyone. Instead, her fists, balled tight enough to drive her nails—short and unglamorous but practical, because Sam believed in things practical, like having two legs—to drive her nails into her palms. The fists started pounding the floor, a trick she'd picked up from Colonel O'Neill. He'd use it to channel pain, but after a while the slow thud-thud also became soothingly hypnotic. Besides, there was little else she could do.

Thud-thud. Lie on her back, stare at the ceiling, pound the floor. It wasn't the end of the world. Thud-thud. Not as long as she kept her fitness reports up to scratch. There were plenty of amputees in the armed forces. Thud-thud. *Amputee.* She rolled the word over in her mind, not ready to say it out loud—if she'd ever be. She'd get a desk job. Not the end of the world. Thud-thud. Except, it looked like a damn close second when the thing you loved more than anything was the thrill of going through the Stargate. Thud—

A barely noticeable drop in temperature stroked over her incomplete body. Someone was standing in the doorway, blocking the light, casting a shadow. The fists froze mid-thud, and her right hand unfurled and, obeying years of training and habit, shot to her hip, where the holster used to be and her sidearm.

"You won't need your gun, Major, even if you had it." The voice sounded calm, almost diffident, and vaguely familiar.

Familiar enough to pique Sam's curiosity, and she finally tore her gaze away from the ceiling. Nothing much there, anyway. The shadow filled the door, broad-shouldered and well over six feet tall. Teal'c's bulk, but not Teal'c's voice. She levered herself up on her elbows, watched him slip into the room as furtively as he'd arrived at the door. She *was* curious now—even if it didn't translate into caring what happened to her.

At two meters distance she recognized him, resisted the impulse to scuttle backward and away from him. After all, she didn't care. "You!"

"Easy, ma'am." He crouched by her side. "I've got no intention of harming you."

She almost believed him. In the past three days he seemed to have aged ten years—they had to be traveling in the same time zone, Sam thought wryly. His eyes were bloodshot and heavily ringed, and the haggard face clashed with the folkloristic outfit. Bare chest, baggy pants, and no shoes—the latter explained why she hadn't heard him coming. Then she noticed something else, and it tipped the balance. "Last time I saw you, you had a pouch and a tattoo."

"No, ma'am." Master Sergeant Macdonald shook his head emphatically. "You didn't see me. I'm the original."

"Sure," Sam grunted noncommittally. "So you're saying you're not the one tried to shoot me out of a tree?"

More headshaking. "That was the prototype. If it's any consolation, when Nirrti heard you'd kicked the snot out of him, she got so pissed she terminated him and the entire line."

"While letting you stroll around at will?" There probably wasn't much point in picking at the inconsistencies in Macdonald's story, but what the hell? Sam pushed herself up a little more. Her shoulder ached.

"She isn't. Letting me stroll around at will, I mean." He winced and shrugged it away, whatever *it* was. "Look, I probably haven't got much time. We need to get going."

That settled it. If blind men could be Marines, she could stay with the flyboys. "Where? And how? You gonna carry me?"

"Come again?" His eyebrows headed north. "Look, Major, I realize you're Air Force, but even you guys have been known to walk on occasion."

Holy crap! He really did have vision problems—or was lacking some basic numeracy skills. "Sergeant, last time I looked I was a leg short." Sam's breath hitched for an instant. She'd said it. It was real now. "I may be wrong about this, but I think it might put a crimp into that walking thing."

"Goddammit, not you too!" Macdonald started swearing a blue streak. When he came up for air, he leaned closer, mumbled an apology, and slapped her hard. "Look at it! Look at your legs, Major! What do you see?"

"Stars!" she hissed, but for a moment—maybe because stark fury blotted everything else from her mind—the veil tore, and Sam saw empty folds of silk fill out, take shape, taper down a calf to reveal an ankle and foot, complete with five toes and a set of blisters. She reached out reflexively, responding to a need to let other senses confirm the impossible, but before her fingers could touch the fabric, it deflated again and the image—vision—delusion—dissolved.

"You saw it, didn't you?" Macdonald asked quietly, a pinch of triumph spicing his tone.

"What? Why?" She had no idea how to phrase the question, let alone what the answer might be.

"It's that b—that witch, Nirrti. She's messing with your head."

"How?" It provoked a shrug. Sam thought of Janet and that inconceivable act of betrayal. "Dr. Fraiser?"

He nodded an affirmation. "Dr. Fraiser, me, my men, too. We

started killing each other to get here, to be *chosen*." The lines of fatigue on his face deepened, and his complexion turned gray in the mellow light fingering through the screens. "We—"

"If what you're saying is true, it's not your fault, Sergeant."

"The hell it isn't! That clone of mine has got my body, my mind, he's me—and he goes and strings one of my own men up on the temple wall to be eaten alive."

The kid's pale face, pleading eyes, bloodied body leaped out at Sam in living color, and she struggled to breathe under that crushing weight of guilt and responsibility. "For what it's worth, he wasn't eaten alive," she whispered. "I shot him. There was nothing else I could do for him. I'm sorry, Sergeant."

"His name was Gonzales." He held her gaze for a long moment. Then he glanced at the door, the hallway. "We have to go. Here, let me help you up."

Threading his arms around Sam, Macdonald lugged her to her feet... foot. Knowing—or having a strong hunch at least—that her leg was exactly where it was supposed to be didn't make a difference. She felt as though someone had ordered her to levitate. "This won't work," she muttered.

"Hey, Major, you ever hike someplace really cold?"

Antarctica sprang to mind. "Yes."

"Ever froze your toes? Same difference. You can't feel them, but you still can walk."

The memory triggered by his query had nothing to do with Antarctica. It was fresh, and it hit hard enough to make her gasp.

"Major?" The sergeant's voice barely registered.

Daniel is gone.

Two identical Jaffa, a pair of twins in a tug o' war over a floppy toy, have Colonel O'Neill strung between them. He doesn't seem to notice; a mix of rage and grief boiling behind his eyes, he stares at the spot where the ring transporter disappeared.

Sam, like so much deadwood, is still lying on the floor of the vault. One Jaffa pins down her shoulders, another her ankles, and Nirrti crouches next to her.

"What the hell do you think you're—" A backhand across the face snaps off the Colonel's protest.

Nirrti's hand opens on a healing device concealed in her palm. "You do not wish her to die, do you?"

The device hovers over Sam's leg, its glow rising from amber to deep red. It's wrong. All wrong. All freezing. The pain is icy, eating its way outward from the bone, freezing nerve and muscle, and wrapping Sam in a glacial cocoon she can't escape. Somewhere outside Colonel O'Neill is shouting, the sound of his voice blending into a fabric of agony that seems to draw down the ceiling to stifle her. She hears herself scream, thrashes against the hands holding her down, and finally, mercifully, passes out.

"Major!" Macdonald was shaking her.

A ruse within a ruse within a ruse, like some goddamn Russian doll—or the mirror cabinet at a fun fair, and Sam was rapidly losing track of which way to turn or what to think. Or whom to trust, for that matter. She pushed the sergeant away, her balance precarious on an unfelt leg she'd tentatively ordered not to give under her. Like St. Peter following Christ across the Lake of Galilee—if she lost faith, she'd sink. But it seemed as though Macdonald had told her the truth on this count at least. Her weight poised in a way that should have sent her sprawling again, she remained vertical. It *was* in her head—but what else had Nirrti done to her?

She shelved the question as not immediately relevant and glared at the sergeant. "Why are you here? What do you want?"

His hands flew up in a *Whoa!* gesture, and he smiled at her coolly. "Common sense and training kicking in, Major? Don't worry, I probably wouldn't trust me either. Fact is, your reputation precedes you. They say you're smart." He closed in a step, making it a struggle for Sam to hold her ground. "You asked me why Nirrti lets me wander at will. She knows I can't run. If I go anyplace I shouldn't go, she reaches in there"—he tapped the side of his skull—"and I stop breathing, simple as that. If she wants me to come to her, I come, like a dog on a leash. If she says *contact your superiors*, I do it, and I tell them what she orders me to tell.

"What I want? I want to get out of here. Go home, get reinforcements, free my men. You're gonna make it possible. You're gonna knock out whatever gadget Nirrti uses to screw with my head. In exchange, I'll take you along with me. Fair enough?"

He sounded convincing. *Sounded* being the operative word. Sam decided to sniff at the bait. A little. "How does Nirrti communicate with you?"

"I told you." He did that skull-tap thing again. "She reaches in there."

"So what makes you think she won't notice what you're up to?"

"I never thought that for a moment. But she's a little busy right now, so we've got a window. When she starts looking for me, you'll be the first to know." Macdonald sucked in a deep breath and looked straight at her. "There's a good chance I'll sell you out."

And that, Sam admitted, had to be God's own truth. He couldn't be that stupid, could he? Unless it was a ruse within a ruse within a ruse. Then again, her options were few and far between. One point needed clearing up, though. "It's not fair enough."

"What?"

"Your deal. Before I do anything else, we go and get Colonel O'Neill."

"Out of the question, Major. Who the hell do you figure is *keeping* Nirrti busy?"

Reeling back might have been a relief. As it was, Sam didn't dare to, for reasons static and tactical. Nirrti, who enjoyed turning children into bombs or programming their bodies to self-destruct, was *busy* with the Colonel. It didn't bear thinking about, so why did her brain, with the brutal zeal of a fire-and-brimstone preacher, latch on to the notion of blood and screams?

"If you're trying to persuade me, you're failing, Sergeant." She choked it out, bristled at herself for that weakness.

"We've got a motto, ma'am." Macdonald's voice carried a trace of pity. "*Semper fi*. Don't for a second believe I forgot."

"We got something like that, too," she replied softly but didn't elaborate. Macdonald was right. If Colonel O'Neill was to have any chance at all, she'd have to play it the sergeant's way. "What kind of gadget are we talking about?"

"Damned if I know, Major." He gave a crooked grin. "I was hoping you'd tell me."

"Great," muttered Sam, already starting on a mental sift of everything she'd ever read or heard about mind control. Holding out an arm for the sergeant to steady her, she added, "Let's go. I can think and walk at the same time."

"To sum it up, the men are in good health and symbiote acceptance is one-hundred percent across the board." The nerdier of the two xenodocs stabbed the air with a white, maggoty-looking finger and leaned further into the table. "However," he intoned and followed it up with a theatrical pause.

"*However* what?" barked Frank Simmons, whose tolerance for histrionics had reached zero.

His arm hurt, he'd had too much excruciatingly bad coffee while waiting out the medical exams, and he was tired to death of the posturing and the monumental waste of time these people subjected him to. And now the hatchet-faced brunette set her features into a scandalized pucker, van Leyden made placating noises in his direction, and Crowley gave a long-suffering sigh.

Simmons allowed himself a couple of breaths, inhaling air so depleted of oxygen it felt like chicken soup. No wonder he was getting fractious. For the past two hours they'd been cooped up here, in the com shack, the chosen conference venue by virtue of its being off-limits to practically everybody, and had listened to an interminable litany of test results, which could have been summarized in two minutes flat.

The minuscule room was stuffed with electronics gear, leaving just enough space at the center to accommodate a table and a handful of chairs. A single window looked out across the plain, toward the moon's horizon and a sky filled with the swollen belly of the planet above, which did nothing to ease the encroaching sense of claustrophobia. What was more—and Simmons finally admitted it—he had a pretty good idea as to the precise nature of *however*.

"*However* what?" he asked again, trying to sound apologetic.

The nerd made a prissy show of straightening out his dented ego and offered, "*However*, in all cases the subjects' metabolism runs well above normal parameters. They burn vastly more energy than non-enhanced subjects."

Dammit. With some difficulty, Simmons controlled a grimace. No use getting all excited. It might be a normal side-effect of the enhancement. After all, given the rapid healing and recovery from exertion, plus the increased strength and stamina, it stood to reason that the whole system needed to be sped up, didn't it?

Apparently Crowley thought as much. "Well, so we feed them protein supplements and stuff. So what? I mean, they're eating for two now, aren't they?"

Van Leyden's aide spotted a chance to kiss ass and burst into uproarious laughter. Hatchet-Face stared at him as though he were an insect she'd fished from a tub of cold cream on her dresser at home, and Nerd performed an eye roll.

"You might want to think of a campfire, General," he addressed Crowley in the tone of infinitely strained patience one would use with a dull child. "The hotter it gets, the faster it burns."

"Don't patronize me, Doctor!" snapped Crowley, making the lingering chuckles subside into a hiccup. "Just spit it out, whatever it is you're trying to say."

"What my esteemed colleague is trying to say, sir," Hatchet-Face took up the gauntlet, "is that accelerated cell metabolism means accelerated aging. We've also noted that it becomes more pronounced the longer the subject has been modified."

"And?"

"And if this trend continues, the long-term prognosis is grim, to say the least."

"What's to say that the trend will continue?" Simmons asked, knowing he was clutching at straws. "It may be a natural reaction to the symbiote and work itself out after a while."

Nerd piped up again. "It may, but so far our results indicate otherwise, Colonel. Two of your Marines, Sergeants"—he shuffled the papers in front of him and eventually retrieved a crumpled name list—"Poletti and Keefe, were among the first men to be enhanced, is that correct?"

"Yes."

"Actually, they were the very first," offered van Leyden's aide.

"Yeah, well, that would seem to corroborate our theory. Tissue samples from both these men show evidence of cell death. In addition, their bodies have started to burn muscle tissue in order to fuel an exponentially increased rate of metabolism. In the simplest of terms, gentlemen"—Nerd peered at them, one at a time—"these two men are starving."

"Impossible!" Crowley's face suggested that he considered this to be an affront against the US Marine Corps in general, and against himself in particular.

The xenodocs responded with synchronized shrugs. "It's what the tests say," Hatchet-Face proclaimed in a monotone. "Although there is always the possibility, as Colonel Simmons theorized earlier, that this is a temporary and normal side-effect of the enhancement."

Nobody looked convinced. Van Leyden cleared his throat and asked the million dollar question. "So what do you recommend we do, Doctors?"

"The safest course of action," stated Nerd after a quick glance at Hatchet-Face; they seemed to have argued over that one, "would be to recall the two men"—more shuffling of papers until he found the list again—"Poletti and Keefe. We propose to take them to Area 51 for observation. One of the possibilities we discussed was a high-protein, high-fat diet. It may solve the problem."

"Fine. Let's do that," confirmed Crowley. Then he turned to van Leyden. "Are Poletti and Keefe with the team that's embarked to the training site?"

"No, sir. Poletti, Keefe, and two others are on guard duty at the gate."

"Well, that's easy enough." Crowley looked at Simmons. "You can just pick them up when you go back. We'll send a couple men with you to take over from the sergeants. So, if that's all," he added, rising. Clearly, this was to be all. "Dismissed, gentlemen... and lady."

Snapping of briefcase lids, rustling of documents, and scraping of chair legs blended into the usual symphony of exodus. Simmons wanted to shove aside this assembly of small-minded small-talkers and barrel out the door for some fresh air, but that would only have betrayed his anxiety. If the xenodocs—and Conrad—were right, before long they'd be back to a hundred percent failure rate. He banished the thought. He wouldn't let it happen, simple as that. Jaffa had thrived for millennia, so there was no earthly reason why *his* Jaffa couldn't do the same—and never mind Conrad's doomsaying.

Van Leyden headed outside and popped back a second later. "The golf carts are waiting, sirs, ma'am. We can start back as soon as you like."

"Right now would be good," snapped Simmons. "We've been here long enough."

"I was going to get a snack for the journey," Nerd protested.

"Doctor, it's a fifteen minute trip back to Earth. I trust you'll last, even if you don't go pee before we start out."

Ignoring the academic splutter, Simmons nodded for van Leyden to join him and climbed into the first cart. As soon as the agent had dropped into his seat, the driver, an as yet un-enhanced private, set off. Simmons supposed he should admire the 'planetset,' but he had no mind for it now—if ever.

"I want you to contact our friend," he said. "I'd do it myself, but I'll have to stay at the SGC for the next couple of days."

"Yes, sir," van Leyden replied blankly, hedging his bets—or maybe he just was that uninspired. Then again, efficiency was more important than inspiration, and the man sure as hell was efficient.

"And I mean *her*. Don't use that tame jarhead you've got in place as a go-between. That'd be about as effective as sending a note of protest to Saddam's valet. It's time the lady understands who's boss."

"Yes, sir."

"Tell her she's been sending us defective goods. She's got twelve hours to come up with an acceptable solution to the problem. If she doesn't, the deal's off."

"*Off?*"

Barely suppressing a sigh, Simmons stared out across the plain and thought that it closely resembled the intricacy of some people's brains. "It's a bluff of course. She'll suspect it, but she can't risk to call me on it. She depends on us for delivery of the symbiotes."

"Yes, sir."

In the ensuing silence, the golf cart rattled on into the gorge. The towering rock seemed to stifle any form of conversation, not that Simmons minded. A couple minutes later, they rounded a narrow bend and rolled toward the opening into the crater. Thank God for—

His prayer of thanks was interrupted by a sharp jolt. The driver had slammed on the brakes hard enough for them to be all but rear-ended by the second cart. "What the hell?" he enquired of no one in particular.

"What the hell?" echoed van Leyden.

Simmons refrained from making it a trio, but he shared the sentiment. The gate and DHD were deserted, the guards nowhere in sight. They hadn't come back to camp—they would have been seen—and they couldn't have flown out of the crater. The only explanation that made any sense at all was that they'd left through the gate. But why?

"Take us closer," he said to the private. "Slowly."

The close-up revealed nothing new. The men were gone, seemingly without a trace. Van Leyden leaped from the cart and ran over to the DHD, where he dropped to his knees to unfasten the lid of an inspection hatch in the base of the device. For a long time he stared at what looked like some kind of early learning toy—colorful crystals arranged in no pattern Simmons could discern.

At last van Leyden closed the hatch and straightened up. "It hasn't been tampered with, as far as I can tell. The changes still are as per your diagram."

Conrad's diagram, to be precise, but Simmons wasn't about to correct the mistake.

"They're not here," observed Hatchet-Face.

"Gee, really?" the private muttered under his breath.

Nerd sniffed, dolefully glanced skyward, and said, "Let's go. I'm feeling watched. This place has a bad aura."

Bad aura. Christ almighty! The guy probably saw purple and green halos around everybody. Then again, the underlying notion wasn't too far off the mark. Simmons, too, felt exposed—watched. "Van Leyden, dial up Earth. No point in us hanging around. Notify Crowley and tell him to find those men. When you've got them, send them back. In the meantime, keep me posted. I'll be at the SGC."

The holographic screen showed liquid swirls of red, throbbing, transforming, until they flowed into the shape of two helices embracing one another. They would link, their joints would bond, and they would be functional as before. Only more so. Much, much more so.

Nirrti smiled. The Tauri's genetic profile was surprising, to say the least. It contained material she had never encountered before, and he had been subtly altered, as though someone had meant to prevent him from doing the things his genes said he was able to do. In some ways he already was *hak'taur*—all she needed to achieve was activation of his programming. It proved more difficult than expected.

A fraction of a second before the marriage of the helices was completed, golden starbursts erupted at the precise center of each link, tearing the bonds, forcing the strands of red apart to dull and fade. Again. She cried out in shrill frustration, swiped her hand over one of the luminous control pads. The slender white beam aimed at the area of his body where the umbilical cord had been attached once—her host called it a *chakra*, whatever that meant; and what a curious way of gestation the Tauri had—waned and winked out. The same instant another hologram rose from the console; a pumping lump of muscle that twitched erratically, as if to flash out a warning or signal its distress.

The energy flow that altered the subject's genetic structure—was *supposed* to alter the subject's genetic structure—also supported the vital systems during the transformation process. Once the process was concluded—successful or not—the subject's body was on its own again, for better or worse. In the Tauri's case, for worse. His heart was weakening rapidly now.

She dredged her host's mind for a suitable curse and vented her rage. Of course, it did not change anything. Not her inability to break his body's code, not the fact that, before long, that body would give out and have to be revived in the sarcophagus, while she would be subjected to the tedium of waiting for him to heal. Barely quelled, her anger rose again, and her fists struck the console. Then she pushed herself away, and marched across the room to where he lay, unmoving.

Although his eyes were wide open, he neither turned his head nor glanced at her sideways. He could not. The second energy beam, the one that connected to his forehead—another *chakra*, according to her host—rendered him immobile. Not so much as a wink of an eyelid, unless she permitted it, and she had no intention of granting that permission. He was too dangerous, and they were not finished yet. Not for a long while.

But she would grant him a moment's respite. His breathing was shallow, and his face and body were glazed with sweat, despite the low temperature of the laboratory. Across one cheek ran a glittering trail of moisture. Not sweat. He could not cry out, of course—any form of vocalization required movement after all—but tears were entirely possible.

Nirrti cupped the side of his face with her left hand, thumb brushing at the fluid. Yes. Tears. She briefly wondered if there was a way of suppressing it, decided that it was immaterial, and leaned closer.

"What is your secret? What is it? What are you?" Her right hand lightly stroked his chest. "It is unfortunate that you cannot tell me. It would be easier on you. But I shall do my best to work quickly." To her amazement, Nirrti recognized that she meant it. "I promise you," she added, the phrase feeling odd and unfamiliar, as though her host had regained control and were reciting words first spoken in a distant past. "I—"

"Lady Nirrti!"

She whirled around, instantly furious at her own carelessness—she should have heard the door slide open—and at the impertinence of her First Prime. "How dare you intrude here?"

"Forgive me!" The man prostrated himself, shaking. At least he knew he had transgressed. "Forgive me, Lady Nirrti. I had to notify you immediately. There is… an aberration."

The only aberration she could see was the sniveling cretin at her feet. "What do you mean?"

"You should see for yourself, Lady Nirrti. That's why I've come. Colonel Simmons's Jaffa have returned."

Which, if true, would indeed merit the name *aberration*. What was Simmons trying to do? Tax her patience until she had no choice but to annihilate him? Presumably, the actions of his Jaffa would answer that question. She would have to see for herself indeed. What a pity. The timing was regrettable, but the experiment need not be interrupted. She focused her thoughts, imagining she could feel them vibrate and amplify through the minute crystal behind her right ear, and summoned Mrityu. And that, Nirtti admitted, was a most satisfactory idea. Mrityu would agonize over this, yet she would have no choice but to obey.

By the time the woman arrived, Nirrti was smiling again. Frantic to be of service, to be wanted, after her earlier dismissal, Mrityu shambled into the laboratory. Her gaze held a thoroughly gratifying mix of dread and eagerness and, predictably, wandered to the surgical table and the supine form of the Tauri.

Ah yes. You find it distressing, do you not?

Mrityu gave no reply other than to exude a mangled flow of despair and fear and outrage. It was good enough. Deciding to amuse herself for a moment or two, Nirrti relinquished her hold on the healer. She could regain it whenever she pleased, and this brief spell of freedom would serve to torment the woman even more.

As if pulled on a chain, Mrityu darted toward the table and to the Tauri's side. Fingers, slight and trembling, wrapped around his wrist, feeling for a pulse. What they felt clearly displeased Mrityu. Her features knotted in shock, and her hand released the Tauri's wrist to touch his face, much in the same way as Nirrti had touched him only minutes ago.

"Colonel?" whispered Mrityu. "Can you hear me, sir? Colonel O'Neill?"

"He can hear you. However, he will not be able to answer until I allow it," Nirrti advised her.

Mrityu's head shot up, and she stared at Nirrti. "What the hell have you done to him?"

"What needs to be done. When I have finished with him, he will be immeasurably more useful than the pathetic creature you choose to call your daughter." Nirrti slid closer, as if to reassert ownership of the Tauri—and to drive home the invisible blade of guilt. "I am indebted to you. By denying me the girl, you have forced me to look elsewhere. And of course, you were kind enough to deliver him to me."

If the loathing in Mirtyu's eyes had been a weapon, Nirrti would be dead. Sadly for the healer, wishes could harm no one. "I had no choice," the woman hissed. "I had no choice, and you know it."

Nirrti relished her pain. It was sweet-scented and savory. "Do not blame your weakness on me. You wanted to live. You could have permitted yourself to drown in the pond, and none of this would have happened. But no. You were so desperate to survive you could not wait to offer your fealty. You betrayed him and the others so you could live."

Shuddering under Nirrti's words as though they were physical blows, the healer turned back to the Tauri, took a limp hand in hers to stroke it. "It's not true, sir. Please, Colonel, don't believe—"

"He will not have to believe," Nirrti said gently. "He will know. Because you shall perform a service for me."

The way Mrityu recoiled was almost comical. "No!"

"Yes. We both know you will. Now listen carefully." Tightening her grasp on the healer's mind slightly, to ensure that Mrityu would indeed listen and retain the information, Nirrti explained the workings of the console and how to calibrate the beam. "You will repeat the procedure continuously either until I return or until you obtain the desired result. Do you understand me?"

Thoughts and emotions were pummeling the walls of Nirrti's awareness like puny fists. The healer was fighting her, more stubbornly and angrily than ever before—not that it would change the outcome. "No!" Mrityu gasped again, a flopping little fish, on the hook and already hurled from the safety of water. "It would kill him."

"It almost certainly will," retorted Nirrti. "He is weak. When he dies, revive him in the sarcophagus and continue." She forced herself further into Mrityu's mind, felt the healer cling to a fragment of an imperative embedded too deeply for Nirrti to eradicate.

First, do no harm.

"What does that mean?" she demanded.

With a scream of rage, Mrityu pushed her back and clutched the Tauri's hand in a death grip. "Stop me, sir! For God's sake, stop me! She'll make me do it, if you—"

"Enough!" The game was beginning to get boring. Nirrti thrust the full force of her will at the healer and sensed the barriers crumble. It was less sensual than taking a host. But it was far more challenging. Taking a host meant coercing a body. This meant coercing a mind. "Do it," she said and smiled.

Mrityu's hand relinquished its hold on the Tauri, jerkily, like the limb of a puppet manipulated by two players, one of whom was inept. Then she staggered across the laboratory and to the console, to study panels and recall Nirrti's instructions. Embraced by soft light, her fingers crept over the control pad, reactivated the transformer beam.

With a brief, satisfied nod, Nirrti turned to her First Prime, who had been watching impassively, still kneeling on the floor. "Come. Show me this aberration," she said, delighting in the smooth play of muscles as he rose.

CHAPTER EIGHTEEN

Kin Selection: Behavior that lowers an individual's own chances of survival in order to enable the continued existence of a relative.

Teal'c approached the end of the tunnel wishing, not for the first time, that there were two of him so that he could guard Daniel Jackson's back while, simultaneously, taking point. However, in light of what the young man had reported, it seemed preferable to remain unique, despite the shortcomings of the condition. Besides, these corridors showed no sign of recent occupancy, and unless the two Marines had been discovered and overrun, his and Daniel Jackson's backs were reasonably secure. Any palpable danger lay ahead.

Which was reason enough to focus his attention that way, instead of engaging in fruitless speculation. The tunnel ended at a waist-high heap of broken masonry that extended into the small room beyond. That room, in turn, had three doorways, two of them—leading off to the left—dark and uninviting, the third—straight across—a narrow portal onto brightness and the sounds Teal'c had heard earlier. Boots hammering down a set of steps, he was certain of it.

"Somebody's bricked this off at some point." Daniel Jackson had joined Teal'c and picked up a lump of stone, squinting at it in the dim light. When he spoke again, he sounded pleased. "Looks like the cave-in had no help from our friends out there," he said, one finger tracing a brittle crest of mortar still stuck to the stone. "It's possible they don't even know the tunnel exists. Which means we've got ourselves a bolthole."

"Perhaps." Teal'c directed a pointed glance at the doorway opposite. "Although it might prove unfeasible to return here."

"Didn't Bra'tac ever tell you that negativity is bad for morale?"

"He did not. He did, however, tell me that undue optimism damages one's health."

"He would."

Daniel Jackson's mien darkened, and Teal'c knew that his friend was lost in the same memory as he. Trapped in the cargo hold of Klorel's *ha'tak*, Master Bra'tac had vowed to go down fighting. O'Neill had embraced the idea of fighting but—predictably—refused to go down. As so often, his stubbornness had saved them, because it had forced them to consider options they might otherwise have disregarded.

"We shall find O'Neill," Teal'c said quietly. "I would not abandon my brother."

"I know."

Without another word, Daniel Jackson began to climb across the heap of debris. Fatigue and injuries made him clumsy, and he slipped frequently, his boots kicking loose rubble. Pebbles rolled to the floor, their clatter amplified a hundredfold through the confines of the room and the corridor behind. To Teal'c it sounded like thunder. But nobody outside that small room appeared to hear or respond to it, and he finally conceded that adrenaline might be playing tricks on his awareness.

By the time Teal'c reached the other side, his friend was exploring the two passages to the left. Both were dead ends, blocked off long ago. "Shame," Daniel Jackson muttered.

Teal'c concurred. But it could not be helped; the only way ahead led toward the noise he had heard. He eased along the wall and into the third doorway. Past the opening lay a vast round space, tiled with stone, and a stairway spiraling to dizzying height along a wall covered in friezes. It partly explained why the anteroom and tunnel were abandoned. The doorway, narrow and uninviting to begin with, was overhung by steps and cloaked in shadow; also, it was located at the lowest level of this structure. Given that there was only one other room off the central stairwell, Teal'c presumed that few people would have reason to come here.

He slipped out into the rotunda, keeping a wary eye on the floors above and ready to duck back into cover at the first sign of company. Further up, alcoves clad in wooden lattices protruded from the wall at irregular intervals, possibly concealing prying eyes. It was a risk they would have to take. A hum of distant activity mixed with words torn free from conversations and drifting down on him like stones thrown into a pond. Though whoever or whatever caused the sounds remained invisible.

"My God." Daniel Jackson had stepped beside him and was craning his neck to stare up the seemingly endless shaft and at the patch of blue sky at its top. For a split-second his face wilted into a mask of hopelessness that reflected Teal'c's own fears. If this was the only access route, their chances of reaching the upper levels unobserved were so slim as to be nonexistent. The young man swallowed hard. "It'll have to be very fast and very quiet."

"Indeed. I suggest you remain here, Daniel Jackson."

"And I suggest you get stuffed, Teal'c." With that he dropped into a crouch and proceeded to take off his boots. When there was no reply, he looked up, his features drawn and determined under the lurid display of bruises. "You decided I was the brains, remember? You need me. Having said that, if I slow you up or get in your way, feel free to push me off the stairs."

"O'Neill would disapprove."

"Yeah, well, Jack isn't here, is he?"

Teal'c disapproved at least as much as O'Neill might have, but he merely removed his own boots, watched while his friend stowed both pairs in the anteroom. "You shall take point," he said, not for a moment deluding himself that his intention of letting the injured man set the pace would be missed.

Zat'nikatel ready to fire, Daniel Jackson tapped Teal'c's chest. "Tag. You're it," he whispered and set off up the stairs at a speed he could not possibly sustain. Of course, Daniel Jackson was at least as stubborn as O'Neill.

After each full revolution around the interior of the shaft, the steps leveled to a gallery that circled the stairwell and gave access to various rooms and corridors. On the first level they reached, they passed two such openings, both tight and unlit, but the third was a wide hallway, suffused with light that glittered from golden walls. Daniel Jackson skidded to a halt and stood staring down the corridor toward a set of closed doors.

"Looks familiar, doesn't it?" he panted softly. "Maybe we should—"

At that moment, the doors at the end of the hallway began to slide open, and Teal'c fancied he could feel chilled air brushing his skin. "We should not!" he gasped, one arm snapping around Daniel Jackson, scooping the young man away with him along the gallery and through a fourth doorway into a musty storeroom, empty except for dust and cobwebs. They slammed into a wall, Teal'c's body covering his friend.

From the corridor, gradually getting louder, drifted the sound of steps; the resonant stomp of a Jaffa's boots and beneath, barely audible, the patter of bare feet. The footfalls reached the end of the hallway and continued to approach. They would come past this room. Teal'c held his breath, dedicated his whole attention to listening.

"We counted twenty of them," a male voice said. "They came through the gate, but of course the, uh, watchdogs hadn't been alerted."

Momentarily Teal'c indulged in a fantasy of much-needed reinforcements having arrived at last, then he discarded it, realizing the impossibility. He never doubted that General Hammond was searching for them, but since the General did not know where to look it was a barren hope.

The voice outside carried on. "They left no guards at the gate—for obvious reasons—and are headed straight for the city, heavily armed."

"Weapons will not help them," replied another voice, unmistakably Nirrti's.

A tremor of muscles tautened to the point of cramping betrayed Daniel Jackson's tension. Teal'c felt fury radiating from him like heat. He shared the rage, and the part of him that had remained untamed by a century of training and discipline wanted to kill Nirrti and kill her now. It would be so very easy. It would also alert her troops, and he and Daniel Jackson would never be able to accomplish what they had come here to do.

"Take your men to the sanctuary. They are to attack at my command," she said. "I shall remind Simmons not to come here uninvited."

"Yes, Lady Nirrti."

The Jaffa's bootfalls moved away rapidly, running up the stairs. The tread of Nirrti's bare feet receded at a less hurried rate. When Teal'c was sure he could no longer hear it, he straightened up.

"Thanks," gasped Daniel Jackson. "Next time try not to suffocate me."

"That was not the intention."

"Apology accepted, but you still need a shower."

Teal'c smothered a grin. "As indeed do you, Daniel Jackson."

"I was afraid you'd say that. By the way, am I hearing things or did she mention Simmons?"

"She did."

"So how does he come into this mess?"

"In no small measure, I would surmise."

"Glad you cleared that up." Daniel Jackson eased himself away from the wall and cautiously proceeded to the entrance to survey the staircase. "Looks quiet. I'm thinking we should go before—"

The mournful blare of a horn cut him off. Teal'c recognized it only too well. It was an alarm signal. Almost instantly shouts and the beat of running boots cascaded down the stairwell, tumbling and echoing and bouncing into pre-battle frenzy. Two levels above a stream of men emerged onto the gallery.

"On second thought, maybe not!" Shouting to make himself heard, Daniel Jackson recoiled from the door and settled back in the corner he had just left.

After a moment, Teal'c joined him. "They are coming this way. There must be an exit on this level."

First shadows trampled across the puddle of light that seeped through the doorway and into the chamber. The footsteps did not slow down but continued around the gallery, then changed cadence as they raced down the bottom set of stairs, proving Teal'c wrong.

"I know where they're going," Daniel Jackson declared suddenly. "The second room on the bottom level? Has to be the vault where Janet sent us last night. There's a ring transporter there, and it's linked to some kind of shrine—probably the 'sanctuary' Nirrti talked about." He fell silent for a minute or two, while Nirrti's Jaffa continued to run past, then he added, "That's why the tunnels were blocked off. Somebody wanted to make sure the ring transporter is the only way in or out of here."

Teal'c had to agree with this assessment. Nodding briefly, he resumed his count of the shadows flitting across the door. It took a long time until the last one raced past, the clank of boots fading down the stairs.

"Fifty-eight," he whispered.

"She's been busy," murmured Daniel Jackson. "You know, I never figured I'd be grateful to Simmons for anything. But whatever he's up to, it got those Jaffa clones off our backs."

"There will be a large number left behind as guards," Teal'c reminded him.

"So what else is new?"

From below came the rhythmic whine of a ring transporter. Teal'c sidled to the door and carefully, so as not to be spotted by a straggler, checked the stairwell again. It was clear.

It was rabidly green, humid, full of unidentifiable sounds that were best ignored. Not the easiest thing to do when the stench of the past clung to you limpet-like and almost alive. Hammond was breathing through his mouth so as not to smell it, and he'd never in a million years have expected his reaction to be this strong. Of course, he'd never tested it. He'd developed a preference for vacationing in temperate climates and refused to consider even Hawaii.

This was the last thing he'd anticipated and, shamefully, the first thing he'd fretted about—even before the missing DHD—after a thirty foot drop from the wormhole into a mud bath had knocked the stuffing out of their little expedition force. He liked to think that he still would have come, even if he'd known. Freeman would have, he was sure.

Maybourne, who was weaving through the trees some five meters off to the right, changed to an intercept course. Reaching Hammond's side, he slid over a glance, too penetrating for comfort. Hammond kept going, tried to ignore that, too.

"You've been to 'Nam, haven't you?" Harry asked softly.

"What gives you that idea?"

"You're the right age. Plus, you look like you're gonna keel over any second now. Cold sweat, is it?"

"I don't handle heat very well."

"Yeah, that usually makes a guy jump each time he steps on a twig." When he got no reply, Harry continued. "You wanna hear something funny?"

"What?"

"Mice."

"*What?*"

"I'm scared of mice. Embarrassing, but there it is. I just freeze up. No good reason—I mean the stupid things don't even carry guns." Harry's voice dropped to a whisper. "Unlike Charlie."

"Dammit, I—"

"Take it easy." Maybourne clapped his shoulder. "For what it's worth, I happen to think you got two big brass ones, General." With that he broke formation and slipped back between the trees.

Mice, huh? Hammond grinned and, to his astonishment, found the jungle a little easier to bear. Just as well, else he might have shot Bra'tac, who appeared from between two bushes like a phantom—or a Vietcong soldier. In a flash, unbidden and unstoppable, Hammond heard the screams of dying men, saw the look of horrified realization in Colonel Freeman's eyes. His fingers cramped with the effort to control the instinct of pulling the trigger. But it was just Bra'tac. Just Bra'tac, the other four Jaffa remaining invisible.

"Don't do that!" Hammond hissed.

Unaware of his almost-demise, Bra'tac fell in beside him and grunted disapproval. "It is a miracle that you have survived this long, human. You make more noise than a temple bell." He paused a moment to let his admonition sink in—to no effect; Hammond and Maybourne moved as quietly as they knew how, but they were no Jaffa—then he changed the subject. "We have found the Marines."

It wasn't exactly in the same league as finding the *Titanic*. The Marines seemed to have vacated the clearing by the Stargate at a run—a profusion of king-size trotter prints in the mud might have had something to do with it—and left a swath of trampled vegetation in their wake. A kindergartner could have tracked them.

"And?" Hammond asked.

"They have halted. We shall approach and try to discover their plans. Come!"

Motioning for Harry to join them, Bra'tac headed away from the trail and for the undergrowth, which was the last route Hammond wanted to take—no, the penultimate; tunnels would have been worse. He felt an urge to make small-talk, distract himself from swirling mists and dripping foliage and stewing heat.

I spy something starting with a 'D'.

He didn't, of course, which would be the point. So where was the DHD? It might not be crucial since the two Jaffa they'd left on M3D 335 were to follow in the *tel'tac*. But for all he knew, the planet—a place called Yamalok, as Bra'tac had determined from the gate coordinates—could be at the other end of the galaxy from '335, which meant the trip might take more time than they had. George Hammond had learned the value of fallback options the hard way—especially when the mission objective was bringing his people home.

His people. He didn't spy anything starting with an 'S' either. What if SG-1 and Dr. Fraiser weren't on Yamalok at all?

Ahead, Bra'tac's shadowy figure crouched in a bank of mist, his upraised fist barely visible through the vapor. Hammond crept closer and squatted next to the old warrior, who wordlessly pointed at a glade that opened about ten meters away. A few seconds later Maybourne settled in as well.

Out in the glade sat the Marines. Twenty men, some sipping from their canteens, all relaxed, none of them chatting. They were focused on their task—which would be what exactly? The answer came quicker than Hammond had hoped.

"Listen up, guys!" The speaker's insignia made him a gunnery sergeant.

This was odd. Where were the officers? A quick scan of BDUs revealed that there were no officers. All enlisted men. Hammond felt a fist of anger knotting in his stomach. He'd come up through the ranks, he'd been there and done that, and he despised the kind of attitude that had put the line animals out here on their own. Then again, if these men were Jaffa, it made sense in a twisted sort of way. An officer who was part alien would be an unacceptable security risk, at least to people with the mindset of Simmons and Crowley.

"You all know the lay of the land, so I'll keep this short," the gunny carried on. "We're gonna leave all heavy gear and head straight for the city, 'cos chances are that they'll be hiding out there—provided they're still alive."

Provided *who* was still alive?

"Inside the city, we split into three teams—two of seven, one of six, which I'll be joining, 'cos my little critter is worth two of yours any day of the week."

It provoked some good-natured protests and chuckles, and it confirmed that the men did, in fact, carry symbiotes.

"Now, in case any of you has second thoughts about this, I suggest you keep in mind what General Crowley told you. This is a matter of national security. You're to hunt down and eliminate the colonel, the major, and the geek, and you're to capture the alien alive. Are we clear on this?"

"What about the doc?" one of the men asked.

"Don't worry about her. The lady's taken care of her."

The *lady*?

"Anything else?"

Shaking of heads all round, and the brief bout of sympathy Hammond had felt for the Marines shriveled in the jungle heat. A gnarled hand clamped around his forearm, painfully tight. Bra'tac sent him a look of warning, and Hammond realized that he was grinding his teeth. He forced his jaw to relax, let the tension trickle down his back together with the sweat. At least they had the right planet.

"We'll stay in radio contact throughout," continued the gunnery sergeant. "Once you've achieved your objective, you're to return here, not to the gate. We'll want these"—he nodded at a grenade launcher—"to take out the boars and get to the dialing thingy. Right, if there are no more questions, move out!"

So there *was* a DHD. It would simply be a matter of finding it.

The Marines stacked the launchers and some of their packs by a tree, covered them with camouflage-netting, and filtered back into the jungle. Less than a minute after the last one had disappeared they were inaudible. Bra'tac still motioned to wait. His hearing was better, of course.

Harry lasted another minute, then he shrugged, scrabbling to his feet. "Let's go."

In a move so fast it looked like a blur, Bratac's hand shot out and yanked him back. "Let us wait."

Eventually Hammond realized what they were waiting for. One cry at a time, animal hoots and cackles replaced the dripping silence that had fallen while the Marines were in the glade.

When the full cacophony of jungle noises was restored, Bra'tac rose. "Now let us go."

"Who the hell put you in charge, old man?" snapped Maybourne.

"This!" The staff weapon twirled up in a swift arc and held, tip cracked open and buzzing with energy, an inch away from Harry's nose. Bra'tac flicked a glance at Hammond. "He reminds me of O'Neill."

"Whom is he trying to insult?" Harry's hands had risen, placating and palms front, and he angled back from the tip of the staff weapon. "Me or Jack?"

Somewhere in the canopy some animal crowed a reply. The staff weapon whirled again, came to a rest again, still pointed at Harry's nose, except now Harry was lying on his back, a fern frond gracefully draped over his forehead. Bra'tac had knocked the legs out from under him.

"Not bad for an old man of one hundred and thirty-seven," said Hammond, trying to keep a straight face.

"Ha! You have heard of our match!" Bra'tac barked a dry laugh. "O'Neill did well for a human. Few could have taken me then. Now, of course, it is different. I am older."

"And meaner," Harry muttered under his breath.

"Indeed! You would be wise not to forget it." The staff weapon swung upright, and Bra'tac took a step back. "If you wish to survive, you will do exactly as I say."

Scowling in Hammond's direction, Harry came to his feet. "Thanks for all the support, Huggy." Once he'd dusted off his wounded pride, his gaze settled on the mound of launchers. "We should borrow a couple of those, just in case."

"He's got a point," conceded Hammond, remembering the outsize trotter prints and what the gunny had said about needing the artillery to get to the DHD, wherever it was. "They might come in handy."

"What purpose do they serve?" Bra'tac looked doubtful.

"They blow holes in things. Big holes."

"Very well. Jaffa! *Kree!*"

Hammond noted with vague surprise that this time he barely started when two Jaffa materialized like mushrooms popping from the ground. Bra'tac gave his orders in hushed Goa'uld, and the men quietly retrieved two of the grenade launchers and draped the netting back into place to make it look as though nothing had been disturbed.

By now the light in the glade had begun to dim, and the slide of the day into late afternoon recalled the urgency of the situation. They had been issued an ultimatum. They needed to find SG-1 before the Marine Jaffa did. Bra'tac knew it, too. Eyes even darker than usual, he aimed a slow nod at Hammond, then turned, cloak swirling, and led the way back onto the trail of the Marines.

Knowing her leg still existed was one thing. Translating that knowledge into locomotion was quite another. For the time being, she concentrated on skipping along on the cognitively and sensually verifiable leg, which had its own drawbacks. The thigh muscles she could feel were cramping, and her head objected to being jolted every five seconds.

"I need a break," panted Sam. More than anything she was getting fed up with wandering—jumping—around aimlessly.

"You should use both legs," Macdonald retorted. "Ma'am."

"Easy for you to say. Why don't you just climb out of a window?"

"Point taken. Come on."

Sam suspected it was a trick to keep her going—hopping—at least for a little while longer. She wanted a beer and a wheelchair, in that order. Some twenty minutes ago an alarm had sounded, and he must have assumed that her escape had been discovered. He'd led her from one flight of rooms to the next, each deserted, some windowless—a shuttered procession of ghostly habitats, festooned in faded silk and dry rot. Eventually they'd come out into the corridor they were in now.

Ahead lay a T-junction. Macdonald parked her against the wall and quietly slipped out of sight. Half a minute later he was back. "You wanted a break. Round the corner is some kind of an alcove. We can hide in there for a while."

In real terms, the alcove was a balcony that clung to the wall like a barnacle to a ship's hull and looked out over an enormous round stairwell. Enclosed by wooden lattices and no larger than a wardrobe, it offered just enough space for two people to sit down opposite one another. Macdonald eased her to the ground, pulled the door shut behind him, and slid down the panel until he hit the floor.

A warm evening glow trickled in through the latticework and cast his face into an untidy mosaic of dark and light. One eye had disappeared completely, the other stared out at her from a patch of gold. Sam looked away, gave up on the mind reading, and let silence ratchet up the tension until the air seemed to crackle around them.

A split-second before something—Sam's patience or the alcove's struts—snapped, he asked, "You done any thinking yet?"

"What?"

"The mind control thing."

As a matter of fact, she had, and she wasn't sure at all that this really was mind control. "What if it's posthypnotic suggestion, Sergeant?"

He gave a soft snort. "I'm Force Recon, Major. Same caliber of training as your Special Ops boys. Brainwashing techniques and how to defuse them are pretty high on the agenda. I know how posthypnotic suggestion works. This ain't it. Besides"—he did that curious head-tap again—"it doesn't explain how she can know what goes on in here. And I'm not nuts, ma'am."

No, Macdonald seemed perfectly sane. And he was right. Posthypnotic suggestion didn't explain Janet either. Her behavior had been far too complex for that. But the notion that Nirrti was a telepath was equally farfetched. They had absolutely no prior evidence for that.

Which left Sam with what? An abiding wish to have her team around, so she could bounce ideas off Daniel, Teal'c, the Colonel. Thinking of them raised a cold wad of anguish that threatened to swallow her whole. She couldn't allow that to happen; she'd be unable to function.

Next.

Suppose the *gadget* was exactly what Macdonald said it was—a gadget. It made sense. Nirrti loved gadgets. So, if Sam were her, where would she put it? She reached up, laced her fingers through the lattices, and pulled herself to a stand.

"I thought you wanted a break," Macdonald hissed.

Ignoring him, she stared out into the rotunda, spiraling stairs, rooms and corridors spoking off from galleries, and more alcoves above and below. "I need a floor plan, Sergeant. What's what."

"Why?"

Talk about wringing water from a stone. "Dammit, Sergeant, do I have to make it an order? Right now I only have the vaguest idea of what it is we're looking for, but knowing *where* to look for it might help firm it up a little!"

He came to his feet with a grunt and squeezed in next to her, rubbing up against her shoulder and hip. The touchy-feely stuff wasn't strictly necessary; on the other hand, it wasn't overt enough to call him on it. If he needed to play his little games, fine. "This is the only connection between the different levels," he said, nodding at the stairs. "Well, the only one I've found, and believe me, I've been looking."

Superb from a strategic point of view, Sam admitted, but for their purposes it sucked. "What else?"

"This level and the level below, barracks—quarters—and armory."

"*Armory?*" Sam cocked an eyebrow. This sounded better.

"Don't get your hopes up, Major. That's one of the places where the air gets real thin for me real quick."

"Too bad, but it probably won't for me."

Another snort. "Leaving aside your mobility problem, ma'am, do you even know how to use the weapons they've got?"

Well enough to damn near kill my CO, you arrogant goon! Aloud she said, "Do you, Sergeant?"

The reply was unintelligible.

"I didn't get that, Marine."

"Ma'am. No, ma'am."

"If you ask nicely, I might teach you someday. What else?"

"Everything you see there"—Macdonald pointed up some forty meters worth of shaft—"is Nirrti's private domain."

"*All* of it?"

"She only really uses the top level. That's where her rooms are. There's also some kind of roof terrace. The floors below are kind of a buffer zone, I expect. To separate her from the rabble," he snarled. "Access to the penthouse suite is by invitation only."

"Who's invited?"

"Her personal guard, Lennox from third platoon—well, a copy that's her, uh, First Prime I, think she calls it—and her servants."

"Servants?"

"Some guys who didn't make the cut for cloning." He gave a crooked grin. "Like my copy."

Which could be useful. Sam filed away the information, then realized that one item remained conspicuously absent from Macdonald's list of facilities. She thought she knew why. "What about Nirrti's lab? That's up there as well?"

"What makes you think she's got a lab?" His eyes narrowed. Evidently the distrust was mutual.

"She's cloning people, right? You can't do that in the bathtub, so there has to be a lab. Where is it?"

"You want me to tell you where O'Neill is? Forget it!"

When hell freezes over. Besides, Macdonald had just told her. The Colonel was in the lab. As, in all likelihood, was Nirrti. And if Nirrti was the only one who could operate the ring transporter, she also was their only ticket out of here. Sam tried her best smile. "Look, Sergeant, first of all, it's *Colonel* O'Neill to you. Second, has it ever occurred to you that this gadget may be *in* the lab? Whether you like it or not, you'll have to tell me and we may have to try and bust in. So stop second-guessing me and tell me where the goddamn lab is!"

"Two levels down." He'd probably broken a tooth or two grinding it out.

"Thank you." She raised herself on her toes and craned her neck to peek down. Yeah, two levels down and diagonally across she could just make out a wider than usual corridor that shimmered golden. Looked about right to her. Looked Goa'uld to her. "Oh, hang on…"

"What?"

She wasn't sure she'd seen what she thought she'd seen. A wisp of movement, caught from the corner of her eye—it might have been nothing. She kept staring at the area, a shadowy recess one level up from the lab where the stairs reached the gallery. Ten seconds later she knew it was *some*thing alright. She and Macdonald weren't the only people creeping around in the fortress. A dark figure emerged from the niche, then another.

"My God!" she breathed.

"What?" Macdonald asked again.

"Take me out onto the gallery. Now! And this time it *is* an order!"

His eyes widened. "With all due respect, ma'am, are you crazy?"

"No. I got us some reinforcements. Move it, Sergeant!"

"Reinforce— Yes, ma'am!" Patterns of light and shade madly gyrated across his face as he nodded.

While Macdonald half dragged, half carried her from the alcove, along the hallway, and toward the exit to the stairwell, Sam tried to compute timings. Six corridors for cover around the gallery, and up a flight of stairs—how fast? She had to head them off, because the one thing she couldn't risk was calling out to them. And what if they didn't come up here? What if they disappeared down a hallway on the level below? What if—

"That's far enough," whispered Macdonald and ground to a halt. "We don't want to be seen."

Wrong. Five meters ahead, the corridor opened onto the gallery and the void beyond. Sam disengaged herself from the sergeant, dropped to the floor, and began to crawl. Just as well she could do at least that on her own, because Macdonald wasn't happy. There was a novelty. She headed for the shadows by the wall and stopped with six inches to spare. Out in the stairwell everything seemed quiet, no noises, and she could see half of a flight of stairs from where she lay. Empty, and so was the gallery. Had they gone past already? One by one, she scanned the doorways on her level for a flicker of movement. Nothing.

Damn, damn, damn! Where—

On the level below, a figure broke cover and hurtled up the stairs, two steps at a time. Yes! It was Daniel. So—

"Freeze!" yelled a voice from somewhere above. "Identify yourself!"

The ID came in the form of a staff blast from the same corridor where Daniel had appeared. A split-second later, Teal'c raced after his team mate, who'd stopped and turned.

"Go!" Teal'c roared, loosed a second blast, and kept running.

Except, he was drawing fire now. Whoever was upstairs had recovered from their surprise. Three plasma bolts in quick succession exploded around Teal'c, raining chunks of masonry down the stairwell. Sam gritted her teeth in frustration. She couldn't recall ever having wanted a weapon so much, but all she could do was pray.

CHAPTER NINETEEN

Teal'c's shout should have catapulted him up the stairs. The tone had been flavored with *That's an order!* But Daniel had a pretty good idea of what was going on behind him—besides, he couldn't see the steps for dust.

Nobody gets left behind.

Another staff blast zipped past, close enough to singe his hair, and Daniel fired wildly in the direction where the flare of light had come from. What was the range of a *zat*? Further than expected, obviously. He heard a scream, and a dark, blurry shape toppled from the gallery above. One of the blurry shape's colleagues took exception. The next plasma bolt damn near charbroiled Daniel's toes. He returned fire, simultaneously with Teal'c, who came storming up the stairs, snagged Daniel's arm, and hauled him along.

"Which part of *Go!* did you fail to comprehend?" wheezed Teal'c, never breaking stride.

Daniel didn't bother to reply, too busy trying to keep up and struggling to draw oxygen from air laden with dust and the fried-wattage reek of energy discharges. A new blast dented the wall behind them, sent stone heads popping from the frieze. Whoever was doing the shooting was in serious need of target practice—then again, even the biggest dud hit the ten-ring once in a while.

Their only chance was to reach the gallery and the cover there. How many steps? Thirty? Fifty? And did it even matter? They'd been rumbled, and—

The floor evened out, and Daniel almost tripped because he'd been expecting another step. A few meters ahead was a corridor. But the guys upstairs weren't stupid; their fire now zeroed in on the entrance, ready for Teal'c and Daniel to run into the blasts.

Teal'c let go of him, swung around, staff already flying up, and loosed two bolts. One hit home. It bought them five seconds. Daniel darted for that inviting patch of shadow and safety, was about to dive right into it, when he heard the shout.

"Daniel! This way!"

He couldn't see worth a damn, but he recognized the voice. He also recognized that it came from the next corridor along. So he ran on. A plasma bolt tore into the doorway behind him, ripped free a spray of stone and mortar. Amid a barrage of rapid Goa'uld, Teal'c fired back. Daniel could make out a really juicy curse, knew that he was the addressee.

Sorry, Teal'c.

"Keep going! Next hallway! Cover me from there!" Daniel dropped into a crouch—for all the benefit that would bring; he was the proverbial fish in the barrel—and *zatted* blindly at the guards above. They were moving along the gallery now, headed for the downward staircase. Not good. At least the nice thing about Teal'c was that, in situations like this, he could be relied on not to stop and discuss the issue. He sprinted past, straight toward the entrance. With Jack it would have been different.

The thought cut like a knife, and Daniel was almost grateful for the staff blast that singed the other side of his head. He ducked, kept *zatting* people he couldn't see, thought he'd got a hit—somebody hollered—and then Teal'c had reached the entrance to the corridor and began laying down cover fire. Daniel shot up, swayed for a moment, disoriented by a head-rush, and ran for the doorway. Propelled by the heat of another plasma bolt, he flung himself through, dived for the floor alongside Sam, landing hard.

"Nice to see you," he observed to Sam's left foot.

"Amen," replied her top end.

"Get up, Daniel Jackson!" Teal'c was heaving Sam up to sling her over his shoulder like a sack of potatoes. "More guards are on their way. They will arrive shortly!"

"Crap!" Daniel muttered into the floor.

A hand hooked under his armpit, pulling him up relentlessly. *Jack?* He looked up, winced. He didn't recognize much else, but he recognized the coif and had a dizzy vision of Jack applying at a USMC recruitment office and getting turned down on the strength of his hair being incapable of conforming to a proper crew cut. Not Jack. A Marine.

"You heard the man," Not-Jack grunted and shoved him along the corridor. "Move it, mister! Go, go, go!"

Daniel lost track of just how long they were running or where. Directed by the bellows of the Marine who never bothered to introduce himself, they ran left, right, straight, and hallways blended into rooms blended into other rooms, until they arrived in a small, gloomy chamber. Not-Jack finally let go of him.

"Who the hell are you?" gasped Daniel, and every syllable felt like it might rip out a bit of lung.

Sam, deposited on the floor by Teal'c but looking a hell of a lot better than she had the night before, was saying something. Her words dissolved into an odd electric sizzle that filled Daniel's ears and turned into high-voltage cotton wool inside his skull. The next thing he realized was that he lay flat on his back and his head hurt worse than ever—a possibility he'd have denied categorically before... before whatever had just happened.

The pressure of hands on his shoulders nailed him to the ground. Probably Sam's hands, given that the very large fuzzy blob by the door had to be Teal'c, keeping watch. Bingo. Sam's worried face bobbed into view. "Stay put, Daniel. You passed out."

Great! Dollars to donuts the Marine was smirking. Daniel groaned. "Sugar high must have worn off."

"Uhuh. You're concussed." Sam patched a smile over the worry lines. "I kind of forgot how dreadful you look."

"Thanks. Love the costume," Daniel retorted and suddenly remembered that he wasn't concussed enough to have missed the obvious. "Where's Jack?"

The smile disappeared, nudged aside when she shook her head. The unknown soldier piped up in her stead. "Colonel O'Neill is doing us all a favor."

"That paragon of tact over there is Master Sergeant Charles Macdonald. USMC, in case you hadn't noticed. What he's trying to say is that Nirrti's... busy. In her lab. With the Colonel." Sam took a breath, then added, "You can imagine what it means—though I wouldn't recommend it."

Golden doors at the end of a golden corridor. Daniel squinted up at her. "The lab's two levels down, right?"

"Yeah. How do you know?"

"Educated guess."

It was nothing of the sort. What had forced him to a grinding halt outside that corridor was the fact that Daniel had sensed something—he'd *sensed* Jack there for a second—though how or why was beyond him. Then again, Jack had had the combined knowledge, abilities, voodoo of the Ancients downloaded into his brain. When the Asgard had siphoned all that stuff out again, who was to say just how much they'd missed in the race to save his life? Or what they'd seen and not told Jack or anyone else about? In any case, Jack being Jack, he wouldn't have opted to communicate in ways whose existence he'd deny until he was blue in the face. Not unless he had no choice. Daniel struggled to forget the bone-deep distress rushing in on him at that moment and recalled something else.

He pushed himself up on his elbows. "Nirrti's not in the lab anymore. Teal'c and I saw her leave."

"You sure?" A sliver of hope, barely acknowledged, brightened Sam's face. "We need to get in there to—"

"Sam, we can't get him out yet." Daniel could barely believe he heard himself say it, but if they didn't knock out the transmitter first, they wouldn't stand any chance at all. Neither would Jack. "We—"

"It's two birds with one stone, Daniel. Nirrti has way of controlling people's minds—including mine. If it weren't for Macdonald here, I'd swear blind that I'm a leg short. She's controlling Janet, and she's probably controlling the clones as well. We've got to take out whatever helps her do it."

"I agree." Breathing slowly through his nose until the nausea subsided and the room stopped rotating, Daniel sat up. "Except, you won't find it in the lab."

"Why not?"

"Because the lab's too deep inside the building. We're looking for a transmitter. Teal'c figured out how she does it."

At Sam's questioning glance, Teal'c moved in two steps from his post by the door and plunged into an epic tale of naked plant guys and sound frequencies and deaf Marines. She listened quietly. When he'd finished, she sat staring into the middle distance for a while. Eventually, she said, "HAARP."

"You mean as in plinkety-plink?" Macdonald mimed strumming

a set of strings.

"That's a lyre, not a harp," Daniel commented tiredly, foregoing the eye roll in the interest of protecting his head.

Sam didn't even twitch. They were too used to Jack, compared to whom the sergeant was a rank amateur. "I mean as in High Frequency Active Auroral Research Program."

"I thought we're talking *low* frequency, Major," Macdonald cut in.

"I'm getting to it. The assumption is that they're conducting experiments to prove the viability of certain technologies Nicola Tesla discovered, including mind control. So—"

Macdonald snorted. "Tesla was a fruitcake!"

Pretending she hadn't heard him, Sam carried on. "It's definitely possible to impair rational thought and induce certain moods—aggression, paranoia—through radio frequencies. We all know that. Sergeant Macdonald and his men started killing each other."

"Don't remind me," Macdonald said bitterly.

"But we didn't start killing each other on PJ2 445," objected Daniel. "Though I got pretty damn close to throttling Jack a few—"

"No, we didn't, because what we ran into was around ten Hertz; mood swings and migraines only. For thought control you'd have to be able to hook into brain frequencies—probably Theta waves, which are in the seventy Hertz range." Sam scrubbed a hand over her face. "I think Nirrti's piggybacking a mind control frequency on an ELF wave. In other words, we're looking for *two* transmitters, not one. I also think that the second one will be on her person. In close proximity it may still work *after* we've taken out the ELF transmitter."

"Wonderful," groaned Daniel. If anybody hit him with any more good news, he'd start screaming.

Sam shrugged. "Not nearly as wonderful as the fact that we have to get to the top level somehow."

Okay, that didn't qualify as news, good or otherwise. He and Teal'c had already figured that one out. They'd also delivered proof positive that the central stairwell was to be avoided at all cost. There had to be another way. Nirrti had built neither the city nor this fortress. The Goa'uld didn't build, they adapted. So Nirrti had *adapted* this place to her requirements. But what about the folks who had *built* it? Early Cambodian, at a guess. Hindu at a further guess. So what did that mean?

Daniel studied the room. It was small, unadorned, and two opposing corners still held beds made from rough wooden planks and sprung with woven rope that had frayed and sagged to the floor. Not exactly palatial. Plain. Poor. Servants' quarters. Obscure. Out of sight. Set apart. That was it! He scrambled to his feet, vaguely noting that his headache hadn't become any more bearable.

"Are they still looking for us, Teal'c?"

"They are not," Teal'c replied, one eyebrow lifted in a delicate enquiry. "They appear to have retreated toward the stairwell, presumably planning to trap us when we return."

"Good." Daniel opened the door, took a peek. The hallway was as unprepossessing as the chamber they were hiding in. Either side there were more small doorways, more servants' chambers. The far end of the corridor opened into a cavernous room. It couldn't be that easy, could it? On the other hand, they were due at least one break. Without turning around, he asked, "Teal'c, would you mind carrying Sam again? It's quicker this way."

He slipped into the hall, listening, almost sniffing the air for company, but it was quiet, as Teal'c had said. His bare feet ground over a layer of dust that cushioned the stone tiles. Nobody had been here in decades—centuries maybe. Daniel smiled.

Furtive footsteps behind him told him the others were following. "That way!" he murmured.

"Where are we going?" Macdonald, sounding petulant.

"To find the second staircase."

"There is no other staircase!"

"Yes, there is."

Okay, so it was conjecture, but he wasn't about to admit that to a Marine.

The hallway led into an enormous kitchen. For a moment Daniel's imagination populated it with men and women, sweating in the blazing heat from clay ovens and the open fireplace, shouts and chatter and clanking of pans, thick wads of steam and the sweet scent of exotic spices. Then the images faded, leaving behind long-cold stoves, a black and empty fireplace, copper pans dulled by grime and silently dangling from racks.

"See?" asked Macdonald. "I told you there's nothing here."

Slowly, Daniel turned full circle, squinted past Sam who was perched on Teal'c's back. It had to be here. It was the most logical place. Everyone came through the kitchen. One of the great constants of the universe.

Yes!

There they were. Across the room two tallish, fuzzy shapes sat in front of an otherwise plain wall. As he approached, gray patches solidified into the forbidding faces of the *dikpals*. This time it took him less than a minute to release the door mechanism. The stone slab swung aside to reveal a steep, narrow flight of stairs.

"Okay, I bite." Sam peered at him over Teal'c's shoulder. "How the hell did you know?"

"Going by the cultural pointers all over this place"—Daniel gave a sweep of the arm meant to include fortress and city—"I figured the people who built it had a caste-system; strict social hierarchy from princes and priests all the way down to laborers and servants."

"So?" asked Macdonald.

"So suppose you're a prince, Sergeant. What happens if you come down the stairs and the stable hand, who's on the way up, bumps into you?"

Macdonald shrugged. "I smack him?"

"Spoken like a true Marine. And no. You run to the nearest priest for a round of ritual ablutions and spiritual cleansing, which is both expensive and time-consuming and should be avoided whenever possible."

"By having separate servants' corridors and stairs!" Sam exclaimed.

"Exactly. It explains the tunnels Teal'c and I found, and if I weren't such an idiot, I'd have realized it hours ago." Fuming with annoyance at himself, Daniel gazed up the seemingly endless staircase. "We should—"

A loud thud made him whirl around. Macdonald had collapsed, gasping for air, his face contorted in a bluish rictus.

"What the…?" breathed Daniel.

Teal'c looked impressed. "O'Neill predicted that your explanations would have this effect one day."

"I want you to tell me what's wrong with them, that's what!" Simmons's minion snarled.

"There is nothing wrong with them!"

How many times had she said this? Two? Three?

Nirrti had lost track of the conversation. Mrityu's suffering, a constant groundswell in her awareness, proved to be more of a disruption than anticipated. It was pleasurable, and normally Nirrti would have welcomed it, but she could not afford to indulge under the circumstances. The man staring at her from the viewing mirror was at least as shrewd as his master—and twice as insolent.

"Look, you think we're stupid?" He spat the words as though he wished to spit on her. "We've run a whole battery of tests, and the results all say the same. You screwed up somewhere, and you'd be better off admitting it, because I doubt the Jaffa you kept are doing any better than ours."

"You lie so that you can justify your invasion of my territory!"

The man smirked. "You wish, lady! And this isn't an invasion. We…"

A wail of anguish from Mrityu blotted out his words, and Nirrti found her attention distracted yet again. Was it merely more of the healer's yammering, or had the Tauri died at last? She hoped the latter was the case. That way she might get a reprieve from all this pitiful emotional turmoil, amusing at it was.

The creature in the mirror looked at her keenly. It seemed he had asked a question and expected an answer.

"I will not tolerate your invasion," she said.

"Yeah, you mentioned that." His smirk deepened. "This conversation is getting a little circular. Not quite up to our usual acumen, are we? But I'm a nice guy, so don't mind repeating myself. It's a search party. You've got a bunch of people running around who shouldn't be there. I'm guessing they stayed under your radar so far. 'Cos you would have mentioned it if you'd noticed, right?" He stared and waited. Finally, receiving no reply, he continued. "So, as I was saying, we want them back."

She stared at Simmons's crony, teased a smile of sincere regret from the memories of her host. "I fear the intruders are dead. The planet is most inhospitable, and I suggest you recall your men before they meet the same fate. After all, you claim they are unwell."

"And *I* fear that's not just a claim. It's a fact!"

For the first time his mask of superiority slipped to reveal anger, even alarm. He was telling the truth. If that was the case, and assuming the humans, in their elemental ignorance, had contrived to actually obtain reliable test results, then the Jaffa were defective. All of them, including hers. The most obvious explanation would be an error during the cloning process—but cloning was too basic to make mistakes. It would be tantamount to committing an error when adding up two and two. Besides, had she made a mistake of such magnitude, the clones would not have been viable at all. No, it was impossible. He simply was a better liar than she had given him credit for.

"Show me records of your tests, and I might believe you," she demanded, bored the moment she said it. Why did they insist on these rituals? Mrityu was quiescent now. Had the Tauri died? Nirrti wanted to return to the laboratory.

Simmons's creature must have anticipated her request. Without a word, he held up two sheets of paper—paper!—for her perusal. The scribblings on it meant nothing, might have delineated the pedigree of his favorite dog. Nirrti pretended to study them and, for a moment, allowed her boredom to show.

"Very well." She had to be seen to comply, even if Simmons's threat of withholding the symbiotes was ludicrous. She could clone her own, had been cloning them, because she did not trust the human scientists. But it would be unwise to let these people know that their ploy meant nothing to her. As long as they felt in control, they were harmless, could be manipulated. "I shall study the problem," she said. "Once you have withdrawn your troops."

"That's got nothing to do with the problem!" he blustered. "We'll withdraw our men once we've found what we're looking for."

"I told you these people are dead."

"Including the Jaffa?"

He had tried to make it sound like a taunt, but she had lived too long, seen too much, not to detect the flicker of worry in his eyes.

Fool! He wanted the *shol'va*. Simmons wanted the *shol'va*. Why? Why would they need him when they had new Jaffa?

New Jaffa.

Here was the solution to the riddle, the connection whose existence he had so adamantly denied. The claim that she had committed an error was designed to hoodwink her—a ruse to deceive the goddess of deceit herself. In different circumstances Nirrti might have found a spark of admiration for the sheer gall of it, but not now.

That disgraceful travesty of a Goa'uld, who had let himself be captured by the humans, must have recognized the cause of the problem, while she had been blind to the most basic of facts. Unforgivable—if understandable. You acquired Jaffa and ensured they did your bidding; you did not concern yourself with the minutiae of their existence. They simply were. But as young animals needed to hone their skills by following their parents example, so Jaffa needed to learn how to coexist with their symbiotes. Failure to master that skill was lethal, for animals as well as Jaffa.

Simmons needed the *shol'va* to teach his Jaffa how to be Jaffa. It was almost grotesque enough to amuse, especially as, to her, the remedy would come so much easier. She would summon one of the Jaffa manning her last *ha'tak* to help train the clones properly. Simmons, on the other hand, would not get his wish. He would have to crawl to her for help.

Barely suppressing a smile, she said, "They are *all* dead."

This time the man's face gave away nothing. "In which case I'd like to see the bodies."

"You shall see them," she promised and cut the transmission.

His image dissolved at last.

She might have told him that her pet boars left no evidence behind; a truth, and he knew it. But it was far more satisfying to pretend to give in to his demand and decimate his and Simmons's hopes. "Jaffa! *Kree!*"

Her First Prime, a mere shadow against the wooden paneling of the wall, eased away from his post by the door and approached. With less grace and strength than he should have displayed—or was it merely a trick of her imagination? No. When he stepped toward her, sudden light flooding his face, she found the telltale signs of exhaustion marking his features.

"Yes, Lady Nirrti."

"Kill the Tauri if he is not already dead and kill the woman. Have their bodies brought here. Also, send some of your men to retrieve Jackson and the *shol'va*. If they are still alive, kill them and bring me the corpses. And do so before those fools out there find them."

"Yes, Lady Nirrti."

As he left, a warm breeze swept through the open door, stirred the silken drapes, and flooded the room with the scent of jasmine. Nirrti inhaled deeply, letting the fragrance ease her tension. Somewhere in the back of her mind the mewling of Mrityu blended with the ancient despair of the host. But she could not allow herself to drift into its music too deeply. She had to—

The door crashed open, driving jasmine and quiet from the room.

"Lady Nirrti!" Her First Prime was shaking, and this was not attributable to insufficient training. "Lady Nirrti, the woman has escaped. My men say Macdonald is with her, and so are Jackson and the *shol'va*."

She almost laughed. Survival instincts were a peculiar thing. They would drive a creature on in search of continued existence, even when the quest itself promised nothing but death.

"They should not have taken Macdonald with them," she said softly.

Master Sergeant Charles Macdonald? Where are you?

There was no answering thought. Impossible.

I command you to reveal your location!

When he still refused to answer, she let her rage slam toward his mind at full force. The agony of it should have guided her like a beacon, but instead of burning his mind, her thoughts ineffectually frittered into a cold, dark void. It might mean that Macdonald was dead. Or perhaps unconscious.

"Find them!" she hissed at her First Prime. "And inform the commander of my *ha'tak* that I may wish to leave." Nirrti felt a knot of worry tightening in her stomach, and forced herself to focus on the woman, Carter.

Somewhere high above gleamed a little speck of brightness,

though Sam doubted it was the proverbial light at the end of the tunnel. Once they reached that light, chances were that brown smelly substance would start hitting the fan at an unprecedented rate.

Macdonald was flopping head-down from Teal'c's shoulder, out cold but still breathing—barely, though he seemed to be getting better with increasing distance from the hidden doorway. They'd briefly considered leaving him in the kitchen, then discarded the idea, because they couldn't be sure whether or not it would be a death sentence. So Sam had relinquished her comfy perch on Teal'c's back and gone back to doing the hop, heavily leaning on Daniel.

The steps seemed to be getting higher as they climbed, making it harder and harder to jump, and the stagnant air in the passage had had several centuries to heat up undisturbed and unventilated. Sweat matted her hair, trickled down her face and neck, her back, soaking the fabric of the sari until it clung to her limbs like swaddling clothes and strangled her movements.

This was crazy. Absolutely impossible. They'd never make it. She and Daniel were injured, and their only able-bodied man, Teal'c, was lumbered with transporting a half-dead Marine. Or maybe Macdonald was dead. It hardly mattered. They'd all be dead before long. They'd die right here. They were dying already. The smell of rot—gangrenous and putrid—wove invisible tendrils through the air, tightened the mesh until it became a blanket of stench that followed her wherever she went. Like Daniel.

Daniel?

When she stole a look up at him, she knew he was the one causing it. Of course it was him. His face was a mass of frothing flesh, skin sloughing from it in pale, rubbery folds to reveal the decay underneath. Nausea racing up her throat, she tried to push him away, but his hold on her tightened. Where his fingers clamped her bare waist, her skin had begun to blacken and split. It was him. He'd been in league with Nirrti all along. How else would he have known about the door? He'd lead them into a trap, just as Janet had done last night.

What door?

"The hidden door," she whispered around the thick need to scream or throw up. "The hidden door in—"

"Sam?" The voice was hollowly resonant like that of a Goa'uld.

Nirrti rising through the remains of Daniel.

Do not speak aloud.

"Do not speak aloud," she parroted.

"Sam?" The cadaverous grip around her hardened some more and forced her closer to that terrible decaying face. Rotting lips pulled back into a skeletal leer. "Sam, who are you talking to?"

"Let go of me!"

I could help you, sang the voice inside her mind. *I could help you, but I do not know where you are.*

Up above, Teal'c had turned, and his face, too, was melting, the tattoo beginning a cockeyed slide from his forehead. "We must be quiet, Major Carter."

Tell me where you are. Let me help you.

"We're on—"

"Shh!" hissed the Daniel creature.

Do not speak aloud.

We're—

"Teal'c's right, Sam. We've got to be quiet."

"I know what you're trying to do!" She shoved him away, hard, fought to retain her balance, watched him stagger into the moisture-coated wall, trip down a step, and nearly fall. "I know what you are! You can't stop me!"

Where are you?

"Daniel Jackson!" the Teal'c thing crowed from an oozing mouth. "Do not let her—"

Sam never heard the rest of it. All she heard was a high-pitched whine as the blue, spinning discharge leapt at her like a giant spider from its lair. Blue tentacles feathered over her body, their delicacy wholly out of proportion to the agony they caused. Nerves wailing and sending muscles into an uncontrollable spasm, Sam collapsed. The last thing that registered before she blacked out was Daniel, wide-eyed, *zat* held out in front of him.

When she came to, the *zat* was gone and Daniel was cradling her head. The real Daniel, not the obscene thing she'd seen.

The real Teal'c was towering a couple of steps above them, Macdonald still slung over his shoulder. "How are you feeling, Major Carter?"

"Like crap, thanks." Sparks of blue pain kept sizzling through her body, rising and ebbing and shoring up the walls of her mind against a pressure that squeezed in relentlessly. She wouldn't last much longer, and Daniel couldn't *zat* her again. Not without killing her. "Nirrti," she breathed.

"She tried to get to you, didn't she?" asked Daniel. "Did you—"

"No, I didn't tell her where we are. At least I don't think so. I didn't get a chance, thanks to your blessed tendency to interrupt people."

"Make sure you tell Jack when we see him." Daniel grinned, bruises spreading in all directions.

Answer me!

The command splintered into her mind in a shower of ice, and Sam felt her skin contract in response to the cold. "Teal'c! She's getting through! You've got a gun. Do it!"

"I cannot, Major Carter. Any shots fired in here might deafen Daniel Jackson as well and would give away our position as surely as you would if you let Nirrti succeed. You know what she is attempting to do, and you can and must fight her."

"Then leave me here. Go! That's an order!"

Carefully, Teal'c lowered himself into a crouch to slip the sergeant off his shoulder. "I shall—"

Daniel's hand on his arm stopped him. "No. He might come in handy. I'll carry Sam. It isn't far now."

"As you wish."

"Out of the question. I gave you an order." They weren't even listening to her. Trying not to cringe in another blast of arctic—*Ant*arctic—cold, Sam glared at Daniel. "Who the hell put you in charge?"

"Teal'c." With that he hauled her up in a fireman's lift and started heading up the stairs. "Let's go!"

I demand to know where you are!

No longer the gentle wheedling that promised help and safety. It was a constant battering, brutal and determined, and the pain was icy, eating its way outward from the bone, freezing nerve and muscle, and wrapping Sam in a glacial cocoon she couldn't—

She *had* to escape!

"Daniel!" She croaked it out, barely able to speak. "I can't stop her. I—"

"Of course you can." His voice was impossibly calm, even through the ragged breaths of exertion. "Tell me about HAARP. Macdonald cut in just when it got fascinating."

He was about as interested in HAARP as he was in butterfly farming, and Sam knew it. But it would keep her mind busy, and maybe it would be enough. Staring down at stone steps bobbing away beneath her, she started talking. "HAARP's a giant radio transmitter array in Gakona, Alaska. It's run jointly by the Air Force and the Navy, and it emits high frequencies into the ionosphere to study the Van Allen Belts and create ionospheric lenses—the broad idea is to microwave the bad guys' satellites. It also does ELF. Extremely low frequency transmissions for radio contact with subs."

Do not dare to mock me! You shall be punished for your insolence! Where are you?

"Sam? Sam! What are Van Allen Belts?"

Eyes closed, she focused on invisible magnetic fields, incandescent with the dizzying dance of aurorae and horseshoed, one inside the other, around a blue and white planet. It was cold up here, bone-crushingly cold, and there was a funny rattling noise. Almost like—

"Sam? Van Allen Belts!"

"They're…" Trying to speak, she realized that the rattling noise came from her teeth. "They're named after Dr. James Van Allen who was in charge of the first *Explorer* missions. The Geiger counter aboard *Explorer 1* picked up the inner belt in 1958, and—"

The bobbing motion of Daniel's steps stopped suddenly, and she opened her eyes. They'd reached a landing. To the right was a door, similar to the one in the kitchen and guarded by the same type of statues. Ahead, another twenty or thirty steps up, daylight filtered through a carved screen. Daniel contemplated the door for a few moments. Eventually he shook his head.

"Don't know what's behind that," he muttered and signaled Teal'c to continue all the way up to the end of the staircase.

Twisting her neck a little, Sam stared up at the screen and the bands of light that flowed through delicate arabesques of stone or wood. Dust motes glittered in the beams, rose and fell and—twirled into blackness. The shadow was shapeless, but it made her instincts holler loud enough to drown out even Nirrti's voice rampaging through her head.

"Take cover!" she yelled, her shout steamrollered by a staff blast that slammed through the screen, trailing a flurry of shrapnel that peppered her face before she managed to turn her head.

Daniel dropped flat, and they slid down a couple of steps. She rolled off him, allowing him to shuffle free and *zat* the jagged remains of the screen. The shadow danced away, unharmed. He swore, and started crawling up the stairs to get a clear shot. Behind him, Teal'c shucked off Macdonald's limp body, flung up his staff, and returned fire, pulverizing carved filigree.

From the doorway below came the frantic hammering of something hard on stone—Nirrti's guards trying to find the release mechanism and get through. Sam had no idea whether she'd unwittingly betrayed her whereabouts, or whether Nirrti knew the layout of the fortress well enough to hazard a guess. It hardly mattered now.

Nails clawing at steps, Sam hauled herself past the sergeant and alongside Teal'c. "Give me that gun!" she gasped. "And any ammo you've got left." For an instant, just long enough to flag up his conflict, his eyes flitted away from the hole in the screen and the potential targets beyond and bored into hers. Sam didn't blame him. She'd have the same doubts. "I know what you're thinking, Teal'c, and we both know you haven't got a choice. I'm compromised alright, but they'll be coming through that door any second now, and our six needs covering."

A minute inclination of his head conceded the point, then he tossed her a Desert Eagle—a testosterone-driven doomsday machine of a gun, lifted from one of the Marines, she supposed—and two clips, one of them only half full. Great! If she didn't run out of ammo first, the recoil from the .50 caliber would probably knock her senseless. At the very least she'd get her wish and be deafened. Then again, it was guaranteed to punch extremely large holes—and there might be a way of marrying up the effects. She tore a couple of strips of fabric from the sari, shoved them at Daniel. "Plug your ears!"

There was no time to check if he'd understood. Below, the door exploded in a hail of stone—they'd given up on finessing and used their staff weapons—and she fired at the first shape that materialized through the smoke. Though expected, the recoil slammed into her wrists with punishing force. Bring down the weapon, aim again.

Mouth yawning in a cry she could no longer hear, her target was tumbling down the stairs. The guard behind him ducked back, startled. Part of her registered that Nirrti's psycho-vise no longer clamped her mind, filed it away. Daniel and Teal'c were right. Next to her, Macdonald shuddered, chest flaring as he sucked in a breath. His eyes popped open, and his lips formed words—*What the hell...?*—face slipping into a grimace of surprise when he couldn't hear himself. It was wiped off by a plasma bolt slamming into the wall above his head.

A blind shot, badly aimed—the shooter had angled the weapon around the doorframe and hoped for the best. The staff still pointed at them, tip gaping on the charge building inside. Suddenly, Sam grinned. Taking into account distance and the oomph the Desert Eagle packed, this might just work.

"Run!" she bellowed at Macdonald, hoping he would get it, hoping that Teal'c at least would still hear her.

He did. He slapped Daniel's shoulder, and together they started scrambling up the stairs, covering one another and the sergeant on their heels.

Sam fired at the open tip of the staff weapon. The round tore into flickering brightness and struck, the abrupt release of kinetic energy superheating the weapon's core for just a fraction of a second. A fraction of a second was all it took. The core—barely enough *naquadah* to coat the tip of a needle—detonated in white-orange violence, burying staircase, doorway, and guards under an avalanche of debris.

A roiling, bubbling ball of fire funneled up the stairs toward her, but she'd already flipped around, was racing toward the top, two steps at a time, flames licking at the bare soles of her feet—both feet, both, a leap of faith taken when she'd felt Nirrti's control shatter. She'd had no time to count toes. The sari caught fire, and she ripped away burning fabric as she ran, flung herself through the hole in the screen, thumped sideways into someone's body. Flames shot past her, tongued across a terrace, swept two Jaffa clones over the parapet. Limbs flailing, mouths screaming silently at the ringing in her ears, they fell as the blowout lost steam and retracted at last.

Gun up and ready to fire, Sam rolled into a crouch. A colonnade, sturdy wooden pillars providing sparse cover. Ten meters to her left, arcade met parapet; to her right it marched around a corner. In front, past the columns, stretched clear space, maybe three meters wide, and beyond that, thin air, the roofs of the ruined city, treetops, and a fat red sun, setting. No hostiles in sight—though they probably wouldn't be long. She checked on her team.

The someone she'd landed on was Daniel, moderately singed and goggling at her from one good eye. Teal'c and Macdonald were peering out from behind a couple of pillars, equally dumbstruck.

Dr. Jackson regained a modicum of countenance, pulled the last intact shreds of sari from his ears, and mouthed, *Wow!*

"What?" she snapped, looking at Teal'c for enlightenment.

Teal'c's right eyebrow climbed to a nuance she was sure she hadn't seen before. The sergeant's lips, on the other hand, were pursed in what could only be a wolf whistle, audible or not.

"Never met anyone in a bikini?" Sam checked above, decided it would do. If nothing else, it'd throw the clones a curveball—besides it was best to get going before her burns woke up and started to hurt. "We'll take the high road, gentlemen. As soon as you've recovered."

Courtesy of some broad-shouldered assistance from Teal'c and Macdonald, they climbed the colonnade in no time. Its roof had a slight slant, but not sheer enough to slip, despite the moss that covered the stone tiles. Above rose the roof of the fortress proper, much steeper and encrusted with ornaments and statuary. It spiked into a quartet of pagodas, all of them inaccessible, growing in height as they receded from Sam and her team's position. Atop the highest perched Brancusi's idea of a porcupine; a large metal sphere, bristling with silvery prongs and crystals that glowed blood-red and vicious in the evening light. A hell of a lot more compact than HAARP—which was the good news. The bad news was the distance.

"Teal'c? Can you take it out from here?"

His response was a tiny twitch of a smile, and the eyebrow gave another cock, this one familiar; Jaffa for *You gotta be kiddin' me!* Suddenly the whole sophisticated communiqué collapsed in a frown, and he motioned them into a crouch. Company. She saw his fingers spell out the details: five clones on a search, heading for the staircase below.

Macdonald had been watching intently, taking in the information. His hand shot out, slipped the diving knife from its sheath on Teal'c's thigh. Without interrupting that slick flow of motion, he rolled toward the edge and slid off the roof, knife between his teeth. Sam could only hope he'd done it as quietly as it seemed to her. *Semper fi.*

"Damn," she breathed. "Daniel, try to cover him. I've got Teal'c's six. Teal'c, you're on."

CHAPTER TWENTY

It was how the frog felt, come vivisection time—had lost all meaning—apart from lasting too long—and even if his life depended on it—for all his life was worth now—Jack couldn't say how much—time had passed since Nirrti had driven a stake of light through his skull and nailed him in place—paralyzed but feeling—oh yes, he could feel alright—he and the frog. Vivisection.

Mercury beads of pain—hundreds, thousands—eddied through his body, and all he wanted was the unimaginable luxury of being able to scream—or go *ribbit*, whichever. He couldn't. Neither could the frog. They couldn't even twitch, he and the frog. Muscles perversely relaxed—when he needed to tense up till tension broke bone—he and the frog couldn't even twitch. All they could do was lie there and take it. Vivisection.

Eternal vivisection. Always hated sarcophagi—guses? Worst nightmare. Never found one when you needed one—don't you dare die, Carter!—but it helped to imagine his body bucking in desperation—a little—little—Fraiser. How could she even hope to lift him into a sarcophagus? He'd explained to the frog that it wasn't Fraiser doing this. Not that it mattered—no more—no more, quoth the frog—

When it stopped without warning, reality seemed to stop with it. Jack tumbled into a blank, disorienting void. He was dying now, wasn't he? Supposed to walk toward the light, except that was gone. He held on to a croak—his croak, and the frog approved—meant to be a scream, squashed into croakitude by the tight-chested stumble under his ribs and the panic-stricken certainty that it would all start again and again and again.

A small hand slipped into his, and, remarkably, he felt his fingers curl in response.

"Colonel? Can you hear me, sir?" Fraiser. She'd asked that before, a mercury-beaded eternity ago. "Look at me. Look at me! Jack!"

Jack?

More than usually moribund then. She only used his first name when he was a hair away from folded flags and flyovers—kinda like Carter.

Determined to prove her wrong, he forced his eyes open and coughed up another croak. "I'm not dead yet, Doc. Stick with the *sir.*"

She looked like a ghost. The ghost of a raccoon, to be precise. Something or somebody had punched circles under her eyes, bruise-purple and shouting misery from a gray face. But that headachy squint was gone, and she seemed ready to fall on her sword. She'd also switched off his personal procrustean bed against milady's orders. Unless he actually *was* dead and too dense to notice it.

"Janet?" he rasped. "Is that you?"

"Absolutely, sir." Fraiser nodded so hard, he was afraid her head would fall off. "Nirrti's gone. Something must have happened. And—"

"Let's speculate later. We've got to get out of here while we can." He tried to push himself up. His chest clenched around a mad jig of stutters that had no discernible rhythm to it and scared the hell out of him. "Help me up. And then take a step back, 'cause I'm definitely gonna spew, and I don't want to do it all over you."

Oh yes, and this was definitely Fraiser. She suddenly sported that mulish medical expression, the one that proclaimed *Do as I say, or enema.* Nirrti couldn't reproduce that one in years of trying. Eventually the expression relented, and Fraiser threaded an arm around his shoulders. "Just so you know, this is against my better judgment. If we were at home, I'd have you hooked up to an ECG so fast it'd make your head spin."

"And that's different from usual how? Don't forget the putting me in restraints—"

The rest of that was cut short by the threatened spew. Fraiser didn't retreat when he doubled over. She just slipped sideways out of the line of fire, one cold little hand rubbing his back, anchoring him between heaves, and he was pathetically grateful for her touch. All around them, the clones in their glass tubes looked on while he was losing a lunch he couldn't recall eating. At last he ran out of bile, too.

"We've got to go," he gasped, trying to ignore the taste in his mouth.

"In a minute. Don't move."

The tone brooked no argument, and the hand disappeared, leaving an oddly empty patch between his shoulder blades. Jack decided that *Don't move* didn't extend to his head, so he looked up to watch her make a beeline for a U-shaped counter that embraced the control console for Nirrti's hellish contraption. It obviously was some kind of drug cabinet, except the goodies seemed to be synthesized rather than drawn from little bottles. Fraiser came back with a large glass of clear liquid and the type of hissy hypodermic used for flu shots.

She thrust the glass at him. "Drink it. All of it."

"What is it?"

It damn near provoked an eye roll, then she seemed to concede that a certain amount of trust issues was excusable. The attitude wilted to guilt. "Just water, sir. Really. You're dehydrated."

He took a sip, rinsed his mouth, spat, drank properly. Nodding at the hypo, he asked, "And that?"

"That's what'll keep you going for the next hour or so." She gave a bitter grin. "Good job I assisted Nirrti. At least I know how to work the synthesizer."

They'd have to talk this out, wouldn't they? Personally, Jack figured the sooner this delightful episode was tucked away alongside Iraq and everything else that hurt, the better. Which worked fine when only he was involved. Except, in this case he had somebody else to worry about. They'd definitely have to talk. But not now.

"It wasn't your fault, Doc, and you still didn't answer my question."

"Electrolytes and a pinch of nitro."

"A pinch of *what*?"

"Nitroglycerine. It'll help with the arrhythmia, though it won't fix it."

"Dynamite. You know me, Doc. I never suffer from stuff I can't spell, and I never inject explosives."

"Shut it. Sir." She'd almost smiled, so that was something. Her fingers felt for his jugular, and she placed the hypodermic there, triggered it. It did hiss. "Express delivery. You should start feeling better in a couple minutes."

"Yeah. Let's not wait for that. In a couple minutes Nirrti might show up with a crew of Jaffa to check why you're offline."

Fraiser didn't look convinced but held out an arm to support him.

Inching off the table to start the fun part of the evening, he remembered what had happened immediately before Nirrti's attempt to fry him in mercury. "I think I'd better try this on my own. Nothing personal, but I don't need my ribs squeezed."

"You'll fall flat on your face if you try that, and your ribs are fine, Colonel." Another wry grin. "Nirrti was good enough to fix those."

Amazing what slipped past you when you hurt all over. "Remind me to send her a thank-you note."

The floor was no warmer than the rest of the lab. It was useful, though, in that his freezing toes provided a solid focal point when the clones and the tubes and the entire room embarked on a whirl around him, dancing to the insane stutter of his heart.

"No way. Sit down again." Fraiser, sounding half a million miles away and disconcertingly adamant.

"It'll get better once I'm moving. Where's the damn door?"

"This way."

Jack had no idea whether or not he actually was walking or where. All he could see past the starburst lights exploding on his retinas were the eyes of the clones, all alike, all staring at him. What the hell were they going to do with these things if they made it out of here? Take them home?

He must have said it out loud, because Fraiser muttered, "They're not sentient. Not beyond limbic instincts."

Not exactly an answer, though it suggested the solution, grim as it was. He'd worry about it later. From somewhere beyond a barrier of fog and eyes, he heard the whoosh of a door sliding open, felt air warm enough to replace cold sweat with the real item. The barrier thinned to admit a vista of corridor and Goa'uldy gilt walls—or maybe Fraiser's cocktail was kicking in at last. His heart seemed to have abandoned its efforts to leave his body through his left nostril.

The hall was as long as he recalled and had sprouted no side-exits since he'd last come through here. Not good. They'd have to make this fast. Hoping it wouldn't result in a crash-landing, he disengaged himself from Fraiser's grip.

"What are you doing, Colonel?"

"Testing your therapy. Run!"

It was more of a stagger, fingers trailing one of those golden walls, just to give him a direction in which to topple. Of course Fraiser didn't run. She paced him, prepared for a quick catch. At the mouth of the hallway he stopped, flattened himself into the shadows and sucked in a surprised breath.

Judging from the activity he'd witnessed—when? A thousand years ago?—he'd expected a steady flow of Jaffa clones cavorting through the stairwell. Instead, peace and quiet. Odd. Definitely not to be trusted. Lately his lucky breaks had been too thin on the ground for that.

The bargain basement was one level below them, and he recognized the entrance to the vault where they'd been captured. That might work. It had a ring transporter.

As though she'd been reading his mind Fraiser whispered, "The outgoing transporter can only be activated from Nirrti's ribbon device. Trouble is, as far as I can tell, it's the only way out of here."

She probably was right. Just like Nirrti's lab on Hanka—if on a somewhat grander scale. He shrugged. "So we'll get the ribbon device off her. But first we get Carter. Any idea where she is?"

"Two levels up." There was a beat, and Fraiser continued, "She's not guarded. She can't walk."

For a second Jack believed the lab door had opened. Then he realized that shock was tracing a cold finger down his spine. "You're trying to tell me she—"

"No. Nirrti cured her, but Sam doesn't know that."

Swallowing a curse, he stuck his neck out a little further and, prompted by the memory of a dozen mystery Marines swinging from the rafters—two thousand years ago?—checked the upper levels. Wall and stairs between the third and fourth floors were pocked with blackened craters, the signature brand of destruction left by plasma bolts. At the bottom of the stairwell lay an assortment of arms and legs, clad in Jaffa armor and flung wide in death. Clearly somebody else had taken exception to Nirrti's hospitality, and along the fourth level gallery guards were blockading all the corridors, waiting for the demolition crew to scuttle from its burrow.

Jack scanned the stairwell again and—for the first time in two millennia—felt like smiling. Things seemed to be changing on the lucky break front. "They never clean up after themselves."

"What?" whispered Fraiser.

"There." He pointed at an orphaned staff weapon wedged under the stairs. "Quickly, before somebody complains to housekeeping."

George Hammond hunkered in the shadows by the city gate and, like Harry and Bra'tac beside him, stared at the coil of smoke that twirled up from a tall pagoda about two klicks northwest of their position.

"What do you think caused this?" Bra'tac murmured.

"SG-1." Hammond grinned around a whole mouthful of hope. "They tend to exhibit a certain degree of carelessness with Goa'uld property."

"I noticed that," groused Maybourne. "Jack can be real clumsy around advanced alien technology."

They'd reached the city just in time to witness the explosion. A staff blast had risen like an emergency flare, streaking for the pinnacle of that pagoda, missing narrowly. The second blast, less than three seconds later, had struck home, and something atop that building had gone up like the Fourth of July. Something vital, presumably. Now there was a pitched battle in progress up there; more staff blasts slicing through the dusk, a much weaker flicker that might be a *zat*, and, unless Hammond was hearing things, gunshots.

Ignoring Maybourne's observations, Bra'tac nodded slowly. "Then this is where we shall go."

"Get real!" Harry gawped at him as though he'd lost his mind. "Did you see what's *under* the boob-shaped thing with the missing tip? Where I come from, we call that a fortress!"

"Where I come from, we call it a challenge." Bra'tac flashed one of those predatory smirks. "Hammond of Texas. I thank you for providing an old man with such entertainment. Come!" He rose easily, belying his old man act, and without looking back set out across the square by the gate, evening light gleaming red on his skullcap.

"Jeez!" Harry groaned. "He reminds me of Sister Mary Evangeline back at school. Is he always like that?"

"Pretty much." Hammond pushed himself to his feet. "Let's go before we lose him."

Bra'tac was heading straight across the square, so it was safe to assume that the Marines had fanned out into the city, his Jaffa on their heels. Hammond and Maybourne caught up with him in an alley that burrowed in northwesterly direction between crumbling houses and tilting statuary. Art and architecture were ancient and distinctly Asian, and Hammond wondered which conclusions Dr. Jackson might have drawn. He himself couldn't read anything into it, apart from a sense of threat that seemed to waft from behind empty casements and lopsided doors. Not the surreal fear of the flashbacks he'd had in the jungle, but something new, something he hadn't lived yet. Preferable, to his thinking, because whatever the danger might be, it didn't come embroidered with dead familiar faces, dead accusing eyes.

You don't know that, George.

The thought chilled gooseflesh from his skin and didn't bear contemplating, so he upped his pace to stay abreast of Bra'tac. An instant later an outstretched arm slammed into his chest, stopping him dead in his tracks.

"Do not move!" murmured the old warrior, head cocked like a deer tasting the air.

As always in the tropics, night had fallen abruptly. Under the faint shine of stars the alley—a different one, narrower and rising steeply—had turned into a gray chasm, doors and windows gaping like fathomless mouths. Some fifty meters ahead was an intersection, a patch of not-quite-charcoal between the houses. It looked deserted.

At first Hammond couldn't make out a damn thing apart from the thudding of his own heart and Maybourne huffing down his neck like an asthmatic seal. Then he heard it. A high-pitched chitter and the scraping of metal on stone, barely there, intermittent—and stationary. It was too faint to pin down distance, at least for human ears. Bra'tac, on the other hand, seemed to have gauged it to the millimeter.

"Come," he murmured and led them toward the intersection.

Three houses from the end of the alley he signaled them to stop, molded himself to the wall, and moved on noiselessly and virtually unseen, shadow among shadows. The chitter was much more pronounced now, though the scraping had all but ceased. Bra'tac sidled up to a window, peered inside. An instant later starlight glanced off the blunt head of his staff as he swung the weapon into readiness. A hand came up briefly, waving them on, and they followed him into the house, guns drawn and unsafed.

The upper floor and roof had disintegrated long ago, and the wan gleam of stars frosted a large open room—probably a combined kitchen and living area. Piles of rubble rose from the stone floor like a miniature mountain range, and strewn in among them lay broken furniture and crockery. Hammond's boot toed something hard that rolled over, clattering; a pottery bowl, absurdly intact. The chitter was loud in here, ringing with greedy, needy excitement. What the devil was this?

Bra'tac nudged his arm, pointed. In the farthest corner of the room lay two shapes, human or at least a pretty good imitation thereof. Hammond felt a fist of terror slam into his gut, forced past it, did what he had to do, what came with the job, same as the letters that started *I regret to inform you*. If nothing else, the godforsaken exercise that had triggered this whole mess had proven conclusively that SG-1 wasn't immune to things that killed you. He'd just blindly clung to a belief in miracles—which was what happened when you were fool enough to care for those under your command. Unhappily for him, George Hammond didn't know how not to give a damn when he sent his people into harm's way.

He stepped closer, straight into a weak-kneed puddle of relief when he saw drooping heads, scalps half-bared by crew cuts. Not his people. Definitely not! Air slipped from his lungs in a surprised little gasp as he tried to yoke USMC follicular fashion to Jaffa armor and failed. Surely they couldn't be part of Simmons's mob. Not with that outfit.

"What the hell?" he whispered.

The words penetrated where the noises of their approach hadn't. One of the men lifted his head, and his eyes snapped open, dim light glinting in the whites. "Who are you?" Slow and labored and, had he been able to summon the energy to make it sound that way, baffled.

"I'm Major General Hammond, Stargate Command. What's your name, Marine?" Obeying an instinct, Hammond was about to crouch next to the man.

Bra'tac clamped his arm in an iron grip. "Do not move any closer!" he hissed.

"This one's safe. He's dead." Maybourne, who'd been hanging back, shoved past them, dropped into a squat, lifted the second man's head to see his face. "Whoa! Take a look at this! He's—"

"*Hasshak!*"

This time it wasn't a game. The staff weapon arced around, whipped into Harry's midriff to snap him double, tore him off his feet. Neatly folded like a piece of laundry, he flew back and into a heap of debris.

"Are you nuts?" he yelped.

Darting toward the spot where Harry had crouched, Bra'tac brought down a booted foot, hard. To Hammond it sounded as though he'd stepped into a plateful of fortune cookies—except, there were wet, squishing noises mixed in with the crackle.

"*Hasshak!*" Bra'tac growled again. "Do you wish to become a host?"

"A *what*?"

The old warrior lifted his foot. The thing underneath was writhing in its death throes, and Hammond could see the dorsal spikes, black on gray in the gloom, flaring a threat no one would take seriously anymore. Up close and personal he'd only seen its like twice—two times too many by his reckoning—but he recognized it alright.

Calmer now, Bra'tac whispered, "When the symbiote sensed this man's death approaching, it left the pouch to search for a host."

"Isn't it a bit young for that?"

"Indeed, Hammond of Texas. But it would have tried, and it might have succeeded with that fool there."

"Mutual, to be sure," groaned Harry, scrabbling to his feet in a susurrus of dust and pebbles. "Before you knock me senseless again, oh Cranky One, you think you might wanna check what killed our friend? Don't know about you guys, but I'd kinda like to know, with a view to avoiding the COD and all that."

"There is no risk to you, Colonel Maybourne. Or to Hammond of Texas."

"Oh yeah? So what're they dying of? Old age?"

"They are dying because they are *not* Jaffa. Their symbiotes have weakened them to the point of death."

Which, in the strict biological sense, would make the Goa'uld larvae parasites — intelligent tapeworms — which was about as apposite as it got. Hammond stared at the Marine who'd sagged a bit further into his corner, wheezing for air and listening to all this. Whatever had been done to the man, whomever he served, they couldn't just stand by and watch him die. "Can't you help him, Master Bra'tac?"

"It is too late, Hammond of Texas. This man has never learned to practice *kelno'reem*, therefore his symbiote was unable to sustain his body's function." Bratac's cloak swished; perhaps he had shrugged. "I cannot teach him in the time he has left. Nobody could."

"Look," said Harry, an edge of disgusted fascination in his tone.

The Marine's hands had been clasped over his stomach. Now the fingers were nudged aside by the thing rising from his pouch and snaking through the chinks in the armor. It reared five, maybe six, inches high, head swaying sinuously, as if it were sniffing for something. And perhaps it was; aroused by scent of potential hosts, it chittered eagerly. Bra'tac snatched it up and, with a swift jerk, snapped its neck.

"Hey!" The edge in Harry's voice bloomed into full-blown disgust. "Why did you do that? You got any idea what these babies are worth on the open market?"

"You will *sell* Goa'uld?" Bra'tac seemed intrigued by the idea. "As slaves?"

"Kinda. Charged a million bucks for the last one, and—"

Their unexpected bonding session was interrupted by the Marine Jaffa — or whatever he was. He extended a shaking hand in Hammond's direction. "You... you are from Earth?"

Hammond shot a quick glance at Bra'tac, received a nod to indicate that it was safe, and squatted next to the dying man. "Yes, we're from Earth. Well, two of us, anyway. We—"

"I dream of Earth. Strange dreams. I've never been there, but I dream of it. It's beautiful, isn't it?"

"Yes, it is." This was getting weirder by the second. Hammond decided that the man was confused and played along because he didn't know what else to do. "Where are you from, Marine?"

"I was made here."

Made? Here? And perhaps the kid wasn't confused at all. "Who made you?" Hammond asked.

"My goddess." The specter of a smile flickered over his face, died when smiling, too, required too much effort. "The goddess made me. All of us... even those who were sent back. They've returned. They shouldn't have. She has commanded us to destroy them, and we will." Then the obvious seemed to percolate through, and his face folded into a mask of suspicion. "You're not with them. Who are you? What do you want?"

"We're three powerful lords, and we have come to revere the goddess and to offer our services." Hammond hoped that tricking a dying man would count as venial sin at worst. "If you could tell us where to find her, we'll present her with our gifts."

"Take the stairs. The stairs to the sanctuary," the kid breathed. His eyes rolled up, lids stuttering shut.

"Where are these stairs?" It took all of Hammond's self-control not to shake the man. "I asked you a question, Marine! Where are the stairs?"

"Left... left..." The kid's body shuddered and went slack.

After a moment of stunned silence, teeth glinted white in the darkness; Maybourne was grinning. "Three powerful lords? With gifts? Nice going, Huggy. Gold, myrrh, frankincense, and a couple grenade launchers. So he was *made*, huh? Figures."

"How?"

The white gleam broadened. "As I was about to point out before King Balthazar over there whacked the crap out of me—again!—this goddess is the proud momma of twins."

Harry was right. The men looked identical. And it was a fair assumption that the goddess, so-called, hadn't stopped at twins. Clearly, Bra'tac was thinking along the same lines.

"How many of them do you believe there are, Hammond of Texas?"

He never got an answer. Somewhere in the city, reassuringly far away, the stillness was shattered by bellowing machineguns and the sizzle of staff blasts. Evidently the Jaffa who had returned and the Jaffa of this goddess had found each other. If the two dead men in the corner were anything to go by, it would be a very short battle.

"We'd better get going." Hammond wanted to find those stairs.

"Indeed." Bra'tac was already on his way out the door.

They reached the junction without incident. Straight across, the alley curved toward the base of the fortress they were trying to reach; a right turn would have taken them closer to the battle noises and the bursts of muzzle flashes and staff fire that occasionally lit up the night sky. To the left rose a flight of stairs.

"I suppose that's what he was talking about," Hammond said softly.

"I don't know." Harry shook his head. "Direction's all wrong. He mentioned a sanctuary, right? What if he went all metaphysical in his last moments, talking about a place of worship where he met his goddess in spirit?"

"Then we return here," Bra'tac decided. "But I, too, believe that he meant a way of meeting his false god in person."

CHAPTER TWENTY-ONE

Gause's Rule: Two species cannot live in the same way in the same place at the same time.

"Where the hell do you think you're going?"

He looked young and scared, his face recurring no fewer than five times among the Jaffa who were guarding this level. He also looked oddly exhausted; not something you'd expect to see in Jaffa with new symbiotes. They all showed the same signs of fatigue—reddened eyes, sallow faces, labored movements—and a part of Janet's brain snapped into diagnostic mode. If Teal'c were presenting in this state, what would she suspect? A problem with Junior, obviously, but she'd seen the symbiotes these guys carried. They were healthy. So—

"Hey! I asked you a question!"

"Sorry. I was a little surprised." And a little suicidal. She couldn't afford to lose focus, tempting as it might seem. Janet vaguely pointed upward. "Lady Nirrti wants to see the Tauri. She must have notified you."

This was the tricky part. Success or failure of Colonel O'Neill's idea hinged on one crucial assumption; that fear or arrogance would prevent the Jaffa from admitting they'd lost touch with their deity—especially if Janet made them believe that her direct line was still up and running.

"Lady Nirrti did inform you, right?" she snapped, to drive it home.

"Of course." The guard actually blushed. "Just being careful. A couple of prisoners escaped."

"Not my problem, and I don't see what that's got to do with Lady Nirrti's orders to me. Now can I pass? Lady Nirrti doesn't like to be kept waiting."

He stepped back, glaring at her. As far as Janet was concerned, he could glare all he liked, just as long as he let them go. She gave the

Colonel a push, hating the necessity.

"Move!" she snarled, trying to sound like a good little Goa'uld minion and hating that, too.

Colonel O'Neill shuffled on, timing and degree of reluctance just right—then again, he'd had more than his fair share of opportunities to practice the skill. If... *when* they got home, she'd have to find a way of dealing with the fact that it had fallen to her to make this last experience a particularly memorable one. The thought made her want to howl, so she shoved it down to fester in her subconscious and concentrated on the guards again. One of them was swaying as she passed, hanging from his staff weapon, barely able to prop himself up.

They'd passed the second corridor, coming up for the third. Suddenly the first guard called out. "Wait!"

In front of them, two Jaffa stepped out, effectively blocking the gallery. From behind came footsteps. Just one set, though, so it might be alright, might be just another goddamn query. Don't lose your cool, Doctor.

Aiming for a mix of fury and boredom, she turned as slowly as she dared. "What?"

"That!" Number One Jaffa was pointing at the staff weapon she carried. He wasn't as dumb as all five of him looked. "Where did you get that?"

"Where do you think I got it?" she barked, feeling her fingers lock around the staff, knowing her knuckles were going white. "Lady Nirrti ordered me to take it. Seeing as you're hunting escaped prisoners, obviously you don't have any men to spare for an escort. You don't expect me to accompany someone as dangerous as the Tauri unarmed, do you?"

Face scrunched in a frown of concentration, he mulled it over. Higher reasoning functions weren't among the intellectual makeup Nirrti had allowed her creatures. Neither were the original's memories. After all, the clones might start to think. Seconds stretched away, interminable and simmering with impatience. Any moment, Nirrti might stop being otherwise engaged and decide to *really* send for Mrityu and the Tauri. If that happened, they'd be up crap creek without a paddle.

Finally he nodded, and the two clones blocking the way scooted back into their corridor like the birdie into its cuckoo clock. Janet prodded the Colonel again. Under the watchful eyes of the Jaffa they rounded the gallery, reached the bottom of the stairs, and started on their way up.

"Nice job," whispered Colonel O'Neill. "I had no idea they did acting electives at med school."

"They don't." Janet fought an urge to swap hands on the staff and wipe her sweaty palm. The Jaffa were still watching. "Chalk it up to panic."

Up here the walls showed a lot less damage—the battle must have been confined mostly to the level below, and whoever had started it was still alive and out there. A reassuring idea, and Janet clung to it. To such an extent that she practically collided with Jack O'Neill, who'd stopped dead in his tracks.

"Showtime," he muttered.

Two levels up, a troupe of five Jaffa was coming toward them, and the fact that they were pointing rather excitedly put paid to any notions of a chance encounter. Up crap creek without a paddle.

"Stop!" hollered one of the Jaffa upstairs.

"Time to run, Doc."

Staggering and stumbling, the Colonel scrambled up the last steps to the fifth level. In his wake, Janet wanted to recite every article she'd ever read on cardiac conditions. That temptation went out the window when the first staff blast broiled past them—a hit would kill him a lot quicker. The boys downstairs had woken up, and within moments she and Colonel O'Neill were hop-skipping through a crossfire of plasma bolts.

He tripped, fell hard. "Keep going!"

Not likely! Janet stayed in front of him, swung around the staff—too damn unwieldy, not designed for people her height—and fired blindly through roiling smoke and dust-laden air.

"Keep going!" he hissed again.

"Shut up and get up! Sir!"

She continued firing, not caring whether she actually hit anything aside from masonry. The whole point was buying him a few seconds to regroup. Behind her she sensed movement. He'd given up on being stupidly heroic and concentrated on rising instead. And then some.

"Give me the staff!" He tugged at the end, sending her next blast wildly astray.

To her utter surprise, a clone came tumbling from the sixth level. Janet grinned. "Nice shooting, sir. Now quit distracting me and find cover."

Obviously he realized that resistance would be futile. Hugging the wall, he headed for a corridor a few meters down the gallery. Janet sidled along on the outside of him, still firing, trying to make herself as tall and bulky as she possibly could to shield him from the blasts. It wasn't fair really; a mother hen had wings to spread, she had a goddamn stick she could barely—

Stairwell, Jaffa, the corridor entrance just behind her exploded into a fiery, liquid plume of agony. The plasma bolt knocked her off her feet and into the Colonel, who caught her and dropped backward into the passage, cushioning her fall with his body. Her shoulder was screaming, and the world around her flipped in and out of existence like a slideshow; the pain-flooded images after each spot of black changing subtly. She held on to one where she sat slumped against the wall, Colonel O'Neill wresting the staff weapon from her, anger and concern ghosting through his eyes.

"Dammit, Doc! A simple *I'm sorry* would have sufficed!"

"We gonna do something about them, Jackson, or what?"

"Or what," muttered Daniel.

The sergeant ducked around the corner, let Daniel's *zat* sing out twice, and snapped back into cover. From across the terrace came the thud of a falling body. Originally, Macdonald had grabbed a Jaffa's staff weapon. When it turned out that firing very long and top-heavy guns was trickier than it looked, he'd grudgingly swapped arms with Daniel. "Hey! I asked you a question."

"Or what!" Daniel mouthed in his direction.

A few minutes earlier a group of Jaffa had peeled off from a unit that defended the marquee on the opposite side of the terrace. All guns blazing, they'd risked a suicidal dash across open space. Two hadn't made it, and now lay draped between statues and flower pots. The remaining five had disappeared inside the building. Clones on a mission, which wasn't a happy thought, given that Jack was still trapped in the lab and Janet, presumably no longer under the influence of Nirrti, holed up God only knew where.

He heard a soft scraping noise behind him, whipped around, saw Sam dangle from the roof over the colonnade and lightly drop to the ground. Crouching low, she threaded between the pillars and over to Macdonald's and his position.

"I don't suppose you've got any spare clips for this elephant gun?" She brandished something silver and enormous at Macdonald.

He shrugged. "Can't hear you, ma'am."

"Nah, didn't think you'd have any. Next staff weapon's mine."

Daniel got that urge to roll his eyes again and nudged Sam to make her look at him. "Where is Teal'c?" he mouthed.

"Covering us from the roof." She risked a swift look around the corner to scan the vast pillared patio that formed the transition from Nirrti's quarters to the roof terrace and outdoors. The whole place seemed to have been transplanted straight from a glossy magazine article on gracious living in tropical latitudes; warm light from garden torches, gently babbling fountains, orange and palm trees, marquee by the parapet to watch the moonrise, eight-o'clock martini optional. The only thing marring the picture were the bodies. "Funny," muttered Sam.

"What is?" No reply. He nudged her again. "What is?"

"It's almost like they want us to get back into the building. I mean, there's what? Two? Three guards there. The rest of their defense is concentrated on the marquee."

"So?"

"So I'm guessing that either they're being a tad careless with the life of their goddess or—"

"There's something in that tent Nirrti wants protected at all cost," Daniel finished simultaneously with her. "What do you suggest?"

"Either way we have to try and find out. And we need to get Nirrti anyway, because we need the ribbon device."

"Why?"

"It activates the ring transporter in the vault, and that's the only way out of this joint."

"Actually, no." Daniel shook his head. "Teal'c and I found the back door."

Eyes widening, Sam grinned. "Of course you did. What was I thinking? I—" The grin died abruptly, replaced by a frown.

"Sam? What's the matter?"

"I'm not sure." A line of goose-bumps raced up her arm and across her shoulder—a bit of a impossibility, given the sweltering heat that still infused the air and radiated from the stone around them. She swatted at it as though it were a spider. "Almost like somebody's touching me."

"I think you've just found Nirrti!"

Incredulity clouded the woman's eyes. "We kept that invisibility belt when we were stupid enough to let her go the last time, Daniel."

"So what if she has a spare? For when the other one's at the garage for a service?"

The woman stared, blank-faced and unable to hear him, just as Master Sergeant Macdonald was. They had been deafened, which explained why Nirrti had lost control of them.

In a blur of monochromatic distortion the Jackson creature whirled around, fumbling with his staff weapon. The swing sliced right through her, would have struck her had she been in their phase. She wished she had killed him while she had had the chance, wished she could afford to force him into butchering his companions. But, now that the transmitter was gone, controlling the clones who defended the marquee required all her mental energy—and it was more important. It was her route to safety. Her fingers flexed inside the ribbon device, wanting to reach across phases and boil the Jackson creature's brain within the shelter of its skull. It almost appeared as though his return had started this... entropy.

Nirrti stifled her craving, knowing that, here and now, revenge was impossible without revealing her presence. There were few things more satisfactory than vengeance, but the chance to breathe another day—with satisfaction merely postponed—was one of them. Her left hand, clad in the ribbon device, reached out and stroked gold-tipped fingers across the woman's neck one final time.

Then she abandoned the humans to their fate, headed past the pillars and into the building. Her rooms were in tatters, small fires springing up here and there, shimmering tongues setting ablaze the silken hangings and licking at wooden columns. On the viewing mirror a silent battle played out. In the alleys and squares of the ruined city her and Simmons's Jaffa had found each other and clashed with what violence was left in them. Not much, not that it mattered now. They would die one way or the other.

Walking unscathed through flames, she stepped out into the central stairwell. She would begin again, that was all. She would regain the stars, no longer be hunted like an animal from planet to planet. She would recoup everything Lord Yu had stolen from her and more. She would own the stars, rule them. The only thing she needed was—

Her rage should have shaken the fortress to its foundations, and perhaps it had. For a moment the skirmish three levels below her ceased, and though they could not possibly have heard her furious scream, the Jaffa, the very men she had dispatched to bring her the Tauri dead or alive, looked around in confusion. Whoever had engaged them made no such mistake. Two plasma bolts in quick succession streaked from a corridor and across the void, killing a clone. Through the strange optics of the phase shifting device it seemed like a shining mirage, and for the briefest of moments, before he ducked back into the safety of the hallway, the Tauri glanced up and straight at her as though he knew she was there. The Tauri!

Nirrti felt the stars slip from her grasp. Bereft of a *hak'taur*, yet again, and again it was he who had cheated her. There would be no third time. She would make sure of that, would make him rue his paltry triumph as he was buried alive.

Her anger tightly controlled now, she spun around, hurried back through the blaze in her living quarters—a strange sensation, cold fire, but it was a fitting simile for her state of mind—out onto the terrace, and toward the marquee. A staff blast strafed past and struck a Jaffa, a copy of her First Prime. He dropped into her path, hands clenched over a smoldering hole where his pouch should have been, pain contorting his handsome face. Pain and bewilderment, because he had been promised near-invulnerability and was dying all the same. She passed through his body—a gesture of farewell from his goddess, she thought—and entered the marquee. It, too, was ablaze, but it did not matter. High above her *ha'tak* orbited the planet, an impervious refuge.

Caressing the ribbon device, she stepped into position, pressed a crystal. The last thing she saw before the brilliance of the ring transporter enveloped her were the humans and their *shol'va*, gawping at transporter rings that had mysteriously sprung up around nothing. An instant later, Nirrti arrived on the *ha'tak*'s bridge, swept past a line of kowtowing Jaffa and positioned herself in front of the control console. Fingers spread across its glowing surface, she entered a simple command, and a red lance of energy issued from deep within the mothership.

For just a second longer, Teal'c stared at the spot where the transporter rings had appeared and disappeared, then he tore his attention away. He knew what had happened, and there was nothing to be done about it. Except leave, as quickly as they could, because Nirrti would not let it rest here.

The clones, bereft of the will that had governed their actions, seemed frightened and confused, and for the moment they had ceased firing. Perhaps it had finally occurred to them that, unless they gave up a futile fight, they would be trapped here as surely as their quarries. Teal'c took his chance, leaped off the roof, and bolted into the cover of the colonnade as soon as his feet struck the ground.

His team mates and Sergeant Macdonald were still in the same position, hunkering under the arcade.

"Now we know what was so important in there. They kept the door open for Nirrti." Major Carter scrambled to a stand. "Dammit, I should have seen it coming! It's not like she hasn't done it before. We—"

"Why the devil did those rings go off?" Sergeant Macdonald never received an answer, either because he had not been heard or because there was no time to explain.

Smoke was rolling from the building, thick and black, blotting out the stars and forming reddish domes above the torches that illuminated the terrace. Through it, seemingly out of nowhere, stabbed a thin, vertical line, not unlike a target laser. It was aimed at the center of the fortress, directly into the open stairwell. By Teal'c's count it lasted two seconds, perhaps three, then it vanished again.

Daniel Jackson frowned. "I'm thinking this is probably not a good thing. As a matter of fact, I'm thinking we should get the hell out of here."

"Indeed."

"We'd better go." Major Carter, not privy to these musings, rose. "Cover me!"

Without waiting for a reply, she darted out into the open and toward the building. The clones by the marquee loosed several halfhearted staff blasts that fizzed through the smoke harmlessly off-target. When Teal'c and Daniel Jackson returned fire, they desisted almost immediately. Major Carter reached the covered patio and began to rip silk curtains from their fastenings. Lengths of fabric trailing after her, she raced for a fountain outside Nirrti's quarters, dunked the silk into the water.

"What are you waiting for?" she shouted.

Teal'c, Daniel Jackson, and Sergeant Macdonald made a break across the terrace. This time it drew no reaction from the clones. Firelight trilled across the patio, cast orange highlights on the stone and flickering shadows from the pillars. The heat was dry and stifling, a mere promise of what was to come. But they had no choice, and O'Neill was still imprisoned in the laboratory. If he was still alive—as indeed he would be. Teal'c refused to contemplate any other option, snatched one of the sodden sheets Major Carter held out, and wrapped it around himself.

"Okay, Teal'c's on point; I'll be bringing up the rear," she said and turned to Teal'c. "Last time we checked, there were two guards left in there, though I don't believe—"

"No." He shook his head. The men who had defended Nirrti's rooms had either fled or burned. Even with the aid of a symbiote it was impossible to survive this for long. Which meant he would have to find the shortest route and commit no error. There would not be time to double back.

A flap of wet fabric tugged over his nose and mouth, Teal'c ventured into the blaze, grateful that the floor was stone—uncomfortably warm, but not combustible and therefore safe. The smoke was thick enough to virtually blind him. Still, logic dictated that the entrance to the suite would be off the central stairwell, which had to be at the other end of this room and to the right. Using his staff like a machete, he swept aside more silken hangings, all furiously alight, burning pennants. Each sweep shook loose a blast of incandescence, and the unprotected skin around his eyes and on his forehead felt as though it shrank in the heat, too tight to contain his face. Like a fiery heart, the room seemed to pulse around him, expanding and compressing, hypnotic. From the corner of his eye he saw tall, dark figures, dancing in shrouds of flame to the roar of combusting oxygen. He turned, only to find that it was a row of burning pillars, realized that it was as good as a warning. Before long, the ceiling would fall.

Within some invisible conduit the temperature rose just high enough to trigger a freak draft. It momentarily cleared the smoke, dragged it toward the roof terrace on coattails of fire. Teal'c found himself less than six feet away from a wall he had not expected to be in this location and with no means of telling whether the exit would be to the left or to the right. If he chose wrong, they would die. His instincts told him to go left, and he obeyed. If he wasted time on hesitation, they would die anyway.

He kept the wall in sight now, yelling—and coughing—in frustration when it led him to a window, not a door. How could he have been so wrong? How could he—

Not a window; it could not be. The heat would have shattered the pane that even now seemed smooth and undisturbed. Eyes tearing from the smoke, he saw that it was an observation device—a communication globe stretched flat, like the television units the Tauri preferred. It showed an area of the city he did not recognize and three men running up an endless flight of stairs. One of them was Jaffa, and the way he moved appeared oddly familiar.

The stately dance of the pillars exploded into a fury of sparks and noise and splintering wood, and the ceiling near the terrace collapsed. Flames began pressing in toward him, and his silk cocoon had stopped dripping and felt hot. Briefly assuring himself that his team mates were still following, Teal'c hurried on. Unless he found a way out within the next—

And there it was.

A dark shaft, punched by cool air that fed the fire, and at its end an open door.

"Come!" he shouted, smoke delving into his lungs and making him choke.

He stayed by the door, counting them off: Sergeant Macdonald, his scalp blistered where embers had burned through the fabric; Daniel Jackson, blindly staggering along, his already damaged eyes red and swollen; Major Carter guiding him, soot-blackened, hair singed, but otherwise intact.

They had barely reached the safety of the stairwell when a deep rumble shook the fortress and for a moment seemed to still even the blaze behind them.

"What the hell?" enquired Daniel Jackson of no one in particular.

"What the hell?" For a second Jack thought he was about to keel over after all. Despite the upbeat medical bulletins he issued to Fraiser at regular intervals, he wasn't all that steady on his feet.

Staff weapon tucked against him in case he lost his balance, he closed his eyes for a moment. He wanted to sleep for a year, but even sitting down would have been a relief. Except, if he did that, he probably wouldn't be able to get up again.

"Colonel?" came Fraiser's voice, way to reedy. She sat tilted at an odd angle, one elbow propped into the crook where floor met wall.

"I'm peachy." Jack slapped on a smile.

This time she didn't call him on it, and it scared the crap out of him. That, and not knowing where Carter was or Teal'c—or Daniel, with that bizarre notion of his.

… if I buy it out here, it won't be because you're there but because you're not…

What if Daniel was right?

The thought splintered in another rumble, and it dawned on Jack that the phenomenon was objective, not subjective. First somebody seemed to have fired an *intar* straight down the center of the stairwell, and now this. Lousy experience showed that there more than likely was a causal connection between these events.

The umpteentuplets also found it kinda weird. You could tell because, for the time being, they'd quit trying to fry him. Staff weapon ready to fire, Jack edged out onto the gallery for a peek. Nicely lined up on the levels above and below, the 'tuplets stood staring into the hole. Maybe they'd been bred from an unusually dumb germline. Maybe it was their incubation-day, and the sperm donor had beamed down a strip-a-gram.

Yeah, you should be so lucky, O'Neill.

He could start picking them off now, but then he wouldn't get to see what was so damn fascinating down there. Another rumble, and he used it to slip just far enough toward the edge of the gallery to get a full view of the bottom floor.

"What the hell?" he whispered again.

A mosaic at the center of the floor—presumably the target area for that beam earlier—had turned a glassy, luminous green, shadows pulsing through it. It seemed to be growing, and they'd have to get past to reach the vault. *After* they grabbed the ribbon device and found Carter—neither of which was likely now, not with Fraiser injured. The best he could do was get her out. And then he'd drag his sorry ass back in here and look for his 2IC.

But first he'd end this current party.

Without bothering to duck back into cover, he took aim—and never fired the shot. The germline couldn't have been all that dumb. Or the clones knew more about pulsing green floor-fungus than he did. They turned around and ran for the exit, which meant downstairs, which meant the gang of four holding the upper gallery was headed his way.

He dived back into the corridor. Fraiser still looked like Casper after hitting a wall, not that he'd expected any improvement. The black and red scorch mark on her shoulder was digging wider and deeper—if left untreated, staff weapon burns could swelter on long after the actual hit—and underneath he could see the faint white gleam of her collarbone.

"What's happening, sir?" she whispered, barely audible over the ongoing rumbles.

"Company. We're gonna have to drop off the radar." Squinting against the gloom, he scanned the hallway. No doors either side, but thirty meters along was a cross-passage. Not perfect, but it would take them out of sight and hopefully out of mind. He leaned the staff weapon against the wall and crouched. "Brace yourself, Janet. This is gonna be fun. I'm sorry."

"No, sir." She knew the drill too well not to get what he was doing and tried to wriggle away from him. "You can't carry me. You—"

"We haven't got time for foreplay, Doc. Either you let me carry you round the corner there, or we both stay here and wait for the clones to declare open season. What's it to be?"

Her glare promised that his next medical would include a prostate exam, but she stopped fighting him. Jack hooked under her good arm, pulled her onto his shoulders, and somehow just knew that he'd never in a million years get up from his squat. Somebody yelled, a furious howl of frustration—his own, he realized, startled—and then he was on his feet. Fraiser's weight shifted subtly, grew a fraction heavier. Grateful she'd passed out at last, he grabbed the staff and staggered for the intersection, waiting for shouts and running footsteps and the sizzle of plasma bolts to catch up with him.

They never came.

An eternity later, Jack rounded the corner and allowed himself to catch his breath and listen past the rumbles that shook the building, the roar in his ears, the thumping stutter of his heart. On autopilot, his mind took in details of the location and filed them away. The cross-passage, lit only by the residual light spilling along the corridor, probably formed a ring around the stairwell; on its outside stretched a parade of doors, mostly gaping on empty rooms. A little further down the hall two were shut. No 'tuplets anywhere in sight, which was good news. He tried to figure out where to go from here. Follow the passage and hope for another corridor or wait a few more minutes and head back the way he'd come?

He wished the thumping would stop, so he could think straight. How was he expected to—

Okay, so his ticker wasn't responsible for the thumping. Too rhythmic for starters, and it came from the direction of those two shut doors.

Carter.

Sucking in a dizzy breath of relief, he eased Fraiser to the ground as gently as he could and edged along the hallway. "Sam?"

The thumping picked up pace and vigor.

"Sam!"

"In here! Hey!" A male voice, hoarse and commanding and, as

far as Jack was concerned, the next-best thing to a boot in the groin.
"Get us out!"

You're an idiot, O'Neill! Fraiser told you she wasn't locked up!

But 'Sam' and whoever else was in there might be of help. *The
enemy of my enemy*, and all that. Jack decided to ignore that lump
of misery in the pit of his stomach and brought up the staff weapon.
"Stand back from the door!"

The lock showed excellent workmanship and took two blasts
before it gave. Somebody yanked the door open and dispelled any
residual hope he might have held of Carter having contracted a bad
case of strep. Nicely lit by the lone torch in the cell, 'Sam' was an
easy six foot six, distinctly male, and African-American. Behind him
thronged four more faces, all of whom Jack recalled seeing on the
clones.

He froze.

CHAPTER TWENTY-TWO

George Hammond watched in dismay as the night sky above the fortress blossomed into flickering red.

"It's on fire," observed Harry.

"Oh, really? Thanks for pointing it out."

"You know, there's a reason why people run *out* of burning buildings rather than *into* them."

"You are afraid, Maybourne?" Bra'tac's voice struck that fine balance between amusement and contempt.

"No. All I'm saying is I've got a million bucks coming my way when I get home, and I'd like to live to enjoy it."

"The Jaffa have a saying. No pain, no gain."

"That's not—"

"There!" Hammond cut in. Above, just about visible, rose the end of the staircase and, set back from a small plaza, an ornate structure, like a shrine. "The sanctuary."

Predictably, Bra'tac upped the pace, and by the time they crossed the final step and reached the top, Hammond was determined to reassess his fitness regimen.

That's why they don't send two-stars into the field anymore. Nothing to do with protecting strategic assets. Most of us are just too out of shape to hack it!

His only consolation was to hear Maybourne panting nearly as hard.

A high, elegant archway flanked by statues formed the entrance to the shrine. Beyond lay darkness so complete, you could have cut it with a knife.

"Anybody seen a light switch?" quipped Harry.

The reply was a metallic noise Hammond recognized as a staff weapon opening. For a moment he found himself hoping that Jaffa shot people who consistently cracked lame jokes. The tip of the staff began to glow, casting its light over wall friezes, well-trodden floors, and a dark shape crumpled against the wall. Another dead clone. His symbiote lay nearby, fins limp, body still.

The passage opened out into a round, high-ceilinged room, empty except for a seam of pillars, and he tried to fight back a black wave of despondency. There was nothing here. The kid had been lying—or he'd been too confused to understand what Hammond wanted. They'd just wasted a half hour they might not be able to make up.

"It was not wasted," said Bra'tac, and Hammond realized that he must have been talking out loud. "Observe!"

The old warrior pointed the staff weapon at the center of the floor. The halo from its tip lit up a mosaic—concentric rings, crenellated around the outsides, the widest about six feet in diameter.

"I don't—" Hammond began, then something about the pattern triggered an association. "A ring transporter?"

"Indeed."

"Where are the controls?"

It was Harry who found it. He'd wandered off along the pillars and suddenly gave a surprised grunt. "Hey, this place has Nirrti's paw prints all over it. Literally. Didn't Dr. Jackson play with one of these on the planet where your bomb kid came from?"

"Who?" Hammond squinted in the direction of the voice.

"The girl Dr. Fraiser adopted. Look!" He indicated the faint outline of a palm print halfway up a column. When he brought his own hand closer, the outline grew brighter.

"Do not touch it!" cautioned Bra'tac.

For once Harry obeyed. He took a step back, and the palm print dimmed again. Bra'tac motioned them to stand at the center of the mosaic, briefly placed his own hand against the print, and ran. "Ready your weapons!"

He made it in the nick of time, all but vaulting over the first ring shooting from the ground. The remaining four zipped up in quick succession, and Hammond watched the world around him being swallowed by light.

Almost instantly it transformed into an eerie green glow, pushing through a narrow doorway into some kind of vault and backlighting eight armed figures, frozen in surprise. The rings whopped back into the floor, and before the men could react, Bra'tac opened fire. A thundering mêlée of gunshots and staff blasts tore away any sense of time.

Then, abruptly, the fight was over.

Too soon, and for the first time Hammond truly appreciated why Bra'tac refused to consider these men to be Jaffa. Against fully trained warriors, the three of them could not have won this, at least not without taking casualties. But the clones, tired and ragged from what must have been a previous skirmish, fought with unfamiliar weapons unsuited to the tactics their originals had been taught. They'd never stood a chance. Bra'tac, in a lethally graceful burst of motion, had dispatched four of them, Harry and George Hammond had taken care of the rest. Hammond had tried to shoot to disable, not kill, aiming for his opponents' legs. In one instance his aim had been too good; the round had nicked the femoral artery, and the clone had gone down into a rapidly widening pool of blood.

"Shouldn't his symbiote stop the bleeding?" murmured Harry.

"Not if he can't *kelno'reem*," Hammond replied curtly.

He knew that, perversely, the clones had very little in common with the men who'd been deployed to '335, but technically—genetically—speaking they were US Marines. Killing them went against everything he believed in. Disgusted with himself, he turned away and to his second victim, a burly, dark-haired man, who was in somewhat better shape and who seemed vaguely familiar. Perhaps he—his original—had participated in the exercise.

"Do you know who I am, Marine?" Hammond asked.

"You're dead, whoever you are!" The man glared up at him, undiluted hatred in his eyes. "Lady Nirrti will destroy you!"

"I don't see her. Do you, son?"

"I'm not your son, human! I have sprung from the goddess. And she'll return to reward me."

"Sure she will. Where are Colonel O'Neill and his team, and Dr. Fraiser?"

"The Tauri?" The clone's mouth curved in a sly smile. "The Tauri has suffered much, and he'll suffer more. Lady Nirrti has taken him. She ordered us to kill the others. You're too late, old man."

"You're lying, you son of a bitch!" Perhaps it was the green glow that suffused the vault, but Maybourne seemed pale. Which didn't keep him from planting a boot on the bullet wound in the man's thigh and stepping down. "Where are they? Where's Jack?"

"I told you!" The Jaffa grated out through clenched teeth.

"Stop it!" Hammond clutched Maybourne's arm. "This isn't—"

"It's why you brought me along, isn't it, Huggy? To do the dirty work. But don't worry, it's purely old-testamentary; an eye for an eye. If they had the bad taste to torture Jack…" He didn't finish the sentence, shook off Hammond's grip, and this time put a little more gusto behind the macabre step aerobics that punctuated his question. "Where? Are? They?"

The clone screamed, sweat beading on his forehead and trickling down the side of his nose. He gasped once, twice, and finally hissed, "They're somewhere in the building. I don't know if they're dead. They escaped."

"Told you he was lying," said Harry, his voice flat. "Let's go find them and get the hell out of here."

At that moment a low growl seemed to rise from the foundations of the building. Masonry creaked and a shower of dust rained from the ceiling. The smile crawled back onto the clone's face.

"You can't leave. The fortress is falling, and the ring transporter doesn't work from here. We tried it. You and your friends'll be buried right here. With us."

Hammond whirled around and stared at that pulsing green aura.

The rumbles had gotten worse, and something on the bottom floor was glowing green and growing—which, according to the iconography of every horror movie ever shot, was Not A Good Thing. Sam had held off on pronouncing a scientific opinion until they got closer, while Macdonald had opined that it might not be wise to *get* closer. Not that they had a choice.

At least the screaming had stopped, and Daniel didn't think he'd ever been so grateful for anything. Trying to persuade himself that it couldn't possibly have been Jack, he stumbled down the last few steps to the sixth level, and almost bumped into Macdonald.

The sergeant, Sam, and Teal'c had ground to a halt outside a corridor. Daniel blinked past them. His eyes had quit streaming, tears drying to itchy trails of salt on his skin. He resisted the temptation to swipe at them. The way his face felt, even a feather duster would cause too much friction. On the other hand, the guy lying prone in the doorway was worse off. Daniel could smell the telltale stench of plasma burns; the clone had been killed by a staff blast. But why? Palace revolution? Opposing factions of clones, having a go at each other after Nirrti had left the sinking ship?

And Jack trapped in the middle of it. He and Janet.

Looking at Sam, Daniel saw his own throat-clutching fear mirrored in her eyes, refused to listen to the memory of those screams, went for a travesty of encouragement instead. "We've got to get to the lab," he mouthed, pointing downward.

"Yeah." One syllable, bitten off, all she could safely let past that bulwark of discipline. If she screwed the self-control any tighter, she'd snap. Lips compressed to a thin, stressed line, Sam dodged his scrutiny, picked up the dead clone's staff weapon. "We need to find Janet."

They hurried along the gallery and down the stairs to the fifth level. More signs of fighting; another dead clone, burn marks around doorways, torn steps, reliefs in splinters, a sconce and torch ripped from the wall, all bathed in that sickening green glow. The next set of stairs was coming up ahead, and Daniel picked up his pace. Passing a doorway, a shadow of movement caught his eye—too late. The arm snapped around his throat, jerked up his chin, sent his headache squarely into migraine territory and all but drowned the shout that echoed from the corridor.

"Don't!"

While Daniel still wondered if he was hearing voices, the pressure on his carotid ceased, restoring the oxygen supply to his brain and sparking a festive shower of stars—uniquely apposite. "Jack!" he wheezed, reeling into the wall.

A Marine who made Teal'c look dainty ballooned into his field of vision. "He with you, kid?" Goliath hollered back over his shoulder.

Kid? The guy was Jack's age, if that, but managed to convey the impression that he'd been at it since the Marines landed on Okinawa.

"Yes, dammit! So's the rest!" Definitely Jack.

Taking a step back, Goliath cleared the view. Definitely, definitely Jack.

The rest gradually lowered their weapons and inched closer, as if a faster approach would dispel the apparition. Teal'c gave one of those rare, all-enveloping smiles, and Sam had gone still enough to suggest that any kind of motion might irreparably crack her armor.

"Colonel," she whispered. "Sir... With respect, sir, you look like hell."

"Thanks." The bottomless relief written all over his face couldn't mask it. Half-naked and filthy, Jack was drained to within an inch of his life, and if he went any paler, he'd start to glow in the dark. And he knew it. Skirting any discussion of what had happened to him, he made a show of taking in Sam's dishabille in open-mouthed disbelief. "Interesting, Major. Love the legs. Especially the left one."

"*Colonel*?" Goliath boomed out. Introductions had been postponed, it seemed.

Jack pointed at his bare chest, which probably wasn't anywhere near hairy enough to impress Goliath. "On the rare occasions when I actually wear a uniform it says 'Colonel' right about here. I'm thinking of getting a tattoo."

"Uhuh. Next we'll find us a general," mumbled Goliath, not entirely convinced but tagging on "sir" to be on the safe side. Then his eyes settled on Macdonald, and he grinned. "Hey, Burger! Glad to see you made it."

"Look, kids, it's all very touching, but we'd better blow this popsicle stand before it blows us." As if on cue, a new rumble rattled through the building. Jack started shooing Marines from the corridor and toward the stairs.

Daniel exchanged a glance with Sam, who shook her head barely noticeably. No symbiotes.

"No clones," supplied Jack, joining in the silent conversation. "They're the originals. Nirrti kept them, just in case."

"O'Neill." Teal'c hovered behind him, unobtrusively making sure that Jack wouldn't keel over. "We have not yet succeeded in finding Dr. Fraiser."

"I have. Long story," he added in a tone that precluded any questions.

Roughly at that point Daniel knew for certain that what he'd sensed outside the lab had been real and it had been bad. And he'd gone on a wild goose chase instead of trusting his instincts. The weight of the mistake dropped into his gut, squirmed and started gnawing. This was how you got ulcers, Daniel supposed. How did Jack do it without practically living on antacids? By throwing knee-jerk reactions, being insufferable, and, ultimately, resigning when he thought he couldn't face making one more mistake.

"Daniel?" Sam was staring at him.

"I'm okay. I—" He forgot the rest, thunderstruck, and his stomach twisted into another knot.

One of the Marines was carrying Janet out onto the gallery. Teal'c's eyes went wide, then he stepped into the man's path. "I shall take care of Dr. Fraiser." The stare he sent the Marine made clear that refusal would be a very dumb idea.

Nodding, the man handed over his charge. Without that larger-than-life energy and determination to drive her, Janet seemed tiny, like a child in Teal'c's arms. The large, vicious-looking plasma burn on her upper chest made Daniel's own shoulder twinge in sympathy. Been there, done that, died of it. And chances were that he was responsible for this, too.

Sam had gone white as a sheet, fist clenching around the requisitioned staff weapon. "Is she—"

"No. And she won't, if I've got anything to do with it. Instead of ducking, she decided to save my life," Jack said grimly. "Let's go, folks, before that fungus down there takes over the joint."

"*Fungus?*" Daniel couldn't help it. He smiled.

"Space fungus." As if to make sure the green blob was still doing its thing, Jack cast a glance down the stairwell and snapped into a classic double-take. "Holy cow!"

"What?"

He looked past Daniel and at Goliath. "Hey, Shorty? You ordered a general?"

Stay where you are, sir!

It didn't make a whole lot of sense, given the dire predictions of the clone Jaffa, but George Hammond assumed Jack knew what he was doing. Currently he was herding his little flock toward his would-be rescuers and the vault and a ring transporter that couldn't be activated. Then again, he wasn't the type to curl up in a dead-end set to self-destruct—not anymore. Which suggested that he might just have a way out.

Green stuff speckling the toecaps of his boots, Hammond studied the odd procession rattling down the stairs and felt a little redundant. A day late and a dollar short, though it was preferable to any number of alternatives. Led by a guy half a head taller than Teal'c, ten tattered specimens of the Marine Corps' finest arrived first, saluted on spec as they filed past and edged along the wall, trying to keep to the very fringes of that glowing green blight. Some of the faces he'd seen on the casualties in the vault—multiple times—but these men didn't wear Jaffa armor.

The tall guy in front—a gunnery sergeant, going by the stripes—called them to a halt, and watched the tail end of the rag-tag assembly negotiate the final steps. Teal'c, surefooted and solemn, carried Dr. Fraiser who had a nasty staff burn on her shoulder; behind him Dr. Jackson; and, bringing up the rear, Major Carter and Colonel O'Neill, both so far south of military dress code that Hammond's eyebrow gave an involuntary twitch.

When they came closer, the facial tic subsided abruptly. As a matter of fact, they confirmed a suspicion he'd held for some time now; that, whenever possible, SG-1 tried to spruce up before gating back Earthside. Hammond felt a bit like a mother paying an unexpected visit to the playground and witnessing firsthand what the kids really got up to when they thought nobody was looking.

Except, there was no way on Earth even SG-1 could have spruced up this one. Dr. Jackson looked like something that rightfully belonged in among the Halloween decorations, and Sam Carter's clothes seemed to have been burned off her back, leaving the blisters to prove it. As for Jack, Hammond had seen that same gray complexion on his father, just before the man had had a heart attack.

Jack must have read it in his face. He forced a grin. "I know. We look radiant. Nice of you to drop in, sir, but what the hell are you doing here? On second thought—what kept you?" The grin faded when he swayed a little, and Hammond's hand shot out to steady him. He shook it off. "No time for that, sir. It'll all be in the mission report." Grabbing Sam Carter's arm and turning her to face him, he mouthed, "Check out the fungus but make it fast."

The form of communication alone sparked a whole barrage of questions, but Jack was right. They didn't have time for any of this.

With a brisk nod Carter corralled Dr. Jackson. Together they headed into the vault to investigate the green stuff. Bra'tac, having convinced himself that Teal'c was unharmed, went to join them, just as Harry pushed through the ranks of the Marines. Jack gave Hammond a disbelieving stare.

"What did you bring him for?" he muttered. "To scare the children?"

"I'm hurt, Jack." Maybourne actually pouted. "Besides, Huggy didn't bring me, I brought Huggy."

"*Who*?" Jack's grin returned, positively beatific. "Hug—"

Before Major General Hammond could find cause to slap Colonel O'Neill with insubordination charges, chunks of gallery tumbled from above and landed in the middle of the floor. By rights the impact should have resulted in a crash and shrapnel flying everywhere. In actual fact, it resulted in slurping noises and masonry stuck off-kilter in what seemed to be—

"Green Jell-O," Jack said. "I hate green Jell-O."

"Sir!" Major Carter shot from the vault and came sprinting over to them. "Sir! Hi, Maybourne. Colonel, we've got to get out. Now. Whatever Nirrti's triggered here, it's basically turning stone to—"

"Green Jell-O."

"Exactly. The foundations are sagging, and it's spreading exponentially. Bottom-line, the place is digesting itself. There's no way for me to fix this. To be honest, I wouldn't know where to start. We've got to outrun it before those tunnels Daniel and Teal'c found come down around our ears."

"Okay. Let's—"

"Major," Hammond cut in. "What if it starts digesting… people?"

"She can't hear you, General."

Jack pointed Carter the right way, and Hammond repeated the question more slowly.

"Won't happen, sir. We checked out the dead clones in the vault. Floor's softening all around them, but the bodies are unaffected—apart from the fact that they're starting to sink."

"Great!" With a visible effort, Jack straightened up. "Daniel, Teal'c, take point. Shorty, you and your boys go next. Harry, you stick with the General—lose him and I'll break your neck. Carter and I've got your six. Move out and don't stop!"

"And I shall be watching you, human," Bra'tac barked, all five foot six of him squaring up to Jack's six-two, toe to toe, brooking no contradiction. "You look to me as though you might delay us. I shall find ways to prevent it."

For a moment protest hovered in Jack's eyes, then he backed down. "Thanks, Bra'tac," he said softly. "And quit calling me *human*."

Dr. Jackson and Teal'c already were wading through the gunk and toward a nook under the stairs, the Marines following close behind. When Hammond's turn came, he realized why Bra'tac had been so adamant. It was worse than running through wet sand, and Jack would need all the help he could get. The gunk—Jell-O, fungus, whatever—had better suction than most vacuums.

The nook concealed a doorway and an anteroom behind, and the exit from the latter was blocked by chest-high pile of Jell-O—fallen masonry, once upon a time. Now glowing an unearthly green, it complemented the noises that had begun to fill the tunnels. The fortress seemed to be groaning in pain, hollow moans interspersed with sharp cracks whenever stone split somewhere. One more incentive to hurry up.

Hammond started scaling Mount Jell-O and at the third lumbering step sank hip-deep into the goo, floundering like a beached whale to pull his leg free again. He managed—just.

Behind him, Harry hollered, "Don't walk, General! Lie flat and crawl up!"

Good idea, though it had been a lot easier in basic training, forty-odd years ago. Hammond pushed and pulled and tobogganed down the other side in a wake of muck. Panting for air and soaked with sweat, he picked himself up and plodded on at best possible speed.

Sam had expected they'd outrun it. Anybody would bet on being able to outrun, outsmart, outsing some pesky microbe. So much for the validity of the anthropocentric world view. In real terms, they barely managed to stay abreast of a massive case of architectural athlete's foot. No, actually, they didn't even manage that, she thought with another glance at the walls. The green, pumping malaise had risen to shoulder height, and God knew what would happen once it reached the ceiling. Well, God knew, and Sam Carter could take an educated guess. She could feel the vibrations that shook the structure each time another part of the building collapsed or subsided.

And subsidence definitely was starting to be a problem. As the softening foundations compressed under the weight of the fortress, the ceiling was sinking at the same rate. The top of Sam's head occasionally scraped stone, and the Colonel had to run hunched over—if you could call it running. Glutinous goop stuck to their soles, making each step twice as hard as it had to be. Occasionally, globs of it would hit Sam's shins, stick there, warm and itchy, until they died from lack of food, winked out, and confirmed her initial impression that it wasn't directly harmful to the human anatomy.

Up ahead, Maybourne and General Hammond slowed to a halt—their trek seemed to obey the same obscure laws as highway traffic, jamming without any apparent reason. She turned around to check on Colonel O'Neill. Despite the green wash she could tell that his lips had turned blue. Bra'tac slipped her a worried glance from behind him and said something that obviously improved the Colonel's mood to no end.

"What?" she asked. "I can't hear you, Bra'tac."

"Air quality sucks!" Colonel O'Neill shouted very slowly and promptly started gasping.

Damn! She'd never noticed it—one of the reasons why they kept canaries in mineshafts—but Bra'tac was right. Damn, damn, damn! Faced with relentless Day-Glo green, she'd automatically assumed photosynthesis, but that didn't make sense, for all kinds of reasons. Whatever this turned out to be, fungus or bacterium, it was aerobic, and there was a lot of it, siphoning off oxygen at the rate of knots.

At that moment, the column started moving again. "Go, Carter," the Colonel mouthed, giving her a little shove. His hand felt ice-cold and clammy.

She nodded, spun around, and sprinted to catch up with General Hammond. "Sir, can you pass word to the front that they have to keep moving? We're running out of air back here."

The Chinese whispers traveled quickly enough, and after about a minute the pace picked up considerably. They passed a sturdy stone gate, edged in green; the place where Daniel and Teal'c had left the two Marines who now would have joined the exodus. Past the door the tunnel broadened, appearing less claustrophobic, with large dark patches interrupting the green pest—tree roots. Hopefully those would add stability, too.

At last they reached a hall, and Sam sucked in a deep, grateful breath. Soaring pillars were streaked with fungus, its tendrils lapping at the ceiling, but the room was large enough for the air to be considerably better than in the tunnel. It also seemed familiar; she, Daniel, and the Colonel must have hobbled through here—how many days ago?

Way in front, Daniel's fist flew up, signaling a halt.

Blurred vowels—*owyiouou*—not unlike a bathtub draining penetrated the ringing in Sam's ears; her hearing seemed to be on the mend. Then she spotted Daniel and Teal'c, headed her way and trailed by the two new recruits. To her surprise, she recognized her friendly corporal from '335. He caught her eye, beamed at her, then his gaze dropped under a withering stare from Colonel O'Neill. Sam bit back a grin and tried to figure out what was going on.

Between snatches of half-formed words and a whole lot of gesticulation from Daniel, she grasped that the debate revolved around escape routes; take the stairs into the city or find the wardroom where Daniel had hidden her and the Colonel and reach the gate through the jungle?

A hand patted her shoulder, and someone said *ao aa* or words to that effect. Corporal Wilkins, cocking his thumb at Janet who still lay cradled in Teal'c's arms, barely conscious. He held up a plastic container he'd dug from his backpack.

Sam could have kissed him. Instead she snatched the medikit. "Thanks, Corporal."

Having picked antibiotic cream, sterile dressing, and a single injector with epinephrine, she handed the kit back to Wilkins, disengaged Teal'c from the discussion round, and gently brushed sweat-matted bangs from Janet's forehead. "Hey, Janet. Let's see to that burn, huh?"

As Sam dressed the wound the doctor briefly focused on her hands. Then Janet's concentration seemed to slip and her gaze wandered, only to return to the injector. Suddenly her fingers snapped around Sam's wrist. "Not me!" she whispered, and Sam read that just fine.

"Funny, but I always suspected you'd make a dreadful patient, Doctor. You're in shock. I've got to—"

"Triage!" Going by that glare, Janet was perfectly *compos mentis*, shock or no shock. "Colonel O'Neill… heart problem…"

"What?" Sam damn near dropped the epinephrine.

By the looks of Teal'c, who couldn't have avoided listening in on their little exchange, he'd damn near dropped Janet.

"Do it," Janet mouthed.

"Alright." Sam heard that *ao aa* sound again, only this time about an octave lower than before. She glanced up, met Teal'c's steady gaze.

"Should O'Neill resist," he said, enunciating very clearly, "have Master Bra'tac hold him down."

"Yeah." Funny as the idea was, she couldn't quite manage a smile.

The powwow had finished, it seemed, and at least she wouldn't have to go chasing him round the hall, injector cocked and loaded. He came over, eyes dark with concern. "How's the Doc?"

"She's holding surgery and prescribed this." Sam uncurled her fingers, showing him the injector.

He stared at it for a moment, nodded slowly, and jerked his head in the direction of a pillar. "I don't need an audience."

Sensible compliance meant he felt dreadful—or planned to lose the medication. Sam bit her bottom lip and followed him to the green-lit semi-privacy behind the column.

"I'll do it." He grabbed the injector, buried the needle in his arm, waited, drawing a few deep breaths. "Still want to puke."

"Why the hell didn't you tell me, sir?"

"Why the hell did you ask Daniel to chop your leg off while I was gone?" The look he shot her said an answer was redundant. At last, one corner of his mouth curled up in a small, crooked grin. "I'll be okay, Carter. Come on, it's about time we got home."

Home.

Quite a lofty ideal to aspire to from where Jack was staggering. There still was the minor matter of the absent DHD.

In the short term, they had other problems, though. They literally were up to their ears in fungus now, which at least had the benefit of adding a sense of urgency to proceedings. Up ahead Daniel skidded

into a right turn at breakneck speed, and Shorty—Gunnery Sergeant
Samuel Walker Adams, USMC—posted himself at the corner to
make sure that nobody galloped off straight by mistake.

Reaching the corner, Jack sent the gunny on his way and suddenly
realized that he hadn't heard any squishing behind him for a while.
The next rumble almost floored him as he spun around. Carter and
Bra'tac stood midway down the corridor, staring transfixed at what
was happening at the far end. The ceiling was coming down in large,
lazy globs of gunk, meeting walls that oozed inward.

Bra'tac grabbed Carter's arm and started running like the furies
were on his tail, dragging her along with him.

Scooting past Jack, she yelped, "Looks like we're committed,
sir!"

"Yeah! Move it!"

Looks like your decision not to lead injured and unarmed people
into the city to join the Clone Wars wasn't such a hot idea after all,
sir!

Mercifully, there was no time to wallow in 20/20 hindsight. Jack
sped up, some remote corner of his mind registering that he actually
felt a little more with it. The maddening tingle in his hands and feet
had stopped, too. Probably to allow him full enjoyment of the intermittent tremors.

As if to make up for that stray piece of good news, he turned the
next corner only to find that the procession had come to a grinding
halt. Jack knew where they were now and couldn't for the life of him
figure out what the hold-up was. Ahead lay one last staircase, and
after that the wardroom and the rainforest and no voracious fungus
from outer space. Bra'tac and Carter flapping after him like a pair of
overzealous chaperones, he pushed past the Marines and to the front,
about to snap at Daniel and Teal'c. The tirade died halfway up his
throat.

"Oh crap!"

"Uhuh," Daniel said softly.

The stairway looked like the waterslide in a Stephen King theme
park. Minus the water. The treads had melted into green, pulsing
welts and, given the rate at which the walls were buckling, the whole
thing was going to slurp in on itself within the next ten minutes.

"We shall have to turn back," whispered Teal'c.

"Ah, no. We don't want to do that. Trust me." Jack gave an unhappy snort, then he looked up. Standing around and shaking their heads wouldn't change a damn thing. There was only one way out of this. "Teal'c, you and Fraiser go first, then Daniel. It's a left at the bottom of the staircase. When you get there, find a shovel."

Teal'c's eyebrow hitched up to signal confusion.

"That was a joke. You may have to dig us out. Never mind. Go!"

Fraiser in his arms, Teal'c hopped onto the soggy stairs and slid down, followed by Daniel. Jack turned to face Shorty and his Marines. "Okay, you know what to do. Take the high heels off, ladies, do not inflate your lifebelts inside the plane, and—"

"Place your head firmly between your legs and kiss your ass goodbye. Sir!" Shorty finished up, counted a dozen Marines—including Macdonald and Carter's Romeo—onto the slide, and flung himself on last.

By the time it was Harry's turn, the slide looked a darn sight narrower. He backed up, sighing. "No offense, Huggy, but maybe you'd better go first!"

"Shut up before I forget myself, Maybourne!" Snarl aside, General Hammond conceded the point.

Jack grinned. "Having fun yet, Harry?"

"You *so* owe me, Jack!"

"I know. Scoot!" The air was running out fast. Gasping for breath, Jack watched Maybourne zip down the slide. "Carter! Your t—"

His order was cut short by a shove. Jack pitched forward, lost his footing, and hurtled head-first through a pumping green tunnel. He arrived in a goop-smeared tangle, only to have Carter slam into him at top speed.

"Dammit, Major! I hope for your sake it was Bra'tac who pushed me!"

"Can't hear you, sir," she retorted. "Get up, Colonel!"

Somehow he managed to struggle to his feet, furiously clenching and unclenching his fists. That tingle had come back with a vengeance and brought along a weird sizzling pressure in his ears and a shower of sparks that danced in front of his eyes. Through it he saw Harry wading toward the wardroom, knee-deep in fungus.

"Go, Major Carter! I shall bring O'Neill!" Bra'tac, sounding a million miles under water.

The sparks changed to black dots, and Jack realized that, while his lungs were working overtime, they weren't getting much oxygen into his system. An iron-hard grip cinched his waist, and he felt his arm pulled over Bra'tac's shoulder.

"Move, human! Or do you wish me to carry you?"

Apparently he was moving, because Bra'tac didn't sweep him off his feet. The going was agonizingly slow, to the point where Jack doubted they'd ever get out in time. Then, through a whirl of black dots, he recognized the wardroom, glowing bright green, the smug faces of the three Rickshaws melting off the wall.

Told you I'd get you a nose-job!

The thought entertained him to such an extent that he stumbled out into the open giggling like an idiot.

Hypoxia'll do that for a guy.

Bra'tac possessed the tact not to fling him to the ground and commence CPR. Instead he leaned Jack against a tree and stepped back a bit, head tilted, to observe further developments. Jack thought he heard an enormous roar, which could well have been in or for his ears exclusively, closed his eyes and breathed. Very New Age, that—fresh air and starlight. Once he felt reasonably sure that he wouldn't pass out, he risked a look. The city wall had sagged into the wardroom, squeezing out a huge pile of glowing green mess.

"When the hell did that happen?" he wheezed at no one in particular.

"About two seconds after you and Bra'tac came out." Somehow General Hammond had materialized beside him. "How're you doing, son?"

Feeling disinclined—with all due respect—to discuss the subject, Jack mounted a counteroffensive. "You realize, of course, that going after us was an insane thing to do, sir?"

"Nobody gets left behind." Hammond smiled. His face was glazed with sweat and shimmered in the fungus-light. "And you're welcome."

"I thought I'd taught you better. No crazy stunts just because a bunch of people have gone AWOL. No sticking your neck out till the giraffes get jealous. By the way, General, the mossy look suits you. Takes years off."

Hammond barked a laugh, snuffed it. After having watched Jack rub his face for a while, he asked, "What's on your mind, Colonel?"

"We might have a problem getting these folks out of here, sir. None of us could find the DHD."

"Neither could we." All things considered, Hammond sounded remarkably serene. "But two of Bra'tac's men are on their way in a *tel'tac*. They're probably here already."

"Oh." Jack tried hard not to whoop. He couldn't spare the breath. "Did I ever tell you that I love you, sir?"

CHAPTER TWENTY-THREE

The chatter and cackle in the canopy, its natural rhythm restored now that Nirrti's transmitter no longer disrupted the animals' instincts, ebbed at their passing and resumed behind them, telling him that there was no imminent danger. This might change before long, Teal'c reminded himself. Returning to the glade by the temple was a calculated risk, but the options seemed worse. Even Major Carter had agreed and, out of all of them, she had most reason to fear the beasts.

The only other landing site suitable for a *tel'tac* would have been the large square just inside the city gate, which almost certainly had been devoured by the fungus. Besides, should the *tel'tac* fail to arrive—a possibility, given that Nirrti's *ha'tak* had been in orbit and perhaps still was— they at least would be in the immediate vicinity of the Stargate and could resume their search for the DHD.

"Teal'c?"

The voice was soft and breathless, but it startled him nonetheless. Since he carried her, Dr. Fraiser had drifted in and out of consciousness, but the only time she had spoken was to refuse the medication that O'Neill needed more urgently.

"O'Neill is well, Dr. Fraiser. Do not trouble yourself."

"I wouldn't call it *well*," she whispered. "And it's not what I was going to say. I'm so sorry, Teal'c. I—"

"You are not to blame."

"I almost killed you!"

"No. You stopped yourself from killing me. It took exceptional strength of will to resist Nirrti's command. You should be proud of yourself."

"Sure. I'll work on it." She made a bleak little sound, not quite a laugh, then she asked, "Is that what it's like to be taken host?"

"No. If you had been taken host, you would have watched from within your body as Nirrti killed me, powerless to prevent it."

"I don't know what's worse," Dr. Fraiser murmured after a while.

"I *wanted* to please her."

"I do know what is worse. However, my opinion may be biased. I am, after all, still alive." Teal'c smiled. "Please, do not concern yourself any further, Janet."

Perhaps it was the uncustomary use of her given name, perhaps her guilt had been allayed somewhat. She fell silent again.

The trees were thinning now, and past them Teal'c could see the dark gray walls of a building. It had to be the temple, as yet unaffected by the fungus—if the blight would indeed reach this far. His vigilance increased, and he found himself listening and looking for any sign of the beasts.

Ahead, O'Neill's fist flew up to signal a halt. Hesitating a moment, Teal'c passed the others to be by his brother's side. They had stopped barely within the edge of the trees. Beyond lay the clearing at last, watched over by the giant stone face that contained the Stargate—itself a dark, still hole to match the emptiness and quiet below. But it was not all empty and quiet. Someone was there; Teal'c could sense it. Suddenly a figure appeared from the trees opposite, and a soft call sounded over the glade.

"Jaffa! *Kree!*"

Instinctively, O'Neill raised and primed his purloined staff weapon, but Bra'tac was quicker, stepping between hunter and prey. "They are my men. Do not shoot them." He turned to face out across the clearing and answered the call. "*Cha'hai,* Jaffa!"

A second man slid from the shadows and, behind him, six others.

O'Neill gave a low whistle. "You bring an army or something?"

"I did not. Those"—Bra'tac indicated the six men—"are not mine."

"Then whose are—"

Above the churned earth of the glade, the air began to roil and stretch, distorting the figures behind until they abruptly vanished altogether, blotted out by the uncloaked bulk of the *tel'tac*.

"Sweet," O'Neill remarked to General Hammond. "I think we should get ourselves at least five of those, sir. They do eighty light-years to the gallon, and the"—his fingers fluttered in search of a description—"super-stealthy camouflage doodad comes as an optional extra."

The hatch slid open, spilling warm, inviting light into the night and outlining the silhouette of a warrior.

"*Tek ma te* Bra'tac. You are late!" he shouted, and Teal'c recognized the voice. It belonged to Tabal, an apprentice of Bra'tac's. "Come quickly. We have to pass Nirrti's *ha'tak*. The longer we tarry, the greater the risk of discovery."

"Or of waking Carter's wee beasties," muttered O'Neill. Aloud he said, "You heard the man. Let's go home, folks!"

They arrived in the golden pool of light outside the hatch at the same time as the eight men from the opposite side of the clearing. It seemed that the six new arrivals were Marines who had surrendered to Bra'tac's Jaffa in the city. As he took in the assembly waiting to board, Tabal's eyes widened and his lips began to move silently. He was performing a headcount, and Teal'c knew the verdict before Tabal pronounced it.

"There are too many of them, Master Bra'tac." He shook his head for emphasis. "I can take twenty, twenty-two at the most. We already have the four prisoners aboard, and even if we left them here, two of you still would have to remain behind."

"That'd be the drawback of the model," O'Neill observed quietly. "Troop capacity's a little on the stingy side."

"Do the math! Just leave those guys here." Colonel Maybourne cocked a thumb at the Marines who had surrendered.

"Oh yeah?" snapped O'Neill. "And call it what? A blue-on-blue incident? They're coming."

"For God's sake! Jack, their orders were to kill you and your team! What's the bleeding heart say now?"

"They're still coming. We don't execute men who give themselves up."

"So what do you suggest we do?" Their difference in heights made Colonel Maybourne look like a pugnacious terrier squaring up to a tiger. "Draw straws?"

"No. That'd put Daniel at a disadvantage. He usually ends up with the short one." O'Neill exchanged a quick look with Daniel Jackson, then pointed at the temple behind them. "There's still the gate. All I have to do is find the DHD."

"*You*? Dammit, Jack, you can barely stand up straight!"

On this point Colonel Maybourne was exaggerating. Either the fresh air or the medication had helped. O'Neill seemed considerably better, and his mind was set. Changing it—if at all possible—would devour an amount of time and energy none of them had. So Teal'c chose the next best option available to him; he returned Dr. Fraiser into the care of the Marines and retrieved his staff weapon. "You may require some help searching, O'Neill," he said.

"Teal'c—"

"As a matter of fact, you'll need an expert," stated Daniel Jackson, joining them.

O'Neill gave a soft snort of resignation. "Do we have one who can actually *see* what he's doing?"

"I can, sir." Major Carter was grinning.

"Great!" snarled Colonel Maybourne. "One invalid and three wise monkeys. See no evil, hear no evil, speak no evil. I've got news for you, Jack; evil's out there, and it's gonna have your butt for breakfast. You're in no shape to—" He cut himself off and whirled around. "General! Do something!"

"I fully intend to, Colonel," General Hammond said placidly. "I'm staying, too."

"As am I," announced Bra'tac.

"That makes six," said O'Neill, turning to Tabal. "Load up and get out of here before that *ha'tak* starts taking potshots."

Too fast for anyone to intervene, Colonel Maybourne had drawn his sidearm and pressed the muzzle to O'Neill's head. "You owe me, Jack," he said, almost gently. "And you've got to be alive for me to cash in. So do me a favor and get your ass on that ship and go home. 'Cos, so help me, I'll blow your brains out if you don't. You go, I stay."

In truth, part of Teal'c wished O'Neill would submit. It was a futile hope, of course.

Standing perfectly still, O'Neill remarked, "I didn't know you cared, Harry. But the argument's a little self-defeating, wouldn't you say?"

Colonel Maybourne shrugged. "I don't—" The rest of the sentence fell victim to an elbow rammed into his midriff.

O'Neill spun around and followed up the blow with a right hook straight to the tip of the chin. Colonel Maybourne sent him an accusing glance and collapsed.

Shaking the sting from bruised knuckles, O'Neill murmured, "Like you said, I owe you, Harry." He looked up, taking in the crowd still gathered outside the *tel'tac*. "What the hell're you waiting for? Show's over. Get going!"

"Colonel O'Neill!" One of the six newcomers stepped forward. "The DHD? It's inside the temple. Good luck, and thank you, sir."

"Your powers of persuasion never cease to amaze me, son," Hammond said as they watched the *tel'tac* lift off and cloak in thin air.

The sight made Jack feel almost as vulnerable as he'd felt that night in Iraq—though that had been worse. Much worse. He'd been alone then. Besides, Tabal had promised to return if they hadn't made it back by the time the *tel'tac* group arrived on Earth. Of course, if they didn't make it back, there might be nothing left for Tabal to find. Aside from green gunk, that was. Jack filed the thought away under 'P' for 'pointless' and slapped on a grin for Hammond.

"What else was I supposed to do, sir? And, let's face it, we've both wanted to clean Harry's clock for years."

"Speak for yourself." Hammond chuckled.

And here was hoping he would never realize just why Colonel O'Neill had been so damn keen on getting Colonel Maybourne onto that *tel'tac* or what he'd discussed with Tabal just before the hatch had closed. Jack *did* owe Harry, and he always paid his debts.

"Sir?" I'm guessing you'll want one of these?" Carter was holding out one of the two GM-94 grenade launchers she'd retrieved from Bra'tac's Jaffa, stock unfolded and ready to use.

Jack stared at it briefly, then shook his head. "I'd rather stick with the staff weapon. All yours, General."

"Been a while since I handled one of those," Hammond muttered, testing the launcher's weight and balance.

"It's got one grenade chambered and three in the magazine. Pump action reload," explained Carter and flashed an encouraging smile. "Think shotgun, sir."

"Can't promise I'll hit anything."

"Caliber forty-three? You won't be able to miss, General."

The sky had taken on a faint greenish tinge. Jack, whose sense of time seemed to have eroded under Nirrti's ministrations, was unable to tell whether this was what passed for dawn on the planet or whether it was the sheen of the fungus-riddled city.

"Jack!" Daniel, Teal'c, and Bra'tac were headed across the clearing, returning from their foray along the temple walls. Going by Daniel's face it had been less than successful. "No joy," he growled. "Your friend, the reformed Marine Jaffa, said when they were sent back to '335 they got into the temple through a tunnel, but that's long gone. Fungus is gobbling up the foundations. No side entrances, either, so it'll have to be the front door, I suppose. Preferably before it belches and snaps shut."

Front door—the maw of the stone face on the temple, home of the beasties; hell, if Carter was to be believed. Eighteen-inch teeth backlit by goop glow, it looked the part. Thirty feet above, a dark hole opened in the forehead of the face—the Stargate, which they hoped to reach from the inside. Jack cast a quick glance over his shoulder to see if everybody was present and correct. Carter, right behind him; Daniel, squinting at the shadows flitting behind the teeth; General Hammond, launcher raised and ready to give the nearest hog a bad case of heartburn; Teal'c, unruffled as usual; and finally Bra'tac, who seemed to be having the time of his life. Jack couldn't think of anyone he'd rather have watching his team's back.

"Bra'tac?"

"What is it, human?"

"Thanks!"

The reply was a grunt, and it sounded embarrassed—Jack would have to ask Teal'c if Jaffa got embarrassed. Not now, though. "Stay together and stay behind me. You got that, Daniel?"

"Just go, Jack!"

The stone tongue lolling out onto the clearing was already striated with fungus, and Jack carefully tested its stability. It dipped a little under his weight, and he hurriedly persuaded his body that this was no reason to futz out on him again. His body seemed willing to reserve judgment, which was about as good as it got. From inside the mouth came faint grunts and snuffling noises. Staff weapon primed,

he crept up the tongue… ramp… reached that hump just above the
teeth. One step further, and he'd trigger a gag reflex on the thing.

Get a grip, O'Neill!

At that moment the stench hit him, putrid and old and thick enough
to feel solid. "Holy crap!"

"What?" Carter, a barely perceptible edge of fear in her voice.

"Stone guy's got the worst case of halitosis I've ever come across
in my life."

"Yes, there must be another ramp inside," she replied. Evidently
her hearing hadn't recovered quite as much as advertised.

"An ulcer, more like," Jack muttered to himself. "Unless it's a
perforated ramp."

He crouched and sneaked deeper into that hellish bouquet of feces,
stale blood, and decay that somehow went with the giant teeth rearing either side of him. And then he was inside the temple. Carter's
hearing might not be all there, but she'd been right about the ramp.
Not as artistic as the tongue outside but a lot steeper. Its lower end
was patrolled by a Volkswagen Beetle with bristles, one of more than
twenty similar models, and they didn't like the fungus either.

"Crap," he whispered again. It wasn't that he hadn't believed
Carter about the hogs; he just hadn't expected her description of their
size to be accurate. After all, she'd had a fever at the time.

"Uh-oh." Daniel had crept alongside him. "This doesn't look
good. I think."

"Yeah, that's what *they*'re thinking, too."

Below lay an enormous stone-hemmed pit, its floor pulsing green.
At the bottom of the pit milled Carter's hell hogs, snorting and
squealing at the squishiness under their trotters and clearly agitated
by the whole affair. Directly opposite a narrow set of stairs ran up to
a gallery—Jack had had enough of those to last him a lifetime—that
circled the room at about thirty feet height and hopefully led to the
DHD.

He scanned the temple for an alternative route, came up empty
and gritted his teeth. Through the pit it was. God knew how the hell
hogs would react if you threw six people into the equation. *Badly* was
a fair guess.

Beside him, Carter rose and aimed her grenade launcher. Jack's hand shot up, pulled down the barrel. "Easy, Major! Let's not upset the applecart. Right now they're busy figuring out the fungus. Maybe they're preoccupied enough for us to get past them."

And they also can fly, carrying little olive sprigs in their snouts!

The point was, though, they couldn't kill all of the hogs at once. One of those grenades could take out a lightly armored vehicle—close enough where it came to the hogs, though Jack wasn't too sure about the *lightly* part. They had eight grenades, a kill each if they were lucky, which still left the question of what the surviving dozen or so hogs would do.

Carter seemed to have arrived at a similar assessment and gave a terse nod. Fear lurked in her eyes; nothing concrete and directed, but a purely atavistic terror he'd never seen in her before.

"When you and Teal'c and Fraiser met them, Nirrti was running the show, Carter. For all we know, they might be perfectly harmless in real life."

Okay, so they didn't *look* harmless, but Jack didn't feel that needed pointing out.

Another nod. "I'm fine, sir. Whenever you're ready."

Never?

Jack got to his feet and slowly started down the ramp. Herbie downstairs grunted and squealed and backed up a couple steps, its little red eyes ogling each move they made. Two more steps down the ramp for Jack and his team; two more steps back from Herbie. Kinda like tango. If they didn't get their feet mixed up, they might just be okay. The final few meters of the ramp were coated in fungus, and Jack slipped a few times. Each time, Herbie snarled and hissed.

And then they'd reached the bottom of the pit, carefully turned toward the stairs opposite—and all hell broke loose. Screeching, Herbie planted its bulk between them and the access to the ramp; its pals started circling, closer with each revolution, forcing them toward the center of the pit. The room rang with squeals and grunts.

"Great! Pack behavior," observed Daniel, a little shakily.

Trodden into the green slime lay countless cracked bones, hunks of rotting flesh, and scraps of olive drab material. Marine BDUs. Jack winced. "I think they want us to join them in the dining area."

"O'Neill?" Teal'c's face beaded with sweat; and he was wound as tight as a spring. Staff weapon lowered, he followed every motion of the lead animal, Herbie's momma, by the looks of her, easily the size of a station wagon.

"Not yet, Teal'c."

Momma had planted her broad hindquarters in front of the staircase to hiss at them. If they brought her down where she was, they'd never get past the funeral banquet her grieving relatives were likely to throw. Somebody would have to draw her off.

"General, Carter, blow her to Kingdom Come as soon as she's cleared the stairs! And then you and everybody else run like hell!"

"O'Neill—"

"We do this my way, Bra'tac!"

Blanking out everything except Momma, Jack broke left, slipping and sliding in the gunk and tripping over bones. The hogs gave a universal snarl of surprise, then a delegation of three galloped across the pit, separating him from his team. A split-second before they could obstruct his line of fire, he loosed a staff blast that struck Momma squarely in the rump, with about the same effect a peashooter would have on him; she was pissed. Real pissed. An ear-piercing shriek, then she shot from her post and toward him with the brio of a freight train.

"Now!" he shouted, barely able to hear himself over the noise of the hogs.

Two grenades hit home, and Momma was knocked off her feet, skidding sideways. An instant later she literally flew apart, showering him in blood and hog entrails and raising a cacophony of squeals and grunts that drowned out the roar of the explosion. The three animals that tried to drive him off stopped dead in their tracks, whirled around and made a beeline for her carcass, oblivious to the human roadblock. The rest of them also converged on Momma, and Jack hit the gunk, rolling and crawling and trying to stay out from under their feet. For a fleeting instant and between a pair of churning trotters, he spotted Daniel, Teal'c, Hammond racing for the stairs, then they were gone again, and he was scrabbling on hands and knees to get away from the heaving, stinking, bristling bodies and finally flinging himself into the clear.

Everyone else was up on the gallery, staring back down, shouting.

At him? And where the hell was—

Carter stood frozen at the center of the pit, ashen-faced, eyes wide, lips moving. Even from where Jack lay, he could see that she was shaking like a leaf.

"Go, Carter! Go!"

No use. She stared past him, not taking in anything except the feeding frenzy that now buried Momma. Swearing, he shoved himself up, staggered toward her, terrified by the glazed look in her eyes.

"Dammit, Major!" he bellowed. "That's exactly why they shouldn't allow women in frontline units! You just freeze when the going gets tough!" Okay, he was trying to snap her out of it, but maybe he'd overdone it a little.

"No, you son of a bitch! No!" Her face contorted in absolute fury, she fired the launcher.

Missing Jack by a finely judged hair, the grenade slammed into a hog that had come after the colonel hors d'oeuvres. The detonation propelled Jack forward in a mad shuffle to stay on his feet, and his chest felt way too tight to breathe again. He ignored it, grabbed her arm. "Carter?"

Still pale but focused now, she whispered, "They were eating him, sir. They were eating him, and I shot him."

Jack had no idea what she was talking about. It would keep. It would have to. "Go, Sam!" he yelped. "Go!"

At that moment the entire temple shuddered and erupted into a crash that silenced even the hogs.

Go with Carter! Find the DHD!

Jack's gasp of an order drove Daniel along the gallery, though he'd hardly needed a reminder. Either the fungus had mutated into a more ravenous strain—did fungi have strains?—or it found the temple tastier than the fortress and city. The foundations had crumbled, and the stone maw had indeed belched and snapped shut. Their only way out now was the gate.

In the pit below, the animals had forgotten about dinner and raced around in mad circles to avoid chunks of masonry thundering down on them. The gallery floor under Daniel's feet began to shimmer green. He ran faster.

Ahead, Sam had come to a halt directly in front of the giant round window that was the Stargate. Through it he could see a pale morning sky and the black silhouettes of trees. Suddenly Sam darted toward a niche to the left of the gate.

"I've got it!" she shouted.

Which had to be the first bit of unequivocally good news he'd heard in a long time. Daniel reached her a few seconds later, almost sliding past her in the gunk. Crouched before the console, Sam had opened the maintenance hatch.

"What are you doing? We don't have time for this." The moment it was out, he realized he'd sounded like Jack in the kind of situation where Daniel Jackson liked Jack O'Neill least. "Sorry."

"Bra'tac told me the crystals in the DHD on '335 had been swapped," she explained. "We dialed Earth alright, but the gate read something else."

"Which would explain it," Daniel said slowly.

"Uhuh." Sam slammed the hatch shut. "This one seems to be okay. I haven't got the tools for a full diagnostic and, as you say, we don't have time."

He heard the slight tremor in her voice and knew she had noticed it too. Around the DHD, the floor had turned a poisonous green and the device seemed to be melting. "The floor's going, Sam! Dial!"

"Earth or the Alpha site?"

"Earth. We need to get Jack to the infirmary."

Sam's hand flew over the symbols, dialing in Earth. When she slapped the activation crystal at the center of the console, the DHD groaned and tilted. "Oh God, no!"

Her outcry was overlaid by reassuring clunking and grinding as the inner ring of the gate spun to life. Barely in time. The DHD's console was flush with the floor.

"Nice," came a gasp from behind Daniel.

He turned, saw Jack, dragged rather than guided along the gallery by General Hammond and Teal'c. Bra'tac was watching their collective six.

"Reminds me of Ernest's planet," Jack wheezed with a worried glance at the DHD. "How'd you feel about dialing in manually, Teal'c?"

"I don't think we'll have to, sir." Sam's smile broadened. "Look!"

The seventh chevron had locked. The event horizon filled the gate with a glorious surge of blue, seemed to hold its breath for a moment, and exploded—away from them, across the clearing outside.

"That's... different," murmured Daniel, futilely battling the desperation that spread through his gut like ice water.

"Now what?" Going by the expression on General Hammond's face, he was a hair away from kicking the gate. "Major Carter? Any ideas?"

"How about we just try it backwards?" Jack piped up again, though where he took the air from was anybody's guess. "Just because we've never done it before doesn't mean it won't—"

"I once knew a man who thought the same as O'Neill," Bra'tac reminisced dryly. "His death was most unpleasant."

"Thanks for clearing that one up, Bra'tac. What do we do? Carter?"

"Sir, I—" She was cut off by another burst of grinding noise. "What...?"

The Stargate itself was swiveling around its vertical axis, ponderous and much too slow for Daniel's liking, but swivel it did. He risked a small grin. "Now, that's *really* different."

His grin died when the whole machinery gave a scream of metal on stone and jammed to a stop, some sixty degrees shy of a full one-eighty.

"It's shifted!" Sam cried. "The subsidence must have—"

"So what?" Jack had unhitched himself from Hammond and Teal'c and came stumbling toward the gate. "It's not straight, but it'll still work, and we can get to the right side now. Right?"

This time Bra'tac had no cautionary tales to offer.

"Right. Teal'c, you still have your IDC transmitter. Hit it!"

Teal'c stepped forward, already keying the ID code into the device on his wrist. Sam watched, breath bated, but there was no indication that the gate wasn't functioning normally.

Finally she released a sigh. "Let's go home."

CHAPTER TWENTY-FOUR

Termination Codon: Nucleotide sequence that signals the end of a growing chain.

"Notify me the second M3D 335 makes contact!"

The balding nerd at the dialing computer uttered a grunt that might or might not have been a response. What it did manage to convey quite clearly, though, was resentment. It carried, and Simmons thought he sensed a barrage of sniggers wanting to erupt all around him.

"Am I inconveniencing you, *Sergeant*?" he hissed.

"Oh no!" Harriman looked up at him, blue eyes behind those nerdy glasses brimming with innocence. "I just thought you didn't need it confirmed for the fifth time. Sir."

"I hope you like cold places, Sergeant," whispered Simmons.

Through the semi-darkness of the control room he felt the crew's stares boring into his back, their amusement souring, the air growing thick with hatred. He didn't care. If they hated him, it meant they feared him. Simmons was fully determined to make them understand why, above and beyond any cause for fear they thought they had now.

He'd have his army of healthy and fully functional Jaffa, and then, finally, the White House would appreciate what a detached civilian perspective could achieve. They'd be kissing his feet. They'd put the NID in charge of the SGC and the base on '335, and—

The klaxons blared the rest of the daydream from his mind.

"Incoming wormhole, sir," Harriman announced mechanically.

At last!

A world of tension drained from Simmons's body. Van Leyden should have reported back hours ago, and he would hear a word or two about the value of promptness, but the main thing was the news Simmons fully expected to receive now. Alpha platoon had returned, hopefully with the Jaffa, Teal'c, and the rest of SG-1 was a thing of the past. He was looking forward to the funeral ceremony. "Scramble the transmission and put it through to the monitoring station on Level 16."

"Yessir."

This time Harriman's reply came loud and clear, and Simmons fancied he heard a hint of disappointment in the sergeant's voice. Too bad, but it probably would wear off by the time the good sergeant arrived at his next posting in McMurdo. Simmons grinned and headed for the stairs.

"Uh," said Harriman. "Sir?"

"What?"

"Receiving SG-1's iris code. You still want me to put it through to Level 16?"

For an endless moment his next breath refused to come, frozen inside his lungs. Then Simmons took control of himself, forced his body to turn around, the man's insolence barely even registering. "Do not open the iris," he ordered calmly.

"But, sir, they—"

"You heard me, Sergeant. SG-1 has been compromised. Anybody could be using their code." Simmons didn't like what he saw in the sergeant's eyes. More than insolence—pure contempt. Contempt and defiance. "You're relieved, Mister."

It was the last thing the man had expected. You could tell by the way he heaved his pudgy frame from the seat in front of the computer and, red-faced and flustered, tripped over a chair leg as he moved aside. Groping for support, his right hand slammed down, hit the palm scanner. Simmons heard his own yell of annoyance, but it was too late. Suddenly not clumsy anymore, Harriman reached across the chair, the fingers of his left tapping out a sequence on the keyboard.

"Oops," he said.

Through the control room window, Simmons saw the iris open on the shimmering blue surface of the event horizon. He grabbed the sergeant's arm, yanked him back into his chair. "Close it! That's an order!"

"Sorry, sir." The sergeant's look of imbecilic innocence reasserted itself. "I'm not authorized to do that. I've been relieved of duty."

Below, black-clad SFs took their positions in the gate room, USAS leveled at the ramp. Simmons grabbed the microphone. "You're green-lighted to fire——"

The traveler, stocky and in filthy BDUs, dropped from the event horizon at an odd angle, as if he'd been physically flung into the wormhole. He landed heavily, sending a rattle through the ramp, but the metal clanking was drowned out by his shout. "Stand down!"

It might not have worked for anyone else, but the airmen had obeyed that voice for years. To a man they lowered their weapons. For a second, Simmons was tempted to countermand the order, then he noticed the cheers behind him in the control room and below, among the SFs. Murder was all very well as long as nobody could prove it, but now there would be evidence as well as witnesses. Knowing that he was looking at the explanation for that bogus gate calibration test, he fumbled for an expression that might or might not pass for relief—in actual fact it felt like indigestion. He should have trusted his instincts. Down on the ramp, George Hammond picked himself up, clearing the way for whatever or whoever was to come. Simmons had a pretty good idea and damn near choked on it.

"Medical team to the gate room!" Hammond hollered.

"Ah, excuse me, sir!" That epic idiot Harriman pushed past Simmons and dived for the intercom—evidently he considered himself authorized again—to parrot his fearless leader. "Medical team to the gate room!"

With considerably more grace than Hammond, a cloaked, skull-capped figure appeared from the event horizon; a Jaffa, getting on in years. Close behind followed Major Carter in an outfit—or lack thereof—that left every male in the embarkation room standing slack-jawed in a puddle of drool. In her wake arrived Teal'c—walking confirmation that Simmons's Jaffa had failed on an unimaginable scale.

"I'd better go and see what's going on," Simmons announced.

It sounded lame even to his own ears, and he didn't wait for the sniggers to resurge. He left the control room, already trying to think past the acrid taste of failure in his mouth. Damage control was the main thing now. The exact magnitude of the disaster was difficult to assess as yet, because he had no idea what was happening or had happened on M3D 335 and how much SG-1 and Hammond really knew. Ultimately the goal would be for Colonel Frank Simmons to climb out of this manure pit smelling of roses. In order to do this he needed a bargaining chip weighty enough to offset anything Hammond might have to contribute to the matter.

George Hammond was reasonably certain that the metal grid of the ramp had left a tattoo on his six. Not that this was any kind of priority. Bracing his not inconsiderable bulk against the impact, he just about managed to catch Jack O'Neill who came flopping from the event horizon like a rag doll.

"I can walk," the Colonel muttered as his legs folded under him. "Sir."

"Sure you can." Dr. Jackson, looking only marginally more fit than his CO, had popped from the wormhole and threaded one of Jack's arms across his shoulders. "Let's get you to the infirmary so you can show Dr Warner."

Thankfully that didn't become necessary. Over by the blast door a crew of SFs flocked apart, allowing a couple of medics, a stretcher, and Dr Warner to pass. Though Warner's experience wasn't quite as comprehensive as Janet Fraiser's, he immediately zeroed in on the usual suspect. Inside a minute, Jack O'Neill was on his way to the infirmary, clucked over by the medics.

The rest of his team remained stranded on the ramp in front of an idle Stargate, looking lost and, above all, exhausted. On the floor, the SFs were still milling around, as was a bunch of bystanders who had no real business of being in the gate room. The SGC was a small command and close-knit; word traveled fast, and the return of a team missing in action, together with the base commander who nobody'd known was missing, presumably rated a degree of curiosity and excitement. Sergeant Harriman was peering down from the control room window, a little green around the gills and gesticulating frantically. Hammond tried not to think *Now what?* and failed. He nodded a brief acknowledgement in Harriman's direction, letting him know he'd get to him. Eventually.

"Sir?" Major Carter, he was relieved to see, had requisitioned a BDU jacket from one of the SFs. She still was clutching her grenade launcher as though she expected those boars to come charging through the closed iris. "Permission to go take a shower, sir?"

"Permission granted, Major. In fact, I—"

"I know, General." She smiled. "You insist."

"How did you guess?" Hammond grinned back at her, slowly surrendering to a sense of relief and the realization that he had, in fact, brought his people home. "Have that shower and then report to the infirmary for a full medical, Major. Same goes for Teal'c and Dr. Jackson. We'll debrief once things have quieted down a bit."

"Yessir."

Hammond watched her round up her team mates and herd them through the blast door. One by one, the audience trickled back to their posts, and the gate room returned to its normal state of quiet readiness. With one exception. An unpleasant one at that. So that was what Harriman had wanted him to know.

The man had been leaning against the wall beneath the control room window, observing, biding his time. Now he pushed himself off, started ambling over, a faint echo of his entrance after the exercise. As he came within smelling distance of Hammond an expression of distaste stole across his face. Apparently Colonel Simmons had issues with eau de hog. Well, that was just too bad! George Hammond half wished he'd had the time or the foresight to roll around in a pile of boar dung. Not that it would have kept Simmons away.

"A word, General," the NID Colonel said, picking an imaginary speck of lint from a sleeve by Armani and trying to look genial. It lacked conviction. Close up, you could see droplets of sweat beading on the man's upper lip, a small muscle working nervously in his cheek. Simmons was scared, which made a refreshing change.

"Get out of my way," Hammond snapped. "Better yet, get the hell off my base and don't come back."

"When we've talked." He grabbed Hammond's arm.

A mistake. Behind him, Hammond heard the characteristic noise of a staff weapon being primed, and then Bra'tac announced, "I recommend you cede to the wishes of Hammond of Texas."

Simmons let go, frowned. "Who is he?"

"A witness." Hammond never took his eyes off Simmons's face, searching for even the smallest hint of insecurity, unease, perhaps even guilt, though that would imply the bastard was human. "Together with SG-1, Dr. Fraiser, and thirteen Marines we're expecting back in, oh, about four hours. You're finished, Colonel." He hadn't mentioned the ten Marine 'Jaffa', deciding it was smarter to keep that trump card up his sleeve. And he would need it, by the look of things. The reaction wasn't what he'd hoped for.

"Witnesses to what? The misconduct of a high-ranking USMC officer? You know, for a moment there I thought you might have something tangible. But alas, hearsay won't fly." Simmons actually contrived to sound concerned. "All I want is to talk to you."

Try as he might, Hammond couldn't suppress a snort. "Right. Keep it for someone who might believe you."

"You'd better believe me, General. I'm trying to stop you from making a mistake. Because, unlike you, I wasn't seen engaging in any potentially criminal activity. I've got three words for you—aiding and abetting."

"What?"

The question was purely rhetorical, nothing but a reflex that might or might not buy him some time. George Hammond knew only too well what—or rather, whom—Simmons was talking about.

I could get court-martialed just for being seen with you.

The words, not an exaggeration but hard, cold fact, had come back to bite him on the ass. Maybe he shouldn't have said it out loud. He *had* been seen with Harry Maybourne. Not just by the NID agents, but by any number of independent witnesses; the waitress in the truck stop, airline personnel, the cabbie in Seattle, a goddamn state trooper, of all things. He never doubted that the NID would dig up all of them and more, up to and including the guy at the hot dog stand.

"Do you wish me to kill this man, Hammond of Texas?" Coal-chip eyes hard and unforgiving, Bra'tac had kept his bead on Simmons. If Hammond asked, he would fire, without hesitation, without even knowing his victim—all because he trusted one fallible general. It'd be easy. Unprovable, in fact: an alien ally misinterpreting an exchange between humans and committing a grievous error; Harriman and everybody else in the control room would unaccountably be struck deaf, dumb, and blind—and Simmons would cease to be a problem.

"Unfortunately, at this moment what I wish and what is right are two very different things," Hammond said softly. "Thank you, Master Bra'tac. I'm afraid I'll have to deal with this on my own."

"I see." With a long, measuring gaze at Hammond, the old warrior closed and raised his staff weapon. Suddenly he grinned. "You are correct, Hammond of Texas. It shall be more satisfying to wait for an opportunity to disembowel him."

That last sentence had been directed at Simmons, who had the good sense of backing up a step or two. "He's kidding, right?"

"No," said Hammond and watched Bra'tac leave the gate room, likely as not in search of Teal'c to discuss Hammond of Texas's imprudent scruples. "I'm listening, Simmons."

"Not here."

"Fine. My office then."

Imprudent scruples, indeed. Hammond thought he could hear Jack O'Neill's voice.

One day I may ask you to buy back my soul.

One day Jack might just have to return the favor.

CHAPTER TWENTY-FIVE

"What are you doing here, Colonel? I thought I'd sent you home."

Dr Warner had the look of a person whose carefully husbanded patience was about to snap into psychosis. You couldn't really blame him. Having both Colonel O'Neill *and* Dr. Fraiser as patients was enough to make Mother Teresa run amok. Rumor had it that Warner's esteemed colleague had attempted to assist in the debridement of her own wound. Rumor also had it that Warner had put said colleague under in a last-ditch effort to save his sanity.

"Morning, Doctor." Grinning, Jack pointed at the door Warner had just slammed behind him. "How's the patient?"

"Active." Loaded with a world of connotations, Warner's reply hung there for a moment. Then he said, "On the off-chance that you're here to visit Dr. Fraiser rather than add to my problems, you might want to try and impress on her the importance of rest."

"You want me to do *what*?"

"I want you to—"

"I heard you. It's just that…" Jack cleared his throat. "It's like inviting Ted Kennedy to lecture on the benefits of temperance."

"Consider it a challenge, Colonel." Warner was already heading down the corridor, mumbling something about needing a drink.

"As I was saying. Temperance," muttered Colonel O'Neill and opened the door to the infirmary.

"What are you doing here, Colonel?"

"Sweet." Jack slapped on his best insulted face. "You'd really think it'd kill people to try something along the lines of *Hey, sir, nice to see you up and about.*"

It didn't work. Janet still glared at him, past a nurse who'd just changed the dressing on Dr. Fraiser's wound and now cleared the battlefield at best possible speed. "Warner had no business releasing you without consulting me first." Even the doc's righteous indignation couldn't bring any color to her face. Her complexion rivaled the bed sheets, which didn't stop her from pushing herself up. Going by the wince, it was less than comfortable.

"Janet, I'm—"

"Peachy. Yeah."

Déjà vu all over again. Jack didn't bother to swallow the sigh. "I know. I'm not peachy until you say I am."

She wasn't playing. "Warner didn't even show me your chart. He didn't tell me anything."

"That's because you're the patient, Doctor!"

"I'm still—"

"Look, Doc. They did a stress ECG on me yesterday afternoon. Twenty minutes on the treadmill, maximum pulse of a hundred and five, nice and steady. BP no higher than one-thirty over eighty, which, Warner informs me, is nothing short of spectacular for a guy my age. After that, he admitted he'd run out of stuff to examine me for."

As a matter of fact, in the two days since his return Jack O'Neill had undergone every single test modern medicine could throw at a patient while still leaving him alive, and the distinction between Nirrti's lab and the infirmary had become disconcertingly blurry.

Fraiser leaned back against the cushions, satisfied or exhausted, Jack couldn't tell. At last she said, "Do they know what caused it?"

"Nope." Shaking his head, he wandered closer to her bed. "She—Nirrti—was trying to get me to twirl chess pieces in thin air. Something was blocking the process, though Warner and his merry men can't say what or how, apart from the fact that it knocked me sideways when Nirrti kept insisting."

"You mean when *I* kept insisting?" Fraiser's fingers clenched in the bedspread, twisting it savagely.

"I don't remember that. What I do remember is the reason for this." He reached out, lightly brushing her shoulder. "Carter also told me about the epinephrine. Stupid, Doc. Real stupid, but thanks."

The bedspread was enjoying something of a respite. "Sam talks too much."

"Probably. But she did it all without techno-babble this time. Even I could understand it." Finally Jack saw what he'd been hoping to see. Fraiser smiled. A little. Then it vanished again, like an old memory, and he wondered if it'd ever been there or if he'd simply wanted to see it too much.

She looked distant, miles—light-years—away. "We watched it from the *tel'tac*," she whispered. "The fortress and the city just melted, sagged in on themselves. They're dead, aren't they, sir? Those I didn't kill before."

"As far as I can tell they weren't really alive to begin with," Jack offered. He knew exactly whom—or what—she was talking about, recalled the staring eyes and blank faces and refused to even consider this as a form of human life. If he did, all notions of individuality, of personality, would fly right out the window. Self-protection perhaps, but there it was, and he wouldn't hesitate to admit that he was glad they were dead. One less thing to worry about, and Fraiser was a priority. "Are we okay, Doc?" he said softly.

"I should be asking you that." The bedspread was in trouble again.

"Works both ways, Janet. So, are we okay?"

"We're okay, sir." The smile—definitely a smile—returned at last.

"Good. 'Cos I've got something for you." Jack produced a parcel he'd been hiding behind his back up until now and put it in her lap. "Open it."

She graced him with one of those patented Fraiser looks. "If that's the ladies' model of Sergeant Siler's pajamas…"

Jack raised an eyebrow. "Would I?"

"At the drop of a hat. Sir!"

"Daniel, that's *not* resting. *Resting* is lying on the couch at home, with the shades drawn and maybe a little quiet music playing."

It was a very polite way of saying *Leave me the hell alone, I'm working!* Sam didn't have the heart to put it bluntly. Besides, Daniel *was* concussed and *should* be at home. Unfortunately, he'd got fed up, knew that—with Janet in the infirmary—there would be no one to put him in restraints, and decided that his time would be best spent distracting Sam. She hoped to God he wasn't going to develop a taste for it. Normally this type of visitation was executed in fine style by Colonel O'Neill, usually when he was supposed to write reports. One hyperactive kid bouncing around her lab was plenty as far as she was concerned.

"Does this thing work?" Daniel was poking at an old TV set that vegetated at the back of Sam's lab.

"Turn it on, wiggle the antenna cable, and slap the top," recommended a voice from the door. "*The Simpsons* should be on in five minutes."

Speak of the devil!

"What are you doing here?"

Daniel had beaten her to it, so Sam confined herself to adding "Sir?"

By ways of an answer, the Colonel put on an A-grade sulk and headed for the TV set, leaving a trail of constant mutter. "Hi, Jack! We've missed you. How're you doing? You're looking great. Thanks. I'm peachy. Good to see you, kids. And by the way, what are *you* doing here?"

This last question was directed at Daniel, who grinned. "I got fed up at home."

"Ah," said the Colonel, implying it was perfectly reasonable that anyone suffering from boredom should converge on Major Carter's lab. Then he proceeded to turn on, wiggle, and slap the TV.

Instead of *The Simpsons*, the image established on a reporter in too much makeup and something that was a dead ringer for Donald Trump's toupee. Clutching a microphone and his own importance, he was posted outside the Pentagon. "And we have just received official confirmation of the number of casualties. A total of ninety-seven Marines were killed yesterday, in what can only be described as the most devastating tragedy in the history of the US Marine Corps. No names have been released yet, as the commanding officers are going to personally inform victims' families." The image cut to an unspecified stretch of ocean, a swarm of SAR choppers, and three Navy frigates circling some floating debris. "Early reports indicate that the *USS Kabul*, a Tarawa class destroyer conducting exercises, sank after a massive explosion in the engine room. However, insiders speculate that there may be more to it. This morning a high-ranking Marine, Lieutenant General Philip Crowley, was detained pending a full investigation of the horrific accident. We will keep you informed as the situation develops. This is Dwayne Keller for—"

"I don't believe it," whispered Sam, half convinced she'd misheard. Her next thought was that, all things considered, this version of events would be a blessing for the relatives of Private Joe Gonzales.

"What exactly is it you don't believe, Major?" the Colonel asked dryly. "The guy's hairpiece or the cover-up?"

"*Cover-up?*" Daniel gasped it out, his eyes as wide as the bruises would allow.

"It's obvious, isn't it? They—"

The Colonel's explanation of the implausibly sordid was interrupted by two new arrivals, and Sam was beginning to consider getting an espresso machine and maybe setting up a couple of tables and chairs. She could also serve ice cream with little paper umbrellas in it.

For the time being she resorted to, "Morning, General. Teal'c."

"O'Neill, I am pleased to see you," Teal'c intoned solemnly. "And you—"

"See? Here's a man who knows how to make a guy feel welcome." Jack O'Neill grinned. "I missed you, too, T. How was Chulak?"

"Cold."

General Hammond was doing his best to ignore the exchange, peered at the TV set and finally at the Colonel and Daniel. "What are you doing here?" he enquired.

"I think he means you," Colonel O'Neill informed Dr. Jackson in a stage whisper that probably carried halfway to the commissary.

"I mean the pair of you," clarified Hammond.

"I'm legit. I got my walking papers, sir. Clean bill of health. Daniel, on the other hand, absconded from house arrest."

The General didn't rise to the bait.

"Something on your mind, sir?" Sam asked.

"As a matter of fact, yes." He heavily sat in her computer chair, looked at them one by one. "Seeing as you're all here, I might as well tell you. You've seen the news, I take it."

"Yeah," Colonel O'Neill acknowledged grimly. "Whose idea was that?"

"Simmons's. And mine."

"Excuse me?" If someone had proved to him the Earth was flat, Daniel couldn't have looked more stunned. "General, you—"

"Hold your horses, Daniel." The Colonel's voice held a mix of disbelief and concern, but mostly concern. "I'm thinking there's an explanation. Butt-ugly but good."

"I'm not proud of it, people." Going by the way it came out, the words tasted like cod liver oil. Hammond grimaced. "The crux of the matter is that I was seen with our friend Harry. Simmons lost no time pointing out just what exactly would happen—not just to me, but to the SGC in general and Sergeants Siler and Harriman in particular—if anyone got wind of my shielding a convicted traitor. The rest was pretty straightforward, as you can imagine."

"Let me guess." Colonel O'Neill discovered that month-old donut mummy under a workbench, hooked it with the tip of his boot, and kicked it across the lab and into the corridor. It hit the far wall and disintegrated. Going by the gusto he'd put behind it, he must have been picturing Simmons's ass. "Amnesia all round. Simmons forgets Harry exists, and we forget Simmons climbed into bed with Nirrti. Crowley—and probably Norris?—get to take the fall, and everybody lives happily ever after. Am I getting warm?"

He'd said *we forget* not *you forget*, and Hammond hadn't missed it. He sent the Colonel a grateful smile. "There's going to be at least one sacrificial lamb from Simmons's side. The official version is that one of the agents the NID had on '335 has gone rogue."

"Van Leyden," Daniel said darkly. "My heart bleeds."

"Don't fret. I'm sure Van Leyden's going to have a nasty accident, only to reappear a few months down the line in a different incarnation." Giving up on his search for further footballs, Colonel O'Neill perched on a table. "I'm assuming the base on '335 will be closed down?"

Hammond nodded. "Orders went out yesterday. They'll start evacuating today at fourteen hundred Zulu. And St. Christina's is being scoured by scientists from Area 51." After a little pause he added, "The deal does have its advantages. Simmons has conceded that all bets are off if he doesn't stay clear of the SGC in future."

"He'll be missed."

"I'll make sure to write." Sam felt a smile quirking at the corners of her mouth. "Does he know that some of his so-called Jaffa are still alive, General?"

"No. He demanded that any surviving Marine Jaffa be handed over to the NID, but rather than discussing the ethics of that, I told him Bra'tac's men killed the guards at the gate and everybody else died on Yamalok."

To Sam's ears it sounded a little surprising. "And he believed you, sir?"

"He met Bra'tac. Briefly, but the encounter left an indelible impression."

"Master Bra'tac has always displayed an aptitude for leaving those." Apparently Teal'c had reminded himself that keeping watch wasn't necessary here in the bowels of Cheyenne Mountain. He abandoned his post by the door where he'd been hovering until now.

"And I take it he's doing the same for his new recruits?" The Colonel scooted a little further along the table so Teal'c could perch next to him.

The six Marine Jaffa who had escaped from Yamalok, together with the foursome that had been captured on '335, had been taken to Chulak, to learn the skills they needed to coexist with their symbiotes. None of them would be allowed to return to Earth. A harsh decision, and one that had caused vehement protests, but it couldn't be helped. Nobody was willing to take the risk of importing ten larval Goa'uld to Earth. The only other option would have been permanent confinement to base at the SGC, and that was a prospect people relished even less.

Teal'c had met the men and helped them settle into their new life on Chulak. "There were some initial disputes over authority, albeit short-lived. According to Bra'tac, training is progressing well."

"They're going to make it?"

"Indeed, Daniel Jackson."

For some reason, the reply brought conversation to a standstill, and an odd silence settled over the lab.

They—the Colonel, Teal'c, Daniel, Janet, Sam herself—had made it, too, and it truly was over, even if each of them had picked up a couple new demons along the way. Simmons would live to scheme another day, but at least Daniel and the Colonel had made their peace. That was worth something. Sam would have to make her peace with Private Joe Gonzales who now lay buried under a molten temple on

a planet called Yamalok. Daniel had said it was Hindi for *Hell*. The
Goa'uld sure had an uncanny knack for naming things.

Without preamble, General Hammond rose, a little tiredly, the
strain of these past weeks showing in the way he moved. "Well, I
guess that's all people. As you were."

"Sir?" Colonel O'Neill slid off the table and not quite stepped into
the General's way. "When can we expect to be back on duty?"

The question made a warm little puddle of relief pool in the pit
of Sam's stomach. They'd never discussed his resignation after
their return — even Daniel had tiptoed around the subject — as if,
by unspoken agreement, they'd decided to leave well enough alone.
Evidently it'd been the wise thing to do.

A small, sly smile crept across Hammond's face. "Any time you
want to use the shredder in my office, son, feel free."

"Understood, sir. Thanks."

"You're welcome. And to answer your question, SG-1 remains
on stand-down until Dr. Jackson's face returns to a state that
doesn't scare the natives. Bed rest would help, I suppose." General
Hammond leveled a sharp stare at Daniel and started heading for the
door. "Meanwhile you can look forward to a nice, quiet diplomatic
mission. The planet's called Kelowna. They want to negotiate a trade
agreement."

Barely suppressing a wince, the Colonel listed in Teal'c's direction. "I hope he means Kelowna, British Columbia," he muttered.
"Great wine, world-class golf course."

Hammond ground to a halt, turned on his heels. "*He* means
Kelowna, P3X-4C3. As far as I'm aware, they haven't been introduced to golf. By the way, Colonel, you wouldn't happen to have any
thoughts on what became of Harry Maybourne? He didn't gate back
to the SGC with rest of the people from the *tel'tac*."

"Uh, funny you should mention it, sir." Ears red, Colonel O'Neill
had straightened up, just about coming to attention. "I had an email
from him this morning. He sends his regards. Seems like there were
concerns that he might have to be arrested as soon as he popped from
the gate here. Somebody instructed Tabal to take Maybourne back
Earthside in the *tel'tac* and deliver him to a destination of his choosing."

"In that case, Colonel, you may wish to remind somebody of the value of diplomacy. You may also wish"—Hammond's lips twitched—"to convey my appreciation for somebody's initiative. And now get out of here and get some rest, SG-1. All of you. That's an order!"

SNEAK PREVIEW

STARGATE ATLANTIS: HALCYON

by James Swallow

Teyla entered first, holding her weapon close to her chest, the fire select set to three-round bursts. The inside of the hall was open, studded with thick wooden pillars to hold up the roof. There were dead oil lanterns dangling from beams, but faint illumination came from a long, low counter set along one of the walls. "What is that?"

McKay pointed at a series of dull yellow-green bowls made of glass fitted to the walls. Liquid was visible inside, glowing faintly. "It looks like bioluminescence. Probably extracted from plants or insects. Cheap lighting, if a little gloomy-looking."

They spread out through the room, their eyes adjusting to the dimness, and abruptly Teyla realised the function of the building. "This is a tavern." On a round table before her there were a couple of flagons and a discarded clay pipe. The faint whiff of stale beer was still detectable in the air.

Sheppard swept his P90 around the hall. "No bodies anywhere."

Ronon fingered a fan of oval playing cards on a long bench. There were other hands here and there, and a pile of stamped metal rings in a clay bowl before them. "Someone left their winnings behind."

Hill crouched by a larger table. "Look here, sir. These chairs are knocked over, like maybe the person sitting there got up quickly."

"Whatever happened, they had little or no warning," ventured

Teyla. "There are no signs they had time to prepare an adequate defence."

The soldier frowned. "But there's no indications of any weapons fire, ma'am, no burns or bullet holes. Did the blokes who lived here just put down their pints and give up without a fight?"

"Okay," said Rodney, folding down his hood. "I'm going to put this out there, just say what we're all thinking. *Culled.* The people here were culled by the Wraith."

Sheppard glanced at the ceiling. "They must have swept in with Darts and just beamed them straight up," he said, turning to Hill.

Teyla suppressed a shudder, thinking back to the awful screeches of Wraith Dart-ships buzzing through the air of her own village, trawling for human lives.

"No doors are locked," noted Dex. "Must have been panic in the streets."

"Blimey," whispered the private.

"Question is, how long ago?" Sheppard studied the floor. "There's a little snow in here. It couldn't have been more than a few days."

Ronon sniffed at a discarded tankard. "Maybe less."

"And so we come to the big questions," said McKay, crossing the room. "Are they still here? And why don't we discuss this in greater depth back on Atlantis?"

"This is not the only settlement on the planet, Doctor," said Teyla. "There are several others within a few day's riding."

"The Wraith would have taken this one first," noted Ronon. "It's closest to the gate. Then moved out in a spiral, looking for any more."

Sheppard frowned. "All right. I'm just about ready to call this one. As much as I hate to admit that Rodney might be right about something, we're gonna head back to Atlantis and come back here after sun-up in a Jumper. We can scope out the other villages and look for survivors."

"There won't be any," said Ronon, with grim finality. "I've seen this before, on dozens of worlds. They don't leave people behind. The Wraith don't waste anything."

McKay was leaning close to a support pillar, shining a penlight at a bony disc halfway up the length. "This doesn't look right..."

"What is it?"

"The design looks different from the other manufactured items here—" Without warning, the disc let out a whirring sound and unfolded like a skeletal flower.

Teyla saw a shock of recognition on Ronon's face; in the next second Dex had his particle magnum in his hand. "Get away!" he snapped.

McKay barely had time to duck before Ronon's pistol barked and a flare of bright energy blew the pillar and the disc into burning fragments.

"You could've killed me!" wailed the scientist.

Dex turned on Sheppard. "That was a Wraith sensor pod. They leave them in places they've harvested in case they miss anyone the first time around."

Hill nodded, getting it. "So any poor sods who came home thinking they'd gone would set it off, and back they come."

"Okay, that's it," said Sheppard. "We're not waiting around here to see if the Wraith want us for a dessert course." He toggled his radio. "Mason,"

"*Sir,*" came the reply. "*Heard gunfire, do we have enemy contact, over?*"

"Could be. Get back to the gate on the double, I'm scrubbing this mission."

"*Roger that,*"

Sheppard looked up. "Let's move."

Teyla heard his order, but it seemed as if the words were coming from a very great distance. She felt dislocated, suddenly unconnected to the cold and ill-lit tavern. She could feel something, out in the ice and the snow, out there in the howling winds. A predatory sensation in the back of her mind, the pale shadow of something cunning and hungry. It wasn't the same glimmer of threat she had felt at the Stargate, there and gone, the very barest touch on her senses. This was different, strong and horribly familiar.

"Teyla!"

She found herself again and turned on Sheppard. "Wraith. They're already here."

The clatter of assault rifles met them as they raced from the tavern. The wind carried the sound from the direction of the Stargate, gunshots joined by the shrieking cracks of Wraith stunner blasts.

"Mason, report!" demanded Sheppard.

"*Heavy contact,*" grated the Staff Sergeant, "*they must have flanked us, come back around past the gate. We got no cover up here!*"

"Fall back to the village and regroup," ordered the colonel. He turned to the others. "Hill, you're with me. Ronon, Teyla, McKay, find something defensible, something with thick walls, and hole up there. If they got Darts and they catch us in the open…" John let the sentence trail off. He didn't need to spell it out.

"If we could just make a run for the Stargate—" began Rodney.

"And let them know Atlantis *isn't* a pile of radioactive rubble?" Sheppard shook his head. "Nope. We gotta deal with this here. Go!"

He sprinted off with Hill at his flank, moving quickly from cover to cover in the lee of deep shadows. McKay's escape plan, while crude and direct — and not without a certain appeal, John had to admit — was out of the question. The Wraith siege of Atlantis, months ago now although it still seemed fresh in his mind, had ended with a magic trick that David Copperfield would have been proud of. The city's defensive shield had been turned into a cloaking device to fool the aliens into thinking Atlantis had been obliterated, but now each time an off-world team ran afoul of a Wraith raiding party they were effectively on their own. They had to operate as if they were isolated survivors who had escaped the city's destruction, lest they tip off the aliens that Atlantis was still intact.

And right now, that meant they had no easy way out of this.

Gingerly, the adjutant ventured a question. "Highness, what would you have us do in this engagement? The troops await your orders."

His commander remained silent for a long moment, observing the unfolding fray in the village through a bulky brass monocular. When the answer came, it was another question. "Who are these people? Their livery and wargear is of no manufacture I can place, not from the homeworld or a vassal planet."

"I suspect they are Genii," offered the adjutant.

The commander made a negative noise. "I know those skulks, and these people do not wage war like them." The exchange of fire became furious, reaching them in the cover of the tree line. "Genii warriors would run. These ones stand and fight. They have zeal."

"Highness," said the man, "if you would forgive my temerity to say so, but their zeal will give them little support against such numbers of Wraith. The second group of the predators we observed even now approach from the far side of the village. These people, whomever they give allegiance to, will perish if we do not intervene. Is that your wish?"

The commander snapped the monocular shut and met his gaze. "That would be poor form, don't you think? It would be impolite of us, to say the least."

"Your will, Highness." The adjutant nodded and turned to his troops. "Charge your guns, gentlemen, and ready the horns."

Sheppard and Hill met Mason and the other men at the edge of the township. White fire from Wraith guns sizzled down after them, flaring off the snow. Private Bishop had Corporal Clarke on his shoulder, helping his comrade scramble away. Mason was low behind them, spraying bullets from his L85 rifle. Sheppard and Hill fell against cover either side of the alleyway and set up corridors of gunfire, covering the retreating men. Bishop and Clarke scrambled past them, and the colonel saw the corporal's face slack and numb along the left-hand side, like a stroke victim.

"He got clipped by a stunner," said Bishop, by way of explanation.

"Bathtahds," lisped Clarke, "worz thun been drung."

"Fall back," snapped Sheppard. "We got you covered."

Mason came after them, ducking low. "Reloading!" he shouted, ejecting the clip on the bullpup assault rifle.

Sheppard and Hill kept up the pressure, taking down Wraith warriors with careful aimed shots to the torso. Mason joined in as the colonel's own weapon ran dry. He dropped behind a wooden barrel and levered off the empty magazine.

"*Sheppard!*" Ronon's voice crackled from his radio. "*Teyla found a place we can use as a strongpoint, west of you, a conical building.*"

"Copy that, we're on our way." Sheppard called out to Mason. "You get that, Staff Sergeant?"

"Clear as a bell, sir,"

"Then let's go!"

Moving and firing, the five of them made their way back into the village in an overwatch formation, two men covering the others as they dropped away from the Wraith advance. They turned the corner and sprinted the last few meters to the building Dex had described, half-dragging the injured corporal with them.

Teyla was at the heavy wooden door, her P90 primed and ready. "Did you bring any guests?" she asked dryly.

Sheppard nodded. "Afraid so. And they all want dinner." He cast a look around inside. The building was circular, with only one door but a number of slatted hatches in the walls. The air smelt of mould. "What is this place?"

"A granary," said Teyla. "We are lucky it is summer. In winter this would have been full."

"Summer?" echoed McKay. "That's summer out there?"

Ronon crouched and gave Clarke a look over. "Don't worry, the pain will pass. Can you hold a weapon?"

"Yeh," managed the soldier, his head lolling. "Jus' point me atta door."

Mason directed the other men to firing positions at the slats and Dex approached the colonel. "So, how we going play this, Sheppard? You let them bottle us up, and—"

"I'm working on it," he replied, cutting Ronon off. "We miss our call-in and Atlantis will send out Lorne and a rescue team."

"That's not much of a plan."

"Hey, I'm making this up as I go."

Rodney snorted. "No change from normal there, then."

"I see one," said Bishop. "End of the street, he's scoping us."

"They won't try to wait us out," said Dex, "that's not how they do it. They'll rush us." He sneered. "Wraith like the direct approach."

"Couldn't be more than a dozen of them clowns out there," noted Hill, "even counting those we put down."

Sheppard looked around. "Ammo check. Anyone low?" He got a chorus of negatives from everyone except Teyla. The Athosian woman was stock still, sighting down the length of her gun. "Teyla, you with us?"

She shuddered, and he saw the distant, fearful look in her eyes that he knew meant trouble. "John. There are more Wraith out there. A lot more. They know—"

Teyla's words were drowned out in a howling chorus of blaster bolts as the aliens opened up on the stone building from all sides.

"Return fire!" barked Sheppard. "Targets of opportunity!"

**Continued in *Stargate Atlantis: Halcyon*
Available July 2006**

STARGATE ATLANTIS: THE CHOSEN

A little knowledge is a dangerous thing

STARGATE
ATLANTIS

THE CHOSEN

Sonny Whitelaw & Elizabeth Christensen

Based on the hit television series created by
Brad Wright and Robert C. Cooper

**by Sonny Whitelaw &
Elizabeth Christensen**
Price: £6.99 UK | $7.95 US
ISBN: 0-9547343-8-6
Publication date: May 2006

Series number: SGA-3

With Ancient technology scattered across the Atlantis team is not surprised to find it in use on a world once defended by Dalera, an Ancient who was cast out of her society for falling in love with a human.

But in the millennia since Dalera's departure much has changed. Her strict rules have been broken, leaving her people open to Wraith attack. Only a few of the Chosen remain to operate Ancient technology vital to their defense and tensions are running high. Revolution simmers close to the surface.

When Major Sheppard and Rodney McKay are revealed as members of the Chosen, Daleran society convulses into chaos. Wanting to help resolve the crisis and yet refusing to prop up an autocratic regime, Sheppard is forced to act when Teyla and Lieutenant Ford are taken hostage by the rebels...

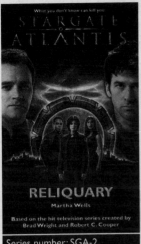

Series number: SGA-2

STARGATE ATLANTIS: RELIQUARY

by Martha Wells
Price: UK £6.99 | $7.95 US
ISBN: 0-9547343-7-8
Publication date: February 2006

While exploring the unused sections of the Ancient city of Atlantis, Major John Sheppard and Dr. Rodney McKay stumble on a recording device that reveals a mysterious new Stargate address. Believing that the address may lead them to a vast repository of Ancient knowledge, the team embarks on a mission to this uncharted world.

There they discover a ruined city, full of whispered secrets and dark shadows. As tempers fray and trust breaks down, the team uncovers the truth at the heart of the city. A truth that spells their destruction.

With half their people compromised, it falls to Major John Sheppard and Dr. Rodney McKay to risk everything in a deadly game of bluff with the enemy. To fail would mean the fall of Atlantis itself – and, for Sheppard, the annihilation of his very humanity…

STARGATE ATLANTIS: RISING

by Sally Malcolm
Price: £6.99 UK | $7.95 US
ISBN: 0-9547343-5-1

Series number: SGA-1

Following the discovery of an Ancient outpost buried deep in the Antarctic ice sheet, Stargate Command sends a new team of explorers through the Stargate to the distant Pegasus galaxy.

Emerging in an abandoned Ancient city, the team quickly confirms that they have found the Lost City of Atlantis. But, submerged beneath the sea on an alien planet, the city is in danger of catastrophic flooding unless it is raised to the surface. Things go from bad to worse when the team must confront a new enemy known as the Wraith who are bent on destroying Atlantis.

Stargate Atlantis is the exciting new spin-off of the hit TV show, Stargate SG-1. Based on the script of the pilot episode, *Rising* is a must-read for all fans and includes deleted scenes and dialog not seen on TV – with photos from the pilot episode.

THE COST OF HONOR

Part two of two parts

by Sally Malcolm
Price: £6.99 UK | $7.95 US
ISBN: 0-9547343-4-3

In the action-packed sequel to *A Matter of Honor*, SG-1 embark on a desperate mission to save SG-10 from the edge of a black hole. But the price of heroism may be more than they can pay...

Returning to Stargate Command, Colonel Jack O'Neill and his team find more has changed in their absence than they had expected. Nonetheless, O'Neill is determined to face the consequences of their unauthorized activities, only to discover the penalty is far worse than anything he could have imagined.

With the fate of Colonel O'Neill and Major Samantha Carter unknown, and the very survival of the SGC threatened, Dr. Daniel Jackson and Teal'c mount a rescue mission to free their team-mates and reclaim the SGC. Yet returning to the Kinahhi homeworld, they learn a startling truth about its ancient foe. And uncover a horrifying secret...

• Available in the USA from October 2006

Order your copy directly from the publisher today by going to <u>www.stargatenovels.com</u> or send a check or money order made payable to "Fandemonium" to:

<u>USA orders:</u> **$10.82 ($7.95 + $2.87 P&P). Send payment to: Fandemonium Books, PO Box 2178, Decatur, GA 30031-2178.**

<u>UK orders:</u> **£8.30 (£6.99 + £1.31 P&P). <u>Rest of the World orders:</u> £9.70 (£6.99 + £2.71 P&P). Send payment to: Fandemonium Books, PO Box 795A, Surbiton KT5 8YB, United Kingdom.**

Or check your local bookshop – available on special order if they are out of stock (quote the ISBN number listed above).

The team is stranded on a doomed world

STARGÂTE
SG·1

CITY OF THE GODS
Sonny Whitelaw

Based on the hit television series developed by
Brad Wright and Jonathan Glassner

Series number: SG1-4

CITY OF THE GODS

by Sonny Whitelaw
Price: £6.99 UK | $7.95 US
ISBN: 0-9547343-3-5

When a Crystal Skull is discovered beneath the Pyramid of the Sun in Mexico, it ignites a cataclysmic chain of events that maroons SG-1 on a dying world.

Xalótcan is a brutal society, steeped in death and sacrifice, where the bloody gods of the Aztecs demand tribute from a fearful and superstitious population. But that's the least of Colonel Jack O'Neill's problems. With Xalótcan on the brink of catastrophe, Dr. Daniel Jackson insists that O'Neill must fulfil an ancient prophesy and lead its people to salvation. But with the world tearing itself apart, can anyone survive?

As fear and despair plunge Xalótcan into chaos, SG-1 find themselves with ringside seats at the end of the world...

• Special section: Excerpts from Dr. Daniel Jackson's mission journal.

• Available in the USA from September 2006

Order your copy directly from the publisher today by going to www.stargatenovels.com or send a check or money order made payable to "Fandemonium" to:

<u>USA orders:</u> **$10.82 ($7.95 + $2.87 P&P). Send payment to: Fandemonium Books, PO Box 2178, Decatur, GA 30031-2178.**

<u>UK orders:</u> **£8.30 (£6.99 + £1.31 P&P). <u>Rest of the World orders:</u> £9.70 (£6.99 + £2.71 P&P). Send payment to: Fandemonium Books, PO Box 795A, Surbiton KT5 8YB, United Kingdom.**

Or check your local bookshop — available on special order if they are out of stock (quote the ISBN number listed above).

A MATTER OF HONOR

Part one of two parts

by Sally Malcolm
Price: £6.99 UK | $7.95 US
ISBN: 0-9547343-2-7

Five years after Major Henry Boyd and his
team, SG-10, were trapped on the edge of
a black hole, Colonel Jack O'Neill discov-
ers a device that could bring them home.

But it's owned by the Kinahhi, an advanced and paranoid people, besieged
by a ruthless foe. Unwilling to share the technology, the Kinahhi are pursu-
ing their own agenda in the negotiations with Earth's diplomatic delegation.
Maneuvering through a maze of tyranny, terrorism and deceit, Dr. Daniel
Jackson, Major Samantha Carter and Teal'c unravel a startling truth – a revelation that throws the team into chaos and forces O'Neill to face a nightmare he is determined to forget.

Resolved to rescue Boyd, O'Neill marches back into the hell he swore
never to revisit. Only this time, he's taking SG-1 with him...

• Available in the USA from August 2006

SACRIFICE MOON

By Julie Fortune
Price: £6.99 UK | $7.95 US
ISBN: 0-9547343-1-9

> Terror stalks the team at night
>
> **STARGATE SG·1**
>
> **SACRIFICE MOON**
> Julie Fortune
>
> Based on the hit television series developed by
> Brad Wright and Jonathan Glassner
>
> Series number: SG1-2

Sacrifice Moon follows the newly commissioned SG-1 on their first mission through the Stargate.

Their destination is Chalcis, a peaceful society at the heart of the Helos Confederacy of planets. But Chalcis harbors a dark secret, one that pitches SG-1 into a world of bloody chaos, betrayal and madness. Battling to escape the living nightmare, Dr. Daniel Jackson and Captain Samantha Carter soon begin to realize that more than their lives are at stake. They are fighting for their very souls.

But while Colonel Jack O'Neill and Teal'c struggle to keep the team together, Daniel is hatching a desperate plan that will test SG-1's fledgling bonds of trust and friendship to the limit…

• Available in the USA from July 2006

Order your copy directly from the publisher today by going to www.stargatenovels.com or send a check or money order made payable to "Fandemonium" to:

USA orders: $10.82 ($7.95 + $2.87 P&P). Send payment to: Fandemonium Books, PO Box 2178, Decatur, GA 30031-2178.

UK orders: £8.30 (£6.99 + £1.31 P&P). **Rest of the World orders:** £9.70 (£6.99 + £2.71 P&P). Send payment to: Fandemonium Books, PO Box 795A, Surbiton KT5 8YB, United Kingdom.

Or check your local bookshop – available on special order if they are out of stock (quote the ISBN number listed above).